D1314451

My Movie

stories

David Pratt

From the award-winning author of *Bob the Book*, *My Movie* showcases the remarkable range and versatility of David Pratt's short fiction, including stories previously published in *The James White Review*, *Velvet Mafia*, *Christopher Street*, *Chelsea Station*, and other periodicals, Web sites, and anthologies. The impact of memories thematically dominates the fourteen stories included in this imaginative collection, from the coming-of-age title story of a young boy's code of secret languages to the magical, speculative world of "Ulmus Americana," where trees yearn for love. Film and video are at the heart of many of these stories, including "Another Country," about a woman who enters a fictitious land created by her son and his boyhood friend for their backyard home movies, and the brilliantly conceived "Calvin Gets Sucked In," where a man is consumed, literally, by a porn video, with hilarious and disturbing results. Pratt also turns an unflinching camera eye on the realities and mishaps of gay life, from a hook-up with a crack addict to the painful and poignant struggles with illness, loss, and mortality. Haunting, funny, surreal, and heartbreaking, *My Movie* brilliantly documents how we come to terms with being queer.

Also by David Pratt

Bob the Book

My Movie

David Pratt

Chelsea Station
Editions

New
York

Cover and book design by Peachboy Distillery & Design
Cover photo by JanVlcek, Shutterstock
Author photo by Eva Mueller

Published by Chelsea Station Editions
362 West 36th Street, Suite 2R
New York, NY 10018
www.chelseastationeditions.com
info@chelseastationeditions.com

ISBN: 978-0-9832851-7-5
Library of Congress Control Number: 2012931519

First U.S. edition, 2012

Some of the stories in this work were originally published, in different versions, in the following: "My Movie" in *Lodestar Quarterly*, Vol. 1, #1; "Another Country" in *Velvet Mafia*, Issue 5; "Calvin Gets Sucked In" in *Chelsea Station*, Issue 1; "Series" in *His3: Brilliant New Fiction by Gay Men*; "All the Young Boys Love Alice," in *Lodestar Quarterly*, Vol. 4, #1; reprinted in *Fresh Men 2*; "One Bedroom" appeared under the title "Use My Face" in *The James White Review*, Vol. 11, #1; "Not Pretty" in *The James White Review*, Vol. 18, #3; "The Addict" in *Christopher Street*, Issue #179; and "Edge," in *Harrington Gay Men's Fiction Quarterly*, Vol. 2, #1. "The Snow Queen" was previously presented in theatrical form, as a collaboration between HERE Arts Center and Dixon Place in June 2003.

Contents

The earliest stories here were written just before the clean-up of Times Square in the early 1990s, when I lived on West Forty-ninth Street, and all-male peep shows and movie theaters still lined West Forty-second Street and the stretch of Eighth Avenue running from the Port Authority Bus Terminal up to the low Fifties. I was aware of AIDS and other contemporary gay issues, but I was more interested in working out in fiction the issues of my closeted youth. In those years I made and remade my adolescent self on paper. Finally, in the mid-1990s, to give myself a greater purpose, I became a volunteer for the Gay Men's Health Crisis. That made AIDS a more pressing issue in my life and in my fiction. In 1998 my partner urged me to think about an MFA in Creative Writing, which I obtained from the New School in New York City in 2001. That opened up a period of more experimental writing—which might mean something with an unusual form, or just a topic or an approach I had not assayed before. All stories were then to some extent rewritten for this volume. One was created from scratch, *"Ulmus americana,"* which, I suppose, describes where I and my partner stand today. This, then, is *My Movie*. I hope you enjoy it!

David Pratt
New York City
February, 2012

For those who wait

My
Movie

My Movie

We're not made of money. That's what they say. My brother works at the Holiday Inn back home. He has a girlfriend. He knows what to do. Up here at the lake, alone with them, I go out to the end of the dock and write in my notebook in code how my brother does push-ups naked and develops his own pictures, how I plot to glimpse his penis dark and substantial like a sausage. At night he does his job. He is hard. I am soft. My father taught me this code. He's good at things like that: tricks, things with punchlines. My mother doesn't know about it, and she wouldn't care. In relentless noon I lie on my belly with my notebook, my legs spread, my penis pressed to the hot wood of the dock. Over there on Cutter's Point I see Camp Assamaug. Laughing, shirtless guys appear from the pines. There's a right way and a wrong way. I search the woods. I find one. I stare stare stare at him until my eyes ache. I love him and hate him and want to be him. He vanishes according to plan, not knowing I exist.

If I leave my notebooks lying around, my mother sneers, "You people talk about 'vacation!' I never get a vacation! I don't know the meaning of the word 'vacation!'"

Neither do I.

Boys sail from the Point. White shirts billow around slender, athletic bodies, flapping like flags. They yell. I can't take yelling.

Later, at the doorway to evening, the counselors appear from the woods. One is rangy with a squinty grin. He is hard and soft. He laughs and loves everyone and everyone loves him. I watch his trunks. I star in a film about a hobo boy found sleeping on a park bench. The townspeople shun him till they discover his hands can heal. He heals an old woman who's been mean to him; she begs forgiveness. He forgives her, and the prettiest girl in town falls in love with him. He makes love to her, he puts it in her and masters her, and then they leave town together without telling anyone.

I watch my counselor razz the other counselors like they were brothers. He stands erect, long arms out. His body his body his body his back his shapely (no! ick!) hairy legs arc and he plunges into the water perfectly. He knows how to do something. He learned it. His father taught him as a boy, and now he is a man and he knows how. His grin pops up. He hoists himself, groin pressed to the raft edge. Big bare feet grip the raft wood as he stands dripping and powerful, slender and free.

I asked them, "Next year, could I go?" I knew camp was expensive, so I quickly added, "If I won the *Super Word Jumble* in the paper? It's $1,200 this week."

"Well, I don't think that's worth discussing," my father said. Same as when I asked how a man could turn into a woman, like in *The Christine Jorgensen Story*, which I tried to glimpse as we passed the drive-in. The screen thrashed while the dark around it stayed still.

So I'd do the *Super Word Jumble* every week till I won, and then they'd see. I'd go to camp and be someone they liked, someone other kids liked, tan and skinny and good, who knew how to sail and yell. "Hey! Watch out, man! You're gonna capsize us, man!" When we fell in I'd laugh. The way I am now, I don't like water. I don't like wearing my bathing suit. I don't laugh around water. Camp would change me.

Saturday mornings when the paper came I hovered. Dad took forever reading it. When I finally got it away from him, I'd say, "Wow, the *Word Jumble*'s eight hundred this week!" Silence. One Saturday my mother strode in, snatched the paper and screamed, "If I have to hear one more word about that damn *Word Scramble*, I swear to God I'll lock you out of this house and you can go beg the neighbors for your stinking money!"

I went upstairs, shut my door, and cried. My mother said "damn."

My dad didn't say anything.

Boys in white sail from the Point, free.

I took my allowance and bought my own paper and hid it under the bed.

By Thanksgiving I hadn't won, then over Christmas I missed two. I never did the *Super Word Jumble* again. In winter you forget what you want so desperately in summer.

I star in a movie where I rescue a girl from a burning building. I get a reward but instead of using it for camp I buy my mother chocolates.

–o–

This is the code my dad taught me:

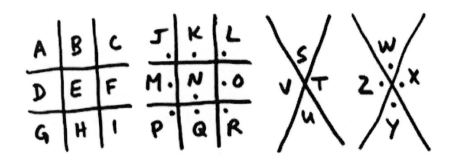

So, "I am not a man" would look like this:

"My parents love my brother more than me" would look like this:

—o—

We don't know the meaning of the word "vacation." We're here because Mr. Violet, who owns the island and the cottages, fits us in for a week, free. He does this as a favor because his father knew my mother's father, who owned the island and then lost it in the Depression. Mr. Violet is portly and bald, with a thick beard, and he always seems annoyed with us. At lunch yesterday my father suggested giving Mr. Violet "some token amount," and my mother yelled at him. She said, "You people don't know the meaning of the word 'Depression'!" My father didn't say anything. Now they're sleeping, my mother in the bedroom, my dad in the living room. I take my telescope and go down to the dock.

I point it across the water, at the counselors from Camp Assamaug. There's the one I love, all jock-ish and smiling squinty-eyed. I call him Eddie Tyler, like Toby Tyler, who joined the circus because nobody loved him. In my movie, Eddie plays the role of the boy on the park bench.

My arm sheltering the paper, I draw in my notebook: "Eddie Tyler in *The Hands of John*. In Technicolor." Eddie would think I was sick if he saw this. I'm ashamed to draw his face. I'm no good at faces anyway, so I blend lots of pine trees into his face. Half his face. One eye. He is a legend. At the top I write, "They hated him at first, but his powers turned their hate to love." Below I write, "Starts Wednesday, Prescott Lake Cinema." The Prescott Lake Cinema sits out over the water at the north end of the Island. I own it, and I run the projectors. I decide what movies play when and what is held over. I decide show times. I don't care about selling tickets. Or popcorn.

-o-

A bell rings. Someone wants the ferry. Mr. Violet built this little ferry you crank by hand, a wooden platform that floats on green, scummy blocks of Styrofoam.

I get an idea.

I can do it. They won't know. I just want to see him and hear his voice and feel his handshake. I want to say hi to him and shake his hand.

I hop up with my telescope, pick my way up the bank and race up-island toward the ferry slip. I have to get there before Mr. Violet comes down from his house. I slip on pine needles, but I barely feel the thud of my butt. I'm up again. I'm on my way.

I leap to the ferry. It lurches and I know it will dump me, but it doesn't. I grip the crank, level with my chest. An underwater cable from the island to the mainland comes up through the crank mechanism, wet and dripping, and goes back down. You turn the crank and the hidden, scummy cable takes you back and forth, back and forth.

I'm alone. Every muscle, tense and gripping, out in the middle of the lake, cranking. I'll never get there. Something huge will fall on me. Everyone can see. Eddie can see. He thinks I'm weird, but he's too nice to say so. "Hey!" It's Mr. Violet. " What the hell do you think you're doing?" He said "hell." Now he's caught me, I can't go back. I don't know what to do. I crank madly, with both hands. I keep my head down; if I look up, I'll fall. Water passes, all mine, but I don't want it! Trees loom. Now I've done it. The ferry worked, it did it's job, because I did something. Something terrible. What now? What will happen to me? The clock on the Chevron station says an hour till dinner. Eddie Tyler will pass a bowl of sweet potatoes to one of his boys. He'll tousle the boy's hair. The boy will give Eddie a love tap. If I could win the *Super Word Jumble*, I could be Eddie's boy. I could give and take love taps. My parents couldn't say no. I'll find Eddie. I'll say hi and shake his hand and he'll recognize me, he'll like me, he'll say my name and he'll say I can stay at Camp Assamaug under a special arrangement. He'll explain to my parents, and they will go away.

The ferry drifts in toward the dock on the other side. Always that terrible moment, leaping on or leaping off. Something will slip away; I will fall, go under. I just hope for the ferry to bump the dock, and when it does, I scramble. People we know wait for the ferry: Mr. and Mrs. Kent. Mrs. Kent wears white pants, a pink blouse, chunky gold earrings, and pink lipstick that goes up into the cracks around her mouth. Mr. Kent's black socks come up almost to his plaid shorts. A little white, veiny skin shows. They carry folding chairs.

"Hey, Schnickelfritz," says Mr. Kent. I think, *They don't know me.* I'm scared. Am I still me?

"Are your parents here?" says Mrs. Kent.

I'm in a movie where I kick Mrs. Kent again and again in the stomach and elope with her daughter and fuck her.

"They sent me over to Muzzy's," I say. "For bread and milk."

"We'll wait for you," says Mr. Kent. He opens one of the folding chairs like a trap.

"It might take a while," I say, going past them, my legs weak. Mrs. Kent hisses, "Jack, the Morrisons expect us at six! I can't go like this!" He says, "Let the damn Morrisons wait!" and he sits. I'll never find Eddie, I will never get anything, ever. I'm panting. There's the Kents' Buick. And our peeling Plymouth. Now I'm on the road. Now...

Just where is Camp Assamaug?

I pictured it to my left. And behind me. On our way here we pass the sign. I think of the map in our cabin. Maybe if I keep moving, I'll overcome space and magically find it. I am meant to be there. I have been there already, more real than real. How can life deny me?

Behind me, I feel the Chevron station vanish. I left my telescope on the ferry! Blood drains from my head, but I can't go back. Once Eddie sees me, I won't need a telescope. After my parents leave, he'll offer for me to stay with him because the bunks are full, and I'll see him naked. I won't need to look through a telescope any more. He will have everything I need.

Dark spikes cross the road. Station wagons with fake wood sides whiz by. I see people from the island, kids' sticky fingers trailing out car windows. Do they see me? I draw close to the back of the Assamaug sign, a stained and weatherbeaten plywood outline of the picture on the front: blond boys swimming, sailing, playing volleyball. I twist my foot on a chunk of blacktop and have to walk lopsided. Pain stabs my ankle and my side. I'm not in shape, like the Assamaug boys. My mother told me to stop complaining and do push-ups. I did them every morning, then I stopped. I think she knew I would. Eddie will teach me exercises to make my stomach hard. We'll do them together. He'll show me, and I'll go back to them in perfect shape and not say anything when they notice. I have to stop and bend over, panting. Then I stand and keep going, going...

The Assamaug sign guards a shaded road that ends in a better world. The afternoon goes chilly. I don't know how long that road is. The raft is empty. The counselors are drying their bare bodies in huts that smell of wood and dirty socks and bygone summers. I start down the road.

Their dinner bell rings. Strokes float like love from a piney night forever. Hair combed, the boys pass bowls of sweet potatoes. We are boys for such a short time, yet I am in eternal pain. Eddie smiles. His forearms ripple as he grips the bowl with big fingers. His bathing suit hangs by his tent. The pouch hangs out. No stains, like in mine. Finally a car slows behind me, a hot rattle pulls alongside, and our peeling hood intrudes. My father snaps, "What the hell do you think you're doing?"

As it was in the beginning.

"Get in, now!" I star in a movie about boys born with an incurable disease that makes them attack people with axes and hack their chests open.

When we get back to the ferry, my telescope is not there. Going over, Mr. Violet gives us a lecture on who gets to use the ferry and when and insurance and how I could have drowned.

-o-

Night. A blurry, murky image of my room obscures the lake. A powerboat makes waves that slap our dock.

My mother says they want to understand, but they just can't. She sent me upstairs, and then they whispered about me. Rather, she did. All I heard him say, once, was, "I don't know."

I sing naked in a Broadway musical. I star in a movie about a man who catches his son when he falls off a building. I am the son. The movie is shown at my school and everyone boos when my name comes on the screen. The teacher shuts off the projector and my classmates will never be allowed to see the movie, even after I win an Academy Award. I press and fuse all my desires into black diamonds that will CUT!

A knock.

"Could we talk, maybe...?" She says it so blubbery, like she's afraid of me. I hate that.

She has my journal. She closes the door behind her and comes and sits on the bed. She asks if I would come up onto her lap? We haven't done that in a long time.

My father found the journal on the dock. He decoded the part about my brother. "Now, I don't know about any 'code,'" she says, clutching the journal but not opening it, but they love me every bit as much as my brother! How could I *possibly* think otherwise? It's just that he can do some things because he's a little bit older. Do I understand?

"Mm-hmm." I feel heavy on her, like I'll crush her legs, and she won't be able to walk ever again.

She strokes my hair.

I didn't run away because I thought they loved my brother more, did I?

I shake my head. Her knees cut to the bones of my butt, but I don't move. My penis is very small now. Her love gives me the inverse of an erection. Her love gives me a hole.

"Look at me." She smoothes back the wet spears of hair. Do I know how much they love me? I nod. Do I know it would devastate her if I ever ran away and something happened to me? I nod. I hate love. So grabby. All a trick.

She holds the journal. I won't write anything about more them loving my brother more, will I? I shake my head. Now she hands me the journal.

I never write in my journal again. The pages will yellow and curl at the edges, but their hearts will remain smooth and empty and unseen. I'll flip through once in a while, just so someone sees them, so they have one friend and can be real.

Did they decode the stuff about my brother's penis? Did my dad decode it and not tell my mother? Did my mother see the movie ad with Eddie Tyler? What is the punishment for making up fake movies? I'll never know. The next day they talk brightly and quickly and joke as though nothing happened.

I never write in my journal again, but that's okay. I am forgiven. The awful thing is forgotten. That's more important than a dumb fake movie ad.

I don't tell them I lost my telescope, and they don't ask. They probably forgot I had it.

I'll never run away again. I don't even have to promise. It's one of those things we just know. Besides, I'm already gone.

–o–

Summer 1979

I'm still here.

After my shift I walk home. At the crest of Mosher Hill I stop to see the Sun rise, July air nuclear-bright over my old elementary school. I'm the only one to see the dawn. Then a cop car rises and stops. They want to know what I'm doing here. They glance up and down, appraising my grease-spattered shirt and baggy pants. I cringe, hoping to hide the stains from their hard eyes. I'm not in movies anymore. I have a summer job as night cleaner in the kitchen at McBurney's Tavern. Patrick, the salad boy with the big, cute grin, got off at 11:00, changed behind the boxes of powdered soap where I couldn't quite see, and with his worn jeans hugging his small, round ass he went out, keys jingling, to seek, to fuck. I worked till four a.m. in the windowless fluorescent palace echoing with AM radio: "Knowing me, knowing you, there is nothing we can do..."

Now I just want to see the Sun rise.

Convinced of my innocence, or not completely convinced of my guilt, the cops slowly roll off. I walk on downhill.

In her nightgown my mother rocks herself on the couch and sniffles. "Hopeless!" she wails, the corners of her mouth pulled down in a mask of tragedy. She dabs at her eyes with a wadded Kleenex. At her feet, a spot on the carpet. I stand in my bathrobe. I did what I was supposed to: shed my uniform on the porch, on yesterday's newspaper, let myself in and went straight to the shower. She wipes her eyes.

Well, don't we have something to clean it with?

She stops rocking, makes a fist around the Kleenex. "Jeepers, no one around here knows anything!" Like she would go some other place. "You have to rent a machine that costs an arm and a leg and take out every stick of furniture!" Dawn makes the curtains glow. I'm tired.

"So, is there anything I can do?"

"You can keep your damn uniform on the back porch where you're supposed to, is what you can...!"

"Hey, I did not do that!" She doesn't look at me, but her spine stiffens. "I've taken my clothes off on the back porch every night this summer! I will not be accused..."

She looks up, eyes ablaze but not meeting mine. Like an electric saw tearing through wood: "I... didn't... say... you... *did*!"

"I'm sorry. I..."

"How dare you say I accused you of such a thing!" Her fist convulses, but doesn't actually punch anything. "I happen to be a *little* upset because there's a spot on a *brand new* rug, paid for with *our* money"— she jabs her chest—"and you won't indulge me *that much*! I see you taking deep breaths. You might choose to understand the totally demoralized state this puts a person in and for once maybe just lie down and take it." She massages the Kleenex. "I guess I'd better never again talk about anything I feel!"

The curtains glow. A cicada starts up: *Naynaynaynaynaynaynaynay*!! What are we talking about?

She stares ahead, her neck is at its longest and most erect. "I work *hard*!" She jabs her chest again. "*I'm* the one who has to worry about how to get a machine the size of a tank in here! *I'm* the one who fixes things around here, you're the one who's enjoying what we laughingly call 'vacation!'"

High school Chemistry: Pressure turns coal to diamonds. Black ones you never see on wedding rings.

"I *NEVER* get a vacation! I keep this place clean for you and your father to turn it like a flophouse! Like I'm some kind of *garbage*! Like I don't even *exist!*"

I have pictures of naked men. I bought a magazine in Hartford after leaving and coming back to the newsstand four times. They have unattainable cocks that hang like my brother's, or curve down like faucets. My brother is gone now. He programs computers in Denver. They all have hard eyes—if you bother to check their eyes—except one. She slips in and out of focus. I turn away. "I wonder," she hisses, "what a *psychiatrist* would say about this!" I just go upstairs. I'm going to break a law. There's a guy in one of my magazines, the only one really smiling. He's dressed like a state trooper, but with his zipper open, thick prick hanging out over his nightstick. He's too young and femmy and pimply to be a real cop. He grins like it's a joke, and that melts what's left of my heart.

Cross-legged, naked on my unmade bed, I dig with my thumbnail at the white flesh of my leg making moons, purple and yellow. With my other hand, I turn pages. I take shallow breaths. My heart knocks as I draw close. There: uniform hanging on skinny body, veins on his thin, strong arm. The joy, the joke, the freedom of that prick. "Knowing me, knowing you, there is nothing we can do..." I touch myself. The cicadas start.

I can't fight the heat and pressure that turn veiny erections and dimpled butts into black diamonds—my family jewels. I jack and shoot on myself, not on the boy-cop.

On all the pages left blank I could write in sperm the sound of cicada wings—not tissue on tissue, but steel scraping bone. *Naynaynaynaynaynaynaynaynay!* "Breaking up is never easy, I know what I had to do. Knowing me, knowing you, it's the best we can do." The fireglow fills my room.

I pull the *Metro News* from under my bed. In the smudgy corner of the personals page, GWMs: "Great loving and dynamite sack action"— two guys in Titusville looking for a third. I sent a letter to the P.O. box. My heart shook my frame as I wrote my address for them. I asked them to send a phone number. I get through each day thinking, today their letter will come. When it doesn't I'm relieved. I can go back to anticipating. At night, alone on my knees, I scrub at glistening grease beneath the fryer. It never comes off. The radio crackles: "Knowing me, knowing you..." I scrub and I think of "Great loving and dynamite sack action." My chance to resume my movie career, lost so long ago.

I won't sleep. I tuck the *Metro News* back under the bed and go down. She sings from the kitchen. "Good morning! Who'd like pancakes?" My favorite.

"Sure," I say.

Cicada sounds cut the screens. They come every seventeen years, but in my world the noise comes every day. In the living room the blinds are drawn. I go to open them but no. They're drawn for a reason. So the spot won't show.

"Okle-dokle!" my father says. "Breakfast!"

The house is a reactor; the heat turns the pancakes and the spot on the rug and "great loving and dynamite sack action" into black diamonds.

-o-

The letter comes with no return address. "Greetings, fellow Sybarite..." A real other male wrote this. I did something and something happened. His scribble speaks of "Epicurean antics" and "forbidden pleasures." Eddie Tyler's dead and gone. I want him back.

There's a number: "Call anytime." I keep the letter for a week, then call one evening when my parents are out. "You wrote..." I clear my throat. I mean, I wrote you, and..." He doesn't know what I'm talking about, or he'll say it's a wrong number, or... "Oh, hey." Throaty and slurred. A trick? His name is Rob. "So I... wanted... to... 'get together.'" "Excellent." We set a time. "Bring some stuff if ya got it." I don't know what kind of "stuff," so I don't say anything. He doesn't mention the other guy, and I don't ask. I picture Rob pliant, with a white body and a red dick standing straight up. But the other guy, the one he didn't mention, is Eddie Tyler. I'll co-star with him at last. Starring in movies together, that's love.

-o-

I hold the keys. I told her I'm going to see college friends. She follows me out: "Now, you don't know this because you've never been out there, but those hills around Titusville are murder. When you shift into second..." And, "Remember, this is power steering, you're not used to it, you're liable to slam into a brick wall." My father stands behind the screen door. She tells me...

Look—why don't you for once shut the fuck up?! Why don't you for once shut that lousy, rotten yap of yours and maybe get the idea through your skull that the rest of the world is grown up and knows what the fuck to do

21

without you sticking your fat, loud, fat mouth into every god damn thing!

Chin quivering: "I... I... don't know what you mean..."

"Let's hold on here a minute," Dad says.

Oh, are we going to speak? After centuries is The Wimp going to break his sacred silence? Gonna be a man? If you're gonna stick up for something, Marshmallow Man, why don't you stick up for taking her down to the booby hatch and having a thousand volts of electricity shot through that drill sergeant brain and then maybe there'd be some peace and quiet around here. The two of you could sit in the corner and drool together, wouldn't that be fun?

She wrings her hands. She turns halfway toward my father but does not meet his eyes. "What's happening? I don't understand..."

I snatch the garden hose and whale the end against the aluminum siding. Water flies in arcs, drops stain the concrete of the foundation and spread. "I'm! Gonna! Do! What I! Want! And you're! Not! Gonna! Stop me!"

-o-

I hold the keys. They watch me go. They assume so much. That brings on a sadness that "great loving and dynamite sack action" can't cure. I want to fuck fuck fuck, lost in mad thrusts. Dynamite. But I love her in her faded house dress, warm breasts I still crave to suck.

I star in a movie where two estranged brothers reconcile in a snowball fight, then head back, arms around one another.

I star in a movie where a boy loses his best friend in a car accident. When he goes back to visit the friend's family he can't bring himself to leave, and he ends up staying for weeks.

I star in a movie where an abused boy escapes Czechoslovakia and comes to America. He looks up at the Statue of Liberty and cries.

I drive. They disappear.

-o-

"Hey." Rob grins. He has a sunburn. His hair is long. Not rebel long. Long because other people have theirs long and he can't be bothered cutting it.

We sit in his parents' TV room. He doesn't mention the other guy. He gets high. I take two tokes and nothing happens. He talks about his car. We eat chips out of a bag and drink beer. I hope the other guy will come. Eddie Tyler. He'll sock me on the shoulder. He'll have hands calloused from football; he'll invite me to his house. I'll tell him about my fight with my parents and how hard it is and how hard it's always been.

Rob gets up, takes me out, shows me his pool. His parents' pool. I'm beginning to hate him. We go in again and talk some more. About the pool, his car, about this girl he fucked. A lot about the girl, and he asks if I want to watch TV. I say okay. He stares glassy-eyed at the glassy eye.

"So," I say, "there's, uh, like, another guy, right?"

"Huh?"

"The ad? That I answered? It said something..."

Rob chortles in kind of slow motion. "Yeah. This buddy of mine. He's crazy... he just... but... um... you wanna have a wank or somethin'?"

I will never forget the way he said "buddy."

I slide my pants down and feel like a fool when he just opens his fly, takes it out and pulls on it. He mostly stares at the TV, checks me out every once in a while. It doesn't get hard, but he's bigger than me so it doesn't have to. "Sorry, man," he concludes. "I guess not today." He puts it back, zips up, and goes on watching TV. I keep going a while. He's making faces at the screen. But I am hard. I can do this. I am ready. But not coming seems to be the thing to do today, so after a couple more minutes I say I have to go. I duck into the bathroom and finish, just to feel strong. I wash it down his parents' drain. I want to kick him.

"Pleasure," he says as I go.

I sit motionless in my parents' car outside his parents' house.

She was right. The hills are terrible.

-o-

Summer 1991

Holding out just in trunks on the overcast beach. Up at 5:00, here at 9:00, past 6:00 now. Loping down the sand with your friends, you have the most perfect squinty grin I've seen all season. Are you a lawyer, Eddie? Or an architect with an espresso machine? You glance. Smile—at all the world, at all supposed creatures of God. Then go on.

Follow you to Antarctica on bended knee, hold you in a sunset meant not for Prince Charmings but for contortionists, hermaphrodites, and men with dead brothers dolled-up hanging from their chests. Offer you black diamonds.

Now comes another, slower, eyes sharper, in just a black Speedo.

23

Inside, black diamonds. His perfect knowledge thrills.

The movies now go unwatched. They're not in wide release anymore, but independent. Limited engagements. Straight to video, really, and all the same.

Eddie, come play on the empty dock, the hollow in the dunes, the enchanted places that thrill!

Instead it will be this sharp-eyed one, not in a lace-curtain bedroom or a chapel or plastic living room, but in nearby hollows where it waited, long before knowledge knew itself. To know his fears might be nice, but his job is unimportant or where he lives. I don't want him, I want you, Eddie, gone twenty-one years but ever here in every movie, I want you to know those hollows, where Christopher Robin and Winnie-*ther*-Pooh still play among the tombstones. We'll get together, make a little package of forever someone else can watch from their dark.

Stops. "Hi." You've gone, Eddie. Gone to humans, whose game I won't play. But I see only you. You are how it should be. I love movies. Love love love! The transaction with the Speedo is weary and blunt, vanishes in dunes blemished with the ruins of used rubbers. He does his job.

"Yeah, oh yeah!"

Everyone does, I guess.

And *The Hands of John*............ will open.......... tomorrow............... .... It will come................. out of................... nowhere............ and win................ every................ Academy Award........................... there is....................

"Oh! OH!!! Oh, shit Jesus Christ!"...................................

It comes out like mother-o'-pearl, but a microscope would show black diamonds. We live in caves of them, where no one else enters. But for just this moment, just for this moment, long gone now...

ΛΕΛ' ΓΟ ΩΕ< ΠΓϽ.

Another Country

When my husband, Dan, lost the way, I drove. Going to Larry, our son, two miles from the house, Dan suddenly drove in circles. He pulled over and began to cry. "Nothing's familiar," he said, although we'd been there dozens of times. The next morning we took him to the hospital. It was a tumor, inoperable. He died the first of the year.

I didn't think I could go back to a hospital, alone, to have my carotid artery cleaned out. It would prevent a stroke, but there was also a five percent chance it would cause one. But I was fine. I've been home a week now. I haven't had so much blood going to my brain since I was upside down in the womb. The world vibrates down to the last placemat and dish. Larry insists I stay home and rest. I stare at old photos by the bed, four dimensional. I'm disappointed when I look up and see a calendar or a clock.

I have to get out. I have to know the world with me still in it. In the sun dress Dan says makes me look girlish, I might go anywhere. I fetch dark glasses and knot a scarf.

—o—

God has made a glorious day! Life rushes up like a boy with a present behind his back. Flowers nod, windows open and wishes meld into memories.

My feet don't know what's happened—they aren't used to walking all over town this way! I can't drive because my neck's stiff, but walking is better suited to my way of seeing now. A film of perspiration forms on my skin; the dress waltzes around me, cooling the sweat. At the bottom of the hill I turn onto the boulevard and realize: that sweet smell of times gone by... I'm in Flombania!—where Percy and Larry set all the movies they made as boys! "Beautiful downtown Flombania!" How often I have wanted to see their world again. I'm a block from Percy's Manicure Parlor and Auto Garage. I stride up to Percy's dark window, trying to see past the flickering neon outline of a woman's hand. I rap and wave.

Percy looks up, frowning. Then he smiles and waves back, almost lost in shadow. I see only his white hand, like a drowning man waving for help. The last time I came Percy waved and turned away. I knew he was busy, God bless him, and couldn't chat. Not that he doesn't love his second mother. With the manicure parlor *and* the auto garage he has so much to do, so it's all right.

But today he beckons to me. I hurry in and I throw my arms around him. The smell of acetone fills my nostrils; I feel its chill on my skin. Percy's hug is stiff and needful.

"Oh, my darling!" I say. "Let me look at you, Percy dear." He smiles, mouth closed, shrugs, looks away. "Is this a bad time, sweetheart?"

"Oh no!" he says, gripping my arms suddenly. "Don't move!" He races to fetch iced tea and cookies, as though he has to have them to keep me here. Percy, darling, I came for *you*!

He sets us up at an empty station by the window and holds the chair for me. We sip tea and look out the window, losing ourselves in the world beyond the glass, as if those people coming and going were in a movie. Now I watch him. On this hot day, he's dressed in a black turtleneck and brown corduroys. The top of his head fades into the light coming from behind him, and I reach for his hand and say, "You know, the heat today reminds me of the day we met—our two families, in July of 1971." He squeezes my hand but doesn't speak. His world consists mostly of memories, and that worries me. Percy's 1971 and '72 and '73 are tiny mirrors mounted in huge, dark frames.

It was so hot by the motel pool, we invited Percy's family into our room for lemonade. Percy was twelve and chubby, and when I spoke to him he frowned at the carpet. He didn't ask for food or use the bathroom. He waited until I offered. He talked about books and movies we'd never heard of. He impressed our son, Larry, though Larry's thing was more athletics. Percy told us about a movie that excited him so much, except he couldn't see it because it was rated R. His mother tried to shush him. Larry jumped up and said, "C'mon, we'll go outside!" I called after them to be careful. They disappeared forever, but came back for dinner.

Us parents hit it off, too, so we made plans for Labor Day. Then Thanksgiving, then Christmas. The years the boys were growing up, we got together five or six times a year, all because of that chance meeting. I believe God meant it to be.

I ask Percy how he is now, and a frown pulls his features to the center of his face. "Business is okay," he says. He never discusses the demands of running a manicure parlor *and* a garage. I've never been back there to see the garage.

He says he's learning slowly how Flombanian business regulations are different from the United States. Still—he motions to the back wall and the garage—where else would he have this kind of opportunity? He looks out at the street. I look at him.

How things have changed!—my Dan gone, Larry with a wife and kids, out of state. Percy—my second son, I always say. From the garage I hear the clank of metal, the hot breath of a grille. I'm not a prude. I've traveled and raised a family and I don't belong to any religious right, though I try to be a good Christian. I do fall short. I wish I could embrace all things, as God does. But Percy knows there are some things I'm not used to, back there in the auto shop, the men and the grease. Still, nothing could make me love my Percy one iota less.

I want to tell him so, but when I open my mouth it's 1975 and I say, "Place a small amount of sauce in pan. Add broccoli and cheese, repeat with vegetables." I touch a finger to my lips. I didn't mean to say that! I try again. "Pour tomato sauce over all. Bake uncovered forty-five to fifty minutes." I clap my hand over my lower face. Tears come. "I'm sorry, darling," I gasp. He takes my hand in his. "Shh!" But I didn't tell him what temperature! It breaks my heart to think of my second son sitting all alone at night, chewing uncooked broccoli. He stands. I feel all my efforts have failed.

He brings me out back to see his garden.

He made it from an oddly shaped patch of dirt left over after they built the parlor and the garage. We stand on the threshold, as though the garden were an exhibit. He's planted holly-hocks, bleeding heart, and purple coneflower, his favorite. He's sunken china plates in the soil, like tombstones. A broken edge sticks up. Only Percy is smart enough to understand each plate's true meaning. I feel as I did when he told me about those obscure movies: I should admire his taste, but I feel chastened. I gave him some of those plates. He turned them into something special. My necessity became Percy's decoration. My pain his redemption.

Percy and I hold one another, and his embrace is more relaxed. It's so nicely arranged out here, like a movie set without cameras, or actors, even. He's placed plastic dragons and knights beneath the leaves, and in the middle, one plastic thing that I'm not going to say what it is. It sits there as though Percy invented it. Maybe that's how we think about the things we need most, though I never thought I invented God.

"Yesterday," Percy says, "someone was supposed to come and ask to stay forever. I shut the garage and opened a bottle of wine. I lit candles and put Messiaen on the stereo." I don't know who that is. A girl files a nail. It smells like burning flesh.

Percy was seeing a man from the garage, but he never brought him by. Since then he hasn't had anyone that I know of. The demands of two businesses, he says. Everyone in Flombania has two businesses—one happy, one sad. You need the sad one because the taxes on the happy one are awful.

He meets my gaze. His lip curls or trembles, then he shifts his stance and draws back, still holding my arm.

"Did he come, Percy?"

He gives an unpleasant snuff of laughter. I glimpse a cynical, unbelieving Percy I don't like. I entwine his fingers in my hands, because those who are broken or buried alive must have our love and know it. There are things I don't understand, but what difference should that make? "He will, sweetheart."

I'm about to add, "You're not alone those nights!" but I just massage his hand. Neither God nor I can give Percy what he longs for. I will not judge Percy. Maybe he hears alleluias I can't.

"I waited," he says. "I imagined a movie camera pulling back till I was this tiny dot of light in the dark, this whole lit up the city behind me."

Lovely! Like an image from a movie Percy might have made.

"Those are peppers," he announces, pointing to a glossy-leaved bush with white flowers. "Or they're supposed to be. The flowers open, but the whole thing falls off at the touch of a finger—little baby pepper and all. I don't know where to turn—no gardening book says anything. Buds keep coming by the dozens, and each new batch I think, these will be the ones that'll stay. And they do, and I'm so... And more flowers open and fall off and I can't make myself fix it. Now they've started dying even before they open, babies falling to their deaths before they've opened their eyes and seen what's in the world. Yet I go on tending them like a lover on a respirator."

Resentment flashes in his eyes, then an afterglow of regret. We take a last look around the garden. I don't know if Percy could abide a man here, loving the garden and readjusting the plates. So much is invested in *that* plate being right *there*. God forgive me for saying so, but maybe a lover on a respirator would be the thing for Percy.

As we step back into the parlor I recall Percy at twelve or thirteen, telling us how he wanted to be in movies and theatre. By fifteen he'd become sullen, and he grew his hair long. He looked like his sister. We were supposed to know he was an actor, but we weren't supposed to ask about it. The day he graduated he seemed happy, but I still saw him holding back—from dandelions, from sprites, from the hungers of his mouth, which was closed in the pictures, even as he smiled. There are things parents can't know, can't help. Percy dreamed, but he wouldn't ask, wouldn't seek. He dreamed, and he wondered why the things he dreamed weren't offered him. He'd visit us every now and then and seem surprised that I loved him the same as ever. Once I asked, "What do you want to do in five years?" His face went white and he smirked. "Let's get through today," he said.

Then we received the letter—or I received it—saying he was in Flombania and had taken over the manicure parlor and the garage. I didn't know what to say, but I knew I loved him same as ever, and I wrote back and told him so. I didn't find out till later that Larry had received the same letter. Larry didn't respond. I asked why and he sounded nonplused. He'd never even thought of it.

The man Percy waits for would upset his garden, loving the peppers like a storm in late July. You have to welcome the water crashing down, the wind that smashes stalks. So long as Percy demands full say over his storm, it will break elsewhere. He'll watch from a distance the terrible baptisms and envy their victims, wondering why those deluges won't come and smash and spank his control, and still he must hold that control and envy what baptisms do to others and so he is baptized, too, by disappointment. Or maybe he's just marked, always convalescing.

There is a baptism that knows no age. It is never too late, if only he'd surrender.

As we sit again by the window I try to form the words. But it is 1971, the boys are movie stars and all I can say is, "In a nine by thirteen pan, melt butter in oven. Sprinkle crumbs evenly over butter, press down lightly."

Can I not find words of love because Percy believes they don't exist, even as he waits for a stranger to say them? I ask what he thinks of God.

"I don't believe in Him." With a smile he adds, "except when something goes wrong, then I'm angry at Him." He concentrates on his iced tea.

I resent Percy for silencing my love. I pray God will lift my resentment. I pray Percy will find Him, in his own way.

Percy stops time. I turn a corner.

Larry was supposed to call Percy after my operation, but there was confusion, and Percy never was called. Maybe he assumed if anything went wrong, he'd hear. But I wish he'd called. Larry's busy, too. Three kids and another on the way—lovely kids! They just bought a new house. I bring out pictures to show Percy. He looks at each one twice, saying, "This is great... great."

"I have such happy memories of you boys!"

Percy nods. He does not take his eyes off the pictures. He's built a wall between youth and adulthood. He longs for what's on the other side, but only in dreams for an instant can he get atop it, then wake.

For Percy it's a different 1971. It's not Larry leaning back, paint brush in hand, hair glowing, bare chest open to Heaven as he painted the church steeple, nor is it Dan's work spread out on the dining room table, where I brought him coffee and sat with him and sipped. For Percy it's a strange, dirty summer. He crouches in a metal box, naked, the radio on. One day soon we'll stand on the beach in the late afternoon, searching the sky for ducks, before we turn into the wind and head home, where everyone waits for us. 1972 will be our best year yet, darling; all your dreams will come true.

Percy glances at customers coming in. I take my pictures and get up to go. We hug. We don't say anything. I don't know if we're so close nothing needs to be said, or if we're separated by what can't be said. Looking back through the door I see his white hand waving.

‑o‑

In the dusty heat I'm anxious and afraid. I have something else to do but can't think what it is. A movie enters my mind. Going to daytime movies is such a luxury. Deep in the velvet seat I imagine myself, timeless, invisible, watching someone else's dream. The Trylon's just around the corner. I could go home after and have another iced tea and lie down. This feels like a thing to do on an eternal tomorrow.

I close my eyes and pray. It comes to me that, if I stop by church, I'll know what to do.

A breeze parts the branches and Larry painted that steeple one summer but it's been repainted since. I draw back the iron gate. The foyer's dark with the smell of hymnals.

"Worship the Lord," it says above the pulpit in spidery letters.

I fit the sanctuary perfectly, like a second skin. I feel His presence. I knew since I was a child that He was everywhere, but only now do I feel permeable. He flows through me, through everything, like a string threaded through us all, some of us not even knowing. Being threaded hurts. But if you release your fortune like doves you will laugh when the needle goes through, and it will be a lovely, treasured imposition. Like bread.

"Worship the Lord." I inhale, feel the chain, paper chain of Christmas, popcorn and cranberries, exquisite shapes, nightingales. I am still of this world. I hear cars in the street, imagine the steeple stretching to Heaven, below me the basement. God knows what is there.

In God there are no surprises. Percy longs to be surprised. But he would have to trade away so many ideas he holds dear. You don't have to sit up at night waiting for God.

Suddenly, I know what to do.

–○–

A shop awning flutters. There's the Trylon and... my word! They're having a Swine International Film Festival! My heart lifts up. Today it's *You Can't Teach an Old Dog New Slime*, starring Larry and Percy, of course. We used to have such fun seeing the boys in their movies. I guess Percy did more with the creative part, but he let Larry have top billing. Larry once said to me, "Y'know, Mum, I'm so grateful to have such a creative friend." Did he ever tell Percy?

You Can't Teach an Old Dog New Slime belongs to a series starring Larry as The Good Dr. Good and Percy as The Evil Dr. Slime, slugging it out in Dr. Good's castle here in "beautiful downtown Flombania," during the reign of Queen Maude the Loud. The posters have what's on every Swine International poster: "During this film, please keep your pettifoggling snickers to yourself. Feel free to voice laughter and/or praise." The boys were so inventive! It's really "pettifogging," but the boys said "pettifoggling." Now they barely smile if I use "pettifoggling" in conversation, but I wish one of them would use it, too, once.

When I buy my ticket I don't say I'm the stars' mother. I pass on into

31

the cool dark, red and stale and comforting, and sink into the plush. The lights dim and suddenly the gray leader of twenty five years ago glows dim onscreen, edges blurry.

A burst of light and I blink. I'm rescued by beautiful, young Larry as Dr. Good, his body sketched by God in a single stroke, standing in front of the church, one of his soccer medals around his neck, big smile showing the chipped tooth he's had since he was eleven. There's something he has to tell me, something he knows that I don't. But that's just a picture of him. Colors faded. Scratches dart across the screen like those little unnamed fish one summer. They scratch my heart.

Dark. The church basement and a pale face floating: Percy as Dr. Slime, stringy hair, construction paper moustache cleaving his face, and this wacky frown. He has on dark clothes, like now, that blend into whatever mess was down there. It's all underexposed. He's squatting on a mound of garbage, gripping a shovel like he's buried something. I remember being concerned years back when I saw first this shot—the dirt, the shovel, like a newsreel from a prison camp. It could have been dangerous in that basement, but try telling that to a couple of kids!

I'm not so sure they should have made this in our church, but they meant no harm, and they never filmed in the sanctuary.

A bit of fuzz dances crazily; the film sweeps it away.

Every Dr. Good Dr. Slime movie goes the same way; that's the fun. Percy breaks into Dr. Good's castle, captures Larry, ties him up and tortures him in some silly way. (In this one he's forced to watch an "I Dream of Jeannie" film festival.) But then when Percy isn't paying attention, Larry slips out of his ropes. Percy gets his comeuppance, and Dr. Good triumphs.

The way they did it was so creative! They took turns shooting. The film cuts so smoothly from one attacking to the other fleeing, I marvel at it. How clever and serious they were! But now I see something else. Really there are two movies. When Percy holds the camera the shots are framed at creative angles. Larry just points at whatever's going on.

When Larry's on camera, he smiles practically the whole time, going through the paces like he was told, yet framed so strikingly, as though Percy's own eyes were the lenses, or as though Larry were clay and the lens Percy's hand, squeezing and molding. When Percy's on camera he squeezes and molds himself, and the frame kind of yaws around.

Then Percy appears in a long shot, his pale hands and face lost down dim corners of the social hall or the corridor by the nursery school, locked for summer. You can see they did use a light. It fills the foreground but doesn't reach back to Percy. Then Larry appears close up, flooded with light like honey poured over him.

Now, a long black scratch yaws down the center. It frightens me, I want it gone, but it pursues me. I run; it looms ahead of me. I fear the film will split. I place my hand over my chest, and still that black horror harrows my heart. The boys play on. They have no idea. Percy creeps to the end of a hallway and disappears. He looks like he's alone, playing Dr. Slime to the hilt for his own benefit.

The scratch ends. Dr. Good wins. He dumps Dr. Slime through the trap door in the church reception hall, where we have coffee hour. It's over so soon! I want nothing more than to be home, sipping iced tea with the air conditioner on. On my way out of the theater I ask the popcorn girl if there'll be more Percy and Larry movies. "Oooh... sorry!" she says, "like, tomorrow's the last day!" She points behind me.

I see a glossy poster for the boys' last movie, *The Search*. I don't think we parents ever saw it. They made it that fall, after the wonderful summer of Dr. Good and Dr. Slime. A chill from the air conditioning makes me goose bumpy. I want to pull my sweater around me, but I don't have it. In my sundress I hug myself and shudder. "Thank you," I say, and I walk to the poster. The lobby lights glare off its folds. I make out two pictures, super-imposed: Percy with his evil grin, like Dr. Slime but without the moustache, and over that a hand (Larry, I guess) reaching but not quite touching a pine twig with a dollop of light on the end. The poster says it's a world premiere—"NEWLY DISCOVERED—ONE DAY ONLY."

-o-

At home I sit with a weeping glass of iced tea. I want to call Percy and tell him I saw him as Dr. Slime and tell him how much I love him and always will. My love could be his shield. But I don't want to think now about the movie, everything the way it was back then but with that awful scratch. I leave my iced tea and go to lie down. I don't mind nights or rainy days, as some people think. Now's the worst—sunset. Every day at sunset, even now, I think, *Well, this is the last day. This is the last day without Dan, and tomorrow he'll be here and we'll be together.* Then it's night and I realize, no, I am alone, again, forever.

I wake in the dark. From my window I try to see the manicure parlor, but brighter lights and my own reflection obscure it. I imagine Percy with his wine, waiting. I go to the phone.

His answering machine plays a terse message muffled in echoes, as though he lived underwater. After the beep I say, "Percy?" He stands in his doorway, unaware I'm speaking to him. "Are you there?" His eyes scan deserted sulfur light cones in the street. "Percy, I won't recite a recipe!"

More words fail me. I hang up and vow to try again tomorrow.

I call Larry and tell him how I saw *You Can't Teach an Old Dog New Slime.*

"Huh!" he says. "I'd forgotten that. Was it a good idea for you to go outside, Ma?"

"Perfectly good! And I'm so happy I did because, why, the things I saw, Larry!"

"Really?" His words dribble out, like bullets.

I tell him about Percy and the movies at Trylon.

"Yeah, that was a lotta years ago, Ma. I doubt those movies exist anymore."

"Lawrence! What did I just tell you?!"

"Ma! It's not even called 'Flombania' anymore! It's got some new name!"

"What do you mean, Larry?"

"It's a whole other country, Ma. Foreign investment, the infrastructure, privatization of the water, U.S. companies own most of it. I tell you, Ma, you have to read the business section! Just ten-fifteen minutes a day, Ma. Stay informed!"

"I am informed!" My fingers want to twist the phone cord, but this is cordless. "You should visit Percy!" Percy with his wine in the night. "Just go say hello. I know he'd..."

"Ma, you've got to understand..." He's doing something while he speaks to me. E-mail or... "Ma, the next time I'm in Flom... Well, whatever it's called now; I can't think... I'm there on the eighteenth to meet with this sheik and this billionaire Brit who's a top authority on guided missile software, I'm there for the day, in-out, I can't be going down to... to wherever he... whatever it is... I can't, Ma, you've got to understand. I have pressures, Ma."

"I know you do, sweetheart."

"Sometimes I don't think you do, Ma. You don't know what the business environment's like. You have to court these people relentlessly. You have to guess what the trend is, what it's going to be. You knock your head against the wall and nothing happens. Deals fall through, people stab you in the back, you'd like to spend a day strolling in good old downtown 'Flombania,' but there's the kids, Ma, and I have... I want to think that I'm doing something, that I've achieved something, that I've reached a kind of apex where it's all important, just for a second. I... I could see him, you know. I don't know what we'd say to each other. I mean, his business and mine... What does he do, anyway, Ma?

I wait a second or two and then I say, "Love goes on forever, Larry!"

"Uh, yeah, of course, Ma. I love you, too. We all love you." A pause. "It's just it's a whole other country, Ma. Whole other country, you've got to realize. Hey, let me put the kids on. Larry Jr.'s right here."

-o-

The ice melts, making the tea gold at the top, shading into dark brown. Its tears sop the tablecloth. I woke up frightened of tomorrow, of having to see *The Search*, for I know I can't avoid it. Larry's meeting a sheik. *The Search* is my destiny. I fear what it has to tell me. I feel chastened to think the boys in those movies know something I don't. Now that they're fifty, I know so much more than they do, but their knowledge at fifteen frightens me. They're my fathers. Innocent, angry fathers with tidings that frighten me.

I reach for the comfort of being told what I know. But I feel in my heart that long, scratch in the film, like a road at night I'm pulled down. My foot presses the accelerator, the film splits. Where are the edges of knowledge? Knowledge is dull knives, nickels and dimes dropped in the street. If I go see *The Search*, God will be with me? In the moment I know everything, nothing will matter.

I wake in gray light and walk the main streets of my house, crowded with shadows. I want this over. I try to get my scarf and sunglasses together but can't decide which scarf, and the first show is starting and I see a black scratch down the center and I think I'll never leave the house. I pray. Finally I leave in time for the second show. I'm relieved to get out where I can be alone.

Only a handful of people have shown up this afternoon. I can't distinguish them, slumped down in those new high back chairs that rock and have soft drink holders. I feel as though we're the chosen, guilty remnants of a once great crowd, come to witness a rite in memory of others, who have gone on. Church, movie theater. The lights dim. The square gray window of projected leader glows dully from the screen. I stare back and try to master my fear.

White and gold knives rip open the gray. From the knives rises an emerald heart. They must have shot this on the fields at Percy's school, late on a fall afternoon after the teams left. There's no dialogue, no music, just the tick of the projector. Larry crosses the field with a straight ahead look. He was the handsome one then, though Percy's turned out nicely. Larry's still handsome, too, of course. He just frowns so much in pictures.

Larry, shot by Percy, squints into the sun, looking toward all things he could not have known, but that with faith he dreamed—a wife, kids, a house, it all happened and I have the pictures to prove it!—then something blocks the light and Larry starts.

Out of the knives of sun comes Percy, shot by Larry. He crowds the camera with a wicked grin. The last thing on his mind was a manicure parlor and auto garage! Larry runs.

This scene repeats: Larry confident, striding, Percy's evil grin, Larry fleeing.

The years have faded the gold green soccer field, the green black end of day, but not a scratch mars this maiden. She aged but was never spoiled by the light. The world looks on her for the first time. She's alone and brave, letting herself be run through that projector, letting light shine in her every corner, letting lenses blow her up while our gazes operate on her mystery. She bleeds what we've been through.

Larry jogs, shambling, but falls and tumbles, the frame whirling from his point of view, bright sky/dark earth/bright/dark/bright/dark. Percy crouches over him with a wicked grin, shoulders shaking. This movie is about something, but I don't know what—and maybe neither did they, in 1972, '73. I wish it were then...

Larry walks again, straight into Percy's shadow, which tapers like a steeple. You can see the steeple has one hand up, holding a camera. Larry freezes. He turns wide eyed and sees: Percy, in close up, setting sun behind him, wind tossing his hair gold, his face a grainy blank. The shot lasts a long time.

Each scene is darker. I'm anxious that they won't finish by nightfall. They'll be late for dinner or won't come home at all. I picture them between scenes, alone in the field, the sun setting, the two of them trying to decide what to do next, the sun setting.

His golden face gone gray, Larry peers at: a bare tree rising out of brambles. I start when I see Percy lounging sinuously along the trunk.

He smirks and beckons to the camera, to Larry. A closer shot: Percy freezes, arms outstretched to Larry, fingers splayed like roots. Closer: hair blows across his face.

Now Larry shakes his head. He puts his palms up, backs away keeps shaking his head, then he turns and runs.

He stops in the center of the field and looks back. Percy advances, fingers like claws. Larry turns and there's Percy again, and again and again, everywhere. Through it all we sit, nearly invisible to one another, sunk in our seats, the only sound the projector ticking. Long arms of light shuffle and reshuffle pieces on the screen. I feel as though my bones have fused.

Light arms draw Larry over black grass, body writhing to escape Percy's steeple-shadow and leer. Percy pushes the camera closer, as though it were a brush with which he's painting his friend. Larry's gaze shoots at us, as though Percy just called out an instruction. Larry obeys that instruction, twisting away, clambering to his feet, running into the last flare of light caught in November branches.

Cut. Now it's so dark I can no longer tell where earth meets sky. They lost a lot of light preparing for this shot. It must be the end. They must have debated. A long time. Fought, maybe. The dark is testament to a clash never witnessed, to boyish passions forever secret and lost. Something moves. Larry's jacket—but I can't make out him in it. It sinks to the green-black earth, then crawls toward a row of pines like judges.

His pale hand rises against blackness. The camera shakes. Percy shivers. He wants to get everything in during that last second of light, get all there is, hold it unchanging, pinned like a butterfly. The camera comes closer to Larry. His fingertips slip out of focus. They extend to within half an inch of a pine twig, drop of sap gold in the last light. But he doesn't reach it.

The Search is over.

The lights come up. No one applauds.

I see now that everyone here but me is a man. Each looks to be alone, as he rises and climbs the aisles, fists stretching black leather pockets, grim, as though he saw something different and private and can't tell the others. Some glance at me. Their looks linger, as though they recognize me, as though they want something from me. I don't know any of them. Percy isn't here. He made the darkness in 1974. It visits him late at the garage. He imagines being here, maybe, to say a word about his life's accomplishment.

Why would the boys make a movie like that? I mean, why would Percy make it? I can't imagine Larry thinking up what I saw. He would have contributed more to the Dr. Good and Dr. Slime movies. Why did they change from making funny things, just from that August to November? After *The Search* they never made another movie. We asked when they would; they just looked at us like we were passé. After that last scene in *The Search*, what more could Percy do? He and Larry... You see, Percy was talented with movies and acting and all, but later, when someone could have given him a real camera and film, he didn't ask. Not that the manicure parlor and garage aren't an accomplishment. The garden's the most creative, but who sees it? Percy shouldn't be spending his life on it. Lord, You're supposed to have a reason for everything. I try to have faith that You do. Help me understand why my second son must spend his life waiting.

I haven't moved. New men fill a few seats around me. I assume they're new, though they look the same as the ones before. I will stay with them and watch *The Search* again. They need me.

Gray eye looks equally upon gold knives, green heart.

My son's athletic stride, eyes on the horizon, Percy with the camera saying, "Okay, you're looking for something, you don't know what it is," and Larry, fifteen and sincere, hope pinned on the future as Percy's will be again tonight. And yes, it has occurred to me that Percy, well, found Larry attractive. I just don't think...

I don't think *The Search* has to do with that, exactly. Maybe Percy wanted to be like Larry. Maybe he struggled with knowing that none of us can be anything than what we are. In *The Search*... When they made *The Search*, maybe they both realized... Because I think Larry did, too... Larry wanted them to be alike, in order to save Percy. Maybe he thought, if Percy were more like him, he'd be saved... Maybe the reason they made movies, the whole reason they were friends... Because after *The Search*, they weren't so close anymore...

Maybe the whole reason our two families met was so one day our boys could learn, so that Percy could accept that he would never be Larry. And Larry... oh gosh... we're all such a grab bag of thoughts and feelings and kids get curious and adolescents are like aliens, anyway, and if Larry felt certain things I could see it, I could see it at the Trylon, a fall night in 1972 or '73, for the Cities of the Plain are gone, always gone down in glory while merciful God lets Flombania stand with its refugees, those of us with more vision, or less. Us buffalo, us pixies.

Percy, turn to Him! He is big enough to contain the hurt you'd feel, but you won't believe. Someone once told you you were outside of Him and so you went wandering beyond His golden city, and there you stay, believing only in... right there, prone on the ground, beautiful and vulnerable, captured forever acting just the way you told him to. You leer and beckon.

Then you tell him, "Quick! Run away!" And he does.

And you watch him go.

That should have been the end. Instead, you were left with this muddle of Heaven and Earth, human parts swimming in a sea of dark bees. Drowning in darkness Larry yearns toward the last sun touched twig, but Percy keeps him from touching it. Time to put away childish things; let there be dark.

In the slow rise of yellow light, the latest scattering of men disperses. One or two smile at me. I want to seize their sleeves, stop their slow, weary climb out of my son's quandary, maybe even ask them home with me. Second son, third son, fourth, fifth, sixth, eighth, eleventh, twentieth... For home is what I know, I must go there, and once I'm there I will not leave for a long, long time.

I rise and stretch, reopening my frozen skeleton.

On the sidewalk the light stabs my eyes; I put on my dark glasses. Once I wanted a business. Not a manicure parlor but a shop with yarn and things, helping people with what thread to buy and suggesting patterns. But Dan didn't want me to work. And I didn't have a daughter, so all that I know dies with me, I suppose. I should have taught Percy.

I should have taught Percy. But how do you begin to teach? How do you begin to say?

To long to be other than what we are is a sin. All sins lurk in that one wish to be someone else: despair, covetousness, all. To be other than what we are is, in the end, the only temptation. When we finally refuse it, then we accept a great gift.

Just one thing I don't understand. Larry was a reasonable kid; he'd go along with anything. Why didn't Percy ask just one time, "Let's have me be the hero this time, you be the bad guy?" Larry would have agreed in a second, and he'd have been such a fun villain!

Tonight I'm determined to call Percy and tell him I love him, and to have him hear it, really hear it.

-o-

Beep.

"Percy, darling, I just wanted to let you know how happy I was to see you yesterday." I tell him I saw and *You Can't Teach an Old Dog New Slime* and *The Search*, and that it was all beautiful. "Percy, you've always been so special in... in our lives, all our lives, and you always will be. Nothing can change that. Someone will come one of these nights, and he'll be a fine person. He'll love you, Percy, as much as I do, and I'll love meeting him. I know juggling the manicure and the garage and waiting like that is difficult sometimes, but I pray you'll find peace. Don't neglect the garden, darling. He'll like the garden, he'll love it, when he comes.

"I hope I'll see you soon, darling. I have to rest since the operation, but I'll come by. I love you, Percy. And no pettifoggling! Good bye, darling."

-o-

For a long time I hear nothing from him.

The weather turns. Leaves fall.

One day I come home to a message on my answering machine:

"You won't believe this. I have peppers—just little ones. I keep waiting for them to fall off and they don't! The cold must have killed whatever was killing them. But the cold's also going to keep them from getting big. They'll stop at a certain point, I won't be able to use them, but at least I finally got something! Last night I closed up early and went out and sat with them. Tonight again. I'm going to hang on as long as I can. I'll stay up all night the first frost, to be with them and watch them die. Well, sorry I took up so much space in your machine, but I have these little peppers, I thought my second mother should know. I'll be the only boy left with dead peppers in December! The only living boy in Flombania.

"Oh! One more thing. The other day, Maria, she works for me, handed me this card someone left on my night off. A business card, I mean; it said 'Larry.' No phone, no Internet, just 'Larry'—in that kind of raised printing? I asked who left it, she said, 'Some kid.' I asked some more; she said he was nice, 'dressed funny,' looked kind of lost. Said he was looking for work. I think she thought I'd like, well, *hire* this kid for... But no. Anyway..."

And so he segués into one of his resigned good-byes. He doesn't say he loves me, but I know he does. I save the message to listen to again later on.

"Larry." How about that. Wasn't there 'some kid' at the Trylon? There must have been, there must have been several. Was one of them 'dressed funny?' Unemployed?

In the kitchen I heat dinner. How tired I am of eating alone. I get through it by pretending each time is the last. I tell myself, "I only have to go through this one last time."

I eat, I wash my plate, fork, knife, and glass, I turn out the light, go upstairs, undress, and slip my white nightgown over my head. The fabric caresses like an arpeggio, setting off longing and joy. Dan, how could you leave me! When the machine beeps it's you I expect, calling to tell me there was some awful mix-up and here you are!

–o–

I ask Larry about the boy with the card. He doesn't know anything, but he says for me to say hello to Percy. "And I'll come see you, Ma, soon as I can." He sounds worried. I tell him not to worry about me. I'm fitter than ever and I am perfectly sane. "We'll come see you, Ma," he says, "soon as we can figure out our schedules. It's crazy here!"

–o–

Now Percy, darling, if I end up in that place where every hour they wake me, if you visit and the halls smell to high heaven and I'm staring out the window and I don't look at you when you say my name, just take my hand. It's all right if you cry when you say "Flombania." No, maybe you shouldn't. I'll be afraid something happened in Flombania and my friend Percy is hurt, or dead. I'll be certified—by Larry, I suppose—but I'll understand. He'll have to. While my first son signs the papers I'll have my second son sit by me and tell me the streets we freely walked are still there, the same, sunny and full of hope, waiting for us tomorrow.

Please Talk to Me, Please

When we finally get out on the street at 3:00 a.m., new snow soundlessly falling on the New Year and Carla stumbling as she struggles to put on her coat, I look at Brian and see that not-quite-there look behind his eyes. I ask, "Did you have a horrible time?" I feel tipsy from too much champagne and too much Howard Stern yelling on the TV in Sharon's bedroom, everyone piled on the bed hooting and hollering. "Did you?" I ask, stepping up to him. "Did you have a horrible time?" He purses his lips, holds up a hand and says, "It's all right." "You hated it, didn't you?" I say. He shrugs. He turns from me to help Carla with her coat, earnestly focusing on her, though he met her just this evening and they've barely spoken. He remains silent as we cross on West Third to Sixth Avenue to find a cab.

As we jounce up Sixth in the cab and then barrel up Eighth, he stays quiet, except when he leans across me to chat amiably about movies with Carla. We drop her off in Hell's Kitchen, then have the driver take us on up to West End and Eighty-Sixth. Walking on West End he remarks how pretty the snow looks falling through light from the street lamps. "Mm-hm," I say, and nod.

I flinch when the apartment door slams behind me. Then I realize I am the one who slammed it. He clumps down the hall to my bedroom. I follow, and find him emptying his pockets onto my dresser. "Seriously," I say, as gently as possible, "was it really that bad?"

I see the anger rise in him. I see him hold it down, as though his impassive features serve as a dam that shows strain but won't let the water through. He says what he said before: "It's okay. Don't worry about it."

"I *do* worry about it," I say. He flinches and I modify my tone. "It is *not* okay if you had a horrible time and you don't *tell* me. You can *tell* me, Brian."

But he insists, "I did not have a horrible time." He sits on the bed to unlace his shoes.

"Don't turn away from me," I say. "Please, Brian, whatever you do, don't turn away from me." Dutifully he turns and looks at me, handsome in the half-dark with his lips pressed together and his regretful eyes. "You did have a horrible time, didn't you?"

He looks down at his shoes and says, "It's just not my kind of thing."

"*What* isn't your kind of thing?" I ask, sitting down beside him and taking his hand. We lace fingers.

"That kind of party. The drinking."

"Then why can't you say to me"—I tick these things off on my fingers—"'Greg, I hated Sharon's party, I didn't like the drinking, I had a terrible time.' Why can't you *say* that? What are you *afraid* of?"

He shrugs. I am used to that. And I am tired of it. He rises and goes to the dresser.

"Come on," I say. "What did you really think of that party? You hated it. You must have thought it was insane. You saw the same stuff I did, right?"

"Look," he says, and his face shows not just anger but an underlying pain, as though communication actually hurts. "Can't we just say it wasn't my kind of party? It was your kind of party, it wasn't mine. I don't see why we have to say any more than that."

"Because," I say, pulling him back down beside me, squeezing his hand to make him look at me, "if you can't tell me how you feel about things then we have no relationship!" As I hold his gaze I see the discomfort, but I tell him that is not an excuse. "You have arranged your whole life around trying to be comfortable, Brian, but dammit, I am really beginning to care about you, and I am not going to let you off the hook just because something you feel is hard to say."

He looks down. I release his hand. I take off my shoes and crawl across the bedspread on hands and knees. I pull at his arm. "Lie down with me," I say, sweetening my voice, exposing another raw chamber of my heart. Slowly he removes his shoes, then slides over to me and we lie down side by side.

"I just have a difficult time with that sort of thing," he mumbles as he places his arms around me carefully.

"*What* sort of thing? Brian, tell me what you *feel!*"

"The sort of thing," he answers, "where there are a lot of people... drinking."

"'Drunk,'" I say. "Those people were drunk. You don't have to be nice. Some of them were, anyway. Come on, say it: 'Those people were drunk.'"

"Whatever," he says. I let out a deep breath and roll onto my back. "And it happens that I choose not to drink, and so I am not comfortable around people who are... whatever they were..."

I don't mean to roll my eyes, but he's holding on with such a death grip—to what?

"Look," he says, laying his open hand on my chest, "Why do you insist that I call your friends drunks when I've never met them before. and..."

"Because I want you to be honest with me!" I say, sitting up.

"...and Carla was there," he continues, "who I'd never met before..."

"Forget the rules!"

"...and we were right there in the taxi with her..."

"Brian..!"

"...and *she* was drunk and I'm supposed to just pop out and say, 'I don't like being around drunk people'?"

"For Chrissake, 'popping out' is part of being human! Why are you so afraid? You could have sat there in that taxi and popped right out and railed at me for ten minutes about how much you hated that party and it would have been okay." He folds his arms across his chest. "So long as it was *honest*. All right, okay, look, forget Carla. Forget the taxi. You're just with me now, and at least when you're with me, I want you to be able to say what you feel, because without that we're just going out to dinner and a movie once a week and there's no partnership!"

After a moment—the moment it takes him to digitize what he's heard and craft a reply—he says, "I don't see what's wrong with dinners and movies. We've only been going together three months..."

"But people who are going together have to have somewhere they're going to!"

His mouth draws in at the corners. He is prepared to wait out my speech, but I can tell he has not given any thought to this. I see I'm going to have to do the thinking, and I am tired of it. Some days I have a tough enough time just thinking for myself. That's when I would need *you* to take care of *me*, Brian. But now I relent. I like Brian, and I think he is a good man. We have fun with those dinners and movies. I look forward to them. But at the same time he's holding on so tightly. He was not comfortable at Sharon's party, and I admit, that's not the kind of party I would go to every week. I mean, the cops came and arrested Sharon's ex-boyfriend for being drunk and disorderly; he peed out the window and yes, absolutely, I admit it, that's insane, I suppose maybe I'd even forgotten a little bit what Sharon's parties could be like, but that's just *one* guy, *one* night of the year, and we could still *talk* about it, couldn't we? I wish he cared enough about me, about us, to just up and say, "Greg, these people are fucking nuts! What did you bring me here for? Don't bring me here again!" We'd be okay now. Instead, as Sharon waved us off and I asked him if he was okay, he shrugged and said dispassionately, "I guess I'm just not a party person."

Add to that, he was "not a sports person," when I suggested he play handball with me at the Y, and when I told him how I was looking forward to summer, I found out he's "not a beach person," either. (The two seemed related because he has "body issues," which I get; I have a few myself, but, "What do you do for fun?" I asked. "This is fun," he replied, looking wounded and nonplused. We were watching TV, I think. Or eating Chinese food. If I press him about having fun or taking risks, well, "We've only known each other three months." He wants to keep things on this nice, safe level of dinners and movies and sex—during which, by the way, he always has to be on top. Which isn't bad in itself. He's sexy. He's okay. He's got that energy and passion I always wanted in a lover, and he's strong—I like having him on top of me. Or did at first. But if I gently say, "Couldn't we try it this way, instead?" he looks wounded, as though I'm saying that what he's doing is deficient.

I touch his arm and say, "I really like you, Brian, but you can't remain safe all your life."

He digitizes this, then asks, "Do you think it's unreasonable that I wouldn't be comfortable at a party with so much drinking when I don't drink? Do you think it's unreasonable that I find it difficult to say something is insane when... how do I know what your relationship is to those people?"

"Say it anyway! Do you think I'm so thin-skinned? Do you think I don't see the insanity, too?"

"Then why did you take me there?"

"Because I wanted you to be intimate with people I am intimate with!"

"While they're drunk?"

"Not everyone was drunk! I saw you talking to Robin for must have been half an hour, and she wasn't drunk. You know what I think the problem is?"

"Okay, tell me what *you* think the problem is," he says, as though I am asking for all the authority and only because I am hopelessly unreasonable is he giving it to me.

"I don't think the problem is who drinks and who doesn't. I think the problem is, you don't know how to have fun!"

"Oh, that party is your idea of fun?"

"Not all the time, but what's your idea? More dinners and movies? I'm sorry, I don't mean that like it sounds, dinners and movies are fine, I like doing that with you, it's been nice, I like you, I really do, but what I really think you look for in life is not fun or *engagement*, but comfort, and you can't always be comfortable! You have to take the plunge! Why do you think they call it 'engagement'? When two people make a commitment to one another, why do you think they call it 'engagement'? Engage with me, Brian. Start by telling me where you are and I will tell you where I am. You didn't like Sharon's New Year's Eve party. Fine. What *happened* to you there?"

He frowns. He massages my hand.

"Brian?" I ask, "Is it about your dad?"

Brian's dad is an alcoholic. He tried AA, but from time to time he still drinks, though not as much as he did. Brian has made allusions to growing up with slammed doors and family outings wrecked, but he talks about these things as though they were only minor annoyances. Things that would traumatize most kids, things that would enrage me against the old fuck, seem barely to have touched him. Once when he was little he spent a month building his dad a box out of popsicle sticks as a present, but his dad smashed it in a drunken rage before it was finished. Brian told me this as though he were reporting it. Now I say, "What did it feel like when your dad smashed that box you made for his birthday?"

"What?"

"What it was like for you? Was it somehow like what you felt tonight? Tell me a *story* about being the son of an alcoholic. I would have wanted to kill someone who did that. I would have wanted to bash their face with a fucking brick if they did that." His hand stops massaging mine. "Didn't you *feel* any of that?"

He runs a fingertip up the inside of my arm. It slows thoughtfully as it nears my elbow. His face in repose, in the light from the one lamp, looks so good, the line of his jaw so perfect. I've told him that he is the handsomest man I have ever been with, and he tells me I am "beautiful."

You see, we can be good together. On the phone, checking in at night, going over the trivia of the day, it can be fun, easy, warm. I could talk to him all night about movies or books, but not, I guess, about the difficult stuff, the stuff of life, as far as I'm concerned.

"I was angry," he says, in response to my question about the birthday present.

"But... tell me a story!"

"I've told you that story a couple of times."

"You told me what happened. You did not make me feel an experience, something so that I can understand how you felt and what it made you want to do! In class," I say, "when we do a scene, my acting teacher always asks: 'How does this make you feel? What does it make you want to *do*?' And to do that you have to risk being uncomfortable!"

"You have a lot of rules for how I should talk to you," he says, his hand cupping my arm and squeezing.

"I do *not* have rules!"

"Yes, you do! It has to be the way it is in your acting class, I have to feel by numbers."

"That's not it at all!"

"How I am is not okay with you, I have to... to be pushed into some feeling state I don't necessarily want to be in, just to please you. You don't leave any room for... for just *how I am*..."

"I've left *plenty* of room for how you are! I've been leaving room for how you are for weeks."

"Why can't you just let me not like the party and have that be it?"

"Because that's closing a door on me."

"And that's my business."

"It's my business, too, if I'm going to be your partner." I suddenly feel weighed down.

He looks away and says, "Maybe I don't know what I feel."

"Bullshit!"

"Well..! Maybe I don't! Not everyone knows every last little thing they feel! Do you know every last little thing you feel?"

"No, obviously not every last little thing. But for the most part, yes, I do know how I feel, and I do communicate my emotions. I believe that's fundamental! If you can't do that, you can't make love, you can't make art, why bother to even get up in the morning?" Suddenly I want to take back the part about "you can't make art," because Brian is a painter, or, I should say, Brian paints; he hasn't been exhibited yet. I've probably just invalidated both him and his work by saying no art without communicating feelings, but he doesn't say so. He just looks glum.

"But you are an artist," I assure him, and the pleading tone I hear in my own voice annoys me. "And you're a good artist"—after much coaxing he finally showed me his paintings; I loved the colors and the textures, but even in the realistic canvases I had to search for the objects he said were there—"and you are a good lover. You're the best I've had..." And this is true: No one has ever touched me the way Brian has. He tries very hard. But when he refuses to speak, except in defensive bullshit, I come up against something that scares me. I don't want to descend into his dark space; my own has been dark enough, thank you.

Now he places his face against the side of my neck tentatively—yes, he is a good lover—and I close my eyes as I feel his warm breath. "So you know what I mean," I conclude, no longer certain that I know what I mean.

After a moment during which we simply hold one another I say, "Tell me what's in your heart," and I probe with the tip of my finger into the coarse hair visible in the V where his shirt opens. "Tell me anything, Brian. Anything at all. Please..."

He curls around me and begins to kiss my neck, insinuates his tongue into the hollow behind my ear, and with his tongue and teeth he toys with my earlobe. "You like that?" he asks hopefully.

"Mm-hm..." I draw him closer and kiss his neck once. It will be all right, I tell myself, as I have told myself several times before. He does move me. He is a nice man. Aren't I just picking on one little problem? Well, not so little, but... Plenty of gay men have trouble opening up, don't they, what with our backgrounds, our isolation, our playground incidents resonating through the years, all that stuff that makes us walk the streets eyes front, sunglasses in place? We all have dark places. I have trouble sometimes. Shouldn't I give this a chance to get better with time? He begins unbuttoning my shirt. I help, from the bottom. Our hands meet and he kisses my fingertips. Maybe I'm just what he needs to bring him out a second time. Maybe I'll be good for him. And Sharon's party was an anomaly, maybe not a good idea, I admit that; when you haven't introduced your boyfriend to your friends before, Sharon's New Year's Eve party might not be the best situation to bring him into, tossing him off the deep end. But people do learn to swim that way.

I start to undo his shirt. "Hey, Sailor," I say, as I watch his shirt open. We smile briefly at one another.

Soon we are bare-chested, embracing, our tongues exploring one another's mouths, gliding and sucking and hanging on. He moans perfunctorily. He breaks the kiss to tell me, "God, you are so beautiful.

49

I have never seen a man as beautiful as you!" I am beginning to believe that. And I'm beginning to see that he means it in a different way than the procession of guys who've said, "You're cute," "You're pretty," blah-blah. Brian looks at me in wonder.

I ask him to look in my eyes and he does. I ask him what he is feeling now, and with a grin he tells me: "I feel great, I swear, you totally transport me!" Too easy, I tell myself. But I file that thought away. When we are naked his hand works my cock with such firmness and dedication that I surrender completely. I let his grip take over. Veins bulge on the backs of his hands and in his forearms. I shoot, effortlessly as a flower blooms. He straddles me and with my cum smeared the length of his shaft he gets himself off onto my chest, the way he knows I like it. Afterwards we lie in one another's arms, still but for gasping, bespattered. "I love you," he offers.

"I think I love you," I say. He says nothing but the tempo of his breathing alters. I make no explanation. Can I learn to love reticence? His reticence? The death grip with which he holds onto what little he has collected in that smashed popsicle-stick box? Are those warm and funny phone calls a trade-off? Is the passion worth it? Or is nothing worth it if that partnering doesn't happen? And while I go back and forth in my head about whether or not that will happen, does my heart already know the answer? The questions blur in my mind. I have to pee. When I pull myself away he makes a joke about us sticking together, and we both grin.

I examine my face in the mirror, the face he's called "adorable," "beautiful," "sweet." I don't look adorable or beautiful or sweet right now. I look exhausted, my features heavy. I know that look. It comes from being untrue to myself. That exhausted look comes from doing something I know I shouldn't be doing. I flush the toilet. When I return to the room he rises. He pauses long enough to pat my ass and kiss me again, the insinuating tongue behind my ear. I like that.

While he's in the bathroom I light a couple of candles, set them in front of the mirror, and look around at the home I have made for myself. I wonder what place is here for the stranger I hear running the sink. Did I say stranger? I've known him three months. Or have I? I lie beneath half-turned-down covers, and I try to imagine what he is like with friends and family. What people does he gather around him? What is he like with his father now? To whom does he open himself, if not me? Oh, he shares some with me; he's educated, intelligent, he has ideas. He has more than that. We laugh together, and I suppose those are the times I love him, late at night, talking about nothing. A couple of nights ago he told me how he had spent the morning working out some transaction with the bank, and as he talked on about the most mundane details I ached with love for him. Or did I ache with desire? If so, was it even desire for him? Or for the ordinary life of balancing check books? But that stuff he's afraid to give away haunts me. I am lost in thinking of myriad little strategies I could employ to make him give it up. But the face I saw in the mirror looks back at me and tells me: You can't make him do anything.

I am not your teacher, Brian. I am not your mentor or your guidance counselor, and I sure as hell ain't your therapist. I don't want a fixer-upper. At least not for a boyfriend. When he reappears, so much himself in his nakedness, as though I weren't there, I put it to him this way:

"I do want to be your friend, Brian."

"Oh," he says, suddenly still, looking aimlessly at the corner of the bed, trying to grasp some emotions that are welling up out of control and that finally can not be digitized. I guess I'd hoped he wouldn't hear the full meaning in that, or I'd hoped that meaning wasn't there, or that I could fudge some kind of in-between meaning, so that for the rest of the night at least we could occupy some in-between state, a crystal ball of night and falling snow, a state of not quite letting go. But I see the woundedness dawning in his eyes and I know what I should know by my age: romantic limbo exists only in theory (or in more lyrical pornography), like a point in space you can discuss but can never represent, never possess.

"Can we please talk?" I ask tenderly, but underneath I feel anger well up as frowning he surveys the room. His eyes settle on his clothes, scattered randomly in the heat of sex. At last, with a shudder of mortal pain he pulls on his socks, enraged, no doubt, hurt, unbearably confused, but not about to risk the real experience of these things. Anyone else who had just heard that his relationship was over would have a reaction—from "What the fuck do you mean, 'friend?'" to "I want to be your friend, too," to anything in between. But not Brian. I'm about to try again, to say something more, but as I take a breath to speak I clamp my mouth shut. Why should I always have to yank it out of you, Brian? Grow up, for Chrissake! Oh, fine, I'll teach him, I'll bring him out, I'll be the caretaker... NO! What about when I need to be taken care of? What about that, Brian?

Oh, Brian. I've had a good three months, I suppose. But it won't fly. It won't fly.

He holds his pants out in front of him, suspended, waiting for what won't happen. He casts a rueful glance down the legs and says, "I don't see why this has to happen over a stupid party."

Later I will worry over my decision to say nothing, regretting it tomorrow morning, angrily justifying it in the afternoon, regretting it again by evening. But you know damn well, Brian, that this is not about a "stupid party." I've explained a million times what it is about, and even if I hadn't, you're a smart man. You should know. You do know, god damn it, but you're withholding and pouting in silence to make me do all the work or to punish me, and *I will not be punished*! He finishes buttoning his shirt, waits, reaches for his jacket, waits again. I say nothing. He takes it. I've had people run this number on me before—The Silence. I won't beat on a locked door. I don't even see the possibility of friendship right now, because friendship is about being there for the other person's growth, about mutual *investment*, and right now I don't see anything to invest in. The bank's closed. I can make deposits in the lobby if I want, but the bank is closed.

I am still on the bed when he turns to face the door and pauses, his knapsack over his shoulder, his shoulders bent, his face showing me a resigned sadness, his eyes not meeting mine. I see the physical pain.

"Call me tomorrow?" I ask.

He shrugs.

I say, "Why don't you cry?"

"I am not an ac*tor*," he says quietly. "I can't turn it on and off on command. And he clumps out in silence.

I'm up off the bed. "That is not fair!" I shout. I follow him down the hall, but I am afraid to reach for him, afraid I will catch him and afraid I will not. "That is not fucking fair!" I stop. I repeat again, "That is not fucking fair," but I will be damned if I tell him yet again why it is not.

He pulls the door shut behind him. I barely hear his footsteps on the stairs.

I stride naked to the living room, and stand at the window overlooking West End. I watch him emerge downstairs and suddenly run like a hunted animal for the subway. He doesn't look back.

Take your feelings and run, Brian. Go paint with them. I tried. I really tried. I thought because I liked you... But no, I could not do this. "Not an ac*tor*." God damn it! He knows... He knew... But it's his problem. His problem. He needed to say it, but god *damn* it, Brian!

I drift back to my bedroom, telling him mentally why it is not fair. Repeating the whole evening, argument by argument. I blow out one candle, leave the other burning, and flop on the bed, belly up. I look at my cock, sad that only a few minutes ago I was hard and ejaculating, thinking what a beautiful man was next to me, taking me in his hand, taking me... where? Where would you take me, Brian? I think of you running to the subway as though there were no one in the city but you. I wonder what will become of you. What kind of life will you have? I want no part in it, not the part I'd play as your boyfriend, anyway. And yet I can't help feeling sorry for the lone figure fleeing, shoulders hunched. I don't just talk about feelings because I am an actor. And if I do it's because being an artist, being an actor sensitizes you. It is my life, it is my living (well, I intend I to be), and so yes...

It will be light soon. The New Year will dawn and I will be alone with dishes to wash, plants to water, cat to feed. (He pads into my room now and meows, wide-eyed, and I feel myself about to cry as I stroke him, the uncomprehending beast, and tell him, "Uncle Brian went away. He's not here anymore.") No more excitement of having him there, thinking about me every day, no calls to look forward to late at night when I'm pleasantly exhausted and curled up with a cup of tea.

I know I can live without that. I've lived without it before. I've spent most of my life without it, and I guess I must sort of enjoy it. I'm not one of those people who has to have a relationship. I know people who can't be out of a relationship two days. I know people who overlap girlfriends or boyfriends, always thinking about The Next One. I'm not like that. But I do feel the passion. I do know what it is like to put myself out like that, and I will not compromise. I need someone who can feel the difficult things with me.

I will sleep now. I will wake at noon and feed the cat and take a shower, and I will eat breakfast in the sun coming in the living room windows. I will study for an audition. I will miss his call when it doesn't come and silence fills the house. When I talk to friends I will tell them I broke up with him. They will ask why. I will say, "Because he wouldn't talk to me." I will tell them he was haunted, bound up in his dark world that I could never be a part of. It's not my job to change anyone. I have other things in my life, and Brian is not an investment that would pay off in the long term.

The cat licks my hair. It's always sad when things don't work out between two people. The possibility of Heaven, however marginal, is lost. "Didn't work out." What a sad euphemism. How general and bereft of emotion. But I tell you, Brian, if you're listening, I would rather be home alone with a sad euphemism, than be drawn into a world that feels like death when I get too close.

The brick wall outside my window grows faintly gray. I can't sleep. The cat still licks my hair. Where is he now? Still in the subway, a block and a half from here, alone on the platform or sharing it with a clique of late, drunken revelers, listening to water drip, no headlights in sight, thinking of the weeks he spent on that popsicle-stick box, remembering how he decorated it with gold stars and a picture he liked of a little boy, cut from a magazine, and swearing to himself with a clenched jaw that he will never again so much as glue two popsicle sticks together the rest of his life..? Has the train come? If I ran after him..? No! Even in my head I can't even make Brian talk to me.

Or is he home, asleep? I want to invade his dreams, seize him and force him to see about himself what I see. I must care about someone to whom I would want to do that, mustn't I? Or—I yawn—do I just want to be right? Do I just want to feel that I have an answer he doesn't have?

The cat licks his paws.

I am alone.

It is New Year's Day.

I ask myself, What do you feel?

I feel frustrated, sad, and strangely enough, at peace. Or, I think with a plunging sensation in my gut, is it not peace but self-satisfaction? Did I really score a victory for myself, as I thought a moment ago? Or a defeat?— throwing away the best thing I ever had? I could mope over that a good long time. But no, I couldn't do it, and running after him now won't make me suddenly able to. With a sigh I watch the gray light grow brighter. I pull the comforter over me, but I cannot sleep. I could sleep with a well-ordered victory or defeat. The sharp pain of a draw keeps me awake. On that gray wall, in the gray light, I see that the life that stretches before me will only be one draw after another. Is this adulthood I've come to? There's no here here. I can go on living only to play the game.

7:01 I can't bear it. But I will. But I can't. And yet I do.

7:02 And yet I can't. But I do. But I can't...

7:03 And I will.

7:04 I will.

7:05 I will.

7:06 I will.

7:07

Series

Peachy held on by planning for the next event—just get to Halloween, Thanksgiving, Kevin's memorial service, Kevin's lover Chris's memorial service, just get to Christmas—which was easy because Peachy had seen Martha Stewart on *Today* wrapping presents in tulle and he was, pardon the expression, dying to try it.

We knew better than to tell him, "Get to Valentine's Day." That was not his strong suit. I told him near the end that he could know he was loved and he said, "I was not *loved*. 'I've always been a woman who arranges things.'" I wondered then what I'd meant by "love."

Peachy died on a warm Saturday in January. His mother insisted on a priest. Peachy hadn't given a sign in hours, but when the white collar walked in he opened his eyes and said, "Well! God's judgment we deliver!" Fast forward: what would I die believing?

The parents abandoned the apartment. Our friend Mona and I split up the meds ("meds" is a word you toss around to sound cool and authoritative in the middle of all this) because we had friends who were still alive who could use them. No one we knew wanted the holistic stuff, but we took it anyway. I still have Peachy's bee pollen. I go to the fridge for a midnight snack, and I take out the pollen. I study the smiling bee. I read the directions. I read them again. I put it back. One more day.

–o–

Jimmy went first, in July '95. He was forty-three. We'd known each other since NYU. We weren't lovers, but one of us might call the other of a January or July night to trade the rack of isolation for some timeless play. Afterwards, not having to deal fully with the other created relief, and sadness.

With Jimmy near death and his parents coming to visit for the first time since he'd moved here, he tried to sit up in bed and he croaked, "In... the... closet..." I went in and dug till I found a cardboard box from the liquor store, full of paperbacks with black and white covers and titles like *Pledge's Cherry* and *Milking Baby Brother*. Jimmy tried to sit up again but couldn't. Trapped on his back like a turtle he rasped, "Take them... away..." So I lugged the books to a dumpster five blocks away and heaved them up over. Jimmy lapsed into a coma before his parents came, and he died three days later.

Then Mario went in August, at forty-one. He'd been Jimmy's lover for six years during which Jimmy hadn't called me as much. Mario and Jimmy had split up in August '93, after Mario found his first KS lesion in his mouth.

For the sake of the benefits, Mario had worked at a place where you charge theatre tickets. But he really lived to make movies—first super-8, then video. We had "premieres" with gowns and red carpets and coke. The most fabulous one was for Mario's AIDS conspiracy thriller, a kind of Mary Higgins Clark thing called *Fuck Me Dead*. Mario's *Citizen Kane*, however, was a 40s-style melodrama called *Forever Rectal*. I have it on tape but I can't watch it now. And yet, as with so much stuff left to my guardianship, I can't throw it out.

Back from Fire Island September 24th, I found it on my machine: Brett was gone. Brett had played all Mario's heroines. He wouldn't let anyone tell him how to do drag, though—and Mario wouldn't either, so as to preserve the "purity" of his performance—so in one called *Police Harlot 2000*, Brett played this transsexual cop who held our friend Danny at gunpoint and said "Up against the wall and spread 'em!" while trying to straighten his wig with the other hand. And there was Brett's one straight role, in *Forever Rectal*, where he got to say, in a none-too-masculine voice, "My God, Professor! They want our women!"

I must not to reminisce too much.

In the end Brett grew too sick to perform, and Mario abandoned mainstream entertainment for *cinéma verité* solos in which he detailed each pill and each new lesion. (The best of his Late Period was a ten-minute video called *Tape of My Last Crap*. He's on the john in obvious pain, and it just doesn't stop, and it's fabulous. It kills me how these guys all went before the age of YouTube, dead of hate before the ultimate expression of democracy. Imagine: The Mario Channel, infintely playing, like our favorite, Mary Tyler Moore.) Brett hadn't changed his will since Mario died, so his costumes were left to Mario.

We gave them to Mario's widowed father, who spoke almost no English and who had never met Brett. He clutched the wigs and spike heels to his chest, said "Thank you" over and over, then asked me something in Italian. Danny translated: the old man thought his son had had a girlfriend, and he wondered why she wasn't there. Had she died, too? "Yes," I said, nodding. "Unfortunately, she died." He seemed to accept it. I felt as though someone had liposuctioned out my soul.

Kevin and Chris died in December, within days of one another.

Last of all (I promise), was Howard. Howard lived to see protease inhibitors sashay down the runway in Vancouver in 1996, but he refused to take them. For fourteen years he'd been planning to die, and so he did. His guru, chomping on beef teriyaki at his wake, said it was his "path."

AIDS has shattered the vessels of memory, like lamps unto our feet. When I see a friend who is still alive—when he can spare a moment between pills—our conversation drifts. Did we really know people named Peachy, Jimmy, Brett, Mario, Howard? Did they make movies, wear dresses, wrap presents, read porn? I'm negative-as-of-eighteen-months-ago-and-haven't-done-anything-other-than-oral-sex-without-ejaculation-with-people-I-basically-trust-who-say-they-haven't-done-anything-other-than-oral-sex-without-ejaculation-with-people-they-basically-trust-or-at-least-that's-what-they-say-and-that's-good-enough-for-me. I may live another forty years. For what? To plant marigolds? Read *War and Peace*? Have sex?

-o-

Wesley comes over and we watch Nick at Nite. Wesley is my boyfriend, for lack of a better word. I can't imagine myself having such a thing.

Nick at Nite has back-to-back Mary Tyler Moores. These are our dreams: Mary's French windows, Rhoda cracking wise at weird, harmless Phyllis. Things changed after Mary moved to the high-rise. She was getting ready for the Eighties. Rhoda and Phyllis had their own series. They were getting ready for the Eighties, too. Wesley backs up into the harbor of my legs. I put an arm around him and imagine I am a fireman carrying a child from a burning building.

If I show less interest in sex now, Wes, it doesn't mean I don't care for you. You belong to my life—your back curving in the light as you floss, the way you make signs and call restaurants to eradicate all Chinese menus from our life. The way you leave your juice glasses in the sink without rinsing them. I put my arm around you like in high school wrestling, the sweat and uncertainty but you never speak of it to one another, barely look one another in the eye when it's over.

Wesley is a composer but he hasn't composed anything in over a year. Once in a while he'll shut himself up with his keyboard and play for half an hour. But when I tell him that the simple act of doing so is good, he gets angry. He says he has nothing to say that hasn't been said, so he has a moral duty not to compose. Dishes pile up in the sink. We're at a party hosted by a composer friend who's won a fellowship. Wes proclaims, "The paradigms are moribund." This sounds like something from *Masterpiece Theatre*: "Cook says the paradigms are moribund."/"Lovely! We'll have Freddy to lunch Tuesday week!" Wes ignores me, which gives me my strongest desire for him in weeks. His sharp, overserious features his darting eyes, the lack of confidence in his own anger. He says that artists who refuse to make art are the real winners. He says we should all stop creating, then honor the dead on World AIDS Day by having a "Day *With* Art." On the way home Wes says he pities the "poor fools" out there still composing. "Oh, yeah," I say, "poor Philip Glass!" "Oh, right!" Wes says. "Who can't make four hours of 'One-two-three-four-five!'" "All right!" I say. "How about... John Corigliano?" Wes stares. "*The Ghosts of Ver-fucking-sailles*??? All the ballyhoo, I wanted some kind of big *Parsifal-Boris-Don Giovanni* catharsis and what is it but *Figaro* with dead people!" He looks out at the city passing: "*Ghosts of Versailles...* huh!" Figaro with dead people. Well, what else? Ghosts of Greenwich Village. Of the Pines. Of Provincetown. Ghosts rattling around the mansion of my dreams. This can't have happened.

Back home I kiss Wes and pull his tie off. In bed he marks time, playing with his dick. His sense of duty is attractive. When I come he holds me and whispers "Yes, yes," then rolls onto his side. I reach for his dick. He takes my hand and squeezes it. "'sokay," he says. After a long moment in the dark, he adds, "I know my music is mediocre, so it is better that I not compose." They did not say that in the Century of Progress. You must do better, Wes. You simply must. We all must, we who are left behind. We won the booby prize—life—completely undeserving. The brilliant ones who died would have done more, better, differently. They would have built the new Versailles. We gaze at their castles, their colors flying, their bridges and banners far off in the summer mist. We, who remain boringly, guiltily alive, how can we equal what those mother's sons would do? Invite them to take our hands, teach us how to play with our poo in the few minutes we have left. I take out the garbage, and I know Peachy would have done it better. Peachy understood recycling. The paradigms are not moribund. We are drained of the common, cuckoo energy that would fill and stretch them and make them rise majestic above the ball fields and the parks.

Wes does word processing at a bank. The bankers love him because he's figured out stuff about Word and Excel that even Bill Gates doesn't know. No opera, but mighty proud of his 1,001 Excel tricks. Excel, a program fittingly comprised of nothing but "cells." Wes leaves for his shift with me still in bed and I wonder, "Where do I want to go today?"

I'm seized with a desire to clean. I go on a rampage—living room, bathroom, bedroom. I vacuum desiccated roaches. I dig slime from the soap dishes and soak charred oatmeal from burners. I throw out the shower curtain, once clear, now, without our noticing, clouded by gray dots.

At three o'clock I'm on Lafayette Street, passing antiques stores, the Keith Haring souvenir shop, boutiques so conceptual I'm afraid to go near them. I'm thinking what a fertile age we live in while I'm cruising this tall boy in drooping jeans, who stares at an orange trash thing filled with burning books. Aristotle, Chaucer —classics-by-the-yard blowing away. I ask him, is he a literature buff? Kind of. Mostly Kerouac. Where is he from? Barnstable, Massachusetts. He works for an insurance company there. Red rings circle his eyes. I ask him what he does for the insurance company. It involves an adding machine. I ask if he'd like to go do something. "Like what?" He snuffs back mucous. Gold hairs corkscrew from his chin. His name is Rick. We shake. He stares down at his gray and blue Sauconys, snuffs back more mucous. We take an uptown R train to Forty-second Street and change to the 1 local.

Rick lopes around admiring my house: it's so clean. He wants a beer. I get one and check the time: Wes comes home in an hour and a half. Suddenly I know Rick will not leave. Wes will come home and see him but not see him. He'll say nothing. We'll become a *paralysie-à-trois*. Rick scratches. I think he carries a disease more terrible than AIDS. When you have Rick's Disease you believe that at any minute you could die. In fact you don't die, you never will. The disease is that, because you think you could, you won't touch anyone, for fear of communicating the disease.

Rick has been locked out of his room on Twenty-second Street. If I give him twenty bucks and a token, we could maybe do something. But there's nothing I want to do. Why are we here like this? The thought that we might do something was so compelling. I can't tell if it still is. I wish this had never happened, but if I think about asking Rick to leave, I feel I'll die. He eyes my grandmother's candlesticks. In the end I give him five bucks and the token. He snuffs back mucous. As he shuffles to the door I ask, how old is he? He says sixteen. *Madre!* And he really works in insurance? He glares at my nineteenth-century watercolor of an empty bandstand with red white and blue bunting.

"So," I say, "my boyfriend'll be back soon with our two Dobermans, Himmler, and Goebbels!"

Rick edges out with a last snuffle. Once again, Irony triumphs over Need.

━o━

Wes comes home and starts dinner. He bought goat cheese and red leaf lettuce at Fairway. I wait for him to notice something. He doesn't, and this devastates me. I come up and I put my arms around him. He pats my forearm, not turning around. He remarks how clean the place is. He hopes I didn't tire myself out. *This afternoon, Wes, I brought home a bum and I don't know why.* But goat cheese awaits. It helps the conversation: it's good goat cheese, but not as good as the goat cheese from Zabar's. This takes more energy than cleaning a thousand apartments. 10:30 at last. Wes backs into the harbor of my legs. Mary makes everything okay. Spunky, unexceptional, giving in to what others wanted—no one reassured us like Mary. You could have stepped into Mary's world and been gay, but you never would have "gotten sick" (as we say). Mare just gosh-darn wouldn't have allowed it.

After Rick, I proceed not to straighten up. I don't want to do any of this, but...

Scottie, an NYU film major cruises me at a deli on Eighth Street. We go for lattés, and he tells me David Lynch has redefined the parameters of American cinema. I can't bring myself to tell him that the only individual to do that in either of our lifetimes is Steven Spielberg, end of harsh-but-true sentence. We have sex in the laundry room in his dorm. The next and last time we get together he brings deli flowers to my place. I have to throw them out—*out* out, as in on the street. I could have told Wes I bought them for myself, but I never do that. On my way down I wonder, what would Jimmy or Mario or Brett or Peachy say? We came of age in the hedonistic Seventies, Source of All the Trouble, yet I think my dalliances look pathetic to my dead friends. They wonder why I don't stay home with the nice man I found. While I trash the flowers I explain to them that, if I were single, I'd find this slutting around pathetic, too, and I wouldn't do it. But with Wes, I need a fount of hope.

Next comes Maurizio—nineteen and kisses like trash on fire. He has a thing in his eyebrow and has what Jimmy used to call NFA—No Fixed Address.

You don't remember which one Jimmy was, do you?

Maurizio lived in Tompkins Square Park—which he mentions when the conversation allows, or even when it doesn't—and now he lives on Madison Street with the family of a woman he met at Gray's Papaya and with whom he struck up a conversation based on a shared interest in Malcolm X (the woman is black, Maurizio is white). He takes the carved jade from around his neck and tries to put it around mine. I remind him about Wesley. All I want is to own Maurizio's slender, hairless body, unnaturally thin fingers, and copious ejaculations. He pops three or four times a session, winces and cries out in Italian as he shoots on my chest. My thinner, grayer fluid follows.

Just when we have this routine down, Maurizio wants to talk. He wonders where Wesley is in all this, and he wonders why I seem not to wonder this. (Maurizio belongs to what Peachy used to call "the feelings Mafia." Please tell me you remember Peachy.) I say Wesley is none of Maurizio's business. I apologize for this and say I was just tired. Maurizio smiles sadly, chin on bare knee. He drops the other bent leg onto the rumpled sheets, and traces his toes with a fingertip.

Maurizio moves out of Madison Street and into a shanty at Ninth and C, next to wizened Vietnam vet with a duck. This does not race my motor the way it races Maurizio's. I do not find the guy with the duck to be a cool piece of found art, but I do give in to Maurizio's insistence that I meet him, because after the howdy-doo I want to have Maurizio come on me.

The duck is named Gertrude. She nests in a wheelchair. To make her lay eggs, the guy plays seventies soul. The O-Jays in particular make Gertrude groove, egg-wise. "Smilin' in your face, all the time they wanna take your place..." Gertrude lets out a quack, and *voilà!* But instead of getting naked, now Maurizio wants to show me the organic market on Sixth Street, where he buys mushrooms to put in a duck egg omelet the three of us share. Then Maurizio videos the guy telling stories.

Any day I will tell Maurizio I'm too old for this. But before I can he moves out of the shanty. He leaves a note with Gertrude's keeper, promising he'll call me.

I can't decide what to hope for.

In the *Times* they review a novel—by a Serb or a Croat—in which cabbages sprout all over the hero's body. The reviewer says it ends up like watching someone else's nightmare. Nightmares, however, tend to be disjointed and autistic, the dreamer only acted upon. The critic said he thought he'd stopped reading if he weren't being paid. Then he decided he wouldn't; he'd keep going no matter what, because he believed the author was actually daring him to stop. If he did, the author would win. So he kept reading, as page after page the author offered more absurdities, more cabbages, in lieu of any traditional ideas of love or order. Maybe, the reviewer concluded, withholding transcendence was the point. Maybe transcendence could come only by plowing through cabbages without end.

The end comes in the basement of a porn store on Eighth and Forty-third. There's a boy with Jesus-gold hair. He bats His eyes so bluntly it jolts me. I follow Him back to the booths. Our quarters drop. I punch my button and unbuckle as the curtain goes up. There is Jesus, staring at the video screen, pulling His dick. With fingers with desperately chewed, almost nonexistent nails he holds up a piece of a cardboard box, black magic-markered: "Fifteen years old. HIV negative. For $5 I suck your dick or you suck mine." Video kills the Bible star. Here I am: the only living boy in New York. Peachy on Gay Pride day: "On this Day of Days there are a thousand kids cringing and naked in basements in this City, all desperate for some prick in a uniform to come over and piss on them so they will feel valid! And there's another hundred people. *Right now* in fucking Normal, Illinois there's a six-year-old at the dinner table with his father sneering, 'Don't put your hand like that, it's queer!' and the kid sits there feeling doomed, utterly doomed, at six, and later he's lying awake and Daddy comes in and fucks him and tells him it'll be 'Our little secret!' And now the kid wants the uniform prick's number. Jesus! Any fag wants love in this City should find a straight woman or a dog!"

The world goes to a hot, wet blur. I will not die thinking that! I refuse!

I bash the red button. My icon zips up, folds his sign, and leaves with the video still going. I stumble out of my booth and take the stairs two at a time up to the main level. I plow past videos without end, past women gagged and bound, past Great Danes with bubble-gum erections sniffing vaginas. The sunlight hits. I can't go back underground to the train. I can't be with a cab driver. So I walk home. On the way I buy a T-shirt for Wesley with the Mary Tyler Moore logo, from the opening when her name fans out and comes at you and you enter her world. "Love is all around." At home I shower—can I get all the cabbages off?—and collapse on the bed.

One morning I rinse out the filter cone. Nothing gold can stay. A pigeon flaps on the AC. I must ask Peachy for his zucchini bread recipe. Oh. Right. Well, I can find one online. Midnight, checking e-mail. A Bogart retrospective! I'll call Howard, and we'll... Oh. No. We won't. Not ever again. How awful for the world just to go on. The bougainvilleas on Sixth Street: Jimmy will be just... No. Either he has already seen them, or he never will.

When I wake up, Wes sits caressing me in his new T-shirt. We watch Nick at Nite.

I don't know what Wes or I want. The kid in the porn booth wanted money and maybe love, Scottie wanted to be right about David Lynch. Maurizio... That guy with the duck meant more to him than I could fathom. What do I or the man I share my life with want? We stay together, the once-clear future becoming a snowy screen. But like that reviewer, I'll keep going. Not because I don't want the author to "win." Life—that is to say, death—always wins. I'll keep going because, even after Jimmy, Mario, and Brett, even after Peachy and Howard, I'm still the kind of moron who believes, in spite of all evidence to the contrary and in spite of the overwhelming Thanatos in this world, that *this* time he *will* pull the big Harvey-rabbit out of the hat—no matter how empty the hat looks and no matter how arthritic his hand has become.

You see why Wesley won't compose. An audience brings him that hope, and it paralyzes him. But it's all predicated on hope, Wes. It's why you took up composing in the first place! You also see why Wes and I will probably never break up. Wes backs into the harbor of my body and we watch Mary. Maybe he is boring. Maybe neither he nor I can give or receive love. I thought I loved Jimmy, Mario, Brett, Kevin, Chris, Peachy, and Howard. Now I don't know what people mean by "love."

Maurizio writes: "You probably don't want to hear from me. I know what I did to you was shitty, but I figured cutting you off would make you mad enough to get over me and go back to Wes. He is better for you than I could ever be. You deserve that. I still think of you. I hope we can be friends. I would be happy if we could get together and talk. I really hope to hear from you, but I will understand if I don't. Love Maurizio."

"Love." People did love once. From about the end of the Black Plague to the start of trench warfare. That was the Age of Love.

Wes, you have become a part of my life—leaving glasses in the sink, explaining why the WordPerfect macro editor was better in DOS than in Windows, getting a "No Menus" sign made in Chinese, putting your Mary T-shirt on every night...

We must do better, Wes. Not just at art but at love. The Ghosts of West Tenth Street, the Ghosts of Key West loved insanely, fluids flying every which way, which was the problem, yet I think finally they experienced something worth dying for. Oh, I know half of it was doped and desperate, maybe more than half. But they were pioneers. From the very edge of life their clouded eyes blinked and tremulous voices said, "I love you." Or did they just say, "Fuck you, get me another pillow"? Each death was senseless and humiliating. Only now are they pioneers. And we go on being dupes, just like them.

And when I tell you—Wes, hit the mute button a sec (you do, but continue to stare at the TV) —that last month for a total of about fifteen seconds I went down on a boy named Maurizio-but-his-name-doesn't-matter-and-I'm-sorry-I-don't-even-know-why-but-maybe-we-should-y'know-not... do...certain stuff till I...you know...again—you stare at the TV like a boy whose parents struggle to say "I love you" while the boy just wants to fly his imaginary airplane around the living room ceiling. You massage my forearm till just enough time has passed for me to feel the depths of dread, then you say, "I guess everyone does." Mary's name appears, one-two-three, for the next episode. You hit volume and squeeze my arm and I want to say, "You don't," but I'm afraid. This is a later episode, with no words to the theme song. "Who can turn the world on...?" By 1975 we stopped believing. Rhoda and Phyllis spun off, leaving Mary in her high-rise. I still want them all back together in the house. I want one more Mario premiere. Love all around. Nearly everyone from those premieres is gone, and I take it personally. I have to, to hang on. I squeeze you in return, and thank you. Your thumb keeps massaging.

At the commercial I add, "I just..." You straighten your spine, turn partway to me and say, "It's okay." I pause. I am lucky. If you could write *The Ghosts of Versailles* or *Einstein on the Beach*, you would not have to forgive me. But you do not ride the sea of Glass's *solfège*. Here, beyond the end of time you hug the shore, where once even Mary had to end. Now, she never will. I put my lips to the back of your neck, but I do not know whether your skin is warm or cool. Hang on till Valentine's Day. Then we might know.

Calvin Gets Sucked In

It didn't get better.

A month after his break-up with Rafe, his latest, Calvin was so desperate for bodily contact that instead of using the ATM he went into the bank, hoping one of the cute male tellers would touch his fingers for a half-second as he pushed bills under the window guard. But no. Their skin never touched. "Thank-you-have-a-nice-day" was the most Calvin got, then "Next-customer-in-line-please!" as he drifted away.

Calvin tried the same thing at a deli and was more successful, but the guy there was hot in a kind of criminal way, and Calvin wanted innocence. The barista at Beans 'n Leaves looked about eleven, but he slid Calvin's cup across the bar in a single off-handed motion, barked "Calvin!" as though this were mail call at Camp Pendleton, and was plop-plopping someone else's soy chai latte before Calvin could lift his hand.

Closer now to forty than to thirty, Calvin felt himself surrendering more each day to the inevitable. His accounting job was a Tilt-a-Whirl of increasing demands and changing deadlines to which he clung, terrified, well into the evenings. When he actually did manage to finish a project, two more had landed on his desk. The best he could hope for from his boss was a closed door, but that rarely happened, and when it did, it never lasted. (Actually, the best he could hope for was the man's total absence, news of which, combined with the warm, safe knowledge of a Beans 'n Leaves macchiato in his hand, would fill Calvin with a childlike sense of possibility, like the announcement of a snow day when he was eight.) Tuesdays Calvin scrambled to finish early so he could make it to Strokers, the safe sex club downtown. The thought of Strokers also called forth that childlike sense of possibility, but it was a half-hour by subway (in the opposite direction from home) followed by a fifteen-minute walk to a collapsing building by the highway. The doors closed at nine, and even if Calvin managed to flee work by eight, by then he was sapped of all energy and optimism necessary to assay a room of fifty or so naked men, connect with someone in spite of their hesitations, quirks, and shortcomings, navigate those hesitations, quirks, and shortcomings to get a bit of pleasure, and, often just for courtesy's sake, see to it that the other guy got something in return.

Instead, most Tuesdays—and most other nights he now had free since the break-up with Rafe—Calvin dragged himself home late, ate standing at the kitchen sink, then stripped and fell face down on the bed. He rose at six, and after a sleepy round at the gym, hurried to work to be met by his boss, informing him that this time the Apocalypse had come and it was his fault. His boss's special talent was to be able to plunge him, on every encounter, into the same roiling sea of worthlessness, dread, and desolation into which one would plunge upon being fired, but without actually firing him.

Yet.

On weekends and when he could actually leave work on time, Calvin went to the hospital to visit his best-friend-since-childhood, Tooker. Once, Tooker had been the optimist, the agenda setter, the authority on electoral politics, Kurt Weill, and risotto, the good talker and, every time one of Calvin's more-or-less-month-old relationships dissolved, an even better listener. Now, Tooker could no longer finish sentences. Some days he couldn't begin them. In the cold light, Calvin sat across the bed from Tooker's boyfriend, Sven. They discussed Tooker's blood pressure and his heartbeat and told one another that he looked a little better today, while Calvin ached for the three of them just to vanish together into a half-remembered, half-imagined Neverland of cappuccinos and beach weekends past.

One Tuesday Calvin's desk was cleared by six-thirty. *Strokers, here I come!* he thought, suddenly hunching and darting eyes left and right for his boss. Just then Sven called, crying. Calvin forced down all thoughts of the flesh and assumed his soothing voice. He promised Sven he would be right there. Of course. What else did one do?

Tooker's breathing had changed. The time was nigh. The nurse let Calvin stay till ten. When he could finally sit upright no longer, he stood, embraced Sven, and squeezed Tooker's hand long and hard for what he figured might be the last time. Then, as soon as he turned the corner at the end of the corridor, he fairly ran from the building.

Up on the sidewalk after a long, lurching, screeching subway ride,

Calvin passed Lay-Z Video. He passed Lay-Z Video every evening, but this time it struck him what they might have in there—in the back. Just the thought bathed him in relief, as on that little-kid snow day, as on those beach weekends past, as when he'd just met a new man. He dove into Lay-Z, wove briskly through the aisles, and slipped behind the cheap, unpainted door with the curling, dot-matrix-printed sign saying, "Adult." In the bright, windowless room, he tremblingly surveyed the DVD cases: boys naked and pouting; boys naked and sneering; boys by swimming pools, faces shining in the sun.

One boy in particular took Calvin's breath away—Joey Rhodes, a graceful, beautiful kid with ice blue eyes and sexy moussed spikes. On one DVD case, Joey stood, arms folded, in a dazzling expanse of green-blue pool water. He looked as though he were winking at Calvin. The video was called *Colossus of Rhodes*. Even though the tiny room was empty, Calvin clutched at the DVD case as though another hand might intervene in the fraction of a second it would take him to secure it. He slipped briskly out, took the DVD to the counter (hoping but failing to touch the hand of the swarthy daddy at the register), brought it home, and put it in the machine before checking his messages or eating.

Joey Rhodes and his buddies cruised around in foreign convertibles like big red candies. They were generously hung, with perfect proportions and perfect definition, not a hair out of place, and they had loads of stamina. They ejaculated like fire hoses as their buddies moaned, "Gimme that load!" Everyone did everything to everyone easily and willingly every time, with no negotiation, objection, or pain. Most of all, everyone had time, time for all that sex and time to loll by the pool with drinks and cruise in those convertibles.

Colossus of Rhodes featured no needy toads in black dress socks, like at Strokers. No one worked, except to hustle or deliver pizzas or clean swimming pools. The boys had no families, except the occasional parent seen leaving for the weekend in scene one. There was no prejudice or discrimination, because everyone was gay. But there was also no catty, bitchy gossip because, conversely, no one was gay. They were just guys with needs whose girlfriends were away for the weekend.

The absence of authority figures in particular drew Calvin. By his TV stood a picture of his father, a self-made businessman still raging against the dying of the light at seventy. No matter how late Calvin toiled, when he entered his apartment his eyes went straight to his father's broad brow, thundering, "Not enough!" Mornings, when Calvin shut that image behind him, it was only to throw himself head first into his boss's carping maw. Actually, the first voice to greet him in the morning was liable to be that of the man back home in the picture, who would call his son's desk at eight and leave a message to the effect of, "Thought you'd be in by now. Early bird catches the worm! Can't get ahead if you don't start the day ahead," etc. This made Calvin whimper and stew, because the old man's business had in fact faltered in the last decade, and Calvin had stepped in to help put his kid sister through college.

So this particular evening Calvin turned his father's picture to the wall, along with the picture of him and Tooker in second grade. He turned off his cell phone. Tonight he was finally going to have some fun. He stripped, slid *Colossus of Rhodes* into the DVD player, and lolled and played with himself and wished not only that he could possess the young studs—Joey Rhodes or curly-haired Roddd Packer, whose Jackson Pollack spurts appeared in head-on slow motion—but that he could possess their easy, unbounded lives as well.

–o–

Sven called the next morning at six. Tooker remained barely alive. Again Calvin came to his bedside after work, and again he stayed late. Again he embraced Sven and squeezed his friend's hand for perhaps the last time, and again, after a grim, grinding ride home, he passed Lay-Z Video.

This time, deliberately.

He beelined to the windowless room in back and snagged a Roddd Packer DVD called *Open the Door and Let Me In*. He strode briskly home and popped the disc in before doing anything else. The words "Harrow Video" flashed onscreen, white on black, in a rounded font popular thirty years ago. The Harrow logo was nothing more or less than a stylized erection in a white circle. Calvin undressed as opening credits played. He tossed his clothes on the carpet and settled in to watch Roddd and friends and, of course, to tease his own member.

"Hey, Calvin, buddy, how ya doin'?"

Calvin started. He must have dozed off. What...?

"Calvin!"

"Who is it?" he croaked, and sat up. Was the film over?

No, the TV still emitted a blue glow. "Calvin!" Was someone in the movie named Calvin? No, porn characters were never named Calvin.

"Up and at 'em!" Calvin stared. There stood Roddd Packer, filling the screen, his grin accentuated by his lantern jaw, naked but for a pair of running shorts, massaging the considerable bulge therein and looking straight at Calvin. His dark hair was swept back, and his cheeks and chin bore a roguish stubble. He held a half-sipped margarita in one hand. Calvin slid off the sofa and went on his knees a few inches from the screen.

"Nice!" said Roddd Packer, looking Calvin up and down.

The blue glow suddenly fanned out and surrounded Calvin, a pulsating cocoon. Then the blinding blue walls of the cocoon faded, and Calvin stood barefoot on a deep pile carpet in a glass-enclosed ranch house with a sunny yard. Roddd Packer stood in front of him—big, so to speak, as life.

"Wanna go for a swim?" Roddd asked, green eyes sparkling like pool water.

"Um, sure…" Calvin followed Roddd out to the patio. He found he had developed a confident swagger. He found out why he had developed such swagger when he felt the front of the black Spandex shorts he now wore. In entering Roddd's world, he had, apparently, developed the anatomical dimensions necessary to succeed in that world. His throat constricted with excitement. "I forgot my swimsuit," he said. "You got an extra?" Even though he knew what the solution would be—perhaps especially because he knew what the solution would be—he fairly trembled to hear Roddd say it.

"Don't need one." Roddd set down his margarita and kicked off his flip-flops. "Those hedges are pretty high." Roddd dropped his shorts. Calvin peeled off his tank top. He was impressed by the designer label in the neck. Before removing his shorts he hesitated. Usually he "shrank up" when nervous. But he wasn't shrunken now. What the hell? he thought. If I can own a fifty-dollar designer tank top, maybe I won't shrink up anymore, either. He peeled down the shorts and was impressed not only with his new and positively unshrunken equipment, but with the toning of his entire body—defined bulge of calves, a rippled "six-pack" of abs, and a broad, shaved chest with pecs that seemed like each should have its own Social Security number.

"Lookin' good," Roddd offered.

"Thanks," Calvin said. It felt strange to accept a compliment for something he had nothing to do with and didn't even understand, yet it felt strange in a nice way, maybe even a wonderful way, not to have to worry about his body. He didn't feel naked. He felt invincible. For once, his body could do the work, make the introductions, set the agenda, succeed on his behalf. As he followed Roddd into the pool, he forgot all past dreads and insecurities. He even forgot his thought that not even Tooker had ever had a body like this. Guiltily Calvin realized that Tooker would never have such a body again.

Roddd stood in the shallow end of the pool, running his fingers up and down the center of his torso. "Man," he said, "I am so horny. My girlfriend's been away for a week."

That comment led to a (very) few words about how, hey, guys have needs, then a pause filled with tingling electricity and an enveloping sense of relief Calvin knew well. The touching began, and then the sex—easy, long-lasting, do-everything-in-the-book sex—on a pure white towel by the edge of the pool. In addition to an amazing tan and amazingly toned and sculpted muscles, Roddd also had amazing rhythm, flexibility, and energy. Calvin was pleased to find that his nether regions accommodated the demands of sex with Roddd, who, true to his name, possessed an organ big enough to require a zoning variance. Nonetheless it slipped easily into Calvin (Roddd did use a rubber) and Calvin lay on the towel under the amazingly blue sky, letting Roddd's rod move in and out of him, reaching occasionally for a sip of Roddd's margarita, and in general feeling he had arrived. He thought, *Take that, Rafe!* But he found himself saying *Take that!* to a giggling Rafe rolling over in Saturday morning sheets and batting his eyes, and then, as soon as he banished that image, to an earnest, sad-eyed Rafe in a suit saying, "You are still a very special man" that last morning. He began to lose his erection. He closed his eyes, took a deep breath, opened his eyes again and tried to focus just on Roddd's plunging rhythm, boundless energy, and growling chant of, "Oh, yeah, gimme that ass, gimme that fuckin' ass."

After several minutes Roddd turned Calvin on his side, nestled behind him, and continued plowing. After several minutes of that, Roddd flipped Calvin onto his back. Calvin wrapped his legs around Roddd's torso, allowing him to bask in the omnipresence of Roddd's commanding physique and the sexy loop of wincing and lip-biting that played across Roddd's face, suggesting a capacity for ecstasy beyond anything Calvin had ever known. Finally they ejaculated (the slow motion thing was very cool), and as Calvin gulped air in the wake of the most powerful orgasm he had ever experienced, a bell rang by the gate to the pool.

"That's probably the pizza I ordered," said Roddd. He rose, pulled on his shorts, and went inside.

Calvin felt blood flow to his groin again. Who would it be? He had watched scenes involving delivery boys, but he'd had no clue how to bring such a thing off, when, in real life, he had been visited by a cable guy, twenty-something, of Italian descent who said "Good 'nuff" a lot and betrayed not the slightest interest in whatever else it was Calvin wanted him to be interested in. Now, a delivery boy scene would simply be arranged for him! Calvin ran his hand over his abs and felt proud and excited that now he possessed equipment that would impress the pizza boy, would make him the pizza boy's equal, or even better!

This pizza boy was a beauty—dark hair, slender, rippled belly, with a naïve arrogance. (Calvin believed the actor was Trunk Caldwell, one of many alleged "brothers" of seventies porn superstar Dunk Caldwell.) He came shambling out after Roddd. "Left my money out here," Roddd said. "Sorry."

"That's cool," Trunk said. He glanced at Calvin, licked his lips, batted his doe eyes, and said, "It is, like, my last delivery of the day." Calvin stepped out of the pool and walked up to the boy dripping, his ample chest thrust forward. "Why don't you stay and have a swim?" he said. For what felt like the first time in his life, he was taking charge. He cupped his cock and balls.

"Don't have a bathing suit," Trunk said.

Roddd annoyed Calvin by interrupting his cool, off-handed explanation that this was no problem. Roddd simply dropped his shorts. "Don't see us wearing nothin', do you?" he said. Calvin loved the "nothin'", the blatant double negative like a shot of cum in the face. Suddenly he adored Roddd and wanted him all to himself. Now it was Trunk's presence that grated. Until, with a knowing grin, he disrobed. After that, though, Calvin found himself a wee bit disappointed at how easily it all went. He had been here—he tried not to think too much about where "here" was—not even an hour, and already he felt oppressed by a lack of... what? A hitch did develop once all three were in the pool. "Wait," Trunk said, as Calvin and Roddd began to touch him, "you guys aren't queer, are you?" Roddd assured him no, they just wanted to "have some fun" because their girlfriends were away. So without much ado—without, in fact, anything even slightly resembling ado—Trunk joined Roddd and Calvin in doing everything Calvin had ever wanted to do, in every position in which he'd ever wanted to do it, plus a few things he'd never thought of before.

Yet the encounter failed to top the thrill Calvin had felt when Roddd announced Trunk. That was it: distances vanished instantly here. They were barely there to begin with. At the same time, Calvin could not say he felt "close" to either of the young men with whom he now lounged naked.

They were sticky and spattered, yet Calvin did not feel, nor did the other two seem to feel, the terrible tenderness post-ejaculation, the sweet sorrow of, *Now I have seen all of you. Now you have given everything. More than you wanted.* To think any of that would be so... uncool. And you had to keep your cool here. Calvin was painfully, almost *physically* aware of that. As though the house and the hedges bristled with dozens of tiny cameras, watching. Which he guessed they must, somehow.

The three of them lolled a minute or so, then a voice called, "Anybody home?" A young man in cut-offs and tank top appeared around the hedge, carrying pool cleaning equipment. He didn't know which house he was supposed to be, as it were, servicing, and Roddd thought his pool had been cleaned a day or two ago, but none of this mattered. The pool boy, like Trunk, had no more jobs for the afternoon, so Roddd invited him for a swim. He not only lacked a bathing suit, he did not know how to swim. Roddd and Calvin and Trunk all volunteered to teach him, and the ways in which the swimming lesson seguéd into groping did provide some fresh seasoning for a weary Calvin. And what would Rafe say, if he saw this? Probably what Calvin was trying hard not to tell himself: With this body and this dick and this house and these people, who wouldn't look good?

What caused Calvin a moment's agony was the *way* Rafe would say it—sadly, hanging his head, turning to go.

The "swimming lesson" exhausted Calvin. It relieved him when finally the boys left and Roddd said, "Let me show you your room."

Showing Calvin where to shower, Roddd began to fondle him again. Soon they were pawing one another under the hot spray. The location added some novelty, but Calvin wanted desperately to sleep. "Sleep, sleep," he purred, as Roddd worked his member in and out, whispering over and over with the same inflection, "Oh, yeah! Oh, yeah!" After coming for the fifth or sixth time that day, Calvin stumbled into the guest bedroom, fell face down on the bed, and at last he slept.

-o-

Calvin woke the next morning and stood naked before one of the mirrors in his room. (There were several, including mirrored doors all the way along a wall of closets that turned out to be empty.) He wasn't ready yet for the attentions of Roddd and the others. He felt overwhelmed by the thought of those attentions. He feared doing or saying the wrong thing. Yet in the mirror he saw a body that could not be capable of the slightest wrong. He kneaded his much bigger pectorals and pulled on his much bigger cock. But none of it exactly aroused him. He felt less like another Roddd Packer than like a character out of Kafka. Another Gregor Samsa. Maybe this place was another Penal Colony!

No! Ridiculous! Why would he think that? This was a dream come true. He pulled on shorts and a tank top. It was a matter of getting away from Roddd. There were thousands more boys out there, at least one, probably ten or a hundred, that were exactly what he wanted. Of course, that was what he thought when dating, back in regular life. That was what he had thought with Rafe.

Roddd now appeared in a pair of white jockey shorts and said, "The guy's here to do the deck."

Calvin's optimism was rekindled when he saw that the handyman was one of his favorite objects of desire—the adorably freckle-faced Reddy Toole. Reddy Toole wore white overalls with nothing underneath. He had brought little in the way of handyman equipment, except a hammer dangling suggestively from a loop at his waist, and his hands were clean and callous free. The guys started with a beer (Calvin had been unsettled to see that Roddd's refrigerator held nothing else, except for a cardboard box with two leftover pieces of pizza), which led to a dizzying three-way session during which little carpentry but much drilling got done. The three were interrupted by another pizza delivery, but the delivery guy failed to have change for a hundred. After an unconvincing pat-down of his pockets, he said, stiffly, "Maybe I could give you something else." Indeed he could and indeed he did, and everyone was happy, or at least, for a few moments, sated.

Calvin felt sick at heart when Reddy Toole had to leave. "Call me," Calvin said, slipping his arm around Reddy's waist. Reddy raised an eyebrow and slipped away. He drove off, not in a rusty pick-up, but in a polished, candy-colored foreign car. Calvin stood at Roddd's front door and wished he had a car, too, in which to follow Reddy. This wish brought up a set of practical questions which Calvin felt he needed to address.

He wanted to speak to Roddd about how to get around. He already craved the wide world of boys that had to lie beyond Roddd's house. But Roddd wanted Calvin to join him in the shower. With some difficulty Calvin sat Roddd down and got him to listen, even if he did pull on his dick the entire time.

"I'm going to need *money*," Calvin said.

"I can get you a job at my gym," Roddd said.

"Thanks," Calvin said, "but I was thinking of something in my field. I'm an accountant."

"A what?" said Roddd.

"A CPA?"

Roddd showed no sign of recognition.

"Do you have a newspaper?" Calvin asked. Roddd shrugged. "A *newspaper*!" Calvin repeated, "with want ads?"

"Hey," said Roddd Packer, reaching for Calvin's groin, his brow clouding over, "be cool, okay? Cool is always beyond question, okay?"

"Um, okay..." Calvin said.

"Like before, when you, like, put your arm around the deck guy and wanted him to call you?"

"That wasn't cool?"

"No." In a low, dismissive tone, Roddd added, "It's somethin' a girl would do, okay?" Then, even lower, and so quickly that Calvin could not be certain he'd heard right, Roddd added, "They won't like it." Suddenly, with a slowly-curling half-smile Roddd spoke up in a normal voice. "Now," he said, reaching to play with Calvin's left nipple—"how 'bout that shower?"

Calvin wanted nothing less at that moment than to shower with Roddd. He was too anxious, and certain of Roddd's mannerisms had begun to grate on him.

For one thing, Roddd's topics of conversation were few, and his sexual vocabulary was pretty much limited to "Oh, yeah!" plus instructions to Calvin to do whatever Calvin was already doing. If Calvin was sucking Roddd's dick, Roddd would say, "Oh, yeah! Suck that dick!" If Calvin was licking Roddd's balls, Roddd would say, "Oh, yeah! Lick those balls!" Most distracting, when Calvin was in the throes of orgasm and Roddd grunted, "Oh, yeah! Shoot that load!" Calvin was too reticent (and too occupied) to respond, "I'm shooting, already! Are you blind?!?" Plus, it wouldn't be *cool*.

Also, Calvin feared that if he crossed Roddd, Roddd would not let him stay here any longer, and Calvin was not prepared to leave. So Calvin gave in to the sex again, after which Roddd lent Calvin his car and ten dollars, and Calvin went in search of the nearest town.

–o–

On the drive Calvin wondered, what had Roddd meant by "They won't like it." Who were "they"? But the breeze blew this thought out of his head as he marveled at the number of hitch hikers along the road, most of them blond, all of them in cut-offs and tank tops. What a gorgeous, perfect world, just as he had imagined! All the guys looked willing to do anything Calvin could want. But Calvin wanted to figure out this job thing, so he passed them by. They'd be there later. And if they weren't, so what? There'd be more.

Calvin never found a "town," *per se*, but he did come to a strip mall comprised of identical, rectangular, *faux* brick edifices, where he figured he could pick up a newspaper. But the mall turned out to consist of two video stores, three pizza stands, and three health clubs. The idea of either video or pizza exhausted Calvin, so he went into one of the health clubs.

The boy on duty gave him a blank stare when he asked where he might buy a newspaper. No amount of description could make him understand. Calvin was aware, however, of a stunning parade of guys passing through on their way to the locker room, each pausing to look him over with laser eyes. The boy offered Calvin a tour of the club, and Calvin agreed. He ended up having sex in the locker room with ten guys at once, a warm and relaxing cocoon of masculinity. Oddly, as the guys all came on one another, Calvin found himself wishing he could experience this with his regular body. He felt let down when after a few claps on the shoulder they drifted away. Anxious for company, for someone to *talk* to, Calvin turned to the boy from the front desk. "Want to pick up a slice?" he asked, his stomach turning just a wee bit.

"No," the boy said, recoiling. He added what sounded like, "I have to go do a freeway." The thought of the boy humping hot blacktop turned Calvin on, then he realized he had said, "I have to do a three-way." The boy had a "night job," as it were.

So Calvin sagged off alone to a pizza stand next door to the gym, where he ordered a slice and again asked about a newspaper. The counter boy squeezed his crotch and said, "Maybe I have one in the back. Wanna come look?"

"Not right now," Calvin said. "I have to find a job."

The boy then told Calvin he could have a job delivering pizzas. He told Calvin to come back at noon the next day.

Calvin thanked the boy and took off. He was relieved of his job worries. Now he was ready to find a hitch hiker who would do it outdoors. Calvin had long fantasized that, and had seen it in so many videos he figured it would prove easy.

It did.

He picked up a boy whom he led down a literal primrose path (but only after the boy had asked, "You're not queer are you?" and Calvin had assured him his girlfriend was simply away for the weekend). The two were going at it *en plein air* when a couple of strapping hikers appeared. One sported jet black hair down to his waist. Calvin recognized this as the Native American model Jake Trouser Eagle, one of the more exotic stars in the porno sky.

Calvin relished the idea of an encounter with Jake Trouser Eagle; he felt that, with Jake, he was racking up something particularly valuable. An American Indian—with all the physical, spiritual, and political superiority that implied, to say nothing of rarity—made, well, a great story. A story, Calvin reflected, he would never be able to tell, because who would believe any of what had happened to him?

Calvin marveled at how easily positions and transitions were negotiated in this four-way. In real life, Calvin had stumbled into a four-way just once, and much hurt had ensued when he wasn't so turned on by the guy who most wanted him, and the guy he most wanted was more turned on to another guy. But everyone here seemed to find everyone else equally desirable. Or they all simply found the idea of themselves having sex hot. This possibility was disappointing for Calvin, but then, dick was dick, and the complete and total elimination of any difficulties involved in getting it was wonderfully liberating—to the point that it nearly erased all thought.

–o–

The next day at the pizza stand the boy handed Calvin a hot pizza box, gave him an address, and to Calvin's surprise, told him that this would be his last delivery of the day.

When Calvin reached the address, the customer opened the door, and...

It was Joey Rhodes! Himself! In nothing but cotton running shorts! Joey Rhodes said, "Come in." Calvin could barely speak.

Joey was house sitting for his parents. He brought Calvin out back by the pool where he had left his money. Suddenly Joey suggested a swim and Calvin said, "Well, it *is* my last delivery of the day, but I don't have a bathing suit." After that Joey Rhodes dropped off the tree almost too easily. Calvin had to admit that Joey had a way about him, a confidence, a capability, an effortlessness, all supported up by a rock-solid belief, a knowledge that these were his God-given rights, and that he would never, ever lose them. No, not God-*given*. God-*like*. This, Calvin saw, as Joey grinned down sweetly and told him to "Suck that dick," was what it was like to be God: utter confidence, utter trust, utter ease with self. No move you could not make, no act you could not perform, no tank top or shorts you could not wear, no guy who would not be attracted to you. And to know it! To *know* it, forever! This was the end state: bliss. Calvin himself had tasted a bit of it, courtesy of his new body. Still, if only he were not gnawed by recollections of his other life: the break-up, Tooker, Sven, his job...

Calvin thought of an image Tooker once presented. Tooker said the Universe was created when God tripped and dropped everything he'd been carrying in his arms. The trick in life, Tooker said, was holding onto grace while you were being dropped.

Joey ejaculated beautifully, his sperm thick and white and opaque. Calvin's, too, though back home it was thinner and grayish-yellow, there was not so much of it, and it didn't shoot as far as it did now. In the exhausted aftermath, Calvin tried to think of something to say to Joey Rhodes, a question to ask, data he wanted to know, but nothing came. Joey stared at him. They liked one another, apparently. They were sexually compatible, but here everyone was. Joey kept staring. Slowly Calvin collected his clothes, hoping maybe Joey would ask something about *him*. Maybe he had disappointed Joey. Calvin thought of the scores of lovers Joey must have had. Surely with his new body he was equal to, well, most of them. If Calvin's arrival had registered on Joey's screen, why not his departure?

Now Joey's stare was burning a hole through Calvin. "What?" Calvin demanded.

Joey put a finger to his lips. Calvin opened his mouth. Joey's eyes grew wide. The finger trembled and pressed harder. Silently Calvin mouthed, "What?"

Joey brought the finger down. With his head he made a tiny jerking motion toward the hallway. Calvin followed him down it.

At the end of the hall Joey stopped, turned to Calvin, and put his finger up again. He pointed to a closed door. He mouthed to Calvin, "On three." Calvin nodded. Joey held up one finger, two fingers, three fingers, then the two of them slipped through the door, and Joey closed it behind them. Another empty closet, Calvin ascertained, like all those at Roddd's.

In the dark Calvin whispered, "What is it?"

"Shh," Joey said. Calvin could feel him holding still and listening. Then he lay a hand on his arm. "How did you get here?" he whispered.

"Huh?" said Calvin.

"You're not from here. How did you get here?"

"What makes you think...?"

"You're not cool. No offense. I mean, you're good. You're good looking and everything. And you're kind of cool, but not completely. You want something. You expect something. You *need* something. That's not cool. It's a little too much like what a girl would do, and they won't like that."

"'They' who?" Calvin demanded.

"Shhh!! I know! I know they won't like it, 'cause it happened before once."

"What happened before?"

"Once, this dude showed up, like outta nowhere, like you did. Poor guy, he was so uncool. He didn't know about, you know, sex. I told him to take his clothes off and he did, but then he just stood there and asked what I wanted. He called me 'sir.' He thought I was going to beat him, like, with a board or a stick. Where he was before, that's all they did. He'd been in a place called a 'boarding school,' and in some place called a 'frat,' and a place called 'jail.' Oh, and a thing called 'church.' Some of 'em I think I heard of, except 'church.' I just knew about having sex in those places, though, not getting hit. But he got hit all the time. He'd do bad stuff, and they'd hit him. And what was really weird, it was always the same guy who hit him, no matter where he was, 'church,' 'jail,' wherever. I said, 'Dude, just stop doing the bad stuff,' but he couldn't. It was what he did. He showed me his ass. It was awful. Purple marks and swellings all over. I couldn't even touch him, so he had to go.

"Plus, they beat him on his birthday—I mean, beat him *because* it was his birthday—and they beat him, like, as part of joining a club. They beat him for everything. It was awful. They hung him by his feet and beat him. They tied him to a bench. He didn't understand sex at all. Just being beaten. It was so uncool. I told him he had to go, like, emergency. 'Cause you can't *not* have sex here. Every guy you meet, you gotta have sex. Or else. That's another thing with you. I don't wanna spread gossip, but I heard you, like, turned down sex a couple of times. And you were driving, and you didn't pick up guys who were hitching and have sex with 'em. You got to. Understand? It's not cool if you don't.

"Anyway, this guy couldn't. Have sex at all, I mean. I was almost relieved 'cause it meant I didn't have to tell him I couldn't touch that ass. I just said, 'Please, nothing personal, but you just gotta get out and go far, far away. For your own good' And he did. I never saw him again. I felt bad, but the whole thing was so uncool, I mean, what was I going to do? They would've... I don't know what... I hope he's okay, wherever..."

"So will someone tell me, who the fuck are 'they'?" Calvin demanded.

"*Them!!*" In a whisper intense but so low Calvin could only catch consonants, Joey insisted, "The ones who watch. The ones who wait. Don't you feel them?"

Calvin admitted he had, a little.

"Well, it gets worse. They're *everywhere*. You start to feel them on your skin, and it *hurts*. And it doesn't go away! The only way to make it go away is to have sex. Not talk about it or kiss or make out or that shit, but the actual in-out. That's the only thing that makes the hurt go away, so you gotta have as much sex as you possibly can!"

"But who are *they*?" Calvin insisted. "Who *exactly*?"

"No one knows," Joey said. "We just know we have to do what they want, exactly the way they want it. We have to. It's only right. They love us. They gave us all of this!" Calvin felt Joey make a gesture meant to take in house, yard, and pool, but in reality indicating no more than the dark, empty closet. "So we do what they say. Or else we disappear."

"What about at night?" Calvin asked.

"What about what?"

"When it's *dark*? Are they watching then?"

A pause. "What do you mean 'dark'?" Joey said. As he said it, Calvin realized: yes, he had slept here, but he always laid down in light and woke up in light. He had never seen a sunrise or sunset, let alone the nighttime sky. "It's never 'dark,'" Joey said. "If it was, they couldn't watch, and they have to watch! That's why you have to be *cool*. Understand? You can *act* like you want certain stuff, you can *act* like you need it, but you can't actually want or need anything. Like, the way you looked at me when you got here, like you wanted my body? That's cool. But after we came, when you looked at me like you wanted, you know, maybe something more? You *can't do that!* There were guys who used to live here who maybe did that. There's, like, a little inscription to one of 'em somewhere around. I don't know where. But you can't do that now. It could get us both in trouble. We could end up disappearing, like that kid who got beaten." For a moment Calvin heard nothing but Joey's shallow breathing. Joey stood so close Calvin felt the warmth. Joey sniffled once and said, "I hope he's okay." Joey's breathing became heavier. "You know what the absolute weirdest thing was? This was so... so, like, just *weird*, it completely freaked me out..."

"What?" Calvin said.

Joey leaned even closer and hissed, "He'd never, ever had pizza! Ever!

He practically hadn't heard of it. What are you gonna do with a guy like that?"

"Uh, gee," Calvin said, "I dunno..."

"Anyway... so, I'm gonna open the door now," Joey said. "We're gonna say good-bye, real cool, and you're gonna go. And you're gonna keep being cool. You can hack it, man. You're not like that other guy. You know what you're doing. Just *be cool at all times!* Okay?"

"Okay," Calvin said.

"Cool is be..."

"....beyond question," Calvin said. "I know."

"Good. You get it. On three. One, two, three...!"

Joey swung open the door, and the two strode out. Joey turned, struck a cocky pose, offered his hand, and said, "S'long, guy."

"Uh, s'long, dude," Calvin said. They shook, and he walked out.

-o-

Calvin thought about what Joey said. He did feel "them" watching, and Joey was sort of right: this realization was accompanied by an itch, a kind of prickle that did indeed lessen when Calvin had sex. So as the prickling increased, Calvin tried, successfully, to have as much sex as he could. He also tried, in what little spare time he had, to see if he could actually witness nighttime. Mornings and afternoons were slightly distinguishable, but he always fell asleep exhausted before shadows lengthened, and when he woke up, sunlight streamed in the windows. He began to keep track, and it seemed that six hours was about the limit for staying awake, though it was difficult to confirm, as there weren't a great many clocks about.

Each new pizza delivery was just interesting enough to keep him going. With each he did his best to be supremely cool. His clients were mostly variations on Joey Rhodes and Roddd Packer, though he was surprised and intrigued one afternoon to make a delivery to a small, dim one-room apartment on the edge of town, occupied by the African-American porn star 'da Hōz, whose presence was normally confined to jack-off or autofellatio shorts, or dramas featuring pale, pimply, barely legal white boys who did not speak except to cry out in pain.

'da Hōz's eponymous appendage miraculously fit inside Calvin, though 'da Hōz at no point seemed exactly hard. He had one physical state—large—one affect—sleepy indifference—and one phrase he repeated, "Yo, take that fuckin' Hershey bar, yo!" The confection in question was able to do its work, as far as Calvin could tell, by virtue of its sheer mass. 'da Hōz's greatest hit was *Titanic*, a murky fifty-six minutes which resembled its namesake only in that 'da Hōz croaked, "Yo, I be king of the world, yo!" when he ejaculated, a process which made Calvin wonder about the physiological mechanism required to move bodily fluid such a great distance, as well as what could possibly make a member of that size necessary simply in Darwinian terms.

Calvin and 'da Hōz were interrupted by a knock from one of the aforementioned pale white boys. The kid was badly groomed, not dressed any special way, and gave no reason for being there ('da Hōz seemed not to be visited by repairmen or delivery boys). The boy gave 'da Hōz a brother handshake and stripped. While Calvin easily accommodated 'da Hōz, this boy could not. 'da Hōz had to hold him in a virtual hammerlock as he writhed and begged 'da Hōz to stop. Calvin fretted, but he knew it would not be cool to intervene, and anyway, this was how things went here. He'd seen it before. He also found the boy's terror sexy, and since it was a given, he moved to caress the kid's flat, narrow chest and pinch his pale nipples as his face contorted and he gasped for air. Even if he wanted to report this, Calvin thought, who would he report it to? He'd seen cops here, but they always joined right in.

–o–

The payoffs of these encounters began to fall below Calvin's expectations, but as he increasingly felt the itch and even the pricking pain of "them" watching, and as he knew the infinite supply of boys here and the ease of snaring them, he couldn't quit. It was, in fact, so easy you couldn't even call it "snaring." What was it? Was he "engaging" them? No. "Attracting" them? No. Simply "getting" them? "Get" implied "have" and "have" meant "possess," and regardless of what acts he performed with these guys, he wasn't possessing them. To try to do so would be uncool. There simply was no verb to describe what he did with these men. Well, "fuck," though, except for the pistoning motion itself, he couldn't think what that word meant anymore, or what relationship it might describe. Maybe he needed the verb phrase "to take time." Or "to take *up* time." Everyone was taking *up* one another's time. Or "*occupying*" one another's time. But "occupy" suggested stasis, and time moved. So they were all stopping time for one another.

He told himself he'd stick with the job a bit longer, though, just to see who ordered the next pizza. But all the while, a thought gnawed at him:

Exactly how much time was he spending here, away from Tooker? Were the bright, truncated days equal to the days back home? At first he'd thought this world was timeless (obviating the idea of "occupying time" and leaving Calvin verbless again), and that Tooker would be the same when he came home as when he had left. Now he wasn't so sure. He had to see Tooker before he died. He had to be there to receive the final news; and he wanted to be able to comfort Sven. (In desperate moments he imagined that, after Tooker's death, he would take up with Sven a while, based on the grief they'd shared—though not entirely over the same things.)

And what about work? Where did people think he was? Could he lose his job and no longer be able to help his kid sister? He could imagine his father's recriminations then!

When Calvin came home the next day after delivering fifteen pizzas for a bukkake fraternity initiation, Roddd was lying by the pool with his eyes closed, playing with himself. Suddenly this annoyed Calvin beyond endurance. Maybe it was uncool, maybe it would make him disappear back to his own life, but he could not control himself. "You!" he snapped.

Roddd opened his eyes and raised a notch or two the speed at which he pulled on his peter.

"I have to go home," Calvin said.

Roddd began to work his shaft with both hands.

"I'm serious," Calvin said. "I have to go back where I came from!"

Roddd pinched a nipple with one hand while he continued to work his meat.

"Stop that!" Calvin shouted. "I have a friend who's sick, you have to tell me how to get out of here!"

Roddd stopped jacking. "Hey, this isn't cool," he said. "What do you mean, 'sick?'"

"He has *AIDS!*" Calvin said, stretching the long "A" and quivering with anticipation at the nuclear affect he would create.

Roddd just furrowed his brow.

"AIDS!" Calvin screeched. "AIDS! AIDS! AIDS! AIDS! PCP?? Kaposi's sarcoma???"

Roddd froze—more at Calvin's rage than at his words, it seemed. Roddd swallowed and said hoarsely, "This really isn't cool."

"What the fuck's the matter with you?" Calvin continued, more excited now to shatter Roddd's cool than he had ever been to receive Roddd's rod. "Don't you read? No, of course you don't!" he sneered. "Maybe I should put it in language you can understand: Oh, yeah! Visit that hospital! Visit that hospital! Oh, yeah! Cough up that blood! Cough up that blood!"

Roddd's face was white. The doorbell rang. Roddd reached for his shorts, stammering, "That must be the pizza I ordered," he said.

"*I'll* get it!" Calvin snarled.

"N-no, no!" Roddd objected, as though Calvin opening the door would blow up the house. Calvin bounded to the foyer almost hoping he would. He threw open the door. It was not Trunk Caldwell, but someone else. Calvin hauled him in by his arm (which was quite well developed and which, together with the sexy shock of hair over the boy's eyes, gave Calvin a second's pause).

"You!" he shouted. "Have you heard of AIDS?"

"Huh?" said the pizza boy.

"I don't fucking believe it!" Calvin screamed. "Are you all retarded?"

"Um, is that the thing, like, why we wear rubbers?" the pizza boy ventured.

"Yes!" Calvin snapped. "It is '*the-thing-like-why-we-wear-rubbers!*'"

"I always wondered about that," said the pizza boy.

"What's going on?" Roddd asked. Still dazed he came toward them holding a hundred dollar bill in one hand while the other diddled his meat through his shorts. "This is all totally, uncool," he opined.

"Y'know those rubber things we wear?" the pizza boy said, looking Roddd up and down. "It's because of this... thing. I don't completely get it. Um, I don't think I have change for a hundred. Lemme check." He patted his pockets. "Nope."

Suddenly a voice called from the patio. "Hi! I'm here to clean the pool...?"

Calvin wheeled and yelled, "Get out!"

"Wait a second!" Roddd said.

"You cleaned the fucking pool yesterday!" Calvin screamed. "And the day before! Don't you people keep records?"

"This is way uncool," the pizza boy observed. Then he added, to Roddd, "About your change—maybe I..."

"Yes," Calvin barked, "yes, this is 'way uncool'! My best friend is dying and three guys have ditched me in the past year and I hate my job and I'm afraid of being alone the rest of my life with nothing to do but watch you idiots spooge all over yourselves—and you say that's uncool! Well, that's the first thing anyone's gotten right since I showed up here!"

"Why are you blaming us?" the pool boy asked.

"Yeah," said the pizza boy. "You're the one who came here. We didn't do anything."

"Right again, junior!" Calvin snapped. "You don't do anything except fuck and eat pizza! I don't want to *see* another slice of pizza the rest of my life! Besides, *he*"—pointing to Roddd—"asked me to come here!"

"So you do everything people ask?" the pizza boy said.

"Yeah," said the pool boy, "like, if some guy asked you to jump off a bridge, would you?"

"If you don't like it here," Roddd Packer said, "go home!"

"Hang on," said the pizza boy, going over to the pool boy. "Are we, like, talking about bungee jumping, or what? 'Cause if the guy was really hot..."

"'Go home!'" Calvin sneered. "Right! How do I get home?"

"You've always had the power to go home," said the pool boy.

"Yeah," said the pizza boy. "You just had to find it out for yourself."

"Right!" said Calvin. "Do I tap my heels together and say 'There's no place like home?'"

"It's a little different than that," said Roddd.

Roddd turned on the television. Calvin lowered his bicycle pants, and while all three guys took turns going down on him, he repeated, "Oh, yeah! Suck that dick! Suck that dick!"

The blue of the TV fanned out and formed a cocoon around Calvin, and the guys faded away. Calvin blacked out. When he came to he was sitting on the sofa in his apartment. On the TV the guys were still going at it. Calvin instantly felt a pang. He knew without looking that his body had returned to its old proportions. For a moment the image of the pizza boy, bare and on his knees, made him want back in. It would be better this time. He wouldn't think about anything except sex. Calvin wondered how he failed to appreciate the pizza boy's beauty, Roddd's masculinity, the coltish and adventuresome pool boy.

The clock said ten-thirty. Calvin checked his watch. It was still the same day. He put his hand to the television screen, but nothing happened. He sighed and switched everything off. He would return the DVD to Lay-Z Video tomorrow on his way to home from work.

–o–

In the morning Calvin forgot to take the DVD. That evening he left work at half past five and headed to the hospital. Sven held Tooker's hand. Calvin held the other hand. They sat for an hour. There was just nothing to do. Once again, Calvin squeezed Tooker's hand. Once again, Calvin hugged Sven and told him to call anytime.

This scene would repeat itself only twice more.

After the funeral, Sven returned for a while to the Swedish fishing village where he'd been born. Calvin drove him to the airport. "Call me when you get back!" he told Sven, but he knew Sven wouldn't. He was really Tooker's friend, and, well, Calvin knew how such things went. Sven disappeared into the terminal, and Calvin barely knew which pedal to press or which way to turn the wheel. He could barely read the signs directing him through a tangle of dead ends, non-ends, non-beginnings, out over an endless chasm to a place called home that he could not imagine and thought he could never find again.

But he found it. It was depressingly easy to find. It was depressingly *there*. His street, his home, his rugs, his answering machine, all refused not to exist. All were unbearably hard, persistent, eternal, or at least intransmutable—not like love, fleeting, deceptive, and unpredictable. He thought of taking a hammer and smashing a vase he didn't like anyway, until he realized he would only end up with a smashed vase.

He checked the answering machine and discovered that he had missed or chosen not to hear two messages left over the last week by the video store. They were calling to remind Calvin that he still had the Roddd Packer DVD.

He looked.

There it was, in the tray of the DVD player.

Damn.

Well, he could take it back the next day after work. What was another two bucks at this point? They'd probably charged him for the whole thing by now. He might as well keep it. The promise of watching it again gave him the tiniest lift. Maybe he could get back to Roddd's place for one more encounter. Maybe he could find Reddy Toole again!

The thought had barely completed itself before Calvin was clicking on the TV and DVD player and stripping. The Harrow logo appeared, white on black, purity on nothingness.

To his relief, the guys were exciting again. The sex was exciting again. Calvin began to diddle himself. To be a part of this! To belong! How had he failed to see? Maybe he had not surrendered himself enough. He had tried to be too controlling. "Please," he said, when Roddd Packer's image came on the screen. He reached out and touched it. "I get it now. I won't make trouble. I'll be cool. Totally cool." Roddd kept fucking, totally cool himself. "Please do not ignore me!" Calvin pleaded. "I learned my lesson. I can be totally, totally cool!"

The bell rang by Roddd's pool. Roddd withdrew from the guy he was doing, explaining that the pizza boy was here.

Calvin slumped back on his sofa. He wanted to cry but could not. "Please, please, please…" he repeated. "Please!"

Lounge music droned, punctuated by moans. When Calvin looked again, there was Joey Rhodes, fucking a guy Calvin did not know. Calvin stared at Joey. Joey's rhythm did not vary. The camera cut from the in-out of his shaft to his face. Calvin crept close to the screen and stared. Joey's face barely moved. The camera zoomed in closer.

"Joey!" Calvin hissed.

Joey's face did not change.

"Joey!"

Nothing.

Calvin stared and stared.

Then, for half a second, a tenth of a second, Joey looked at Calvin.

"Joey!"

Calvin grabbed the remote and rewound. There it was, for half a second. He rewound again and again, and called out each time Joey stole that glance.

But the more Calvin watched, the less sure he was that Joey actually did look at him. He tried freezing the frame, but he could never get that frame exactly. So he clicked a frame at a time, forward, then backward, then forward again. In the end he was clicking back and forth, back and forth between just two frames. Still, there was no way to be sure, and no other form of analysis to which he could possibly subject those two frames. He virtually punched the ▶ button, threw the remote at the wall, fell back, and let the DVD go.

Joey fucked and fucked and fucked.

Calvin watched and watched and watched. Eventually he crept up to the TV again. His fingertips touched the warm screen, smooth as young skin, with almost the same give. His eyes ached.

"You are so cool, Joey Rhodes," he whispered. "You are so incredibly cool. I think I love you."

Possession

The Writer was late. Terribly. He had to get back. Everyone else was gone to somewhere safe. A wizened man at a turnstile gave him an old, beat-up bicycle and pointed across a dim field. He shook his head. "You are very late. It is very far." In the very last of the gray light the Writer made out a narrow path through weeds. The wizened man walked away. "So late," he sighed. "So late. So far."

The Writer mounted the bicycle. He could barely see where to put his feet. He missed and tipped over sideways. The bicycle was ashamed and resented it. Every minute, every second, it was darker and darker, later and later, and it was so far to go. The Writer could not begin the long, long journey back to where he had to be.

But he had forgotten to ask the wizened man where he, the Writer, had come *from*. It seemed there was no *from*. Just a field, trackless, and the dark. And lateness.

Now a bridge, high. He abandoned his bicycle and began to climb. So late. Way past time. High, dark, cold. Everyone was safe at home, out of sight, below. He climbed and climbed. It was far across the bridge. The gorge was deep, the other side impossible to make out. The little train meant to carry him could break down. It would be so late, all existence would have passed. Everyone would be in Heaven, on distant planets, he alone in the cold and dark, not knowing what to do, having broken a train, alone on the high, cold, dark bridge, no going forward, no going back.

He had to pee. At the top, alone, afraid to move, afraid at any moment a foot would slip and he would fall into space, plunging, forever separated from those in Heaven. He would never find the train, never get across.

There was an attendant. "I have to pee!" The attendant showed him a tiny, dim house between the girders. He saw no tickets. No till. He would be stuck here forever.

Stacked high on the toilet were rubber hoses, curved like horseshoes and in different colors. Dirty white walls crowded around him, covered with hooks. The attendant told him he could pee only after he had taken all the hoses from the toilet and hung them on the exact right hooks. But how could he know? The attendant shrugged and left him alone. There were dozens of hoses. Dozens of hooks. How could he ever guess? All right, he wouldn't pee. No, the attendant said. He had to pee before getting on the train. Where was the train? It would come. He looked at the hoses. There were hundreds, thousands of combinations to test.

So be it.

This would be his work: to rearrange hoses the rest of his life and never pee, never get back, never see Sean again, Sean whom he had made, *created*... He began to remove hoses from the toilet and hang them just anywhere, taking pleasure in the randomness. "Have to get back, have to get back," he muttered, and he began to cry. Then, "Never get back," he sobbed. Poor Sean, alone...

A tiny tick somewhere. "Better hurry," the attendant said. Tiny, tiny tick, coming just the tiniest bit. The train! Hurriedly the Writer threw hoses on hooks. How could he possibly be right? Should he change one? Or ten or twenty? It was so hopeless he went faster, grabbing, hurling hoses, switching them with bravado. The tiny, tiny tick ticked the tiniest bit closer. He stopped. Without pausing he turned and stared at the attendant, eyes blazing. The attendant shook his head. The tiny, tiny tick ticked tinily a tiny bit closer. The Writer spun, lunged for a hose, changed it, changed another and another. The attendant stood stoop-shouldered, shaking, shaking his head, and the tiny, tiny tick drew unbearably closer without getting there, and time itself crashed down on the Writer.

He would never again get back to Sean. He would spend eternity rearranging hoses while the attendant stood shaking, shaking his head.

The tiny, tiny tick just ticked there too tinily ever to do anything. He rearranged hoses as though it were a joke. The attendant stood with his back to him, shaking, shaking his head.

Suffocating without Sean, without the possibility of the idea of Sean. In this Hell with an old man shaking his head. Now he lacked energy even to change one hose. The attendant turned. "Well, looks like you've done it!"

He held out a ticket.

The Writer snatched it. He turned to pee. No victory, yet. No Sean. So far to go. He zipped up and turned to go.

"Wait," he said to the attendant. "Where am I *from*? I..."

The attendant shrugged and indicated the door to the outside.

There, the tiny, tiny ticking train sat so, so tiny on the tiny track that disappeared into the dark. No conductor. No passengers. Barely room for the Writer to get into the tiny wooden seat. The tracks were tiny copper threads, leading into the black. The train started. It wobbled. The dark swallowed him. The attendant and the little house were suddenly far behind. Was Sean there? The Sean he remembered? Wind blew. The bridge swayed and groaned out of the dark. The Writer's heart thudded, but he could not move from the tiny train. The tiny, tinily, furiously ticking train wobbled, went slow, slow, slow, and the Writer tried not to look down, down into the infinite drop, infinite height, infinite night.

He walked. The town was far. A few people passed, but they would not help. They shook their heads, and the Writer understood: late, hopelessly late, all hope gone, Sean so far, far gone. They had homes to go to. They had Seans to go to. So late. They passed and were gone, gone. He faced a tangle of streets. At first the streets seemed to match his little map, but when he tried to go here, he ended up there; when he tried to come back, he ended up somewhere else. "I beg your pardon? Do you know of a white mansion? I have to get back to..."

No, sorry.

Sorry.

I'm so sorry, Sean. I'd like to rescue you, but I can't. I don't know where to go. I am so sorry.

Mist fell. It got later and later, past time for anyone who didn't have a house to find one. Perhaps Sean had a house, far away on a distant planet. He didn't need the Writer. Didn't remember him. Would not have the slightest comprehension what was meant by his name.

Yes, that was it! The Writer had never existed for Sean. Sean consumed the Writer. Took him over. Owned him, used him. Now Sean had eaten and digested and shit out the Writer and gone to live in a cozy home on a distant, cozy planet, without the slightest clue what he had done.

The Writer had never rescued Sean. Sean had never needed rescue, Sean lived a triumphant fanfare of a life, and the Writer had been trampled under jingling elephant hooves. Still, if he could get the old Sean back. The old Sean was there somewhere, not too different, wasn't he?

The street ended in a dark, dense park that went up, up. The Writer could see a steeple on the other side, but the park was thick with no paths and fences in the way, and he ended up trapped on an playground surrounded by a fence with no way out. There had to be a way out. The children who had been there had escaped, with mummies and daddies to show them. Around and around he went. No gate anywhere. The fence was too high to jump. And the steeple was *right there*!

Then somehow he was in dense forest. The steeple was out of sight and he panicked, panted, climbing, climbing the trackless dark. Fallen branches, stumps, wet and hands injured. Then the top. But not the top. No steeple. Just a glow from over there. Yes! Just there. Just. No. Coming down suddenly. Playground again. No, turn. Go. Up. Go. Foot crashing through a tangle of branches. Leg stabbed. Glow. Up. Down. Around.

If only someone would help. But it was late, and they were gone. There were exact steps he had to take, like the hooks to hang the hoses on, but no one to tell him. Turn. Turn. Where? Still no steeple. It was *right there all that time*! Now just a glow. Back. Forth. Couldn't put his hand on any of it. A glow, beyond. So late, far past the end of time, all good folks safe in their houses.

Finally the steeple, where he never expected it. Finally, the church. Finally the town. Deserted. Dim. No one. No help.

Street.

Street.

Street.

Shops shut. Lights out. Walking. Walking. Yes! This street, on the map! Turn. No. Go back. Yes. Go here. No. Back there. Down here.

The White Mansion! He didn't know it, but he knew it. Exactly. Oh, Sean, I am here for you! I will see you now, as you were! I will save you. You will save me.

Inside the Mansion unbelievable beauty of young women weaving back and forth, laughing in silence, in light, laughing, clapping in silence, clapping in light, bending, dancing, dancing in silence, dancing in light. They implicate Sean. They ascend to a frenzy for him, every one wanting him, moving, dancing, clapping and dancing, in silence, in light. The more they want Sean, the more the Writer wants him, the more the Writer knows Sean was right, that Sean was the most right thing in Creation, Sean was Creation, Sean gave birth to the Universe, without Sean the fires of Creation could not whirl, without him dew would not fall. If dew fell, it fell in him, as proof of him. They clapped and wove, hopped and smiled to call forth the Sean of the world.

He opened the door.

Inside the dance looked subdued, slower, random, the silence merely quiet, the light, just lamps.

A young woman asked, "May I help you?"

"May I sit down, please?"

"Perhaps you can tell me who you are looking for?"

"I am looking for Sean..."

But no matter how he described him, she insisted there was no Sean. She spoke stiffly with a small smile. She had never heard of him. No, there would be no one else here who would remember him.

"He went out with someone named Megan..."

There was no one named Megan, ever. No one ever named Sean. "You are mistaken. If they were ever here, they left a long time ago. A long time before us." The dance went on, slow, random, hushed, seeking Sean.

"That's it! If they were here, someone must know... Are there pictures? Or...?"

"No. There are no pictures. No one would remember. So long before us. If at all."

"Wait."

Both the Writer and the young woman looked.

Another young woman stood a few feet off. The one at the desk seemed disappointed. The other young woman came forward, wearing wire-rimmed glasses and a loosely-fitting nightshirt. Her hair in a tangle. "My name is Martha," she said. "I can help you." The one at the desk flung down a pencil. Martha held out her hand. "Come," she said.

She seated him in a room that ran the length of the Mansion's south wall. She brought him cake on a plate and took a napkin and utensils from a cubby in the wall. The room was comfortable and worn and beautifully furnished.

Martha was not beautiful, but she was very pretty. She was not brilliant, but she was decent. "Maybe you know," the Writer said to her, "where I come *from*. There was a field. And a bridge. And streets and streets. But where did I come *from* to endure all that?"

"You may choose to discover that," Martha said. Now she sat by him and said, "You are a Writer. What do you write?"

It came out of his mouth like a lizard: "I write Sean!" She seemed not to mind. "That is, I write *about* Sean." She seemed to understand. That is, I *wrote* about him. Then I couldn't any more. I wrote less and less. Martha, why can't I tell the truth?" "That's all right," Martha said. "As long as it takes for you to tell, I will listen." Out of the corner of his eye the Writer saw, in the middle of the room, an exquisite Empire Desk surrounded by velvet ropes. He did not know exactly what Empire was, but he knew this was an Empire desk, and he could tell that it was exquisite. "What is that?" he asked Martha. She took his hand. "Why don't you tell me about the writing?" she said.

So he began to tell, though all the time, in the back of his head, he wondered, what if he had been fooled, and the Empire desk were not exquisite, or what if it were even more exquisite than he thought. What if instead it was utterly incomparable? He would be humiliated to have thought it merely exquisite.

"I tried to write about him," he said. "I wanted to write his biography, to capture him at a certain time. I knew him. Once."

"How?"

"Here," the Writer said, and for a moment he felt horribly certain he would die from something more than a sob, something great big and goopy that would tear out of him and leave him a bloody shell of meat. "I was here," he said. He felt naked and tiny in front of Martha. "I knew him here."

"Oh. No. I don't think that's possible," Martha said.

"Why not? You don't believe I was here?"

"No," Martha said sadly. "I do not believe you were here. I think you have come here mistakenly."

"But I was here!" the Writer snapped. He saw clouds of doubt on Martha's face, and he saw what she truly was. How limited. Not a woman in white, but a dark lady, doubting like everyone else. "I was here! I saw him! Every day. Every day was sunny. Every day was hopeful. He left every morning and came back every evening. He loved a girl named Megan."

Martha shook her head.

"Yes, he did! He had the whole world before him. He was beautiful, the way his body twisted in the sun. The way he walked through grass barefoot. The way he put a letter in a box. Beautiful."

Martha shook her head.

"I did not make him up!!" When he saw Martha's head still wagging he added softly, "At first. No. At first I did not make him up. I could not bear my desire for him. I did not know what the 'him' was I desired. I did not know in what universe my desire could go forth. What laws were necessary? If I went forth, would he vanish? Would I then only read about him? That seemed best and safest. So in the long, hissing summer days I retreated to my room and began to write about him. I entered him. Like pinworms up his ass, I entered. I entered him and laid my eggs. My sentences crept in his every orifice. My commas wiggled inside his colon.

Ellipses wound down his esophagus. Metaphors ate at his lungs. I was writing his autobiography and it was destroying him, but at the same time it was giving birth to a new him. When I finished, the old, rotten flesh would fall away completely, and a new Sean would rise to be mine forever: A Sean more Sean than Sean; Seanness, as defined by me. Already he had rotted into paper on which I could read about him. Already there stood in my locked room the beginnings of the Sean that was the correct Sean, according to me."

Martha's head slowly, sadly wagged.

"And I finished, as much as I could ever finish, and then I had nothing to do. His autobiography was not enough, and besides, no one would publish it. I must have sent it to a hundred publishers. So I began something new. All those creatures infecting him would move as one, would animate his limbs and make him do as I wished. The larvae would concentrate together and move his leg. Then they would raise his arm. He would fuck me, moved in his exertions by larvae. He would be a stack of wiggling worms, animated by my commas and ellipses, and he would wiggle his way into me. I wrote over and over about him doing this. And of course you know the kind of publishers that liked *that* kind of story!"

Still Martha's head wagged.

"Those were the only publishers I dealt with now. Snotty and unshaven. They loved Sean fucking. Sean so striking. Sean on a beach head. Sean doing filth. I owned him. He was gone from the world now; I had him. Still, I could not get him in focus. The publishers of *that* kind of story disapproved. I loved him. I wanted more for him. I wanted him free, yet I wanted to be the one who freed him. I wanted him free but bound by love. But in love he gave away his freedom and strength. I wanted him, modest, sweet, tender, drawing near to another man as a bee does to a flower, but I had built him so huge, of such granite he would crush that flower. The publishers of that kind of story told me it didn't matter. Didn't matter that he would become the kind of man I could never be. They slashed those things from my stories. I was a parked car that could not go backward or forward. I made him one thing, then could go no farther nor make him something else. I made him another thing, and the person he loved vanished. I brought the person back, He became something else, all the time displaying the insignia of cock, balls, ass."

The Writer glanced at the Empire desk. Martha tensed. She stopped wagging her head. Was it truly exquisite? Or—and for the first time this occurred to him—what if it was a fake? Sweat broke out on his forehead.

He wanted it gone. Now. If there was any chance it was not genuine. He tried to continue, but he choked on the thought: What is "Empire" anyway? He forced himself to speak.

"So I just wrote, wrote, wrote, heedlessly penetrating and infecting him. None of the stories could end. They dissipated in too many possibilities, too much I wanted for him, too much I wanted him to be. Every morning I resurrected him, hulking conglomerate of worm-marks, to do my bidding. But he never satisfied me, and I could write no more. The remaking of Sean was an exhausted project."

Martha was nodding now. The Writer stole another glance at the Empire desk. He would not be fooled, by God! But the desk would not give up its secrets. He had to cast his lot. Adore it for its exquisiteness…or despise it and dismiss it as a fake.

"Why are you looking at?" Martha asked.

"That desk," said the Writer.

"What desk?"

"That one. The Empire desk," He said, praying it was Empire.

"I don't know about any desk being Empire…"

"That desk—there! I…I believe it is Empire…"

For the first time, Martha glanced at the desk. She did not protest, but she looked uncomfortable. She looked away. Her head began to wag.

"Don't you see it? It practically fills the room, with those ropes around it!"

Her head stopped.

"Don't you see it?"

"Of course I see it. Shh!"

"What shh? Shh for what?"

"Please." She looked around. "We don't discuss it. Especially with the underclassmen. They should not know such things. They never ask, and we say nothing."

He lowered his voice. "Why? It's right there. It's so obvious!"

"I know. Still, people don't ask. People let the days go by and rarely ask. If they do, we try to ignore them."

"Why? What is it about that…"

"Shhhh!!"

Mouthing silently: "…*that desk*??"

"That is Sean," she said.

"What??"

"Shh…"

He looked nonplused. He looked at the desk. He looked at Martha, imploringly.

"It is Sean." She took his hand. She looked left and right. It was now very, very late and everyone had disappeared from the hallway outside.

"It happened long ago. When he was here. Yes, he was here. I didn't want to say it at first, until I had heard your story. But now I do believe you know him. That you were here and saw him. By the time this happened, you must have vanished."

"To my room."

"One day, at breakfast, he complained of a stiff neck. Megan rubbed it. They looked so sweet together."

The Writer looked away.

"By afternoon his neck was worse. Megan worried. She looked at the other girls like... well, like the expression you have right now. She was afraid. They went to the hospital and came back late. No one had found anything. Megan begged, but they discharged him. He told Megan, it's nothing. He told her to stop worrying and go to sleep.

"In the morning the stiffness had spread to his leg. He didn't want to, but Megan insisted they go back to the hospital. You should have seen her eyes, making the rounds of the girls, begging. And Sean: he looked so beautiful in his suffering. Everyone wished they were him."

"I know. I was in my room. Writing about..."

"Again the hospital found nothing and sent him home. By nightfall he had trouble moving his legs. Now he was worried. They couldn't go back to the hospital. He cried when he looked at Megan. He would not let go of her hand. She could not sit by him any longer. She came down to the other girls. She cried and asked what should she do. They could not say. She knew what they thought. Sean tried to follow her. He tried to come downstairs to where they were. Already his legs began to look like... *those* legs." She pointed at the desk. "Already his face—they thought it was a terrible rash—but it was wood. Finely finished wood, in terrible pain, wood crying for mercy, wood wailing for the injustice of it. He held out his arms to Megan as best as he could, but she had other plans. She saw where this was going and that she would have to find someone new. Sobbing she tried to raise her hands to his, but she could not. He filled her with revulsion now. If he had been man enough, this would not have happened. She could not even tell him she loved him. She just fled, out the door, crying for herself, not him, and she never returned.

"He stood, tears streaming down what remained of his face, trying to

95

call her, but he couldn't. He had almost no mouth. He could only make whimpery grunts. The girls looked away. It was so pathetic. He stood in the middle of their circle, holding out what was left of his arms. They had begun to go wooden, too, and reach to the floor. Right in front of them his arms and legs turned into the four legs of that desk. And then he could make no sound at all. And all the little filigrees and the finely finished wood. The inlaid pieces. All were there, bright and beautiful. He grew more and more beautiful. For what he was.

"When it was all done and they could look at him again, even if furtively, when they were sure he would not demand their sympathy or ask their help, they carried him in here. They took him tenderly in their fingertips and lifted all at once and brought him here and put the velvet rope around him. They did not like to talk about him, but they could not let him go. At first they polished him every few weeks and shut those drapes to protect him from the sun. But some of them began to say it was morbid, this furniture that used to be a man. They began to ignore him, but still they would not let him go. He was appraised, and they were offered quite a bit for him. It still happens, sometimes. We could get a lot of money. But no one wants him to leave. Who knows what would become of him out there?"

"I was in my room," the Writer murmured.

"Yes, you were in your room," said Martha.

"Fucking him."

"Fucking him."

"Is there any chance he will come back? Any chance he will go from wood to human again?"

"No," Martha said. "We do not think so."

The Writer stood.

"No!" Martha said.

"I'm just looking..."

"Please!"

He went to the velvet rope. He turned back to Martha. "I could buy him!" he said. "I could buy him from you!"

"With what?" Martha said. "You do not sell your stories."

The Writer's shoulders fell. "I could buy him on time." He turned to the desk. "Oh, Sean!" he said. "This is all my fault. And poor Megan! What did she do?"

"She went far away," Martha said, rising. "You can imagine the heartbreak. Your love turning into an expensive antique! They say that now she has all the things people have. Computers and tablets and phones—

several phones—she calls people all the time—and a nice car and beautiful shoes. And they all smell fresh. But no, you can not buy him. They would not allow that."

"But no one acknowledges he's here; they don't even take care of him anymore."

"They would not let him go. They need him, even if they never talk about him." Martha came and stood next to him. She took the velvet rope loosely in one hand. The Writer looked down at the desk. Poor Sean, who had been so beautiful, so free. He just stood there, decorated, perfectly still. Inlaid. His pretty muscles not capable of being anything—other than appreciated. His smile fixed forever, if visible at all. What did Sean think? Or had thought fled through his pores and left black night? The Writer wanted to kick the desk, in the hope that it would say, "Ouch!" Martha looked around. When she was certain no one was there, she lifted the rope.

"You may go say hello," she said.

"I don't know..."

"Go on," she said quietly. "It will do you good."

"No," the Writer said. "I can't be close to him."

"Yes, you can."

"The rope is there for a reason!" the Writer objected. "He is too precious to be touched. I would spoil something."

"He needs you," Martha said softly. "No living thing ever touches him. He has waited for you. You can't turn away from him now. Imagine the pain. Go. Step inside."

Touched that Sean might actually need him, might crave a touch neither of them had ever had, the Writer ducked under.

Martha dropped the rope. She watched carefully as the Writer put both hands on Sean, bent and pressed his whole body to him. He swore he could feel something, some blood still pulsing, some wish expressing itself. But the wood did not move.

"You look good in there," Martha said, backing away.

"Wait!" the Writer cried.

She held up her hands, thumbs and forefingers coming together in a rectangle before her face, as though she were a movie director. "Perfectly framed," she said.

He called to her: "How long can I stay?"

"That is not the question," Martha said, the rectangle of her thumbs and forefingers still before her face.

And she was gone. No one now. The Writer turned back to the desk.

He sighed. Sean all alone; he had him to himself now, to do anything he wanted. He knelt and tentatively put his face to the beautiful, polished wood. There was nothing he could not do, but this was not the Sean to whom he wanted to do it. Half-heartedly he sat cross-legged and hugged one leg, rubbed it up and down and nuzzled it and licked it. He stopped and looked up. "Martha! Martha?" No one answered. Beyond the well-lit room the house was dark. No tick of a clock, even. No chime. Deep, thick dark and quiet.

Then slowly, softly, something emerged. Not a clock but ticking like... The train. Tiny ticking like the tiny train. The Writer rose. "Martha?" No answer. Definitely ticking now. He stood and in one stroke leapt the rope. He moved toward the velvet dark Martha left in her wake dark that went beyond the walls of the house, within which flickered and ticked one pale lamp.

The ticking was lonely, the little lamp so lonely, so cut off. The Writer drew around a doorjamb and there ticked the tiny lamp, frightened and alone. On the wall a dark image, projected by the tiny, ticking lamp. In a deep gray room a boy bawled on a table. He was naked except for a cloth around his middle. Worms crept across his skin. As the Writer looked closer the worms resolved into commas and periods, semi-colons and ellipses, clutching, creeping, gnawing, sucking, infiltrating. The boy's parents stood by, holding hands. Tick tick tick went the tiny lamp. The boy wailed desperately. He begged, "Please, please!!" Other people stood around the deep gray room. The parents cast their eyes about. "Don't you worry," the mother said. "You will all have your turn. While he remains conscious." The boy burst out wailing and begging again in the most pathetic mortal anguish.

The Writer fled. Back to the light. Back under the velvet rope, shuddering to the floor where he hugged the desk and nuzzled it, hoping against hope it was not fake. "What can I give you, Sean?" he cried, gagging. "What can I give you?" he hugged tighter and tighter.

Now there was no tick.

The light in the room burned bright.

No chime.

In the morning, a beautiful Empire chair sat still within the velvet ropes.

The desk was gone.

On the carpet in the hall, just at the door and pointing toward it, they found the muddy footprint of a sneaker, smudged, as though on the run.

The Island

One more weekend they inch to the ferry: Roy bound to life, Jim and Mags to death. Roy inhales salt air and again thinks, *This time it will be better.* He shows their tickets, and he thinks, *No, it won't.*

Will.

Won't.

Homely wavelets lap at the side of the boat: *Might. Can't. Could. Won't.*

Some days the loop feels new, as though he might break free. Each day is different and the same. Good, worse, better, worst. Bad, better, okay... A gull's cry doesn't help. Young men's tanned calves don't help.

Jim brings the tip of his cane down loudly on the dock. He stops to cough. Two of the young men look. Roy's hand hovers at his lover's elbow. Roy has to caress, crush, scream, smash—right now. But he doesn't. What if Jim stops and hocks and spits in the water again? Roy was speechless as the globule sank. But Jim is angry. Jim is dying. Other men get this way.

Mags' plump arms pull her luggage, while she talks about the forecast (high in the eighties) and the boat being late and what will be for dinner. Will be. Becca bought swordfish steaks in Sayville. They are supposed to be good. They are supposed to be special.

They duck into the musty lower deck. " 'Scuse me, sweetie," Roy says, and moves from Jim's halting figure to help Mags stow luggage: "Careful... Would this go better here?" Fussing holds the truth at bay: the truth that you are fussing instead of loving. Roy steals a glance at the man who cannot be the man he has spent twelve years with. Can not. *Won't be.*

Jim stands still amidst the flow of passengers, almost blocking the steps to the upper deck. Younger men maneuver around him too energized to object. He draws his mouth into a drooping bud and aims his leaden stare out a window. *I no longer spend my life with him, I spend it on him.* The thoughts you have when you love. Roy goes back to the luggage. Fuck what the grief groups say! You aren't supposed to think like that. He helps Mags balance the cooler, which perhaps does not need so much balancing, and he stops himself from seizing her, pulling her to him, and burying his face in her breast. She says again that she can't wait for dinner: Becca bought red potatoes, too, and... Roy makes approving noises and looks again. No change in Jim's furious composure. There are no respites, no we're-together-and-that's-all-that-matters; if you say so, the cadaverous face remains stone, or erupts in hacking coughs.

There is no more story. There is stuff lined up, stuff understood to come before other stuff, stuff understood to come after. Maybe it is order and maybe it is disorder. But there is no more story, except inside them.

Men waltz around him—in pairs, in groups trash-talking or alone they crowd on—" 'Scu-u-use me-e-e!"—anxious for release, for the weight to lift in Paradise where they rule, May to September, in shares and half-shares and quarter-shares and even clinging in eighth-shares—you and an over-cologned stranger scrunched on cots in a friend of a friend's guest room every other weekend because something might happen, because It might happen, because you have no place else. You saw more women now. Better-off lesbians like Mags and Becca rented houses that had belonged to better-off men who would never come back, or would never leave.

A fiftyish man sweeps on with a Vuitton bag. White shorts, white sneakers, white muscle shirt set off a rippling tan. His calves are shaved and tattooed, his smooth face topped by a shock of lemony-blond. Roy sees in his wide eyes and the trenches of his face the blasted look of one who has endured years of rejection or illness or booze or bankruptcy or loneliness or all of the above. Now he has his Vuitton packed and is searching for his moment, which might already be gone, if it was ever there. He swings around Jim and takes the steps two at a time. Roy hurries to Jim, only to be met by The Look, frank and resentful. Beyond resentful; caught stone-faced in the teeth of final humiliation. Roy itches to crush his lover in the kind of embrace for which Jim is now forever too frail. Mags appears, the savior. The three of them wait, upright and still, for one more cooler and one more Vuitton and one more cooler and one more biography of Lincoln Kirstein, and then, together, a staggering chain, they negotiate the steps.

Up top, set free in the late sun and marshy breeze, Roy quickly weaves and sidles up to claim their usual seats. Mags escorts Jim. He smiles for her. Roy watches his love draw near. Jim keeps moving for her. He doesn't stab his cane into the deck, and he doesn't spit over the side. Jim sits, falling in slow motion from Mags's arms. He is shivering. She drapes her shawl around his shoulders. Behind them, the lads with tanned calves and coolers of Heineken crow how shitfaced they got and crawled into the office at seven a.m., ha-ha! What, *AIDS?* So Eighties! A twenty-something in Roy's office said, "Well, since they got a cure..." then seeing Roy's look, "Yeah, I know it's not a cure, but look: no one dies from it anymore," then, "So whatever! You know what I mean. It's not so bad anymore; you can't deny that!" Roy did not tell the kid his lover was dying from it. "I won't give him that," he told Mags. "I come from deception. I come from how to phrase it, when to stop and turn and look and wait and smile or when not to. I come from you and me against the world. I don't chat about my lover's slow death over the copy machine."

The ferry chugs and turns. Roy slings his arm over the back of the seat and absently holds Jim's fingers, sticks with cool, dead skin stretched over them. The prow points toward the Island and suddenly the pale, plump, baseball-capped kid from Sayville (who, Roy wryly notes, has no future, either—he just doesn't know it) guns the engine and the three friends lurch back and the scarf around Mags's bald head flutters and she grins, eye teeth showing. The curls blow back from Roy's ever retreating widow's peak. Even Jim has to let go, momentarily. The lads behind brace themselves and howl, "Woo-hoo!" Why have impossibly beautiful August afternoons? Jim shivers, raised his bony chin and draws the shawl tighter. Roy tries not to look like he is wiping his eyes. Mags pats his hand, hard, and he wants to yank it away.

If only he would die it would be all right. No, don't think it! Like idiots we rearrange his shawl. He'll get there, he'll only want to take a nap, he'll say the room is cold and demand to know how many pills he should take, and then say he didn't take that many yesterday.

Mags rubs the back of Roy's hand. Her right breast, the stuffed one, droops. The cancer has come back, in the left one now, and chemo isn't working so well. She'll begin another round Tuesday and won't be here next weekend. They have known her twenty years: she was their landlady when they first moved in together, on Jane Street. But she preferred *padrona di casa*; her lover then was an Italian. They all bonded over an air conditioner and Indian food. Now, Roy imagines himself, next summer, or the next or the next, dining in silence with Becca on a swordfish steak in a nice sunset, nice waves on the beach, and Becca will say, "Mags liked swordfish," and Roy will say, "I remember," and Becca will say, "You remember that time we had the swordfish together? Wasn't it wonderful?" and Roy would say, "Yes," because in a year or two today would be wonderful.

The Bay calm and lovely, like the brow of God. Roy has decided that God, whatever He is, does not pity, nor does He seek vengeance. Mags watches the shawl slide off Jim's shoulder and does nothing. She knows. *There's only so many times you can fuss with the shawl.* Soon there will be the dock and the next thing: Becca game in L.L. Bean cargo shorts and the purple T-shirt of an AIDS organization, salt-and-pepper hair in a ponytail. The long hug between her and Mags, the hug Jim and Roy can no longer have, the exhausting, seemingly endless discussion about whether to go to the girls' place first or drop the luggage at their own rental—"Whatever you want! Just please decide!"—then dinner, swordfish ("Ooh, Bec—gorgeous!") with red parsley potatoes ("Fresh parsley! Mm!") which Jim will poke at while the others keep talking—about Mags's will for Chrissake!—then a walk ("I really do feel ready for a walk, wouldn't that be nice, Jim, a walk?"), the slowly-descending peach and azure night and laughter from Rachel's bar and Jim announcing poker-faced, "Well, I'm dead!" and Roy's jaw clenching and him praying Mags and Becca haven't seen because he is really not that kind of man. Except he is. More and more. Isn't death supposed to make at least one party noble?

And tomorrow! Better than today. But in the end it never was. Still, Roy looks forward to it. That's what you do. Tomorrow is the only time you could look to, though Roy certainly looks back, too—back to when they'd flown to London, to when he'd been nineteen, fifteen, ten, six, roads not taken. He tries to figure out when he might have been nobler and how. Looking back saddens him, but it gets him to sleep at night.

He lies awake—in a separate room because of Jim's special needs—listening to waves that never cease: Can't. Still. Can't. Tomorrow would be better and Sunday Andy and Edwina would come, more people, making it easier to cover Jim's anguish and resentment with fun things and "Hi, how are you?" and "Feeling better, a little?"

"No."

"Oh."

"Are you disappointed?"

"Oh, Jim! Roy, where shall I put this bread? It got it at Hot and Crusty, the kind I was telling you about, with the herbs and raisins?"

But now, after dinner, on the boardwalk, in the violet twilight Jim stumbles and says it is nothing, stumbles, breathes heavily, draws back from soliciting hands. He doesn't look when Becca points out a deer chewing a bush in the dunes. It raises its black eyes. Becca and Mags address it in juicy squeaks, ask what it is thinking and what it is doing and isn't it pretty, and they make kissing sounds. Roy's jaw clenches. "Look, sweetie, a deer."

"What?"

"A *deer*, for Chrissake!"

The kissing trails off. Jim blinks—eyes red and wet, crippled and enraged.

"I'm sorry," Roy mumbles. Mags puts her hand on his back.

Becca's lip twitches. Roy says again, "I'm sorry. Sorry sorry sorry."

"Don't be," Jim says after a pause, the "t" clearly audible.

"Hard," Becca whispers hoarsely, arms akimbo. She coughs, bounces on the balls of her feet, and she and Mags exchange glances.

Mags rubs her hands and offers to walk them home. She kisses Becca and they squeeze one another's arms before parting. Roy reaches out and strokes the flannel of Jim's back. Jim, not turning, allows it.

Now, later, Roy rocks on the sand hugging his drawn-up knees.

Mags brought them home, kissed them, turned and went, a hunched genius who made the night look friendly by disappearing into it. Then nothing but the grinding of the moon. They climbed the stairs. Dust in the corners. As he helped Jim fall slow-motion onto white sheets Roy fantasized getting his lover supine and pressing a pillow over his face. This messenger from hell was not his lover, the one he'd flown to St. John's with and chosen carpets and a microwave with. This monster had to be destroyed. Then the real Jim would come back and gambol in the sun. Or no Jim. And Roy could finally sleep, finally greet the daylight soberly, go out without being scorched, buy flowers in the street.

But he never would. They'd endure tomorrow's fresh death, locked like grubs in the dark, feeding on one another's flesh.

−o−

Jim turned his face to the window and shut his eyes. Roy stole out, fled the house, padded down the boardwalk, eyed by dim, silent night cruisers, climbed the ramp over the dunes and came here to sit and rock. Two young men run up the water's edge, voices sibilant, intertwined. Had he and Jim been like that? Through his fingers he sifts sand and bits of shell. Those bits made a home, once, watertight. A gull snatched it, dropped it on a rock, the owner died, and the sea took the fragments, polished them till they could never fit together again. They are pretty now, and useless. They will become sand. This morning's tide left billions of tiny shrimp in scrawled lines up and down the beach, dying in the sun. Tomorrow it would be bright sea lettuce in the curl of each wave. I'm sorry, we don't have death today. Today's special is life. Try some!

Every night he said "I love you" and kissed Jim's forehead. Jim might pat his hand or mumble "Me, too" before turning his face to the drumming fan. At odd moments he'd blurt out memories as though they'd happened an hour ago: "That bitch who brought her dog in the elevator—who did she think she was?" "Kevin Costner, you know, was awful in *Robin Hood*." "Make strawberry soup!"

Strawberry soup. Good. A task, with rules and a result.

"What's this?"

"Strawberry soup. You asked for it, remember?"

"Do I like this?"

"You used to."

"What do you mean, 'Used to?' Huh!"

-o-

"Everything's 'used to,' Mags. He's a ghost, I'm a ghost. He has to let go."

"I know." Saturday night Becca is at a benefit in the Pines for a lesbian-owned press. Mags eats with Roy and Jim. Jim left his strawberry soup and most of his chicken and went upstairs. Now Roy sits at the too-big table, arms and head flopped on the oilcloth. Mags runs the remains of a damp towel over the faucets and counter. "For me—for us, I mean—there's BC—'Before Cancer'—and there's…this. Limbo." Moths thrum across the dirty windowpanes. Beyond the open front door, the torn screen, a cricket stops as though it has forgotten its tune. After a moment it resumes, only to forget again.

At dinner Mags coaxed a sepulchral smile or two from Jim, croaked with him a few bars of Gershwin and got him to do Joan Crawford in *Johnny Guitar*. His deadpan delivery made it even funnier.

"I'm so angry sometimes, Mags."

"I know."

"You mean it shows?"

"It's all right, kiddo. He can be a bitch. That shows, too. No one expects you to be perfect."

"I just wish he'd fight... more valiantly Or at least be more polite about giving up. There are things one does and says—at least some of the time. Even when one is dying. Mags, I'm tired of feeling like everything else is trivial. The tyranny of the sick. The minute I get going enjoying something, he drops a little reminder. Raisin biscuits for breakfast mean nothing to the dying. The fact that *The Rose* is on, well, he's dying so there should be no TV! Sometimes he does it with silence. 'Honey, I thought we might go to the Guggenheim this weekend.' Pau-au-au-ause!"

She passes the rag around the sink, then throws it on the table and sits. She twists the gold band on her left hand. "But for him," she said, "or anyone to have *love* end this way, to have your desire be responsible for bringing you to the state he's in. Me, well, women get breast cancer, lots of women"—she gestures to the right side of her chest—"not a fact I especially like, but...

"...for him, to have your own desire, the rich, pretty thing you cultivated ever since you were a little boy, to have that desire let a germ in that one day turns around and burns it all down and leaves you homeless...

"Desire is some people's only friend. A difficult friend: out of control, unpredictable, frank, always there to compensate you on a lonely night. So you wed desire. But your bride has a secret. A virus living in the house, unbeknownst to you. One day men bust in and push you down, hold your face to the abyss, because you desired. Because you wanted to feel for one minute like a character in a movie. And where the hell's desire after the men have beaten you? Still there. Diminished, but loyal. Look at his face. That's what happens to thwarted desire. It can't die, it can't pack up and go away. It turns..."

"Ugly. Now, my desire," Roy says, "I guess it just goes on. I never thought of myself as having desire. I just always wanted everything to be different."

"I know."

"I'm always on not-quite-the-right-island, looking at not-quite-the-right-sunset. And on the other side of those pines is someone on the right island looking at the right sunset, and if I'd done X instead of Y, I'd be looking at the right sunset, too, and I'd have the right salad for dinner and everything. Isn't that boring?"

Mags looks at him with an infinitely pitying expression. He offers to walk her home. Before they leave he goes up and sits by Jim's bed. He strokes Jim's hair and hopes he won't wake. On the bedside table and on the sill, discarded plastic like shells. Jim's eyes pop open. Roy wants to say to him things Mags had said about desire, but he can't find a reason to begin. Roy will escape with his own desire intact—barely. It will drag him on through life, though at the moment those future years are like a foggy desert. Instead he asks, "What do you think about?"

Jim blinks and seems not to hear. Roy feels the rising anxiety and panics. His lover's head jerks: "What?"

"What do you think about?"

"Oh." Jim blinks at the ceiling. "I wasn't aware anyone thought about what I think."

Roy feels the knife. He lifts himself above crosscurrents of rage and grief to murmur, "I do."

"No you don't."

"Didn't I just ask? Didn't..?"

"Do you want to know if I think about you?"

"It doesn't have to be me. I'd hope it was, but..."

"I'm sorry. I suppose I spend more time thinking about myself."

"As you should. Do...I take good enough care of you?"

"You do your best. For one of the living."

"Did I deserve that?"

Jim says nothing. His jaw works and he breathes audibly. "I hate God a good deal," he says. "A good fucking deal."

"I feel so alone," Roy says. "More than if you were dead."

He expected the roof to fall in, but the room lightens. Even Jim's face seems to lighten. Then he closes his worn, thin, red eyelids. There is nothing beyond silence. Roy stands and goes out.

-o-

Mags puts an arm around Roy, and Roy tries to feel the two of them vanishing into some other night, where things are right. Bamboo along the boardwalk leans in and rustles. "Sometimes it's still beautiful," he says.

"It's always beautiful," Mags says. "Slow down."

A boy in a tank top, skirt, and flip-flops sweeps briskly past on their left. A living person's stereo plays Chaka Khan. Men at a party laugh.

"I think about killing him, Mags."

She nods.

"I never would, but sometimes... I imagine... going in there, in the middle of the night... And just taking the pillow and saying, 'This is it, James, I can't take it anymore,' and pressing it down and just pressing hard, hard—and in a panic he'd flail those thin arms and then... everything would go slack... and I'd fling the pillow away and bawl, 'Oh, God, Sweetie, what have I done?' and dive on him and give him mouth-to-mouth and he'd come back kind of retarded but... sweet. Dippy, goofy. And we'd go off into the sunset. It's hideous, I know, I mean, you know obviously, I'd never..."

"Don't you have a right to sound hideous? To think hideous things?" Mags stops, throws back her head and crows into the forgiving night, "Dead babies!!! Let's vivisect pussycats!!! *Let's stuff puppies into the wood chipper*!! Spuh-*lat*!!!" Her echo dies away. Beyond the next rise, unseen waves crash and die: Might still. Never can.

"Mags! People will think something's wrong."

A nasal drone from a nearby porch inquires, "What the fuck is that?" Other guys whistle and applaud. Mags looks at Roy, her eyes wild, her chest heaving. "Something *is* wrong, Roy. Every minute of every day something is very, very wrong. Every minute is survival."

"Some people don't live that way."

"Oh-ho, yes they do!" They resume walking. "They may not think about it that way. But they live that way!"

"I just want *life* back, Mags. My life. My world. Even if I'm devastated, it'll be mine. Him hanging on is killing me, it's killing him, I know, for real. He's lost his humor, he doesn't read anymore, doesn't understand what I read to him, stares at videos, like Streisand or *Madame Butterfly* mean nothing. Is this what it's like to be old?"

"For some, I imagine."

"Well, it's making me old, Mags. It's made him old, it's made me old. My life—our life—is all coda now, like those Beethoven finales that never end. One more stabbing chord and no clue if it's the last one. You might get stabbed again, there might be silence without a proper good-bye. Every weekend we run here, every weekend I think it'll help—sun! sand! freedom! memories! wine!—and it never fucking does. Then we go home, Monday passes, Tuesday, the subway grinds me down but, oh, we have the *WEEKEND*. Now is torturous and shitty, but on the *WEEKEND* it'll be the way it was, we'll laugh, time will turn back! Maybe we should just all walk back into the sea!"

"Whoa, let's not devolve too fast!" Still panting she takes his upper arm and brings him around toward the rise in the boardwalk, toward the beach. "Want to take a look at the ocean?"

"Sure."

There are a few hangers on at Rachel's, raising glasses at the edge of the world. The ocean sighs, "Yes, yes." Damp wind flutters their hair. "You still love him. He loves you. But he can not give you now what he used to: the interest and engagement, the initiative. Now, it's all about him." A slicing motion with her hand. He stiffens. She likes to be definite about it. "I know. I do it, too. Already..." *Oh no,* he thinks. *Oh, no.* "But he still needs you. He needs something for nothing, yes, and it's emptying you out. So come talk to me, talk to Becca, for Heaven's sake. She can give you an earful. Talk to people! Talk to God!"

"Uh-oh! We're going to start in about praying, aren't we?"

"Hey, been known to work! Be there for him any way you can. You know, his desire for you is the only desire that hasn't bitten him on the ass."

He nods. "Thanks for that."

She puts her arm around him again, and they stare out at the black sea, the same as before. "Anytime. No charge." She chuckles. "You know I'm here anytime... when it gets to be too much."

"Oh! No, I'm not... I wouldn't..."

"But when you feel like you'd like to..."

He shakes his head firmly, feels some long-ago demon chew at his heart. How did you get it out? What terrible cleansing would take place? "How do you do it, Mags?"

She stops, draws damp, uncertain air into her lungs. A whiff of pot and the bounce of headlight beams come down the beach. The moon shines low in the east, shines over lives tucked in, over "Where's the remote?" and "Another Scotch?" and "Put the salad there." Shines over laughter. Shines over "Tomorrow we'll buy some more."

"You're... maybe dying, too. We pray not, but you live with the possibility. And yet you... I never know whether I'm going here or going there. I never know what I feel except sad. I look back at my life and it makes no sense. A flat plain with some bumps and broken spots I happened to trip over. I think I should've done differently. Lots of things.

Most things. 'I did my best.' Fuck that!"

They come to the top of the wooden stairs. From behind them two boys in sweatshirts, shorts and Reeboks clumpety-clump up the boardwalk, arm in arm, bound for the dark. Roy thinks of them minutes from now, entwined, sucking each other off in the waves. Sex. Another world. Another lifetime. "Sometimes I think I should have done everything differently, but I can't see how. And yet you... It's like you're at the center of your own life. You have faith."

"Yes. I do."

"How, Mags? Where did you get it? Why does this make sense to you, when I feel like I'm a million miles down a wrong turn with no hope of getting back? Pain shouldn't be joyless. Pain and grief and mourning and hate shouldn't be joyless. Well, hate, maybe. But the ache shouldn't be dull. I bet you weep."

"Sometimes." Below, the boys stride into the black. In a nearer, huddled group, a roach glows.

"And laugh. I've seen you. You shout at Becca and I bet the two of you fuck just great. Where does the faith to do all that come from?"

She chuckles. "Maybe you should kill him." Roy rolls his eyes. "I don't know if I can say where faith comes from. Or why you don't have it. But you can have it, simple as asking. You stand a micron from it. How to get there?" She puts her hand on his arm and he puts his hand over hers. "Roy, I can't tell you! This is the place on the road where everyone has to leave you."

He squeezes her hand. "Now I have it."

"You have me. Not it."

"'scuse us!" Two more young men duck past and clatter to union in the womb of night. Above, clusters of lights coast home. A distant cluster rises, bound for Paris. Possibilities and limitations swirl laughingly at the young men's feet. They are cold. They are startling. They carry corpses and teem with heedless life. They can not be prevented. They do not understand man. They are the ferry. The shuttle. They roll. They sort. They erase. They humiliate.

"I'm not a micron from anything," Roy says, pulling away. "I'm standing in for the better man who should be living my life! I rent; I don't own. God, everyone creates their taxonomy, don't they? But these are not my juice glasses. That is not my day bed. I'm the great pretender, who will live another fifty years. Maybe I should get infected."

"No no no no no, Honeybunch!"

"It would be so easy. He'd be happy to, I'm sure."

"Stop that! What if you just got laid? You're in the perfect place for that, too. And I don't think he'd deny you."

"Oh, don't say that!"

"That you should do it, or that he...?"

"The idea of him sitting there, blessing. Me going off while..."

"I know couples who do it."

"So do I. I envy them their cool. I know a guy who went to Madrid with Boyfriend #2 while Boyfriend #1 lay in the hospital. With Boyfriend #1's blessing. I can't. I like suffering and being a mess and putting up with. And anyway, getting laid is the least of my concerns. I don't think with my dick any more. I've been purified."

"I saw you looking at those boys on the ferry."

"Nostalgia. Wanting to be them. Wanting their lives. Remembering when I had their lives!"

"They're not getting half the kick out of their lives that you are!"

"Maybe not. I have to get back, Mags."

"Honeybunch?"

"Yes, ma'am?"

"Just know that... sometimes you can't kill and you can't fuck and you can't do anything, so you do nothing, and things happen on their own." She winked at him. "Just 'cause you've forgotten God, don't mean God's forgotten you."

"Thank you, Ms. Twelve-Step!"

"You stop that! How do platitudes get to be platitudes? They're true."

"G'night, Mags. Thanks for the walk and for the offer. You staying here?"

"A bit."

━o━

On the way home through rustling bamboo he toys with it: God in the bamboo, in the boardwalk at his feet? In Chaka Khan? He smiles. Out here it is easy to believe the strands of existence are perfectly balled up togewoventher. The City is jagged, fragmented, but out here, no cars, no heterosexuals, talk of surrender and divine purpose come easy on the waves. God is a micron away, but it is one hell of a micron. Does God know his name? Does God carry a grudge against him? The micron holds to its one requirement.

Resentment and doubt are more certain gods. They've gotten him this far, and he can control them. Mostly, yes, he can.

−o−

Always it feels he is coming home to a haunted house. Jim makes not a sound. Roy swears he does it on purpose.

"Sweetie?"

Has the moment finally come? Would he now always remember that evening, the walk with Mags, the talk, the last sight of her wild-haired against the stars waving and him shuffling home godless?

Up the stairs and one stride into Jim's room: "Jim? James? Sweetie?" He stops to impress on his brain the image of his lover like that, wrapped in the chenille, head turned to the window, jaw highlighted by orange from the table lamp.

"Not dead yet."

"I worry, you know."

"Wishful thinking." He does not turn his face from the night air.

"What?"

"You always think this time I'll be dead. Wishful thinking."

"Jesus, James! Do you say shit like that deliberately? To hurt me? I think you do."

"Is it true?"

Roy forces air out his nose. "So interested in truth! Yes. I do, sometimes. I do think that I will be... relieved... if..."

"When."

"I'll be very grieved, too. I am grieved. You know I am. You're my love. Even though sometimes you don't act like it. Nor do I, I know."

Jim's fingers flutter around on the blanket. Roy takes his hand. The tremor is transmitted and quieted. A breeze brings laughter and music. "I've got a crush on you, sweetie pie." Crickets in a sexual stupor. "All the day and nighttime." Behind the dunes men must be gasping, "Suck my dick!" "Yeah, take it!" "Want you to fuck me!"

"Do you love it anymore?" Roy asks.

Jim shakes his head. "I know you don't, either. But you will, again."

Roy watches his lover's breathing. At last he pulls his hand slowly away, but Jim hangs on, tighter than Roy thought possible. No, tighter than he thought Jim would bother to. "You know," Jim says loudly, "people always remember their first time on the Island.

"They remember the ferry pulling in, people on the dock waving as though everyone were there for everyone, meeting refugees in 1903. You pick out a face, arms waving. Or you remember the first time leaving. At night with the chilly air, the stars. The time they met someone at the ferry, coming in, or saw someone off when they were staying... here... Para... dise...

"The day before I left I... grieved, for what I would lose. We'd dress for dinner or toast the sunset. I felt grief in my heart, as though death awaited, as I ordered Margaritas at Rachel's and we took them down for one last look."

Roy wiped away tears. He kept his hold on his lover's hand as he pulled an unraveling wicker chair over beneath him.

"Night came. I wanted to be alone and sob for all the losses of the world and of my life. So many friends. And I was going to lose Paradise, this one place in the Universe where everyone was like me, this miraculous, silly, beautiful, innocent, lovely... lie. I'd feel the weight of the week ahead, four walls... Even if I knew I'd be back in a week or two, I felt I was being exiled, east of Eden. West, in this case.

And that was Jim, yes, the old Jim, wryly amending the allusion, making what they'd known all their lives amusing. "Oh, Sweetie, Sweetie..."

"One a.m. I'd lie there thinking how much I'd lost and how I couldn't get it back, not really, and now I was going to lose Paradise. The bamboo swaying. Who cares if it's a lie? It was the most beautiful lie in my world, ever.

"This was before you came. The truth. The flour and water and soap and wine. Subway rocking and the garbage to go out. Before your elbow in my side when I slept.

"At dawn I'd force myself: do The Next Thing: shower, sweep the hallway, just... sweep... *that corner!*, throw out food. The time for the ferry got closer. Such grief in my heart. One last look around. What I wouldn't do for one more day! Just turn the clock back twenty-four hours!

"With all the babbling friends I'd drag my heart, clunk clunk down the boardwalk, past the Belvedere, watching people pass, envying them. They'd be there that night when the stars came out, they'd ride the breeze, steal through the eyes of needles, dance, drink champagne, never the world would shout them down, always they'd feed at the nectar of night.

"Turn the corner by the Top of the Bay. If the ferry wasn't in we'd have to stand and endure its approach. Maybe it wouldn't come, and we'd all have to stay! But it always comes, on time.

"We'd shuffle on. I'd lose myself in stowing luggage. Just like you, yesterday. Thought I didn't know, hm? We'd go up, find seats, fussing and trying to pretend the Island and the bustle wasn't right there where we could reach out and still touch it. Finally I'd look and look at the Island going on with its business. I would so want to go back. Run off the ferry. One more day in Paradise.

"And then. You know when everyone's on and the gate closes, they back up and turn around?"

"Mm, yes, Sweetness, I know."

"It starts slow. You don't hear the engines. You look back at the Island—right there. People at lunch or buying plants. It turns and you look, and before you realize it, it's turned all the way around. Then they gun the engines and you're thrown back in your seat, and my heart would rise up and suddenly my heart would no longer be on the Island but right there on the boat, and I'd embrace the week ahead: apartment, boss, the shit waiting, my heart and soul, what I was meant to do. I might look back once, and Paradise would be small and far away, like a toy. But the life I'd been dreading and avoiding, I wanted to sink my teeth into it like a plum. I'd tip my face to the sky and think, This is who I am. Not Paradise, but the real world ahead. What I have to do.

"And I wouldn't look again. I think when I die, it will be like that."

Roy shuts his eyes and rocks himself.

"One day I'll come up, in the afternoon, for a nap, while you and Andy and Edwina are on the deck firing up the grill. I'll wake up and come down and call to you, 'Darling, there's extra salad in the crisper!' You won't turn around. And I'll know. I'll hope you just didn't hear. I'll say, 'Andy! Get his attention for me!' But Andy won't look, or Eddi. Still, I'll go to you, I'll place my cheek on your neck. You'll just keep on grilling meat. You'll step away for an oven mitt and slip from my grasp, just like that."

"No, I won't!"

"And I'll stand there crushed, looking at you and Andy and Eddi going about your business. Someone will say, 'We should wake him up.' You'll say, 'No, let him sleep a little more.' And I'll turn and go.

"I'll try to caress your arm one last time. But my heart won't be in it. Then I'll go down the walk, look back once, at you once, through the trees, smiling, Eddi making a joke, laughter filtering through trees like light, like gulls.

"I'll head for Bayview, past the Belvedere, past the living on their way to cocktails, past friends wrangling luggage, clunkety-clunk, here we are! The Sun will be low. When I'm almost to town someone will call:

"'Jimmy!'"

Roy wiped his eyes.

"'Mags!' I'll say.

"She'll be standing alone in the crowd, happy to see me. 'You, too?' she'll say, and I'll take her hand and say, 'Guess so!' We'll hug in the middle of the crowd, and she'll sigh, "Oh, my poor, poor Rebecca!" and then, 'Come on, now, Jim, we'll be late.' She'll turn me toward the dock and clasp my hand. We'll head down together past The Top of the Bay to the dock and the open water. The ferry will be coming in. Some young men jump off, loud and healthy, and we'll get on. No luggage now, just straight up to the deck. The afternoon sun lights the whole Bay. We look back at the center of town, point to things and people, close enough to touch. Suddenly I say, 'Mags, I can't, I have to go back, I have to make sure he knows about the extra salad in the crisper!' and I pull my hand from hers. 'One more night, Mags!' She says, 'Shh!' 'No, Mags, one more night, watching 'In the Life' with my head on his shoulder. Tomorrow we can go. Just let me go to him now!'

"She holds tight to my hand and says, 'No, Jim. I want to go back to Becca, too. There's nothing I want more in the world right now, but I mustn't. And you mustn't go back to Roy. You'll be sorry if you do.' And she makes us sit.

"And now the ferry's backing up, slowly backing away from all we knew, turning with barely a sound. I stare back. Just beyond those trees you are finding me, calling the authorities, crying into Eddi's shoulder, later crying into your pillow, alone. And the boat is turning. I want so badly to spend one more night with you, lie next to you as you soak that pillow and tell you how much I love you, even if you can't hear. Mags pulls me close. We don't take our eyes off the Island.

"And then...

"Then they gun the engines, we're thrown back in our seats, the wind blows our hair, the water sprays and we're on our way!

"And if for just a second we look back, the Island will be just a tiny, pretty trace vanishing, and your grief—I'm sorry, my love, your grief will be as a single star in the Milky Way. And we will go to... another island... where it'll be beautiful and right and hope and sun and wind..."

Roy presses his lover's hand to his lips. "Thank you," he mumbles into the wasting flesh. "Thank you so much for..."

Then with strength so great, so unexpected Roy does not know what is happening, Jim pulls himself up, torso stiff, eyes wide but not looking at Roy, and he cries, "There cannot be nothing! Please, God, there can *not* be nothing!"

"Shh, Sweetie! No!"

"They are coming!" Jim wails. "To hold me down! Help! Me!! I... can... not... *breathe*!!"

"Oh, my God! Yes, Sweetie, yes, you can. You can. Just... you're breathing. Yes, you are..."

Jim's legs flail, as though he would run, and Roy does not know what to do, except say, "Shh, Sweetie," because it always worked before. Jim is still breathing. His face folds up and his voice becomes a tiny, tiny wail. "There can't be nothing!" he whimpers, then a dam breaks and he bellows long and loud, "There can't be nothing!!" and from outside on someone's deck amid the clink of glasses Roy hears, "What was that?" "What?" "Did someone just hear, like, shouting?"

"There! Can't! Be...!" He gulps air. "There can't be nothing..." He says it over and over, softly now, as Roy senselessly pats his hair and the back of his neck and all over him and babbles, "Yes, Sweetie" or "No, Sweetie," it hardly matters, and lowers him back to his pillow. Clear eyes staring straight up he whispers, "I have not lived the life... I meant to live. I have not. I have not..."

Finally he is silent, fingers fluttering, trembling lips releasing air.

That night Roy sleeps in the unraveling chair, body twisted, head lolling, one hand trailing across the sheets, an inch from his lover's cadaverous body.

–o–

Jim does not die that day, nor the next. He dies at home in the City, just before noon the last Sunday of October. People say they are surprised.

Mags dies in March at Sloan-Kettering, on a Thursday evening, after the color has gone from the sky.

Out on the Island, high tide comes at 11:45 a.m.. Low tide comes at 5:37 p.m.

The wind blows out of the southeast at eight miles an hour.

The air temperature is 62 degrees at noon; the water temperature,

48.

Bamboo moves in the breeze.

In the City, alone at their kitchen windows at sunset, Roy and Becca have the same thought, they have every day since the love of their life left:

Thank God this is the last day. The last time I have to endure this. Tomorrow he will be back. Tomorrow she will be back.

In the morning, when they wake to the empty space beside them, they say it again:

Today is the last day. Tomorrow.

Tomorrow.

Tomorrow.

And in the dark the waves lap:

Might.

Could.

Can't.

Can't.

Won't.

Might.

So they deliver life to the sand to be transformed.

Until one morning, no more tension exists between the empty and the full, the sentenced and the executed, between love and rage, slavery and freedom, between the wish and what is said to be the reality. One morning, you look at the barometer or the coffee pot, and you realize you are living a different life. You traveled that micron. How did it happen? When did it happen? Does he know? Does he see? If only it could have been for him. The pang. You sob.

Then you say so long, for now. You have a date Friday. And it's not bad. At home, later, you tell him about it. You hold your pillow tight, but there will be another date. And nothing is wiped away. Not completely. Life grows dimensions. And the roar of the engine falls silent, the wash of waves dissipates, and the million tiny pockets of air sent underneath by the propellor's churn rise to the surface and join the thin layer between life and the question.

All the Young Boys
Love Alice

Did you read Alice Munro's story in *The New Yorker*—how at sixteen she
secretly dated the Salvation Army boy? The tale is touching, forgiving
and wise, with poignant and subtle shades of feeling. I long to write the
same way about my youth and so be approved of, like Alice.

Young Alice is daring, trespassing on a strange woman's property
to lie beneath a tree she loves. She lies on her back and imagines that
the trunk grows from her head. This girl will grow up to tell truths and
touch souls and be loved.

She is caught by the woman, a sharp-tongued horse breeder. As
she flees the property she sees the boy. He works for the woman. Alice
sees him again Saturday night in town, in full Salvation Army regalia,
preaching and making music with his family. They meet again in the
countryside, riding bicycles. The boy is thoughtful, like Alice. He doesn't
find it silly that she imagines a tree growing from her head. They kiss.
She feels his erection against her.

The boy belongs to a lower class, so Alice keeps him a secret. She
accepts his family's invitation to dinner but lies to her own family about
where she is going. How noble, the lies of sixteen, memories I wish I
had.

Oh, I lied at sixteen. But not that way. I just kept silent.

After dinner he walks her home. He wants to detour by the horse
breeder's barn. Alice follows him inside. They kiss, and then... Well,
I won't spoil it. You might read the story some time. You should. It's
beautifully etched (or limned—whichever) and the prose is, you know,
lapidary. Alice writes about important things and evokes universal

feelings. Everyone loves Alice. I will take Alice's idea and fit it to my own life at sixteen. I will make the story I've always dreamed of, that everyone will love.

So—summer, 1974. I am sixteen. With whom would I have gone biking? Who would I have invited home for dinner? Who would have brought me to a stranger's barn for a kiss?

I dreamed of having such a person. Or I dreamed of someone I should be, who perfectly executed such things with others.

But instead of making those things real, silently, inevitably I longed for Jeremy, a night manager at the diner where I washed dishes. Jeremy was two years older than I. His taciturnity, compact body and mop of dirty blond hair, his self-possessed frown and quick little smile, his round bottom and swagger captured what I longed to be. You see, I wasn't really male. I wasn't even really human. To Jeremy and to many others, I knew I appeared a soft, bumbling, impotent girl-boy, awkwardly hoisting beat-up gray bins of dishes, hesitating before I stammered out answers to snappy questions like "How are you?" Seeing the role in which I was forever cast made me despair, but watching Jeremy's swagger, the sweat glistening on his chest where his shirt fell open, obliterated my pain. Jeremy had what I needed to have to make myself real and good, and so I took it, and I used it secretly.

Late, late, after he'd scrubbed down the grill (face flushed, shirt clinging, sweat and rippling forearms setting off his soft skin and his prettiness) Jeremy ducked into the manager's office to change. I made up reasons to pass the half-closed door, to see what I could see, to see what I should be. He was too modest to reveal much. He did sometimes emerge with the clean shirt unbuttoned, his chest now dry, smooth, trim, nothing unnecessary like my flab, an unlit cigarette hanging from his red lips. He lit it and slouched on a stool and spun, eyes narrowed, watching me as he blew out smoke. Or he might come out still tucking the shirt, jeans unzipped an inch or two, and I'd see the elastic of his underpants, flat and snug to his belly.

Once a girl called Jeremy on the pay phone. I knocked on the door, and he came out shirtless. As he murmured to her, I racked the last dishes and the dark grill implements while attending to my life's true, secret work: glancing at his downy triceps, the golden hair under his arms, the gap between his lower back and the waistband of his jeans, rough denim against vulnerable, unblemished skin. How he was in his glory!

Once, when I was on during the day, Jeremy came to pick up his check. He wore a blue flowered shirt and had his arm around a girl. She was pretty and delicate, like him, the kind of girl I wanted in my thin arms.

Maybe it was best I never investigated a barn with Jeremy. He would have disappointed me. I certainly can't get an Alice Munro story out of him.

Nor can I get an Alice story out of Eddie, my fellow busboy who trained me.

Eddie was more gregarious than Jeremy, but not as smart. Rangy, with a big grin, prominent Adam's apple, and black curls, he grabbed pots one-handed, and the veins stood out in his forearms. I couldn't dream of dreaming of Eddie. He liked motorcycles and, of course, girls. Every question he asked about what I done or what I liked I just muttered, "No, sorry," or "Not really," and I maintained a permanent frown in order to appear masculine and discourage further questions. I couldn't tell Eddie that after work I stayed up late reading Moby-Dick. Maybe I could have told Jeremy, though even with him I should have been prepared to add, "Yeah, I was bored. S'posed to be some 'great classic.'" Jeremy would have understood what I couldn't say. But even Jeremy could go down that road only a short way. To go down farther I would have had to be so alone that I would not even have been able to see the road.

Nor is there an Alice Munro story in Paul, another night manager. I felt safe and relieved the nights I saw Paul was on. Smart and funny and bubbly and soft-voiced, with rounded features and feathered bangs, he'd been one of my father's piano students. But in Windsor, Connecticut in 1974 no one talked about what smart and bubbly and soft-voiced and playing the piano might mean. Paul was my sanctuary, so long as I wasn't like him. Jeremy and Eddie were not sanctuaries, and I wasn't like them, either. I wasn't like anyone. My struggle with life on Earth was a singular and disgusting stain on the sheets.

One night Paul burst into the Rice Krispies song. "No-o-o mo-o-ore Rice Kri-i-ispie-e-es!" he sang in his thin tenor, eyes wide, rushing down the aisle at Jill, the waitress with whom I'd gone to Sunday school. "We've run out of Rice Kri-i-ispies!!!" He pulled little cold cereals from under the counter and sang, "But we do have Sugar Pops, Fruit Loops and Frosted Fla-a-akes..."

I grinned from the kitchen doorway. What happened the nights Paul was on with Eddie? I bet he didn't sing. He probably didn't speak, except to Jill. Only thirty years later does it occur to me that, just as I felt safe the nights Paul and I were on together, maybe Paul felt safe, too. I would have made him feel safer still. But I didn't know.

Eddie came for his check one night when Paul and I were there, and Paul spoke a few friendly words to him. Eddie spoke friendly words back—to whoever he'd decided Paul was. I also recall chatter between Paul and Jeremy: Paul chirping, Jeremy nodding with narrowed eyes, reaching for his girl. I think I remember thinking: They... *share* something... *understand* one another... that's why he just nods. Except I didn't think it so specifically. I just stared and wanted more than ever to be Jeremy, to gather a girl to me and please my mom and dad as Jeremy must please his. To make a little Alice Munro story. And the goodness of my longing fulfilled me a moment before its crash.

Or maybe Jeremy listened to Paul to be polite, and later he told his girl, "Those types make me uncomfortable." Maybe, like many people in relation to many things, he didn't think much of anything. You never know what people are thinking, or why they do things, even when they tell you. Maybe especially when they tell you.

Nights Paul and I were on together were nights off, nights off from fear, fear of how I looked, how I sounded, what I might be asked, what someone might say to me or behind my back, what they might expect me to do or say or be, nights off from my face reflected in the stainless steel of the dishwasher. Usually the boy I saw there was a shell—frightened and angry. Nights Paul was on that boy, if I stopped to see him at all, was whole, busy, unself-conscious, in motion as boys his age should be. No stack of dishes was too big, all was right with the world because nights with Paul belonged to a world more right than the "real" world of motorcycles and girlfriends.

I had no sexual interest in Paul. He shut the office door all the way and locked it when changing, but I wouldn't have looked. Not that he was bad-looking. But the bubbliness, the turn with the cereal boxes... People looked up from their burgers and rolled their eyes... I didn't want to be like Paul. I just wished the whole world was like him, so I could breathe and go anywhere and do anything in peace. Well, that's my grown-up rendering of whatever I felt inchoately then. What normal sixteen-year-old would expect the world to sing the Rice Krispies aria along with him? Instead, I had to become strong, simple, decisive, in charge. And leave Paul behind.

I'm not doing very well here with Alice. I haven't offered much hope, and the best fiction is predicated on hope. "Fiction" might be a synonym for "hope."

Maybe if I stop and focus on specific elements of Alice's story. So, here's what I need: ache of youthful love; ennobling awareness as adulthood dawns; rebellion; shock when the boy and the situation turn out not to be as innocent as one thought; sadder-but-wiser ending.

The seduction I wish to practice on you would come especially from the love and dawning awareness parts. So: Whom did I *love*? I felt a longing when I saw Jeremy with his shirt off, but I denied it thus:

    I. I didn't *love* Jeremy, I merely envied:
        A. His easy, boyishly cool masculinity.
        B. His trim body.
    II. So if I mastered Jeremy's cool, if I could make myself trim and easy with the world:
        A. My envy would go away; and
        B. My desire to masturbate after seeing Jeremy with his shirt open would go away; and
        C. I could turn my attention to girls, who,
            (i) if I mastered that cool; and
            (ii) became that trim and easy,
            (iii) would like me.

—o—

It was just envy, you see? It wasn't lust (it certainly was not, you know, *HO-MO-SEX-U-AL-I-TY*), just envy and resentment on the part of a guy who hadn't made it. Yet.

But isn't it sad that, upon feeling first love and desire, I had to call it envy and resentment in order to go on breathing. My love was a mislabeled masterpiece, ignored in a museum basement. The endless desire/cancellation, desire/cancellation made me feel I was disappearing. Love Jeremy?? How? For what?

Lighten up! Adolescent boys have crushes all the time!

But it wasn't a crush! Why exchange one lie—he meant nothing to me—for another—"just a crush"?

You could have made friends with him.

So we could—do what?—shoot hoops? Talk about girlfriends? Go for beers, sit close, give the occasional pat on the back, done too soon? Maybe if I, too, had had a girlfriend, Jeremy and I could have been closer.

Yet, if I'd been like him, he could not have lived for me, in me, in the way he did. O, Alice, help me!

What about Paul?

I liked Paul, I felt safe with Paul, but I didn't want to be Paul. And if he and I did things together, *everyone* would suspect. And my family knew him. And no guarantee anything would happen, which with Paul I didn't want it to. I just wanted to be Jeremy in his flowered shirt with his arm, *my* new and restored arm (sounds bionic, eh?), around a girl...

Don't worry. We'll get this yet. We'll get to a nice story that everyone will love. Now, wasn't there a girl that I did actually go out with?

Ellen, from school. We went for ice cream one afternoon and walked along River Street. I'd imagined a whole romance, but she treated me as a friend, and I was frankly relieved. I felt drained by expectations, leaving me no strength to leap the chasm before me. I felt no primal electricity with Ellen; I had no idea who to be for her. Still, I had electricity for the idea of some girl someday. Or just impotent desperation.

But I must be sage and forgiving. That's what makes Alice's stories glow. That and her loving detail. I've neglected to mention the scalding plumes of steam unfurling from the dish washer as I pulled up its stainless steel doors, jammed with grease. I haven't mentioned the bursting laughter of customers as I scurried by with bins of dishes, gummy with melted ice cream, smeared with ketchup. I haven't mentioned my favorite duty: cube and boil potatoes, frothy pot hubble-bubbling, for next morning's hash browns.

Maybe I should have been able to get a better job, in an office, where a nice boy in a tie...

We exhaust ourselves thinking how our summers might have been different. But now, really set the scene, fill in the nice boy, script an encounter with him. Then the wish, the story, the child of regret, will die, its death rattle: "You were who you were." Stillborn wishes exhaust me, but when they are still in the womb, they are better than reality.

I should be telling you of first love, but I didn't love anyone at sixteen. I believed I couldn't love (it is work to live with that thought), and stories only exist if someone loves, don't they? (One of Alice's more famous *New Yorker* compadres supposedly said that gay fiction is inherently inferior because it can not have a "marriage plot." Of course, it can now. But, back to 1974.)

Young Alice and I did share one true love: books. After the Salvation Army boy disappoints her, Alice retreats to a world of literary lovers—Rochester and Mr. Darcy. I didn't seek men to love in the books I read.

Mr. Darcy wouldn't even see me. There on my bed by the window overlooking the neighbor's unmown yard, not the characters but the books themselves became my lovers, their powers of resolution conferring on me purpose, worth, and hope.

I didn't love Thoreau's *Cape Cod* for Thoreau or his techniques, but because our family went to the Cape at Christmas. I had maps of the Cape on my walls. I wanted to own the windswept dunes of Orleans and Truro. I'd be a naturalist-philosopher, tramping the sand with my walking stick, sketching dune grass, describing waves. I'd meet a girl on the beach, someone soft I could love, who'd love me because then I'd be different. I'd be strong and save her from the rip tide. We'd have babies and live looking out to sea.

I did like girls, but not enough nor in the right way. I wanted to impress them as other guys did, but I failed from the first moment, and they scorned or just didn't notice me. Girls I felt attracted to, like Ellen, slipped away—apparitions for other guys to make real. Sex was a sheer rock face, impossible to climb. I desired those boys who clambered effortlessly up, unconsciously born to climb. What turned me on about Jeremy's chest, glimpsed within the half-shut manager's office, was how his girl loved it, how he felt as she stroked it and whispered, "Oh, Cliff!" Eddie's veiny arms: if I had them, girls would want me. But I had been made too soft and timid, fruity, my mind rotting with warped desire and fantasy.

Like all great artists, Alice is brave. If I liked girls, why didn't I ask one out? If I liked boys..? No, I just gazed over beige dunes. How did love work for those like me? I didn't even ask. It didn't. And there were none like me, anyway. Yet people operate without evidence all the time. Brave ones, like Alice.

My shift is almost over. I guess I won't ever be Alice. How you write is how you live, and I have not lived in a way worth reporting on. Alice lives with vision and courage; she's earned her audience. I've hewed to fear and diminished myself. I won't be writing an Alice story, but can I tell you I'm frightened? Frightened that there can be no victory, that destruction rules the crippled house, frightened now, as then, that no effort can bridge the chasm between what I wish I wanted, and what life reveals me wanting. I should take a graceful bow and leave the stage.

And the curtain comes down.

—o—

I lock the back door, turn out lights in the store room, kitchen and bathrooms. On my way to the door, where Jeremy waits, I pass the cold fluorescence of the fountain.

"All set," I say, emerging into humid night. A cigarette hangs from Jeremy's lips. He presses the door shut. He stands legs spread, denim cupping his bottom, shoulders stretching the thin cotton of his white shirt, stout forearm turning the key. He pulls it out and shakes the door. He turns to me grinning, gives the keys a little toss, snags them in mid-air, and clips them to his belt loop. An almost-full moon lights the parking lot.

"Headin' home?"

"I guess."

"Stay," he says. "Lemme finish my cig."

" 'kay..."

He puffs, shoots me a look, jerks his head toward his rusty Camaro at the edge of the lot. "C'mon!" I follow. Is that a light across the street in the Cymerys Funeral Home, or just a reflection? Jeremy unlocks the door. "Drive ya home?"

I get in.

Slouched by him I watch his small, strong hand turn the radio dial. I lean forward, trying to pull out of the deep, bucket seat. He looks at me. "Relax," he says. "What groups you like?"

"The Rolling Stones," and he must know it's a lie because if I liked them so much, I'd call them, 'The Stones.'"

"Cool," says Jeremy. I try to recall titles: "Tumbling Dice," "Satisfaction." Jeremy can only find Elton John: "Mongrels, who ain't got a penny..."

"Your girlfriend didn't come tonight?" Sometimes she picks him up. He shakes his head. I wait for an explanation. None comes.

"This car yours?"

"Kinda." He blows smoke out the window. His gaze nails me, eyes narrowed. A smile curls the corner of his mouth. "So what you like to do?" He's slumped so the top of his shirt pulls open, revealing clear skin that is so much and nowhere near enough.

"What do I like to do?"

He laughs, leans forward, pats my left knee twice, hard, then flops back again, shirt open, blue denim in a nice, tight V between his legs. I say, "That's a dumb question!" and we laugh. I think he's blushing.

"God!" He regards his cigarette. "Gotta give up these things!"

"You should," I say, and realize that I really do think Jeremy should give them up, so he'll be more pleasing to me and won't die.

He squirms. "Make your blood race."

"Cigarettes? Make your...?"

"Yeah. Feel my heart. Go on!"

"Feel..?"

"Feel my heart."

His fingers circle my wrist and I let my palm open a little. He draws my left hand to his chest and I open my fingers further as he places them on his shirt so my thumb rests on the exposed skin of his chest. I have never touched another boy's bare chest. I don't reach in, though. Through the cotton my palm cups his left pectoral. My face is hot. I nod like, "Yup, sure is beating fast," though I don't feel his heart and have no idea how to find it. I feel him breathing. My hand lingers, then I take it away. He flicks the butt out the window and blows a last stream of smoke. I glance at the funeral home and try to remember the perfect fit of his pectoral in my palm, the cloth of the shirt, moving as he flexed a muscle. He twists around, hunches up to the wheel and turns the key. "Let's go," he says.

On the way up Bloomfield Avenue I keep my eyes front, but I know he's watching me. I ask, "So, you gonna give up cigarettes?"

"I should."

"Yeah, your heart really was racing."

The grin again, but he doesn't look at me. "Was it?"

"Yup."

In front of our dark house I pull on the door handle but don't yet open the Camaro's door. "You on tomorrow night?" I ask, though I already know he is. Is that the light over the kitchen sink, or just a reflection?

He nods. I nod. "Great," I say. His face is so still, so blue-shadowed, so pretty. Softly I add, "See you then." "For sure," he says. I heave myself out, shut the passenger door, then poke my head back into the fetid warmth. "I can..." I clear my throat. "I can check your heart again."

He smiles. "Cool," he says. He nods a couple times more, then averts his eyes as he shifts into gear. We wait a moment longer, but nothing more will happen tonight. Maybe it will tomorrow, an age away. He gives me a last grin, and I step back. My knees are weak.

"Oh, it's you!" My mother stands in her blue-and-green patterned housecoat and slippers once pink, now colorless.

"What're you doing up, Ma?"

"Oh, I heard the car. You didn't walk?"

Suddenly I'm hungry. I want to get rid of her so I can raid the fridge. I need to sit and eat and think of the compact mound of muscle over Jeremy's heart.

"Got a ride."

"Oh. Who with?"

"Jeremy," I say, inching toward the fridge. "The night manager."

"Oh. Isn't he the one you like?"

"Ma! I don't 'like' him!"

"Oh... I saw the way you looked at him that time I picked you up from the day shift...!"

"Mom..!"

"You should invite him to dinner one night when you're both off. Your father and I can get to know him a little more."

"Maybe." I pull the fridge open, putting my back to her.

"You know, we don't want our son going around with just anyone!"

"Mom! I told you: I'm not 'going around' with him. I don't even... Never mind..."

"Well, whatever you say. I just hope you'll invite him over and let us meet him."

"Yeah, well, maybe..."

I busy myself taking three slices of cheese and mustard. When I turn, she's gone.

The top of the house is hot. I smell the damp wood of the banister and mildew in the walls. In my room I start the thrum of the fan. I take off my clothes and stand in the shower.

I lie naked on top of the sheets, turn my face to the window screen, the dark, vegetable-smelling night. The neighbor's yard is a black sea. I place my hand over my own left pectoral and feel the thud. I close my eyes and squeeze. I have a little breast. I have a heart. I think of Jeremy's red lips, his shirt open. The tip of my penis skips up the damp skin of my thigh. Maybe Jeremy wanted me to notice his shirt open. Maybe he thinks I am beautiful and good and exciting. Me.

Life has begun. It stretches as far as I can see, and a hundred times more to be revealed tomorrow. I am loved and nothing touches me, not parents or friends, not my job, not time, for I contain everything. If I yawn or scratch my shoulder it is special. My fingernails are beautiful, and the pimple on my back. Angels envy me. Most of all, I am without fear. I'd jump out of an airplane to embrace the sky; I'd run into a burning building, strip my clothes off and laugh as flames bubbled my skin.

Tomorrow I'll ask Jeremy how his heart is. He'll let me feel, quickly. After we close he'll call me into the manager's office where he'll stand with his shirt unbuttoned. I'll put out my hand and he'll say it's more accurate if I put my ear to his chest. I will, with my right hand on his back, where it narrows. Then I'll straighten up, and I'll bring that heart to mine, and we'll kiss, and he'll blush and tell me that, from the first night we were on together, he thought I was sexy, and I'll say, "Yeah, I thought the same about you."

I'll invite him to dinner. He'll be nervous and keep asking what he should wear, and I will find it annoying yet adorable. The evening he comes to our house he won't smoke. He'll wear his flowered shirt. He'll put on mitts to help my mother lift a dish from the oven. He'll call my father "sir" and tell him about his plans to study accounting, and I will watch my parents' faces; they're both teachers, and I fear they'll think accounting is not enough, but all during dinner my mother will give me little smiles.

The future tense: it is exhausting, isn't it?

Tonight, as I lie in the dark, unchanging breeze, I know none of this. I do not know that I'll walk him home (his brother will have the Camaro). I don't know that as we step out into the dark my mom will catch my eye and mouth, "He's very nice." I don't know that my dad will beam and nod.

I don't know that Jeremy will take my hand on the empty streets of town, or that we'll detour to the darkened restaurant because he has the key. I don't know that we'll kiss passionately against the still warm dishwasher. I don't know that suddenly we'll hear a noise, nor do I know that it will be Gary, the manager. He'll say, "Hey! Who is it? I've got a gun!" Jeremy will shoo me out back, promising to handle this and call me tomorrow. I don't know that I'll linger by the door and hear, "Just me, Gare." "Oh, Jeez. Hey. What're you doing here?" "I, um, left my jacket." "So you're alone?" "Uh, yeah." "You been out somewhere? You look good in that shirt." A chuckle. "Yeah?" "Yeah." Pause and another chuckle. "You doing anything now?" "Not really." "Want to go to Windsor House for a drink?" I will wait for Jeremy to spurn dopey Gary. "Or we could stay here." And Jeremy will say, "We could." I hear the half-smile in his voice. It is my half-smile. Or was. I will see him toss hair out of his eyes. "How about it?" Gary will say. "You ever done it at work?" I will see Jeremy

127

slowly shake his head. "No?" Gary will ask hoarsely. "You never had a guy take you on the counter?" Then silence, except once I will think I hear Gary sigh, "Yeah, that's right...!"

I will go home.

I will go home and bury myself in *Jane Eyre* and *Pride and Prejudice*. I will imagine Mr. Darcy half-dressed, gently moving my buttocks apart, saying, "I want to be inside you..."

I will find that the next week I'm only on the nights that Paul is on. And so summer will end.

But tonight I know none of this. Tonight, pleasantly exhausted, naked with the fan on me, I caress my chest and belly. I imagine a big house with lots of windows, and my parents' car pulling into the driveway on a Sunday afternoon, and I imagine, even before Jeremy and I emerge, that Jeremy Jr. charges out the door and across the lawn, blond hair flashing in the sun, young heart beating faster than it ever will again.

One Bedroom

November met me by the river. The current drew faceless ice to the sea. I stood with the wind tugging my forelock, and I wondered what to do now that God had turned his back on me, now that I felt no trace of Him in my soul, but only the slow encroachment of the Devil, like hypothermia that warms you while it kills you. I longed to feel alive again in the only way I truly understood:

When I was a boy my friend Alex and I went into the barn on the Jensen property and we peed on the dusty floorboards, warm, golden streams, drumming, spattering—dark, redolent rivers running, twisting out of the dappled pool of light in which we stood, off into shadows. We didn't speak, but glanced at one another's penises and grinned.

At night, alone in the dark in my bedroom, a movie opened in my mind, a movie that took place in the Jensens' barn. Alex and I were naked, T-shirts and cutoffs dropped in haste. Alex knelt before me, his sculpted face upturned, eyes closed, mouth with its red lips wide open and tongue extended, and I peed lovingly over every square inch of his face, a steady stream moving from his chin up to his forehead and back down, and then from side to side across his open mouth. He drank voraciously. Droplets danced off his teeth and tongue and scintillated flying through a shaft of light that shone in.

I played this movie over and over in my head as I masturbated. Soon Alex and I stopped going to the barn. We went away to different schools and I never saw him again. But I masturbated to that fantasy for years, through college, through my years of wandering, and now in divinity school. I had just, in fact, come from a session with myself that November afternoon, and now I prayed to God that He would grant me the strength to throw myself into the river and freeze to death as quickly as possible, with no interference.

But the presence of a stranger by the wall, looking out over the water, ready, perhaps, to call for help, discouraged me. He saved me, I suppose, or his serendipitous presence did, so that on my way back to my dormitory I could, for the fiftieth or hundredth time, break my promise to myself and to God, and visit the narrow, malodorous, newsstand just off campus on Elm Avenue, and buy myself one last copy of *Knight* magazine—"Personals for *Real* Men."

Imagine the thrill when I opened that particular issue back in my room, and the first ad that hit my eyes began:

USE MY FACE FOR A TOILET

The moment I saw those words I knew I would answer the ad. I skimmed it, devouring without knowing what I was devouring. The advertiser's age was the same as mine, twenty-eight, his height-to-weight ratio reasonable, and the ad mentioned he worked out. He concluded with the traditional prohibition, "No fats, fems." I turned to the front of the magazine and my eyes skittered impatiently over the instructions for answering ads. Half an hour later I sent off a scribbled letter to "*Knight* Box #5384" in New York City. I described myself, or rather I described my body, and in particular my penis. I wrote in a tough, desensitized tone, quite unlike the way in which I thought of myself. "You'll beg for my hot piss," I promised, and I felt a shudder of revulsion thinking of the face that would stare, mesmerized, mouth open, as it read this. But I kept writing. This was, after all, what I had always wanted.

Three weeks later the magazine forwarded a plain, white envelope to me. In the envelope I found a one-page, single-sided letter, written in green felt tip pen, not in flowing script, but in tiny letters, well set off from one another. The tip of the pen was so thick and the letters so small, that they looked like little, amorphous, balled-up fists. The letter was not signed, but concluded with a Manhattan telephone number.

The voice that answered the telephone spoke in a distant monotone. Yes, he said, with no enthusiasm and with no hesitation, yes, he'd like to get together. I said, "Are you sure?" and after a pause he said, "Yeah." "When?" "Anytime." "This weekend?" Pause. "Yeah." "Saturday?" Pause. "Yeah." "When's convenient?" "Anytime." He said nothing more, so I began to go over the train schedule. The 10:40 would bring me into Penn Station at 12:51—would that be okay? Pause. "Yeah." Get there about 1:15? "Yeah." "Do you have an address?" He had one, though he had to repeat it three times before I understood. He lived on the Upper West Side, in the low Eighties, off Amsterdam Avenue. I felt relieved that I knew that area, knew how to get there by subway, and more importantly, how to get away. "Okay," I concluded, "I'll see you Saturday." Pause. "Okay." "You're sure that's okay?" Pause. "Yeah." "You're sure?" "Yeah." "Okay. 1:15." Pause. "Okay." "See you then." "Okay." Then silence. Then he hung up. Neither one of us had told the other his name.

When I woke Saturday morning the first thing I knew was that I wanted to go anywhere and do anything except go where I had planned and do what I knew I would end up doing. I tried to pray to God to keep me from it, but when I closed my eyes I could only see of Alex kneeling before me in the barn, the joy of release, the marking of a fellow human being.

I boarded the 10:40 to New York. I sat by grimy glass watching rail yards crawl by as the wheels screamed. I dreamed over and over of what might transpire at that apartment in the West Eighties. He might be a hunk. He might be sweet and small, a boy like Alex.

Like Alex was.

I imagined I might not go there at all, but instead buy a half-price ticket to a Broadway matinee or browse in a department store. And I thought about my parents.

I was, as I mentioned, twenty-eight. I had been accepted to divinity school only after I had tried everything else. I was not even certain I believed in God. Certainly I had trouble praying to Him, had all but stopped trying, and certainly He had answered none of my prayers, most of which begged Him to lift the burden of my desire, and upon completion of which I binged, purchasing copies of *Knight* and *Drummer* and *Mandate* and *Torso*, only to purge after a few weeks, carrying the magazines in plastic bags to dumpsters in far reaches of the city, only to go back to Elm Avenue and purchase more.

Not that my application to divinity school had been without precedent. I had felt spiritual longings all my life, like mist around me since earliest memory. Most of these longings had been for upper middle class heterosexual love objects—boys who went on to live successful lives without ever having suspected that I once sat alone on bleachers watching them cross a field half naked at sunset, never having known that I leaned against a portico column late into a spring evening watching their shadows come and go behind yellow shades until their lights went out.

Rejected by the golden, privileged ones, I tried to adopt Lucy's advice in Peanuts, when Schroeder comes to her, wailing that Beethoven, deaf, never heard his own Ninth Symphony. "Try not to think about it," she says. "Five cents, please." Tuition to divinity school? But I couldn't not think about it. Rejected in the halls of privilege, I settled for second best, for God, hoping He would save me from the longing I didn't want to be saved from. I accepted His work as penance—joyless, and yet comforting and pleasurable in its compulsive stringency. My parents were puzzled, yet happy, too, that I had developed new ambition after all my odd jobs and backpacking trips through the West and after my previous attempt at grad school—a single semester of philosophy that I could not complete because every time I sat down to study I fell asleep. At least in divinity school I stayed awake.

And now I sat slumped, rocked gently by a New York train, bound to meet a man whose letter to the world was, "USE MY FACE FOR A TOILET." I imagined that this abject man had more of God in him than I did at that moment.

-o-

When the southbound traveler first catches sight of Manhattan over the bridges and the charred warehouses of the outer boroughs, he doesn't know what he sees, only that he sees more than anywhere else on earth. As the train turns, the City turns, plays hard to get, slides behind smashed factories and reappears in different guises. She reveals more and hides more, now close, now far. On a day such as that, with rain and low hanging clouds and steam rising from a trio of smokestacks in Queens, watchful like Three Fates or Three Furies, she looks like an infernal machine. As the train turns, the machine, ever the same and ever indifferent, seems to unfold, holds out satiation in forms you never knew existed outside your own head, offers an unbearable intensity and isolation, so you run to be satiated again and the fire in the furnace chars your face, stoked by the rage of birds trapped underground like an evil boy humping his mattress or sticking pins in a live beetle and pointing giggling hand over mouth as the beetle heaves and freaks.

"Heavenly Father," I prayed, "give me the strength to go to a movie, better yet, give me the strength to get right back on the next train"—among other things I couldn't really afford this trip—"give me the strength to go anywhere and do anything but ride the local to Seventy-ninth Street."

When the train pulled in I automatically made for the subway station.

You just didn't give up an opportunity like this one. You just didn't.

I found my way through the rain and steam to West Eighty-first Street, just off Amsterdam. The building was a brownstone, surrounded by rubble, its first floor windows smashed. The bell corresponding to the apartment number he'd given was unmarked. I pushed the buzzer and prayed there would be no answer. When, after several seconds, no answer came, I pressed again. And again. Finally the speaker crackled. A voice behind the crackle murmured indistinctly. "Hi. It's me," I said, and the door buzzed and I went in.

The hallway was narrow and high, lit by one flickering violet ring hung cock-eyed on the ceiling. Whole sections of tile had fallen from the walls or been ripped away. The newel post looked as though it had once been nice, but its detail work had been blurred by coat upon coat of brown paint, and it had been scarred by a parade of thoughtless young people moving in, moving out, in and out of anonymous buildings like this all over the City.

Above me I heard the clack of a deadbolt. A door cried. As I ascended I was conscious of the too-loud sound of my footfalls on the stairs. My eyes still had not adjusted when I reached the third floor. I looked both ways along the narrow, tiled corridor. High up, plaster had fallen from the walls. The ceiling was covered with what looked like giant lichens, in fact flaking paint. Somewhere someone held a door open for me, but I couldn't see. Neither he, standing so close yet unseen, nor I spoke. I shuffled back and forth tentatively until I found it. The open door revealed a long, dark hallway, at the end of which shone a distant rectangle of gray light. A radiator tinked and gushed steam; the air emerging from the apartment was stale and hot and pressed against me.

He stood half-hidden behind the door, wearing only boxer shorts. For a moment it occurred to me that he never went out, that he stayed here day in, day out, dressed in the same pair of shorts. Perhaps he didn't own any other clothes.

His small toenails were reddish-purple. Feet white. Legs powerful, sexy, really. He had a sweet bulk, just enough out of shape to feel familiar. His face was pasty but vulnerable, his hairline receding, though he was about my age. His eyes looked everywhere but at me, though I felt instantly connected to him. Why is there no word but "harmless" for how he seemed? Why is "harmless" an insult? I liked him immediately. Or sympathized.

He fidgeted, cleared his throat, looked at the floor. His right arm jerked up, hand pointing down the hall, a gesture meant to welcome me in. I stole by him, toward the square of light. He closed the door, bolted it, as though for my safety, I thought, though his last gesture, putting on the chain, felt sinister. Not that I couldn't get out. There was something he feared getting in. He padded briskly past me, down the hall, head bowed. Halfway down he made a left turn and vanished. I followed him to the doorway of a small room where a narrow mattress lay on the floor. Grayish-yellow bedclothes twisted on the mattress, white socks scuffed brown and a shirt hung over a chair, and a gooseneck lamp and digital alarm clock stood on the floor by the mattress. A dusty Scrabble board lay open, tiles in disarray, some right side up, some upside down. This room was hotter than the hallway had been. It smelled of the stale socks. Paint flaked off the ceiling and walls, and flakes lay on the floor and the Scrabble board. As I crossed the threshold, I saw my host pass head down through a brightly lit doorway on the other side of the room. A harsh gush of steam came from within.

I followed.

A bare hundred-watt bulb glared over the sink in the bathroom, the hottest room yet. Crooked, cracked tiles covered the walls, lemon yellow and black. No window. Steam whined and blasted from the top of a rusted, peeling pipe in the corner. The boxer shorts lay in the middle of the floor. He knelt naked, sitting on his heels in the tub, his face turned upwards, his eyes closed, their lids twitching in anticipation. A ragged length of string hung from the showerhead.

I stripped, stepped into the tub, put one foot jauntily on the edge, placed my arms akimbo, and used his face for a toilet.

It gurgled in his cheeks and under his tongue. It scintillated off his teeth, but he was no Alex. There was no Alex in the Universe now. Had there ever been?

When I was drained he bowed his head, wiped his face with his fingers, then reached around me to turn on the faucet. When the brownish stream went clear, he daintily splashed water on his face. The stench of my urine permeated the hot air. I felt proud, relieved. He stretched an arm out over the side of the tub and wiped his face dry with his boxer shorts. Then, head bowed, he mumbled something.

"Excuse me?" I said after a moment.

He mumbled again.

"I'm sorry..."

134

This time, still not looking at me, he spoke louder and with somewhat more clarity. "Take a shit on me," he said.

He proceeded to lie on his back in the tub. Again he closed his eyes, his face moonlike, blank. He waited, eyelids trembling, as though his eyeballs were darting in a dozen different directions, on the lookout for something.

I had not expected this. I had interpreted "USE MY FACE FOR A TOILET" as fulfillment of my longing for the nonexistent Alex. I associated urination with freedom and innocence, defecation with desperation and need.

"Where?"

He said nothing. The eyelids twitched frantically but the rest of him barely moved.

"Where do you want it?"

"Wherever," he shrugged, then added, "Face."

So I straddled him, bent my body forward, my hands on my knees, contracted my abdominal muscles, and after several seconds made a little fart. But I'd eaten a big breakfast that morning and had stopped for a snack in Penn Station, so after a little more effort I managed to push out a reasonable turd. I heard it land on him with a plop. I stole a glance. It had landed awkwardly on his neck. I knew it would. I could not bring myself to shit on his face. I squeezed a couple more little ones out. Eyes front now on the stained fixtures and the garish tiles I thought of what we called our turds in grade school. Big ones were "grunts," and little ones were "doots." One grunt, two doots. That was my score. After that I farted again, then I just stared at the ragged end of the string and felt empty. What was the etiquette here? "That's all I have," I muttered. "Sorry." A dribble ran down the inside of my leg.

He moved beneath me, legs brushing mine, and climbed quickly out of the tub. I didn't look. I wondered what had become of my turds. Over the relentless blast of the steam pipe I heard the toilet flush, a riptide, quick disposal of what little had passed between us. He ran water in the sink. At last I looked at him. He hunched over the sink, splashing water on his face. He was wearing the shorts again. I didn't move until he had dried his face and had padded out the door, head down, back to the darkened bedroom. Then I stepped out of the bathtub and closed the door. The blast from steam the pipe abruptly halted.

I examined the tub for traces of what we had done, but for a lingering smell, there were none. I looked into the toilet bowl, so stained with rust that I could not tell what else might be there. I examined his towel, damp and rumpled but clean. All traces of our act had been expunged. Disappointed and empty I sat on the toilet, pulled off a length of paper, and wiped my anus. Then I cleaned the inside of my leg.

I flushed the toilet, washed my hands and face a couple of times, dried them on another towel, and carried my clothes into the next room. The dim light relieved me, and it felt cool. I still felt as though I had shit on myself and could not wipe it off.

-o-

He sat on the mattress, facing away from me. The bright light from the bathroom illuminated his back and cast a huge shadow on the wall, blurred and amorphous as the letters adrift on the page he'd sent. I asked the only question I could think of: "So what do you do?"

It turned out, as best I could tell, that he had served as some mid-level sub-assistant in the last administration in Washington. Nonplused, I asked the next obvious question: Had homophobia in government been a problem for him? He shook his head. I bit my tongue. I had known, as soon as that question had come out of my mouth, that it constituted a trespass. I could not apologize, for acknowledging the trespass would also have been a trespass. This man invited men to perform excretory functions on him, yet for me to presume that he spent his passion on the souls and hearts of men, that he lived "the gay life," was a ghastly intrusion. Wasn't it?

"Is there anything to eat?" I asked. I couldn't understand his reply, but he pointed down the hall. I left the bedroom and went to explore.

The kitchen was as bare and under-equipped as the other rooms. Just as I couldn't think of him as gay, or as oriented sexually in any direction, I couldn't think of this collection of rooms as his or anyone's home.

I found a half a ham sandwich and a plastic jug of water in the fridge. I looked in the freezer and noticed something was wrong. The dial was set on nine, and yet no ice had formed. Water dripped from the coils, dribbled through a crack in the catch tray, and collected in the empty vegetable crispers in the bottom. The water in the plastic bottle was barely cool. I stood with the door open for a moment and tried to imagine us having a conversation about how he might obtain a new refrigerator, but I could no more imagine such an exchange than I could imagine us chatting over dinner about the gay life in D.C. There was nothing for me to do but leave.

On my way back to the bedroom I passed another door, open just a crack, leading off the main hallway. Unable to contain my curiosity, I pushed on the door enough to see the outlines of furniture shrouded in dusty sheets. I heard a pleasant bubbling sound and a gurgling such as a baby might make, only this gurgle sounded older, ancient, desperate. Not a gurgle, but a rattle. It responded with hope to the touch of my hand on the door. I pushed again. The rattle asked a pleading question. I moved my head into the space between the door and the doorjamb. A large aquarium, forty or fifty gallons, came into view. Its watery fluorescence gave the only light, save the gray glow that came in around the edges of a grimy shade, pulled down over the one window. The water bubbled happily, but no fish swam within. There was pink gravel and a ceramic castle and what looked like the broken remains of a soft drink bottle, but no fish. The fluorescent glow of the tank illuminated another Scrabble board, scattered with tiles, open on a card table. But unlike the board in the bedroom, this one appeared to have been recently used. The tiles lay in neat rows, forming words.

Suddenly I started and drew back. Then I looked again, my heart pounding. Two eyes stared out at me from the edge of the fluorescent halo of the fish tank—eyes yellow and unblinking.

"Meow?" I said. I stuck my head further in and in doing so pushed the door open another few inches, to which the rattling gurgling responded with hope. But my attention remained fixed on the yellow eyes staring back at me.

"Meow?" I said, as the cat face emerged from the dark. The eyes made no response. I drew closer, passing over the threshold into the room. The rattling became insistent; it reached out to me. It struck me that I was looking into glass eyes mounted in the face of a stuffed house cat. "Did you eat all the fish?" I asked. Having understood what I was looking at, I turned my attention to the rattling.

Next I knew, I was standing in the hall, shaking violently and clutching the ham sandwich for dear life. I did not know how much time had passed, how long I had stood staring at the image that had now imprinted itself on my mind, likely forever, and I do not recall what happened between the time it imprinted itself and the moment I found myself standing in the hall again, but I will tell you, as simply as I can, what I believe I saw:

A bed.

Lying on the bed, covered in a single, wrinkled, mildewed sheet, propped up by pillows, an elderly figure with unkempt hair, hands reaching out, eyes and mouth wide open, the insistent gurgling rattle coming not from the mouth, agape with terror, but from a bleeding gash that traversed the throat. With her left hand, she held out to me a razor dripping black blood. I stumbled down the hall, back to the bedroom, still clutching the sandwich. Before I entered I stopped to collect myself.

As I entered I noticed an avalanche of papers and navy blue ring binders massed in one corner. Upon closer examination, these papers and binders indicated that this young man indeed had had some connection with the federal government, though I must have knelt examining the papers for five minutes and still had not the slightest idea what they were or what they said or what subdivision of the government had drawn them up. Just before I turned to look at him I spied, half buried in the mound of paper, a shredder, a faceless machine of gun-metal gray frozen in mid-act, a fistful of papers yanked halfway into its maw, a spray of shreds hanging from a slit beneath. I glanced at him, still hunched where he had dropped on the edge of the mattress, shoulders bent, head fallen. He had pulled the rumpled bedsheet around him like a royal robe. It spread in wrinkled, dirty swags.

Above him and in front of him, on top of his dresser, a pair of framed pictures, brown with age—one a man, the other a woman—stood to either side of a scattering of change, receipts, subway tokens, cough drops, razor blades, pens, pencils, dust kitties, and an unopened plastic package that contained rubber gloves of the sort used by medical professionals. Above the dresser hung a mirror in a heavy, overwrought gilded frame, ornate interstices caked with dust and grime, something from the Victorian gingerbread house of an aunt or a grandmother. A pair of garish candles stood on the dresser before the mirror, deformed with generation upon generation of over-flowed drips and bits of charred, broken-off wick embedded in the wax. The candles seemed not to have been lit in some time, as they, too, were covered with dust.

I stood over him with the ham sandwich. "Want some?" I asked. He raised his head, looked sadly at the sandwich, then readjusted his position, put his face forward, took a bite, and chewed. I looked down at what was left. I threw it into a box that sat beside the dresser, filled with crumpled papers and pencil shavings and Kleenex and dust bunnies.

Finally I said, "So this is a two-bedroom apartment..."

He stopped chewing.

"I went in the second room," I said. "I'm sorry, but I was curious." From the way he froze, one might have thought I had brought up some detail of his life I could not possibly have known, that I had intuited something. Finally I said, "Is there something you'd like to tell me?"

He stared straight ahead. He chewed some more and swallowed. "There are no other rooms," he said, more clearly than he had said anything since I had come.

"But I was just in there..."

He turned his face toward me but did not raise his eyes. "This is a one bedroom apartment," he said in a voice hollow but insistent. I waited and said nothing. "Did you find the kitchen?"

"Yes, no problem."

"Where is it?" he asked.

"Excuse me?"

"Where is the kitchen?"

"Down there. Down the hall. Where you pointed. That's where I found the other bedroom."

"No," he said. "There's no other room. This is the bedroom. Only one."

As though something inside him had been released, his head dropped and his shoulders slumped. Then in a pleading tone he mumbled a plaintive question that began, "How about..?" Suddenly I felt something crawling on me.

"No. No," I said, before the sentence was done. I didn't want to know what awful act he wanted me to perform now. I rose and walked several paces from the mattress. I stood by the dusty Scrabble board, my back to him, and pulled my clothes on. He didn't see me out, but stood hugging the bedroom doorway, the sheet pulled around him, gazing ruefully, longingly after me. Downstairs, when I reached the door to the outside, I finally heard the clack of the deadbolt.

As I made my way back to Penn Station, I began to feel titillated by the hope of figuring out what he had asked. I began to go back in my mind over his final question. "How about..?" What? I believed I had no hope of salvaging the words, but I repeated the rhythm over and over using nonsense syllables, trying to conjure up a question, as though waiting for a photograph to develop, or for the wreckage of an automobile with a drowned passenger to be winched into view bit by bit from a river bottom.

As the train rocked its way back home, I snatched back a piece of the puzzle: the final sound of that question had been "bl." Okay, I said to myself: hum*ble*, no*ble*, a*ble*, ca*ble*, fa*ble*, ta*ble*, fum*ble*, crum*ble*, stum*ble*, bum*ble*... I didn't come up with a word that had to do with any sex act I'd ever heard of or even imagined. "How about tying me to the table?" I hadn't seen a table. "How about whipping me with a cable?" "How about..?" What?

The train rocked and I drifted to sleep. When I was fully submerged a voice cut through the murmurs of my mind and said:

"How about a game of Scrabble?"

There stood the man from the promenade, the one whose presence had prevented my flirtation, maybe even my consummation, with death, who had saved me only so I could use some poor tortured man's face for a toilet. He stood, as before, with his back to me. Now, slowly, he turned. He revealed the face of a serious and tender young seminarian, slender body sheathed in black. How, I do not know—for he stood on the near side of the protective wall, well above the water line—he reached down and scooped water from the river and threw it on me.

I jolted awake, and now I knew how to pray for myself, and for my new friend, alone, seeking the second bedroom in his one bedroom apartment.

Not Pretty

Robert shrank behind the gate as the ferry angled toward the pier and Sam Ody's assistant, Ben, drew closer. Robert strained to comprehend the bulges of Ben's arms, thicker than his own thighs. He looked and looked at the worn denim on Ben's fly, but the $1.25 he'd paid for the round trip on the ferry ruined any pleasure. By the time he'd reached the slip to come over that morning, peak fares were in effect, but by then he had invested so much future life in seeing, watching, somehow fusing with Ben, that he had to buy the ticket.

So he'd promised himself he wouldn't spend a cent over on the mainland. Once there, however, on the boardwalk, he immediately grew so thirsty he bought a lemonade. Then he thought he'd fall apart if he didn't have something to do with his hands for the two hours till peak fares ended, so he bought a balloon and wound the string tight around his hand. In a crowded, wordless, shuffling men's room, chipped concrete floor a soup of water and sand, his skinny, long-sleeved, long-panted body pressed up to the urinal so tight it might have formed a seal, he pissed away the lemonade. He kept his eyes ahead, trying to avoid his distorted reflection in the flushometer, as free, strapping souls in tank tops and trunks came and went, came and went to either side of him, unthinking, flip-flopping thongs, on their way somewhere.

Now:

The ferry nudged the pier. Pilings groaned and dark water sloshed and echoed beneath. The first car off blared its horn. Ben crouched. The denim pulled up in a bulging V. The car blared again. Robert drew his balloon to his chest and stumbled back into the gutter.

After the last car ker-lunked off, Sam Ody called, "'bo-*oard*!" Robert shuffled down, streams of electricity shooting up his legs. Ben still crouched and Robert shuffled slow, slower, faster, then as he passed Ben, looked down the back of his jeans to see again what he could not believe. He'd done the same on the trip over and the sight had gripped his soul: Ben wasn't wearing underwear. Robert would masturbate to this tonight, if he could hold his spending to only fifty more cents for the rest of the day. Tonight he could eat off customers' plates...

The ferry engines revved deep down, and the horn atop the pilot house blasted its presence to the harbor. Gulls wheeled.

Robert lingered on the lower deck, his gut feeling the wonderful, unsettling sensation of moving on water. Ben swaggered forward and took the metal stairs to the pilot house two at a time. His back, butt, thighs, calves vanished. Alone now, Robert surfaced to the passenger deck.

There in the wind and light and pageant he squinted toward the target ship. Recruits from Wagner Field used the long-grounded wreck for bombing practice. By now they'd gutted it, leaving only the jut of the bow and a faltering piece of stern. Yet for half a second, when viewed head-on, the ship looked intact. Robert liked, for that half-second, to see the wrecked pieces come together into a picture that looked beautiful and whole. But today he'd spent too much time below, watching Ben, and so had missed the lovely illusion of the target ship.

Gonging sounds pounded up to the deck. Robert hunched in the lee of his balloon. Voices of two boys. He peered beneath the bobbling balloon to take in tanned legs, just assuming their manly shape, golden hair coming in. He looked to the rusted, gutted target ship and sighed. How did it feel, having come to this? Soon he would be twenty. He drew from his left pocket his remaining cash, and counted it, again. Then he stared at the horizon, calculating the total in his savings account once he deposited tomorrow's paycheck. A breeze came up. He pressed his few bills tightly between left thumb and index finger.

Robert did not find himself attractive. The face that often caught him staring in store windows had the bereft look of a middle-aged widow. He was painfully thin; he felt brittle, breakable. He had little, lemur-like fingers, not Will's large, capable, grasping hands. He was very white. He burned easily, but he couldn't spend on suntan lotion if he was to save a thousand dollars to show his father. He had played the moment over and over in his head.

And yet Will had... liked him... somehow... hadn't he?

That Sunday, back in June, Robert had stood on their porch, staring into the depths of the stagnant creek out back. Muscled arms suddenly circled him and he felt the warm, needful breath on his neck. "No!" he cried. Will backed away, "Hey, sorry... 'scuse me."

The horn sounded more plaintively over open water. A laughing gull, black-headed and cawing, floated by as though suspended on a string.

Once, Robert had believed he'd be different, down here on his own. He'd become daring, fun, good-looking, an active, decisive, graceful young man at last. Back home, he'd lain on his bed and the island appeared out of his water-stained ceiling, a paradise afloat in golden light. In it he recognized a lost part of himself, lost so long he had no word for it, or for the hole that was left when it was removed. That huge hole in him made breathing difficult. For years, his mother had rushed him to the emergency room with asthma attacks.

The gull rose into gentle swords of afternoon sun.

At first his father had refused the whole scheme. "Kind of thing kids think they can pull off, but you got rent, got food, got one thing and another, things you can't even imagine. In the end..? These morons don't save a dime."

Robert said he knew kids who had made money this way.

"Yeah? Tell me their names."

"What??"

"Tell me their names. Tell me the names of these mythical kids who go away and make their fortunes at the beach!"

Robert began to give names, the capable, the comptetent, the heroic, each name wrenched from his gut, stumbling aloud, obscene across his lips. His father came to the rescue:

"Look look look, I dunno who these guys are, but I do know one thing: these clowns were prob'ly all rich in the first place!"

Robert argued that he could eat his meals at the restaurant that had offered him a job. Finally, his father, throwing his newspaper aside and sitting forward, index finger leveled, offered one of his deals: "Okay. Go on. Have your fun. And come Labor Day, I will give you a dollar for every dollar you've managed to save. and if it ain't enough for school, don't come cryin' to me. Go knock on the goddamn neighbors' doors. Let them feed you, most of 'em have more money than we do, anyway!"

"Fine," Robert said, "I will. You'll see" And his father shrugged and said, "Your money," and went back to the paper.

Robert knew that, at summer's end, his father might not remember, or would squirm out of the deal on a technicality. Still, he threw himself into every one of his father's deals, his fantasies of heroism like the perfect, gleaming curls of the ocean, destroying themselves repeatedly on the rocks.

Robert's Summer of Winning the Deal and Being Someone Different ended the first afternoon, when he found out the restaurant did not give employees free meals, only a thirty percent discount. But sometimes customers left food half eaten—toast in the morning, then French fries and cole slaw. Robert began to make his meals of these.

One of the waiters, Don, six-one, veins bulging in his forearms when he hoisted trays, saw Robert scooping half a cheeseburger with its bite marks from a bussed plate. Don broadcast this to a waitress and two customers, a teenaged boy and girl, tanned vacationers younger than Robert who stood at the register, the boy with a fifty, grinning.

The next day Robert bought a regular meal, but Don announced, "Hey-hey, Rover's eatin' real food!" and Robert slipped out and slammed the whole thing in the dumpster in back. Later, after Don left, Robert went to dig in the mounds of slime for the plate, and the hole in him felt bigger than his whole self. Now he was the hole. He went back to squirreling away leftovers and eating only after everyone else was gone. In this way he made the money part work: by July he had four hundred and fifty dollars in Island Savings. As he worked his shift, he made constant mental calculations. But late at night, after closing, as he gnawed the cold remains of a fishwich or gulped slimy onion rings, he dreamed about the other thing: that this paradise would any day now make him into the kind of young man he should be.

Out of the deal he'd made with his father, he had made more deals with himself. If his daily spending went over a certain amount, he couldn't masturbate that night. Awake at two a.m. he squirmed in damp sheets, images of Don in his head, and Ben. If he masturbated on a day he'd overspent, he had to spend nothing the next day. If he spent on *that* day, no masturbation for a week. The penalties piled up like a tidal wave, and he had to start over.

Some nights, to keep from masturbating, he rose and paced, calculating how he'd ultimately save a thousand dollars, picturing himself holding the teller's check up to his father. In the mirror he practiced the expression he'd wear (like Don's cocky smirk), the way he'd walk (Ben's shamble), the off-handed way he'd present the check. Running the fantasy became more exhausting than spraying seed.

–o–

At first he couldn't find a cheap enough room on the island. He settled for one on the mainland—over a clam shack off the boardwalk. The ferry tickets ate into his paycheck and seeing Ben twice a day made him want to masturbate—in the restaurant's tiny toilet after he came over—as teenage boys tried the flimsy door and slurred, "Lesgo!"—and on his cot above the clam shack when he came home.

He posted a notice at the restaurant: "WANT TO SHARE?" He put his first initial and last name and the restaurant pay phone number on strips at the bottom. No one took the strips, but three days later, Will called, addressing Robert as "Mister." Robert made an appointment to stop by Will's early the next afternoon on his way to work.

Will was a year younger than Robert, confident, changeable, barefoot, a little clownish. He was tan, dirty blond but with golden arm hair, a little calloused, a bit smudged with paint and oil. He'd come to the Island on his own the past four summers to work at Day's Marina. In the living room of the small, tacky ranch house he offered Robert a beer. Robert refused, saying he was going to work. Will first appeared to sulk, then to grow anxious. He shambled about the apartment, pointing out amenities, then looked Robert up and down. Rent at Will's was a hair less than the combined cost of the room over the clam shack plus ferry tickets. Will said he'd help Robert move—his boss could lend him Day's panel truck on Sunday. "We could go someplace," Will said. He pushed his hair back. "You been out to Mattagonquit?" No. Robert hadn't been to any of the places everyone else went. He didn't know what Mattagonquit might cost, yet in just twenty minutes, he'd begun mentally to organize his wants around what Will wanted. He agreed to share the house and go to Mattagonquit Sunday. If he had to, he'd work double shifts and eat only food left by customers. In the course of twenty minutes, Will had been more solicitous toward him than anyone the whole rest of his life.

Sunday they moved Robert in one trip, dumped his belongings in a heap in Will's extra room, then headed to Mattagonquit, Will's left wrist hung jauntily, delicately from the top of the wheel as he waved at the sights, then grinned at Robert, his eyebrows appearing over the tops of his dark glasses. Just when Robert feared the afternoon's adventure was over, Will would have another idea. They drove up to the Heights and Will sneered at the natural-wood-and-glass palaces with no people in evidence. At sunset they ran the other way, past the stragglers deserting Prospect Beach. They flopped side by side on the sand, munching hot, ketchup-drenched clam rolls and gulping Cokes. Will talked about books and movies (Vonnegut, Truffaut) while Robert's insides quivered over the gift of hot, fresh food, and over the need now to somehow make up the price of it. Then Will fell silent and they watched shimmering breakers curl home in the six o'clock sun. Will turned to Robert suddenly.

"You seem like a good person," he said. Then he swiveled his gaze back to the horizon. He held perfectly still, then sprang to his feet. "Lesgo!" he said, swatting sand dramatically from his pants. He ran barefoot ahead of Robert to the truck. His thick calves flexed as each heel pushed bravely back into the sand.

Now, having Will, Robert walked a little faster. He wrapped himself up in and emulated Will's reading and eating habits, in what he wore, in dreams of the places he had been to, in the friends he spoke to on the phone, his large family in Pennsylvania, his hair in a ponytail, the hems of his boxers showing from under his cut-offs, his powerful body slightly out of shape, his loose-limbed gestures—which Robert tried to appropriate, though on him they felt silly—in the sound of water splattering off Will's body in the shower, his razor flecked with whiskers, his gym shorts on the line, straining in the breeze, his pouts followed by a need to take off for Mattagonquit or Quantham Point Park or Gillette Castle (Robert begged off these last two, paralyzed by unknown costs), and then...

Will coming up behind Robert that Sunday afternoon just before the Fourth of July. Hands on his shoulders, then on his bare arms, squeezing, squeezing nothing. Did Will understand what he was?

He jerked away. "No! Sorry... No..."

Will backed off. "No no, my fault, sorry..." He left the room. He did not reappear till after midnight, drunk.

Then, a week later—

Paolo.

Paolo victorious. Paolo chosen. Paolo dark. Paolo wonderfully, fearfully made.

Will spent nights at Paolo's now. He'd grin, his eyes not meeting Robert's, and say, "You're a lucky dawg havin' this place to yourself!" Leaving he howled, "Aroo-oo-oo-oo!"

One pink and gold evening, Robert couldn't bear the thought of going home one more time to the airless, musty silence Will had left behind. Robert ate cold French toast sodden with cold syrup, which a customer had left that morning. He went for a walk on the beach, then headed to the movies. He saw Will and Paolo in line ahead of him. Will made big, dancing-bear gestures as he talked, and Paolo watched, unblinking. Robert broke out of the line. He ran as best he could down Surf Street to where the amesite crumbled and disappeared into sand.

He curled into the lee of a dune. As darkness came he heard boys and girls. A voice that might have been Don's: "Do that thing you did before." A girl giggling. Robert clasped his arms around his head. The compass grass whispered unintelligibly.

-o-

Now:

The island loomed and Sam cut the engine. Still clutching his balloon Robert hurried down to see Ben manning the chains. But Ben was shooting the breeze with a friend, so Robert gave him a wide berth. He couldn't bear their looks or to hear what he heard before: "...slipped it right to her, yeah, and she's moanin'..."

A moment later he was off the boat, looking back, stumbling up the road to town, looking back, looking back again, then with a heavy heart facing home. He'd blown money on a ferry ticket, on lemonade he'd already pissed out, and on a *balloon* for fuck's sake! And now it was over. Ben had offered nothing. One thought allowed him to go on: giving the balloon to Will.

He came in the back door and halted at the sight of Will and Paolo, shirtless, skin damp, hair slicked back. Will nodded. Paolo tipped his chair back and looked out the window. He had uncanny eyes and small nipples that Robert could not stop thinking about. Robert moved through the kitchen, feeling as though he were running a gauntlet. "Balloon," Will said. "Uh-huh," said Robert, not looking back. In the hallway he passed Will's half-open door. Suntan lotion, uncapped, lay on the nightstand. At the bathroom door he passed into a nimbus of damp air. Everything wet and warm, like inside the body. The showerhead dripped. Who did what to whom, when they had their conversation with God? God, who Robert recognized only in rejection. He went to his room, shut the door, set the balloon on the floor, then brought his foot down hard.

He scuffed the plastic rag under the bed.

A moment later, in the living room, Will asked, "What was that?"

"What?"

"That bang."

"I didn't hear anything."

"Where's your balloon?"

"In my room."

"Where you going?"

"Out."

"Where?"

"I'll know when I get there."

Robert congratulated himself on that comeback. It was the kind of thing he never said.

—o—

He did not go to the beach. The beach drew him. All roads led there—Kettle Beach, south of Prospect, little used, kingdom of isolation. He went hands in his pockets, mind gripped by Will's suntan lotion. A cinderblock house rose from the dunes. Over its two entrances, signs that looked like they'd been routed and stained in a high school wood shop: "Ladies" and "Gents." Robert stood in the grass, heart pounding.

He crossed a crumbled parking lot and passed in the doorway that said "Gents." Still air, strong with urine and deodorant. Now he felt of the island.

Two urinals, two stalls. No one there.

He entered the stall that was next to the urinals. A two-inch hole in the transom over the TP provided a view into the other stall. Robert licked his lips. In the opposite transom a smaller hole allowed the gent on the toilet to sight across the urinals at crotch level.

Robert shut himself in. He shuddered as he undid his pants and sat. His penis was shrunken. Electricity filled the air. He waited. Then he rose, did up his pants, and left.

That night he lay thinking about the holes, who drilled them, why, how, the audacious expression of desire like Will putting his arms around him. He dwelt on it the next day at work. While he daydreamed the dishwasher jammed and broke several glasses. His boss said it would come out of his paycheck. The moment Robert got off work he ran to Kettle Beach, as a child flies at the school bell. He sat on the toilet half an hour. A couple of sour-looking, paunchy guys with surfboards came and went. They weren't Dan or Ben, but it thrilled Robert that the hole in the transom actually worked, that he could capture their pure manhood, unawares, detached.

No one else came. It just soothed Robert to sit there. Like church. He could have spent hours, out of the fresh air and noise of the world, snug as Will and Paolo sleeping.

One afternoon, as he was about to zip up, he heard voices. The boom of two young men abruptly filled the room. They quieted as they took their places at the urinals. Zippers ripped down. Urine spattered on deodorant cakes. Robert leaned, and there came into view through the hole a thick, dark penis, uncircumcised. Robert held his breath but couldn't control his trembling. Tanned fingers shook the last drops from the dick with the kind of assurance Will had, the assurance with which Robert wanted to hand his father the check. As the guy zipped up he said quietly, "Donny, man, look!" Suddenly there were no transom. Robert felt entirely, exposed, half-naked, crouching and peering. He wanted to move but couldn't. He wanted to shrink and vanish.

The other one—"Donny"—said: "Aintcha seen them little holes before?" *Don! From the restaurant!* Blood left Robert's head and his skin went clammy. "They're for faggots to go peepin'!" Don said. Each word, soft, cool and penetrating, punched Robert's ear drum. "Shh!" the other one said. "Shut *up*, man, there's some guy *in* there!" His whispers shot across ceiling, walls and floor like snakes. "Oops!" Don said, full-voice, then called out, "Hey, sorry, man! Nothin' personal!" He flushed. The other snorted, "Douche-bag!" and flushed with a bang of his fist. "Hey, I didn't know," Don protested, and giggled. The other guy said, "Hey, if that was a faggot in there, he'd be pretty disappointed in you," and Don said, "Eat me, dude," and the other guy said, "You wish!" and their laughter lifted on the breeze.

Robert put his head back. He put one hand over his shrunken genitals and closed his eyes.

If only it had been true, that there was "some guy" in there.

-o-

Will leaned against the kitchen sink, shirt open, staring down into the carton of scallops in his hand. He forked them one after another into his mouth, chewed, and sighed. Robert wanted to ask where Paolo was. Instead he drifted around the kitchen. He mentioned *Magister Ludi*, the book of Will's he was reading. "'smy brother's," Will said. "Never read it." He tossed the fork into the sink, jammed the carton in the overflowing waste basket and went to his room. It was supposed to be Will's week for the garbage, but Robert said nothing. He tied the plastic sack and took it out.

Will reappeared in front of the TV with a bottle of wine. A soap opera played. Robert sat in the easy chair. Will offered the wine and Robert tried some. The barometer dropped and the wind shifted. Robert said, "I'm sorry about, you know..." Will must have seen what he'd seen: Paolo in a BMW, tinted windows, driven up to the Heights by a tanned, silver-haired man. Seeing this Robert had felt betrayed and excited.

Will smiled indulgently. Robert thought, I don't know what these things are like. "Fuckin' Eye-talians!" Will shook his head and made a forced grunt. As though there were more to the joke that Robert couldn't understand. But Robert did understand. He understood more than Will did what it meant to love, to lose someone, to be drunk. He couldn't wait to get back to the Gents'. He remembered how cozy and meaningful he'd felt, bare thighs on cold seat. He'd seen Don's dick and Don didn't know. That alone could blot out all he felt about Will and Paolo. He and Will should have been together, but now, this side of Paolo, it would never happen.

–o–

Don stopped teasing. Because Robert had nearly stopped eating. He tried not to go back to the Gents' either, but on a Saturday in mid-August he could no longer stay away.

He trembled as he let down his pants. After twenty minutes he heard shuffling up the path. It entered and hastened to the other stall. Shoes without laces. A zipper came down. Grubby cuffs fell. "Psst!" Breath rasped through the hole by the toilet paper. Robert froze, eyes forward. "Joey! Want me to suck ya? Take my teeth out, guys say it's the best they ever had! Wanna make a deposit in the sperm bank, Joey?" Robert leapt up and fastened his pants. He didn't slow down till he hit the shops on Surf Street, their infinite goods beyond his means.

–o–

Two days before he was to leave the Island, Robert came home to find Will in the easy chair with a bottle of wine, staring intently at a blank TV screen. "What's the matter?" Robert said.

"Nothing."

"You sure?"

"Yup!"

Robert thought he might never see Will again. He wanted to ask him to the movies that night. That might cheer him up, and they might have one last time what they'd had before Paolo. Robert stared out the window and calculated: His last paycheck would bring his savings balance to $1,003.39. He had to hold the line if he wanted to get off the Island with four figures. He slipped a hand into his pocket and counted by touch. Three bucks. The ferry would be fifty cents. The movies were ninety-nine, he could forego popcorn or hope Will would treat him. So: ferry and treat Will to the movies was $2.48 total. He could eat what was left on customers' plates tomorrow and Saturday morning. But what if something happened? The $3.39 he'd have over $1,000.00 was his cushion. And he had to have four figures. Nine hundred ninety-nine was nothing. A thousand was a man's number.

After a moment he asked, "Want to do something tonight? Like drive around?" Shit, that could end up costing more!

"Nah," Will said. He got up, went to his room and closed the door. Robert slumped in the easy chair, relieved, and felt the warmth of Will's absent body.

–o–

The next morning he received his last paycheck. He had lain awake worrying what could go wrong; in his head he'd fought with his boss over a wrong amount. But it was exactly right. He flew to the bank, fidgeted in line, fearing somehow the bank wouldn't accept the check. But they did and there it was, exactly as he'd dreamed: $1003.39.

Something had worked. One thing. One thing, in his entire life.

He stared at the teller's check and breathed deeply. Outside in the sun he knew what he'd do the minute his shift ended.

–o–

He ran through the dune grass, swung himself around the doorjamb and into the stall by the urinals.

This time he didn't have to wait. A truck or jeep, far off, then closer... Tires scraped to a stop. One door slammed. Words. Finally others slammed. Robert heard a braying, put-upon whine, male: "Come on! Let's go!" Childish voices complained up the walk. Robert tensed as all three voices moved from far off sunlight into the concrete present.

"Daddy-y-y I don't have to-o-o!"

"Dad, me neither, why do we gotta..?"

"Look, just shut up and do it; it's a long trip home!"

"Dad, we peed over at the other beach! Maybe *he's* gotta go but..."

"I don't gotta go and don't say 'he'!"

"Both of you shut up. I know what's best and you're doing what I say. It's been the same thing all week—whine whine whine, no matter what I come up with you're against it and I tell you I'm sick of it!"

Robert thought "I tell you" sounded wimpy; it was why the kids didn't respect or maybe even like this guy. Same for "I know what's best." Robert felt pleased to identify something weak in another man. He could destroy this man by eavesdropping on him.

"Now you," the man said to the smaller boy, "you stand there. There! Last one. And you, next to him, here. I said stand at the last one!! Now take down your pants. I said take 'em down! Here!" He yanked at his boys' waistbands. Robert's heart thudded. The younger one's entire midsection, from belly button to knees, was naked. Pudgy. "Now, there, now, do your business. Just like that. Just like that. Stand just like that. Now do your business."

Now the kids' voices came from inches away, just on the other side of the transom. Their feet shuffled. "Just like that," the man breathed. "Atta boy."

Robert folded himself in half to look under the transom.

Adjusting themselves before the urinal were two pairs of top-siders, one pair of slender calves tan with dark hair, then a skinnier pair with the barest hint of gold down. This was the younger one, his shorts around his ankles now. Tiny dribbles spattered on the cakes of disinfectant. Robert's heart shook his torso. It had been years since he'd seen a penis without hair. In the junior high showers hairlessness meant nothing; everyone lacked hair then. Now it was forbidden, a trip back in time. He might never see again.

He sat up and brought his face to the peephole. A small, pretty dick, right there, reddish with a scrotum like a flesh-colored walnut. The older boy spoke. "Look!"

Robert pulled back from the peephole.

"What?" asked the younger one.

"There, idiot! Dad..!"

"Look, are you peeing?" sighed the father. "Are you..?"

"Dad, no, look!" said the older one.

Robert grabbed toilet paper and busied himself. He felt sorry for the father. Robert hadn't seen his face, but he thought he wasn't much like a father. More like a friend these boys had been dumped on.

With a tense, sudden vehemence, as though he knew a bomb were about to go off, the father said, "Just do your business. I want to see you peeing."

"I'm done!" It was the young one.

"Then go back to the car."

"I have to wash my hands first."

"No, just go to the car!"

"But Mom says always wash our hands."

Now the man's voice was a hiss, breathing short phrases separated by sharp inhalations. "I don't give a good goddamn what *Mom* says, if you're done, I want you out of here, I want you in that car, I want you there now, and if you don't do as I say and I think I've been pretty patient all god damn week but now you are really really straining it... What, are you done?"

"Yeah," said the older one.

A pause. "All right, both of you, out in the car."

The topsiders scuffed. Then the older one asked, "You coming, Dad?"

"No," the father's voice breathed evenly. "I am not coming. I am going to pee now. It's time for me to pee and time for the two of you to get out to the car!"

"But Dad," the little one said, "why didn't you just pee with us?"

There was a terrible silence. Robert held perfectly still, felt a draft tickle under his balls and clammy sweat in his palms. The father's voice quivered.

"If you... do not... get... Look, look!" A rustling. "Here, look, I'm giving you each a dollar for a popsicle..."

But the young one whined, "Daddy-y-y, I just had..."

"Just *take the money, Dennis!*"

"But I..."

The older one spoke, low. "Take it, Dennis." Then, "C'mon, Dennis, lesgo," the older one said. A quick scuffing. The father shouted after them,

"And don't lose it! You lose it, don't come crying to me!"

Now in the gathering silence of the little gray room he breathed in and out, in and out, tremulously. "Jesus fuck," he said. "Jesus fuck Jesus fuck..!" He paced. Robert wondered whether to stay put or walk out past this guy. The pacing stopped and he looked down. A large, battered pair of topsiders stood outside the stall. Fat, hairy ankles. A whisper, low and conspiratorial, "Hey..."

"What?" Robert snapped. "Look..." He cleared his throat. "I didn't do anything!"

The topsiders inched closer. "You, uh, wanna open up?"

Robert stood and did up his pants. He paused, then came out, body tensed and ready. The man stood hunched with his back to the wall, one hand braced on a sink. He was pear-shaped, powerful in a clumsy way, like he might damage you if he happened to fall on you, but he wouldn't actually do anything. His bitterness would harm you more. He looked like he was in pain, like he couldn't take any more of something. His lower lip swelled in a permanent pout, as though he'd had a stroke, and his wet eyes moved away from Robert and back. An odd thought occurred to Robert: This man might be worse than him. More bound up in lies. He could waltz out past this guy, if he didn't feel a kinship with his need.

"I gotta talk to you," the guy said.

"Look, I have no interest in..." Robert went for the door.

"Hey hey, wait!" Robert felt the voice advancing behind him. He turned and gripped the doorjambs with his thin fingers. The guy came toward him, something between a strut and a waddle. "C'mon, I can talk to you," he said. He gestured broadly, vigorously, like a coach. His chest was out, but his eyes still did not meet Robert's. He put a hand in his pocket. Wet desperation flashed in his eyes and Robert thought, *At least I'm not some fat slob, I'm too skinny, but some people envy that. He might envy me.* He stared at the pear-shaped torso and wide hips and hungry eyes. The man startled him with an edge in his voice:

"C'mon back here a sec."

"I wasn't looking through that hole," Robert shrilled. How easy, how thrilling it was to lie. How true the lie felt in the face of this fat thing.

"No no," the guy said, like it hadn't occurred to him. "I got something I wanna ask you. I just wanna ask you something." His wet eyes sought some place past Robert. Robert turned, felt breeze on his face and saw dunes and sky. He thought he might see the kids, but the beach plum and pine screened the foreground. Still, he imagined that his skinny body, spread-eagled in the doorway, protected the kids from their father. "No, c'mon," the father said, "c'mon back in." His voice was solicitous, automatic, bent on something. Robert felt pulled between the salt air at his back and the crypt before him, all piss and mildew and disinfectant, and this Minotaur.

"That, there." The man pointed to the holes in the transom. "Like, you...you watch guys piss..?"

Robert shook his head. "No!"

"C'mon, you can tell me. You look through that hole, see a guy's dick, right? You see anything else? C'mon in a little more..." The father jingled change in the pocket of his tentlike shorts. "You can't be too careful. I know, I'm a lawyer. You, either. You prob'ly got a girlfriend right?"

"Uh-huh," Robert said.

"See?!" The guy was sweating. "I knew that." The guy jingled his change faster. "Comes from being a lawyer."

The guy kept jingling, or... The discovery of a possible truth thrilled and shocked Robert: inside his shorts the man's hand briskly patted his penis, then changed to a stroking motion. Robert felt his own penis stir.

"You got a girlfriend, I got a wife, ex-wife, don't mean nothin." He took a step forward. "Man comes here to do a man's thing, piss, whatever, it's why it's called a *men's* room... Come in some more! Jesus! Lotta inquiring eyes in a place like this." Same sweeping gesture. "Rich people, right? Do anything they want." Robert checked behind him, then let his arms fall and took a step into the cool, enveloping shadow. The father's eyes drifted to a point above the doorway and he kept stroking, like the flapping of one stunted wing in the shorts, stroking, straining as though the guy thought he could do this yet somehow not be doing it. Robert could see the actual penis, erect under the cloth. The audacity hypnotized him, narrowed his mind. He wanted to join with the audacity and neediness. His own penis swelled. That misshapen body would be warm and strong, and it understood. At least it understood—what it was like to be disgusting in Paradise.

"What d'you do? Tell me what you do. You just look or you jack off? A lawyer wonders this kinda stuff..."

Robert felt suddenly weak. If he touched this guy it could be a trap. Could a lawyer arrest you? He felt ashamed to fear it.

I am thin, I am keeper of thin for all the world, the Jesus of thinness, whosoever believes in me shall be thin, too.

"You ever seen like a freak of nature? I remember this kid in high school—Jesus!—you couldn't believe it was real! He was skinny like you; musta all gone to his dick. And that motherfucker knew! Stood in the shower looking this way and that, makin' sure everyone noticed. It was sick, that kid shoulda gone for an operation! Wonder if they have an operation like that. So regular people don't have to look at that shit!"

"I'm not big," Robert said. Suddenly he didn't care about lawyers or arrests or police. He opened the front of his pants and showed the man. "See?"

"Yeah...yeah..." The guy stroked like mad. "Funny," he panted. "You know... what my kids... look like... down there. Hank, the... the oldest... he's... he's big now, right? You can say it..."

"He's nice... looking..." Robert said, playing with his penis. "Nice looking..." He watched the door.

"Yeah..." The man stared hard at the concrete floor and chewed his lip. "Oh, shit!" he said. "Shit!!" He yanked his hand out of his pocket as though it were on fire. He turned quickly from Robert and waddled to the sink. Robert zipped up. The man grabbed four or five paper towels in quick succession, unzipped and began to wipe at his crotch. "Shit! Shit! Goddamn it!" Robert approached. "No!" the man barked. "Get away from me! It's dead. It's dead." Robert thought suddenly of all the hamsters and lizards he'd woken up to find gone.

Then a voice spoke behind his back. " 'Scuse me..?" Robert turned. It was the older one, Hank. "My Dad here?"

"Wait in the car!" the man snapped. Hank paused. His eyes met Robert's and Robert held steady, abashed at what the boy understood that he didn't. Hank looked away, into the grayness of the room. Then he turned and jogged back down the path. "Go on, now," the man said. "Go!"

"He's gone," Robert said.

"No, I mean you. Go. Go on. It's dead. It's dead."

"Yes... Yessir," Robert said. He drifted backwards into the light.

"And, hey! Hey!" Voice lowered. "One word. One word. I am an attorney. It will never end for you. It will be one long hell till the end of your life. You understand?"

"Yes," Robert said. "I understand. Sir." He wanted to show him the check. He wanted to take him to the movies. To Mattagonquit. Away. Away.

"One word. Now get the hell out. Now!"

Clouds had moved in, yellowish-purple and gray. The air was close, as though he and the man's children were sealed inside something. He couldn't get out no matter where he went. There was no such thing as out. The whole Universe was sealed.

From the end of the concrete walkway he looked back. The father still hadn't appeared. Robert saw their truck, black, in the center of the lot. He walked a wide circle around. The kids were on the other side, Hank in an open door frowning, Dennis kicking at sand. Hank fixed a tough, weary stare on Robert. He had a head of unruly black curls.

Dennis looked up once, then away. Dennis was blond and pudgy. No. Fat. Dennis was fat. Robert kept walking.

He turned and looked from the dune bluff overlooking the lot. The kids had drifted from the truck. The father was still inside. Hank looked toward Mattagonquit. Dennis threw rocks. The three of them formed a triangle. The two down there could not leave, but Robert could. The farther he went the skinnier the triangle would become until it was a needle, pointing north.

-o-

Two a.m. Will not there. The check lay on the kitchen table: $1,003.39. Only numbers now. The summer had been a waste. He had a thousand dollars yet he had failed, terribly.

Where was Will?

He took French fries in a wad of foil from the refrigerator, and ate slowly. He expected pounding on the door at any second. "Police! You at Kettle Beach this afternoon?" He'd rehearsed it every minute since he'd left the bathroom:

"Never looked... thought maybe he... never looked... strange questions... thought he might... never ever looked..."

Tomorrow he'd stay inside all day. His father would meet the 4:30 ferry. He tried to picture his father's face and couldn't. He wanted more than anything then to hug his father and kiss him on the lips.

-o-

Late afternoon sun off the bay. Robert, with his pants rolled up, suitcase in one hand, shaded his eyes with his shoes. Waves lapped at his feet. He felt for the check in his pocket. A breeze made him shudder.

Guys and girls his age but somehow more youthful and somehow more grown up played volleyball in the sand. Their joy made him feel old. Two elderly women in identical bathing suits lugged folding chairs in from a sand bar.

He felt for the check again. Nothing like it had come true for him ever before. How had his grubby self gotten this grail from a normal world? What did those numbers mean? What could his father possibly say?

He'd heard a butterfly could flap its wings over the Pacific Ocean and affect the weather in New York City. The outgoing tide formed ripples in the sand like Don's muscles. What would Don or Ben say? Nothing. Divide by zero equals infinity, or just impossible? Sand ripples converged like chromosomes. Where was that man now? What had he said to his sons? Nothing. Beyond the chromosomes, past the curtain of light waves rocked, *My father's the ocean, I am rain. Rock me beneath your heart, hair on your heart like seaweed makes everything better, I don't want any more deals. I'm tired of proving stuff. You must be tired, too.*

Equations could account for those ripples in the sand, for who got born to whom... With a long, bare toe he broke a quahog shell from wet sand. Just a fragment, trace of purple on the edge. Holes riddled it. It looked crumbly but was hard to break. Did the holes follow a pattern? He looked close and concluded that they were random. Fractals, that was it. He took the shell to the water, washed it off and pocketed it. *There are shells like this and there are boys like this all over the world...*

-o-

The ferry angled toward him through a veil of exhaust. Sam Ody undid one chain, Ben the other. The ferry bumped the pier; wood groaned. Chains ran through their hands like water. Robert edged back to let the cars pass on their way to Paradise. He looked for the silver-haired man and Paolo in the BMW. Not there. Always somebody else, some place else. The last car ker-lunked off and Robert walked down. "Your dad's lookin' for ya," Sam said. Robert looked for Ben's reaction, but Ben's eyes were like a shark's. Passing behind him Robert looked down the back of his jeans. No underwear. The whistle blew. Robert felt for the check. He tried again to picture his father but couldn't. He climbed to the upper deck and walked forward as though he'd see him from there. He looked for the target ship, but couldn't find it. An energetic gonging came up the stairs. A dark-haired boy twelve or thirteen appeared; an older man followed.

A quarter of a mile or so out, "Look!" cried the boy. Robert turned and he met the eyes of the older man, who smiled back at him. Robert followed the boy's finger.

There in golden light the target ship appeared, closer than Robert had ever seen it. His head felt heavy. He felt in his pocket for the shell, right by his penis.

"Land ho!" cried the boy. The Connecticut shore moved to embrace them. Robert saw a man in the parking lot by a car, smaller and paler than he had remembered. He wanted to want to hug and kiss him. He took the check from his pocket and held it up in the breeze. Still his father didn't move. "Look, Dad," Robert whispered. Tears stung his eyes. "I did it. I really did it—for you, Dad!" He relaxed his fingers, shut his eyes, and with one hand on his fly and thinking of the view down Ben's jeans, he released the check. It shot up on the breeze, then pierced by sun it plunged, plopping into foam churned by the ferry. Robert's arm dropped and struck his thigh. The tears almost came.

Shadows fell across the deck. The ferry nudged the pier and rubber squealed. "All ashore that's going ashore!" Sam called.

Head bowed, unable to look at his father, Robert was simultaneously seized by a wish for the man, standing there, having done his duty and desiring what only a son, a real son, could give.

"All ashore that's going ashore!"

He came toward him. They did not embrace. He could call the bank and have them reissue the check

That thought just crushed him.

"Hey, Dad," he murmured, inclining his head but still not really looking. As he walked on past him to the car he added, "Lesgo."

Ulmus americana

They were very old.

They had stood in the park for as long as anyone could remember, keeping watch, sheltering those beneath them, missing those who left and praying for their safety, welcoming back those who returned.

Everyone spoke of them together. No one spoke of one without the other. They were almost one, their root systems so entangled that one could not live without the other. They thought alike, in silence. Picnickers in their shadow raced and called out. Cars whooshed on the highway below. But they spoke only when wind infiltrated their boughs. Still, each knew the other's thoughts. They kept no secrets.

They germinated close by one another in a nursery across the river, and they came to the park the week before its dedication in the spring of 1916. Upon planting, immediately they reached for one another's roots. Those who maintained the park called them *Ulmus americana*. So "Ulmus" seems a good name for the one on the left, as we face the river. "Americana" is not a good name. It means too much. But both belonged to the order *Urticulae*, so we will call the one on the right "Urtic." In so naming them, we go counter to their nature, to be one. Still, the world saw two, so we have named two.

Once, there were many trees like them across the park and down by the railroad tracks. But a terrible disease came, borne by bugs, and many of those trees died. At night the wailing and moaning rose from the tracks and echoed across the park's cliffs and meadows. Through the sobs and groans of their dying comrades, Ulmus and Urtic clung to one another, their roots and branches having by then grown close. It broke their hearts to think of going on, one without the other. They saw dead comrades dismembered, dug up, and hauled away, and each knew they could not endure standing there, seeing such a thing happen to the other. Each wished that, if the other had to die, they would die, too.

And there were the terrors of weather. The trees found it odd that humans talked about "the great blizzard" of one year or another, as though storms were celebrities they knew personally. (They even named the storms of the late summer, as though they were girls or boys passing.) The humans seemed proud of having endured these storms, but they had houses to protect them. Did they not know that trees lived their lives storm to storm? Even August thunderstorms could end with trees uprooted and branches torn away. Ulmus and Urtic had heard it often: the snarl of buzz saws on a clear morning, after little more than a cloudburst the night before. And finally, worst of all: lightning! Many times the trees had clung to one another as thunder blasted, rain and wind swept down, and blazing cracks parted the sky.

Ulmus and Urtic remembered everyone who passed or stopped beneath their branches. Trees had long memories. They even sought certain people at certain times each day or each week: the family that picnicked beneath them every Sunday, the girls in white dresses; the curly-haired mother who jogged every morning with her son in a stroller and a golden retriever on a leash. When someone they loved did not come, they fretted. The birds might bring news of the missing person. Sometimes the trees just waited, and the person returned, perhaps with a new friend or a child. They might stay. Or they might have come back just once, to look again or say good-bye. Some vanished forever, and the trees could only imagine: a job in a far country; a relative needing care; life going on.

Once in a while they learned that someone they loved had died. The bus accident, right outside the gate, that took the life of the woman who supervised park volunteers on Saturdays. They had loved her, and they knew she had loved them back. Saturday mornings, early, before anyone else showed up, she came down the stone steps and hugged them. She sipped her morning coffee beneath them.

A few days after the woman died, her son appeared and came down the stone steps holding a small container. He came to Ulmus and Urtic and sprinkled ashes from the container around their roots. Now his mother would never leave them.

They loved everyone equally: the jogging mother; the woman whose ashes they now absorbed; girls in white dresses; young men disagreeing; newlyweds posing with the river passing at their backs. They loved and were loved by those who had no one else. For many years a man came to their roots at night, dressed in stinking rags. He scratched at his body. He clutched his head in his hands and muttered angrily to himself, then shouted furious words no one understood. He paced between the trees. In rare quiet moments he leaned against them. Ulmus guessed that, in all those years, they were the only living things with which he had bodily contact. One winter the man disappeared in the middle of a modest snowstorm no one would remember. The trees waited. They invented stories: a social worker rescued him; he was in a hospital now, and he could smile. But they never knew. He never came again.

Then, one morning, early, a young man jogged down the path past the two trees, Urtic first, then Ulmus, then ascended through the brush, leapt a stone wall at the top and was gone.

Both saw him, but it was Ulmus, on the left, who was caught. The young man had been so beautifully shaped. He had run with such purpose, young muscles flexing to carry him up, up, up to the wall and over into the morning. The moment he disappeared Ulmus wanted him back. Nothing existed for Ulmus except the moment tomorrow when he would come again and this time maybe stop. Stop to catch his breath, stop to tie a shoe, put a hand out to Ulmus to balance himself. Lean back a moment and feel the rough bark. Look up and marvel at the crown. The crowns. Yes, Urtic's, too. Of course...

Anxiety seized Ulmus that the young man might come back and do these things with Urtic, might lean back on Urtic's bark and gaze only at Urtic's crown. How could this be prevented? How could it be controlled? How could Ulmus guarantee possession of the young man? All these thoughts, of course, had to be kept from Urtic. They could not be, yet they had to be. Not that Urtic would have raged or wept. Hardly. Urtic would have understood. That was the trouble. Ulmus wanted to revel in the young man's existence and the feelings it raised. Urtic understanding, Urtic merely knowing would loosen Ulmus's grasp, and it would all be gone. The young man would mean nothing.

Meanwhile, Urtic already knew of the attraction to the young man and the longing, and of course also knew that Ulmus wished to hide it. Urtic said nothing.

The next morning at the same hour the young man raced by again, past Urtic, past Ulmus, then up through brush and over the wall.

With his parting, Ulmus sighed. Something inside collapsed, though pleasurably. Painfully and pleasurably. And again, Ulmus could think only of the young man's return the next day, and if he might stop.

That is not quite true.

Ulmus thought of other things. Keeping this from Urtic, yes, but then racing on to more pleasurable wonders: what did the young man do from the time he leapt the wall to the time he came the next morning? What was his job? What was his family like? Was there a girl—or boy? This wondering ran so strong, hour upon hour, that Ulmus forgot any real effort to keep it from Urtic. Ulmus decided Urtic just somehow didn't know. Having decided this, Ulmus was now free to imagine every detail of the young man's life without interruption. Without understanding.

The morning came when the young man did stop. He sat on a bench ("Come to my roots!" Ulmus cried, yet ashamed for the first time that they were so gnarled) and removed a shoe and sock. His foot was pale, elegantly curved, strong. Pale blue veins ran through it. The skin looked like you could dip a twig into it that would come out dripping creamy white. The naked whiteness seemed vulnerable in the early morning chill, the toes innocent, yet the tendons flexed capably. Then he put the sock and the shoe back on, hopped up, assayed the hill, leapt the wall, and left Ulmus dazed and aching.

The time came when the young man touched Ulmus. He came running shirtless that morning and stopped, flat, rippled belly heaving. He came to Ulmus and put out a hand. He gulped air as Ulmus longed and longed for him to rest his bare back against the bark. He did not, though. A few seconds later he took his hand away and was gone.

Tomorrow, Ulmus thought. Tomorrow he will. Or the next day, or the next. It doesn't matter. He will, soon. Until then, Ulmus would return to fantasies of what the young man became each day after he leapt the wall.

Ulmus wanted so much for this young man, wanted him to *be* so much, that soon Ulmus's invented narratives began to step all over one another. First the young man was single, allowing Ulmus alone to possess him; then Ulmus felt sorry for him being alone and gave him a companion. Ulmus gave him one job, then, when that job did not serve the fantasy, gave him another. He would be noble and kind and caring—a doctor or a minister. Or strong and decisive and rich, a financier. No, he would be romantic, a painter or writer or soldier. Or maybe a sort of financier-writer, minister-painter, soldier-doctor-composer. But soldiers killed. Financiers exploited. Artists were selfish. Did doctors really care? He would! Wouldn't he? Imagining his life became burdensome. Ulmus still longed for his appearance each morning (he even ran in the rain, wet spikes beautiful against his pale forehead), but his existence, as opposed to his body, was increasingly a problem.

Ulmus felt desperate to find out for certain who this young man was and what he did. Ulmus also wanted someone else with whom to discuss the young man, though it could not be Urtic. Urtic knew too much, though, of course, Urtic was also supposed to know nothing.

So Ulmus spoke to a close friend, Chuck, a large, sleek, black bird that came and went occasionally from their crowns. (Chuck's real name was Corvus, but in flight school the other birds had made fun of him for having a sissy name, so he called himself Chuck and further overcompensated by becoming an expert on flight and weather jargon.)

Ulmus whispered to Chuck very low. Chuck understood and decided not to point out that, as we can imagine, Urtic understood everything already.

"Follow him," Ulmus begged. "Find where he lives. Perch on his windowsill. Follow him to work and fly by his window there."

"You know," Chuck said, "that this is really not in my line of work."

"Please?" Ulmus begged.

"Really," Chuck explained, "my main job as a bird is just to carry messages from Earth to Heaven and vice versa. Though a lot of good that's done. I mean, the Heaven-to-Earth part in particular. No one listens. They have more scientists listening for messages from deep space than studying birdsong. Maybe after another 30,000 years they'll catch on! So it makes your request kind of interesting. Something to do beside cry out to people who ain't listening!"

"Yes, yes!" Ulmus agreed and described the assignment again.

"Well, now, there's the other thing," Chuck said. "'Follow him to work.' You know how hard that is? What if he takes the subway? I will not go in the subway. I tried it once, and it was hideous. I'm freaking out, and this family from Des Moines thinks it's cute. The best I can do is fly over along the route and watch for him to come out. But if he changes trains underground, there's no way I can know. Then his job. Let's say I see him enter 500 Whatchacallit Avenue—how do I know which side of which floor he's going to? I don't want to get too tangled up in all those midtown towers. You know, 90,000 birds die every year in this city from flying into reflective buildings. And I will not go inside. I tried that once, too. They called security. I got called terrible names by these Master-of-the-Universe types. Plus I had to relieve myself before I could get back out, and you know that went over big."

Still, the job appealed to Chuck: something novel to do, secrets to discover and possess, Ulmus needing him, longing for information only he would have. This made Chuck feel the same sense of renewal Ulmus had felt the first morning the young man came by.

Early the next day, before light, Chuck perched in Ulmus's crown. At first light, the young man appeared, long stride, eyes ablaze, muscles longing.

"That's him!" Ulmus hissed, and without a word Chuck flew off.

Soon Ulmus would know! And Ulmus would become powerful! More powerful than...Urtic?

Ulmus calmed down and thought of Urtic. Urtic thought of Ulmus. How important was this, really? While it had all been going on, the jogging mother had been ignored. One of the girls in white dresses was sick. Yet all Ulmus could think of was Chuck's return and the final knowledge gained!

Four hours later Chuck returned, panting, clinging to a branch in Ulmus's crown. As his body heaved, his black feathers shone. As he and Ulmus spoke, they pretended Urtic couldn't hear.

"Well," Chuck gasped, "this is one of those good news-bad news situations."

"Don't play with me," Ulmus hissed. "What did you find out?"

"Apartment: easy. Job: not so easy."

"Tell me!!"

"Calm down; let me catch my breath."

When Chuck had caught his breath, his explanations to Ulmus were full of lingo about "lift," "drag," "wingtip vortices," sideslips" and much about "wing loading." (Chuck assumed correctly that, being a tree, Ulmus would not know he was not a big enough bird for wing loading to be an issue.) Apparently he had gone to a great deal of trouble, and Ulmus made certain to thank him before hurrying him on.

Chuck had an address, an ordinary brick building a few blocks away. Hardly a dump, he said, but not one of those buildings people clamber for or hate for being too chic. "Now as for finding the apartment, well, even with some multi-planar helixing, it was tough, but..." Chuck had flown in circles around the building, changing angles each time, waiting to see a light go on in a window or for a shadow to appear on a shade. It happened fairly quickly, a light in a kitchen, and it turned out to be the young man's kitchen. Beyond that, it was difficult to figure out whether the windows to the left or the right of the kitchen (or both left and right) corresponded to the rest of the apartment. "And I am not going into the apartment," Chuck said. "I tried that once. They hate it. They automatically assume you have lice. They bring out flyswatters and shit. Plus, I'm always afraid they'll have, you know, a bird in, you know, a cage. I could not deal with that."

So Chuck knew the young man's address and what he had for breakfast, but since shades were drawn in the windows to the left and right of the kitchen, he had ascertained little else. "He looked very handsome heading out to work, though," Chuck said. "Tie with no jacket, so it was hard to tell how formal or important he is." After that, though, Chuck had lost him. He had entered a certain subway station, and, by using a "calibrated, multiple-short-duration flight plan," Chuck had tried to catch him coming out of a station down the line, but it never happened. "Some stations have exits blocks apart," he said, "plus, like I said, he might have changed trains. Anyway, I lost him."

Ulmus remained excited, though, because this meant more to be discovered tomorrow. Then suddenly Ulmus wondered, how long would Chuck wish to continue this? Just then Chuck said, "But at least I have a home address, and I can go back tonight. Maybe he'll put up a shade or two." Ulmus was glad. It appeared, as they continued *sotto voce*, that it had become a matter of pride for Chuck how quickly he could get how much information.

Chuck went back that night, then again the next morning.

As days and then weeks went by, shades went up, patterns emerged, and information accumulated. Chuck found out where the boy worked. "It was tough," he told Ulmus, "but I got it. I combined calibrated, multiple-short-duration flights with mixed-method helixing. Planar and nonplanar, in other words." It turned out the young man disembarked just five stations from home, but Chuck had not previously been watching the set of exit stairs he took up to the street.

The boy worked in a small townhouse, so his window had been easy to find. What he did was another matter. Chuck could not get close enough to discern anything more than, "he types a lot. Sometimes numbers, mostly text. He comes and goes. I guess he has meetings. He likes to get coffee." Chuck found that there were three similar businesses all in that townhouse; it was difficult to tell which one the boy worked for. Chuck had, however, ascertained what he had for lunch, and was proud to report this.

As we can imagine, the situation was the same at home. Shades had gone up, and, the way Chuck told it, he had discovered much. But none of it pointed anywhere. No compelling, vivid man emerged for Ulmus to love. A poster on his wall said "Paris," but Chuck could not be sure he had been there, and even if he had, who didn't love Paris? A photograph in the bathroom might be...siblings? Cousins? There was a roommate, an older, stouter blond boy. They watched one TV show or another, laughed or didn't, ordered Indian or Chinese, spent a weekend at a lake or woods, biked or swam. Warm weather came, and they slid up their windows. Chuck heard phone conversations, but never assembled a satisfactory narrative; the boy dodged from room to room while on the phone, and, Chuck noted tartly, "multi-vector micro-flitting is not my specialty." *Well, practice!* Ulmus thought. "It's more of a sparrow thing," Chuck said dismissively.

Chuck did get the boy's name—"Franklin," or "Frank"—and proclaimed it silly.

"Oh, really, *Corvus*?" Ulmus said.

"I'll ignore that," Chuck said. "I saw them trimming your branches yesterday, and I know how you get about that. I'll just say, I don't have to be doing this."

But Ulmus sensed Chuck would not quit. The change in him had been visible. Chuck had begun to desire information himself. He spent hours with Ulmus, speculating. Did a certain photograph on a bedside table mean this or that? He peeked in the laundry room when Frank went down, but what did all the socks and the shirts and shorts mean? He eavesdropped on more phone conversations, ascertaining that someone in Frank's family was getting married, a sister or cousin. Or maybe not a relative, but a friend. Ulmus knew more about the couples that married in the park and never came back!

Summer windowsills afforded Chuck opportunities to uncover intimate details. He described an eccentric way Frank trimmed his fingernails. That excited Ulmus. Rather, gaining the knowledge excited Ulmus—Chuck leaving, Ulmus waiting and thinking this would be time, this would be the bit of data, Chuck spying, Chuck returning with information, the two of them knowing and Frank running by not knowing they knew. But the bits of information never coalesced. They tended, in fact, to make Frank less interesting. When he ran by in the morning, Ulmus tried to pretend nothing at all was known about him, not even his name. Ulmus tried to return to imagining a doctor-poet or musician-financier. If Chuck was not there, it was easy. If he was there, reciting data and speculating, it was depressing.

Frustrated, Chuck broke his own rule and flew into the apartment one morning when the boys were gone. He came back with a mountain of data for Ulmus, but they knew it meant little. Bills, junk mail, a few CDs, books. The CDs were too various to point in any one direction; the books were dragonslaying kinds of things, plus a book on baseball and *Great*

Expectations. Chuck excitedly profiled Frank based on these, but Ulmus interrupted: "You found these in the living room."

"Yeah," said Chuck

"How do we know," Ulmus asked, "which books belong to which boy?"

"Um...well, we don't know," Chuck admitted.

"No," Ulmus said drily, "we don't."

And so it went. Frank took a girl to a multiplex, but Chuck could not tell which movie or his exact relationship to the girl. He took a boat around the harbor with people Chuck had not seen before. Who were they? Why were they there? At work, booklets lined up in Frank's office did not reflect the company name or logo outside. For whom did he work, then? Two mornings in a row he failed to emerge from his subway stop. No number of calibrated, multiple-short-duration flights could find where he went. Then his schedule returned to normal. The blond boy moved out and the girl moved in. (Chuck determined her name was Tanya.) Ulmus became despondent. Chuck did not want to go anymore to the apartment. He stopped visiting—or, as he put it "surveilling"—Frank's job, frustrated that he could not figure out even the name of the company.

"His life is out of reach," Chuck sighed. Ulmus said nothing. "And it always will be. It's been months. What else can I find? I know his brand of shampoo and his cell phone plan. But I don't know whose books are whose, and he never leaves the Netflix where I can see. I thought the parents were divorced; now I'm not sure. And what if they are? So he mountain bikes. So do thousands of people. Loves Paris. Well, that's unique!

"And now," Chuck sighed, "he has someone. Someone to know the things I wanted to know. And you wanted to know. Now, she knows them. She will take care of him. And only God knows everything. We might as well give up."

It was late July. Ulmus gamely said they would try the rest of the summer. It wasn't hope. Ulmus just hated to see Chuck disappointed. They had grown close, and both enjoyed the daily ritual when Chuck reported what he had learned. Ulmus did not want to give that up.

Just till Labor Day, Ulmus said. Chuck agreed. Urtic heard and said nothing. Words are not always necessary. When, for a century, you have waited out wind and hail and lightning in one person's arms, when with that person you have watched children grow and friends die or disappear, when you have stood together listening to buzz saws draw closer, when you have watched one another's leaves move in the breeze or seen one another's boughs bend to charm a girl in her first white dress or a soothe man shouting and gripping his head in his hands, when you have prayed to share death with someone rather than stand alone without them, it does not occur to chide or seek explanations if the other one's spirit wanders, or if they try to keep secrets. The temptation is greater to step in and try to prevent fixation from growing and hurting, like beetles multiplying and swarming under bark. Urtic knew Ulmus too well to chide or to interfere. The only thing to do was wait and be ready when the hurt, inevitable as a summer thunderstorm, finally broke.

Then, for a week in August, Frank and Tanya went away. Chuck followed them several miles upstate, then lost track. "They were in a traffic jam," he confessed. "Suddenly it broke up; they must have taken an exit right after that." To keep up the daily meetings, Chuck reported to Ulmus on events at Frank's building. Or they just speculated on the summer breeze. Frank came back, but not Tanya. Ulmus and Chuck were breathless. What did it mean? Two days later she appeared, and life went on. Labor Day approached.

"Look," Chuck said to Ulmus one day. "I've been kind of holding off saying this, but..."

Ulmus knew what was coming.

"The flyways are going to be jammed in another few days. Monday is Labor Day, and I doubt we're going to find out anything more. They're gonna close the windows. So I hope you don't mind..."

Ulmus had no choice but to say, "No, of course not."

Chuck hung on a few days more. Flying conditions apparently were iffy, even on nice days. ("Cross-currents, upper zone, maybe mid-zone," Chuck muttered, shaking his head.) Chuck also thought they were now on the verge of getting critical information on Frank. Ulmus wanted to believe, and at the same time wished Chuck would just go. Summer was over.

Instead of finding critical information, Chuck watched a movie with Frank, through his living room window. The way Frank watched the movie—"tucked in like a little kid"—captivated Chuck. Frank had fallen asleep, and Chuck proceeded to describe the sleeping boy to Ulmus in great detail. "Sometimes he twitched. His entire body..." Ulmus longed to see this, yet also longed for Chuck to go, that minute. The idea had been to know things: revealing things; reassuring things. Ulmus found it hard to bear when trivial information raised powerful emotions but revealed nothing. All that day and night, Ulmus dwelt on the image of Frank asleep, twitching. It was touching beyond what could be borne, but it told nothing, *nothing* about Frank. It just renewed and renewed and renewed, painfully, every second, Ulmus's initial desire. But fulfillment of that desire now seemed farther off than ever, perhaps infinitely so.

The next morning, after Frank had jogged by, so, too, did Chuck take flight.

"I'll see you in March," he called.

Ulmus said weakly, "I'll be here." But how, without that knowledge? How do we survive, without possessing?

Chuck diminished to a tiny dot in the "upper zone" and vanished.

Ulmus wondered and despaired. March, so far away. Ulmus ached for Chuck, for Frank, for more, to find out and lay hold of and possess one certain thing. Everything had been done, thousands of bits of data were known, and that thing lay as far off as it ever had. It would lie just as far off in March—and the next March and the next. Ulmus had a sudden horror of dying with that thing still not found. Ulmus's thoughts turned to Urtic. Poor Urtic, the day Ulmus would die. Urtic would die, too, their roots were so intertwined. Or perhaps poor Urtic would live and not know what to do.

Ulmus had not been honest with Urtic, and Urtic knew. Ulmus knew Urtic knew. Autumn deepened. Urtic was patient, as trees can be, their lives lasting hundreds of years. One day, having no other place to take it, Ulmus at last gave all the pain and hopelessness to Urtic. Urtic took it, silently.

After some time, Urtic came up with a task for Ulmus.

Name all that you wish him to be, all that you hoped you would discover. Don't worry if some wishes contradict or cancel out others. This is a jewel of infinite facets.

And so Ulmus began. Everything Ulmus had ever wished Frank to be was told: the beauty and virtue, the hopes, the dreams, the strength, the shining future, all the different professions and hobbies, all the random moments, all the gifts, however absurd, however contradictory. When Ulmus was exhausted, Urtic said,

All those qualities you must possess. I know. I see you imagining, longing for them. But rather than summon the courage to possess of them yourself, or perhaps the courage to let them go, you place them in him. When you do, and then dote on him, it shows all the more how you might embody those qualities. You have no choice but to try.

Yet, you hesitate. It is more comfortable to place those qualities in

him. You hope that, because he looks a certain way, he must have those qualities—to give you. He must reassure you that those qualities exist out there. Whereas, if you yourself indeed worked to possess them, for yourself— how lonely, tedious, and unexciting!

Not lonely! Ulmus objected. *I have you!*

Sometimes I may not be sufficient. Our roots and branches intertwine, but you may need something you can not find in me. Maybe a passing human's pretty form will seem to have it. Meanwhile, how many humans, pretty or not, have come to your roots, reached for your leaves in the months since that human first passed? Then Urtic broke the news:

One of the girls in white dresses had died.

Ulmus reeled. How could it have happened? How could it have been missed? Not every hour was passed speculating with Chuck! One of the girls in white, dead? How...?

Very soon, it was proven.

Her father came.

It was early morning. He limped coming down the stone steps. His body was wide and squat and sagging, his face exhausted and red. He did not have all his teeth. He walked uneasily down the lawn, toward Ulmus. He put his hand out to the bark and leaned heavily. His hands were calloused, and his fingers were crooked. One of his thick nails was split. He gulped air. He mumbled something in a language Ulmus recognized but did not understand. His body swayed, and he repeated what he had said. He cried. Not just cried, but sobbed, still trying to speak. Maybe to his daughter, Ulmus thought. Maybe he was trying to tell her things he had not told her in life. Maybe he was trying to call her back.

Then Frank appeared. These days he ran with Tanya. The two of them slowed as they approached the sobbing father, bent over, his calloused hand propping himself against Ulmus. Tanya frowned at him and said something.

"No, c'mon," Frank was saying.

"We should at least ask," Tanya said. They both jogged in place. She came closer. "Sir...?"

"I told you," said Frank, jogging in place, "he's drunk. They come here at night, get blasted, sleep it off. C'mon, please? He could have a knife or something."

"Sir, is everything all right?"

Frank looked away and kept jogging in place. Deep in Ulmus's grain a tension rose, a disappointment in Frank, though Ulmus stopped short of calling it that. Instead Ulmus focused on Tanya, pretty, delicate, her hand extended. The man continued to sob.

"Sir," Tanya said, taking out her cell phone, "I can call the..."

Frank jogged backwards, slowly, moving subtly away but without leaving. Tanya glanced at him, and he quickly hopped back three or four feet. She turned back to the sobbing man. The man kept his head bowed. "Sir," Tanya said, "is there something..?" She looked up at Frank, who jogged backwards several more feet. The man shook his head and continued to sob. Again Tanya looked from boy to man, man to boy. Finally, she gave a little shrug and looked at Frank. The moment she did so, he turned and ran, and after a second's hesitation, so did she. She caught up with him on the hill, almost at the stone wall. She said something to him. He replied, not looking back at her. Ulmus caught two words, "my responsibility," and, a moment later, two more: "probably illegal."

Then they went over the wall—Frank first and more easily—and silence fell.

After a moment, Ulmus felt Urtic's roots reach out and tighten their grasp. Ulmus wept, saying to Urtic, *Forgive me! Forgive me!*

There is nothing to forgive, Urtic said softly. You did nothing wrong. Who would I be to say you did? Confronted by that boy, as we are confronted time to time, you did do less than you might have, and you hurt yourself. For a time you must hurt more, before you set matters right, with yourself.

Ulmus found this as hard to accept as the idea that all lovely qualities formerly placed in the boy were, in fact, Ulmus's to own up to and embody. No wrongdoing, except to the self, yet so much responsibility. For what did Ulmus weep?

Below, a gust of wind swirled their leaves, dead and dry, along the path. Winter set her bags down in the hall.

More leaves fell. Joggers put on sweatshirts and woolen caps. Breath trailed from their mouths. Frank still ran, but without Tanya now. Ulmus pretended he was back to the way he was before. Tanya had been the difficulty. Now she was gone, and Frank was pure again. But he wasn't. His once vibrant muscles seemed to strain. Ulmus thought he ran slower. He would recover, though, wouldn't he? He would get over her. He would realize his mistake about the man. The man still came. He put his hand on Ulmus's bark, or perhaps on Urtic's, and bowed his head and prayed. Ulmus imagined that Frank would jog by and stop and greet the man and apologize for what happened before. He would apologize to Tanya, too, and she would come back. Ulmus missed her. Rather, Ulmus missed Frank having someone. Before, he had felt not single, but singular. Though Ulmus had been jealous of Tanya, she had lent a note of grace to Frank. Now, without her, he seemed alone, abandoned. Some days he walked the last few steps up the hill. He might not leap the wall but might sit a minute, slumped, then get up suddenly, as though whatever thoughts he had had were unimportant. For two weeks there was another girl, but Ulmus did not find her inspiring. Then she, too, disappeared.

Thanksgiving morning the man came and set a red and white wreath on Ulmus's roots. He touched the bark and prayed. He did the same with Urtic, then left quickly. Of course, Ulmus thought. He has a family. Others beside the girl in the white dress. A gust of wind sliced down and dispersed dead leaves.

After Thanksgiving clouds moved in, lower and darker. Wind slashed across the river, more horribly than anyone could remember. Cries and cracks of broken branches competed with the raging gale. People vanished. Even the park's caretakers disappeared. Ulmus and Urtic hung on to one another, their roots intertwined, their branches intermingled. Ice whipped down from the sky and coated everything. How rarely, Ulmus thought, we can truly say "everything," "nothing," "always," or "never." How recently Ulmus thoughtlessly wished to know "everything" about Frank, despaired that "nothing" had been discovered, believed the longing would last "always" and "never" go away.

It is true—some people leave and never come back. But the river would not always be there. Urtic might not always be there. The grip of Ulmus's roots on Urtic's tightened. Now it really seemed that ice covered everything, down to each red berry in the thorny hedge before them and each of the few brown, teardrop-shaped leaves left in it. Ice encased Ulmus's and Urtic's branches and each one of their twigs, and still they hung on with all their strength, yet somehow effortlessly. Wind whistled and moaned. They clung and swayed with it. The second day a branch cracked off Urtic and crashed on the path below. Urtic moaned. They both hung on tighter. That night the wind tore a branch from Ulmus, and tighter they clung. They swore in one voice as they had sworn in winters past, as they had sworn in hurricanes and once even in the roar of a tornado's funnel, that, even if they were uprooted, they would hold tighter than ever with whatever they had left.

Frank was a memory now. He might return, but he would be someone else. They had seen it. People returned and were someone else. Ulmus had sworn this would not happen with Frank, but he was no longer a boy; he was a man now. When next he came he would be sadder. He would expect things and become irritated when they did not happen. He would have a routine. Well, then, Ulmus could not resist thinking that, when the ice melted, another boy would jog by. Not just one but dozens—hundreds! But none would stay.

After the ice stopped lashing down, a few people returned to the park. Dogs slid on glazed fields. A buzz saw could be heard. A caretaker cut up broken branches and hauled them away, including branches from Ulmus and Urtic.

The next day the girl's father came.

He made his way down the stone steps. Salt was scattered in uneven patches. Not knowing where ice had melted, he had to be careful. On the lawn, ice-encased grass crackled beneath his feet. He placed his foot on one of Ulmus's glassy roots and kept his glove on when he touched the bark.

He looked up. Instead of weeping, this time he laughed. "Look at the two of you!" he said. "You hung on. You are not broken. I was afraid you would be broken, but you are not. Ha-ha! Congratulations!" He went over and put his hand out to Urtic's bark and pointed up. "You each hung on to the other, and you did not break!"

The next day, the man came again. This time, a woman came with him. He helped her down the steps so carefully, Ulmus and Urtic knew she meant to the man the same thing they meant to one another. She was the mother of the girl in the white dress. She was stooped and sad. The man spoke to her in another language, but Ulmus and Urtic understood. He pointed up at them and coaxed her to smile. He was telling how they survived the storm by hanging on to one another. The man led his wife to Urtic. He took her hand and placed it on Urtic's bark. They bowed their heads and murmured. Then they went to Ulmus and did the same. Then they embraced, eyes closed.

After a long time, the man opened his eyes. He and his wife looked up. "Ha-ha!" the man said. "Look, you two even have another friend!"

Far out off in the iron gray sky a speck had appeared, darting wildly on the wind. Everyone watched. What had the man meant, "a friend"?

The speck grew. It began to take form, flapping and tumbling, looping and gliding on the icy air. Soon they heard muttering: "Easy, easy, tighten cross-draft control, more lift! Note to self: air pressure gradient force way different in winter!"

"Chuck!!" Urtic cried. "What are you doing here?" With a flourish of his black wings, Chuck came to rest carefully on one of Ulmus's icy branches. The man laughed and pointed. His wife smiled.

"I heard..." Chuck panted. "...about the storm. They said trees were... down ... everywhere. I couldn't...sleep, so I...came back..."

"All that way?"

"It...wasn't...so bad... And I...couldn't stay...knowing... I had to...make sure..."

"But now you have to go all the way back again!"

"Nah!" Chuck took a moment to catch its breath. "I'll stay. I'll be fine. It could be fun! Look, I see some berries down there..."

"And people always put out birdseed!" Ulmus added.

Chuck made a face. "Nah. Birdseed's a sparrow thing! But I'll improvise. I can even try making a nest. I mean, my girlfriends always took care of that, but I bet I could figure it out." He looked around. "Besides, I never got a lot of experience with northern invernal wind systems. It'll be fun to learn! So, uh, how's You-Know-Who?"

Ulmus told Chuck about the talk with Urtic and the scene that precipitated it, when Frank wouldn't let Tanya help the man. Chuck confessed he was not surprised. "He does a lot of things right in his life," Chuck said. "Like, the way you're supposed to. But he rarely considers what things really *are*. He couldn't release Tanya. Urtic's got the idea: you yourself have to face all those things you wanted him to be. And so do I. I got so into finding out one more thing about him and one more and one more, I forgot everything about myself. I disappeared, kind of. But I couldn't finish the job and turn into him. I was stuck being one big craving. I woke up terrified in the middle of the night. I felt like I'd smashed to the ground."

Ulmus first and then Urtic tightened the grip of their roots, one on the other. *That was the worst*, Ulmus said. *Not becoming so attached to him, but forgetting you. I was insensible. I couldn't bear it at night, either. You were right here, and I felt hideously alone.*

You are not alone, Urtic said.

I know, said Ulmus. *I know now.*

The man and his wife walked back across the lawn and up the steps. They stopped one last time to wave to Ulmus, Urtic, and Chuck. Then they disappeared, and silently, the three friends faced the uncertain season ahead.

The Addict

He sidles into the booth. Parkas touch. I close the door, slip the bolt.

Hi.

He nods, stares at the video screen. A black cock plows white cheeks.

He's the handsomest young man I have ever seen in a place like this. Petit, perfectly sculpted face, black curls, large brown eyes in which I crave to be immersed. I put my hand out. Abruptly he turns, puts his eye to the crack between door and doorjamb. He stays like this several seconds, breath shallow, eyes darting, blinking. The cock plows and the counter counts down: 59, 58, 57, 56... He turns to the screen again. Close-up of the white guy, eyes scrunched in pleasure or in pain. I don't know. I attribute no particular reality, no particular origin to this. I better go next door, he says. Okay, I say. I slide the bolt back. He will go next door, and we will each hit our button so that the shades rise between our booths. He takes a quarter from his pocket and puts it in my slot. Now, 1:44, 1:43, 1:42... Reprieve. Kindness. Justice. He slips out. I close the door and slide the bolt again. I stare at the screen and knead my half-hard cock through my sweatpants. I hear the swish of his coat pushing into the both next door. Crack of his zipper on particle board. Shadows at the bottom of the transom. (Some guys reach under. Not satisfying to me, the claw, although the feel of warm flesh, always.) More rustling. Pause. He goes out. After several more seconds my counter hits zero and my light comes on. Dream over. I pull on my jacket and emerge into the dimly lit arcade.

He waits at the end. His eyes dart everywhere but at me. As I approach him I smile encouragingly. His pretty lips curl up on one side. I can not believe my luck after three hours of cruising mostly empty arcades up and down the street. Now he looks. His half-smile vanishes, submerged, drowned.

Without saying anything, he turns. His step is measured, anxious. I do my best to match it as we go out into the main room, where a paunchy old man and a middle-aged queen in a business suit look up from their magazines. Their eyes go from him to me and back to him. I ignore them. I am of the elect now.

We ascend past garish, mirrored walls to the vast, bright emporium where hetero porn is sold, and finally to the street. He looks back, mutters about a guy who tried to get into a booth with him, and he gave the attendant five bucks to make the guy go away.

The conversation is disquieting. I have to ask everything twice. I have to say everything twice. Some things I have to tell him over and over. Did he say he lives with his parents on the Island? No, he has his own place, near his parents. Do they know that he..? No. He works for the phone company, in Queens. Did I say I have a roommate? No (but my lover is due later), so we will go to my apartment. What does he like to do? He likes to, well, he guesses he likes to take things as they come. I nudge him with the double entendre: as they *come*?? He smiles. He doesn't get it. He frowns, looks ahead, keeps walking. I say I like to fuck. Or we can do whatever. The important thing is not to lose him, he is so handsome. He's on another channel now, receiving instructions from...

As we wait for a light he glances up and down the Avenue, his gaze so frightened I look, too.

Nothing.

I test the waters again: if we are going to fuck, I need to get rubbers. He shrugs. We cross the street. For the next block we don't talk. I ask where he is from. He tells me he was born on the outskirts of Amman, and he lived in Toronto for a while before his family moved here. On the next corner he asks if I am going to get rubbers. So he does want to fuck? He shrugs and looks up the Avenue. Whatever I want. So should I get the rubbers? Okay. I turn toward the door of another porn palace and run right into him. He looks confused. He points to the brightly lit window of a camera store and asks if that isn't where we get rubbers. Later I will pinpoint this as the moment I should have known, when I should have said, I'm sorry, I guess I just feel like being alone tonight. But if I am to be honest I should have known—I *did* know—earlier. We know in the first second, don't we? If the answer in that second is no, then from that point on we are kidding ourselves, all the way to the last dribble, as we tell ourselves, Oh, well. That was that.

But this is the handsomest young man ever to choose me. I can hardly believe it. And now he's saying (isn't he?) that he wants me to fuck him.

And guys this good-looking who happen to want the same thing you want are rare. At least for me they are. It's such a crap shoot, and I have been at it so long tonight. Now there is not much time left before my lover comes. This kid would be perfect, if it weren't for something, something I don't know yet, something I can't get past, a demon between me and him. But I want to fuck, to possess who he really is, and I want it so badly that, No, I say patiently, and point to the peep show. We get rubbers in here.

Oh.

This seems to make him anxious.

Are you okay? Why? Do I look like I'm not okay? You seem nervous is all. I'm not nervous, okay? Okay.

This will wear off. Give him time and be kind.

He follows me to the counter of the peep show. His eyes dart at movies and dildos. I buy a box of three rubbers with a picture of a ripped, headless male torso. Back outside he pulls a dollar bill from his pocket and offers it to me. Don't be silly, I say. But I am touched, and being touched is interfering with my breathless anticipation. Always I have wanted a handsome Mediterranean boy who would want me.

On the A train he does not want to sit. He says nothing, only stares out the window as though he thinks something is following down the tunnel, or as though searching for his own face.

As I motion him in the door of my building I glance up and down the sidewalk. He hesitates, then enters. He seems not threatening, but threatened, needing reassurance like a child, a son, my son who wants his dad. Standing close in the shaky, shuddery elevator makes him nervous. I say nothing.

I have no curtains or blinds in my apartment. I moved in a year ago. I keep meaning to. But money...goes down the gullet of famously withholding video machines... So someone sees me naked now and then. So when I bring men home after dark, we have a choice: Do it in the bedroom, in spillover light from the hall; or do it in the living room, with spillover fluorescence from the kitchen. Or in the bathroom, where the tiny window is pebbled glass. (I like fucking in the bathroom; it feels impersonal and tough and the semen goes down the sink.)

This boy can not make up his mind. Living room? Okay, but he says we need some light. I explain (again) that the neighbors will see in. So, on the bed? I tell him no. (I don't say it, but I don't want his smell on the sheets when I lie with my lover later.) So he'd rather do it in the living room. But what about some more light? No, *the neighbors will see in.* Oh. Yeah. And so on. And on. He has no memory. None of this has to do with what room we fuck in or whether the lights are on or off or anyone sees. All this has to do with something else, known only to him. Maybe even he does not know.

He tosses his coat on the chair in the bedroom. He removes his shoes and socks. Reassuring. I remove mine.

One more thing: do I mind if he gets high?

Well, yes, I mind. I can't stand to look on other people's addictions. Their need makes me squirm. I tell him I don't want the smell around.

This doesn't smell.

Is it poppers? (The blue lips. I can't...)

It's not poppers.

What is it?

Just cocaine.

Oh. Well, uh, okay, go ahead. We've come this far. And his perfect round little butt is just inside those jeans, which are just about to come down.

I'll do it in the bathroom if you want.

Okay.

Don't worry.

I'm not worried.

He pulls something from his jacket pocket, his beautifully proportioned, creamy tan fingers curling to conceal it. I follow him at a distance of a few feet. He sits on the toilet. He keeps his fingers curled, but at last I can see that he holds a small, grimy glass pipe and a disposable lighter. He kneads them with those fingers that are not quite so beautiful anymore. His tendons spring out. His knuckles are white. The cords of muscle in his forearm play incessantly. His eyes dart around the bathroom as though demons would leap from the walls. From another pocket he produces a tiny plastic bag with three pure white pebbles, and he lays the pebbles on the edge of the sink, after checking most fastidiously with a trembling long finger to make sure... What? That there is no water there? His finger rubs the porcelain over and over like Lady Macbeth rubbing her hands.

I have never seen these pebbles before. Not live and in person. I tell myself calmly that this is not crack. I don't know enough about drugs to know that, so it is not crack.

He tucks a pebble in the end of the pipe. He puts the other end to his mouth and flicks the lighter. I no longer know what to think. Of him, of myself. I do not know who I am right now or where I am. Every assumption

I had made about myself and my life was challenged with the flick of his lighter.

For the first time I see the gold band on the fourth finger of his left hand. Even now, as it registers, it does not register. I am engaged in a complex dance with my eventual inability to get what I want and my eventual inability to make this end.

He sucks and holds the smoke in. His eyes blaze. His facial muscles knot up, as though something were building inside him. He holds and holds the smoke. Suddenly, with a raging whoosh, he pushes it out. It clouds the bathroom. It has a smell, but not a distinctive or strong one. He looks enraged. His eyes dart even faster. His body tenses, as though someone were jerking strings attached to his innards. Never before have I truly had not a single idea what a person sitting right in front of me would do next.

Are you nervous?

No. Why?

He doesn't look at me.

You seem nervous.

I'm not! I'll be fine.

He looks around

As soon as I come down, I'll be fine.

I resume taking my clothes off. He looks at me as though disgusted or uncomprehending. He looks away. His lips move, but no sound comes out. I have heard that people on crack—though I don't know if this is crack—can kill people with their bare hands, in spite of the victim's adrenaline rush.

It's okay. We can do whatever you want. Or not. I mean, you don't have to do anything you don't want to.

As soon as he comes down, he'll be fine...

What are you talking about?!

He starts removing his clothes, absently, nervously. He is beautiful, no matter what he has done. He stops and watches me, as though to see how it's done. He shudders. Suddenly he looks down the hall. He peers into the dark as though at any second it will disgorge a heartless, hungry beast. I continue to remove my clothes. I am naked. He has unbuttoned his shirt and removed everything below his waist. His calves and feet are beautifully, purely shaped, gifts God never gave me, till now. The perfect little depression in the center of his chest makes me want him never to remove the shirt. But naked is naked. Take off your shirt, I say. I step toward him.

He backs away.

I'm cold.

I move to the door.

Where are you going?

I'm going to turn up the heat.

No!

He steps up and puts his arms around my waist. I want you to warm me. All is forgiven. Everything will be OK. I place my arms around him, gently. His body is rigid.

Are you okay?

Why do you keep *saying* that?

He presses his flaccid cock to mine and pushes rhythmically. I slip my hands down his back to cup his butt. It is firm and hairless and fits perfectly in my hands. My cock swells. This will be perfect, now. Do you want to do it here?

Anyplace you want.

We could go in there.

Okay. Go ahead.

We edge into the living room.

Okay. So where do we do it?

On the couch.

Okay. Could we get some light?

The neighbors will see.

Oh. Yeah.

Why don't you take off your shirt?

I will when I warm up. I want you to warm me.

So are we going to do it?

Where are your rubbers?

I dash to the bathroom and back, not wanting to leave him alone. I dismiss this thought in favor of visions of that firm, hairless butt, mine, almost mine. I want him on his back, looking up at me. He is so pretty, so vulnerable. I must have him. I will have him, and I will shine. I will be someone. I grab some lube, too.

When I come back to the living room, he is preparing another hit.

I wish you wouldn't do that.

Don't worry. You worry too much. It's only cocaine. I want to snap back, It is *crack cocaine*, but I don't. I feel like his father. I am losing my partial erection. What are you worried about? I can handle it. I'll be okay. I like you. You're handsome. I begin to work my cock again.

With cold, trembling fingers I tear the foil and extract the slimy, rolled-up thing. Losing my erection. Tugging, massaging, yanking I pull the latex down what remains of my shaft. I squirt lube into my palm and work my sheathed cock while he takes his hit. I try to think of his bottom, penetrating his bottom... There follow several minutes of tension and jumpy looks while he reassures me: he'll be fine; I should relax. I sit by him. I work my dick, hold my breath, try to get hard again. Jacking through latex doesn't work so well. I pull the rubber off with a snap and work my bare flesh. I look at him and ask, How about taking your shirt off now?

Why do you keep asking that? I want you to warm me.

What does he mean by warm, this boy who could kill with his bare hands? I touch his hair and he flinches. I caress the inside of his thigh. He allows that. What was Amman like? Where? Jordan, where you were born? What do you mean what was it like? What was it like with all the... trouble... over there. What trouble?

He works my cock, but he does not look at it. He seems a little more focused, like he understands what this is about, but still enraged underneath, eyes blazing. I thrust my cock into his hand. I reach for his dick. It is a cold nub. How sad, I think. I wonder when he will leave. I glance at the clock. My lover. Time running out. No longer wanting to deal with the nub, I slip my hand inside his shirt and finger his nipple.

What are you doing?

Warming you—isn't that what you want? Then you can take your shirt off.

He diddles my cock absently.

Grip harder.

Huh?

Grip my cock harder. I thrust.

I'll be fine in a minute.

I put another dab of lube in my palm and try to help him with my cock. His hand drifts away. He looks around the apartment. His brow is knit. He flexes his fingers again and again.

While I work my cock I take a mental inventory. Where is my wallet? Where are my keys? My cash? Is anything lying around with my name on it or my Social Security number or... what else? Viewed in the dim light of this desperate scene my apartment looks feral, like a den. Bones lie around. Bloody cartilage. Feces. I wonder just who I am, who I have become. Who will I be later, when my lover is here, and I turn on the lights? Then there will be no bones. Not for him. Still for me, though.

He reaches again for my cock. I thrust into his limp hand, trying to get him to grip it, establish a rhythm, get interested, He watches my cock go up and down in his dead hand. There is no way back, no way forward. You get hard easy. My fingers still work half-heartedly on his nub. Must be nice. Is he regretful or angry? I am older than he. It shouldn't be this way. He should sound regretful.

The gold band brushes my cock and I shudder. Who's that for?

Who's what for?

The ring.

What do you mean?

Just…

It's not *for* anyone! His fingers flex. What did you mean?

Nothing…

He looks around. Not *for* anyone… Fingers flex. Pause.

How do you want to do it?

Why don't you lie down… Belly down, my cock in him, he will be less likely to kill me than if we face one another. Sex as self-defense.

Where?

Here.

On the couch?

Sure!

Won't the neighbors see?

The lights are out.

Oh.

Lie down. Take your shirt off.

He is on his belly. Then he turns over and rises. Why don't you do it this way? He puts his legs in the air. I kneel on the floor in front of the sofa. Fine. He'd still have a hard time grabbing for my neck. Any weapon would have to be in his pants, and they're over there. I like strategizing this way, figuring out what should be where and why. He rests his shapely, downy calves on my shoulders. He looks past me, out the window to where skyscrapers stand like silent witnesses.

Can we go to the bedroom?

What for? I thought you wanted to do it here. I work my cock to keep it hard.

Come on. He takes his pipe and lighter. He takes me by the arm and leads me into the bedroom. He kneels on the bed on all fours. Are you going to fuck me?

Sure.

Could we have some more light. I want to see.

If we have light, the neighbors will see.

How about music?

I hop back to the living room (what's in the bedroom? wallet? phone bill?) turn on 102 FM and dart back. He's in the exact same position. Is this okay?

What is it?

The radio.

I know that! What station is it?

102. Is that okay?

I like 96.1.

I hurry back and spin the dial to 96.1. My fingers fumble. Those pretty firm cheeks, raised, spread, that little brown pucker won't be there, so vulnerable, so exposed, forever. They could vanish in the time it takes me to change the station.

When I come back he's crouched by the window, staring out. I reach for him. He flinches. Maybe we shouldn't do it here, he says.

You want to fuck in the other room?

Okay. He keeps looking out the window.

Look, do you want to do it or not?

I want to do it, okay? I want to! I am almost disappointed.

Okay.

Give me some time.

Are you nervous?

Why do you keep saying that? You want to do it here?

Here?

Yes.

Okay.

Okay.

He kneels on the bed again, hole so fully given, so right there. He glances around. Reflexively, I do, too, but now I begin to worry—is something lurking, waiting to catch us? Catch me? My life feels this way. My erection is faltering. I run to the bathroom for another rubber. I tear the foil and manage to get the rubber on. I work the encased flesh. He waits, cheeks spread. I kneel behind him. I don't know that I can penetrate.

Take your shirt off, please?

Dead silence. I dread an explosion. But, nothing. Eyes straight ahead. He reaches one hand back to pull his cheeks farther apart. I have to penetrate now. Get this over with. My lover comes at ten. Only now this is it, the moment, the gaining. In the back of my mind: what if he won't leave, even when we are done? He does not know where he is, so how can he imagine he should leave? He does not exist in time, so how can he understand when he should go?

Go slow.

Okay. I'm grateful that what he says matches the situation, that it represents a progression toward a goal. My goal.

Go real slow.

I place the tip of my shaft against his pucker and lean gently into him.

He sucks his breath in through clenched teeth. Slower!!

My cock falls out. I am swollen but not completely hard. I try entering again. Once I am inside him and feel his sphincter alive clutching the base of my shaft, I place both hands on his back and push his shirt up toward his shoulders.

Don't do that!!

In the spillover light, it looks as though his back is covered with bruises.

I pull the shirt back down. I slip out again and re-enter.

Slowly.

I'm trying. A common interest. At last we are together. Who hit him? What should I do? Will they come for me? It was his wife. For some reason I decide, it was his wife. As I re-enter him he takes the pipe and lighter from beside the bed.

No! I pull out and stand away from the bed.

What? That look, as though my behavior were utterly incomprehensible.

You do that, and we are not going to fuck.

It's the last one, he says, incredulous. Look, I don't have anymore. You can search me. It's the last one.

Damn right it's the last one. It occurs to me it's not the crack that bothers me—he's smoked two already—but that he won't do what I want, the way I want it.

What are you so upset about? He climbs off the bed, suddenly holds my face in his hands and kisses me on both cheeks. The kiss of death. I like you, he says. You are a nice guy. This is the last one, I promise.

No. I really want to be alone. You are going to have to go.

Tonight my anger will be satisfied, not my lust.

He sits on the edge of the bed, face turned away. He looks sad and resentful. The green glow of the alarm clock says my lover will be here in less than half an hour.

It's nothing personal. I just need to be alone. Okay?

He says nothing. He does not move.

Time to get dressed, okay?

On his shadowy, turned-away face, some violent drama plays out.

You have to get dressed now, okay? At any moment, he will explode. He has no intention of leaving until he gets what he wants. I have no idea what that is, and I doubt even he knows.

His head turns. He looks around slowly as though someone had sent him here to memorize every object, find out everything about me. Has he already memorized my credit card number? My Social Security number, or a bank card? After a long silence he asks, Where are my clothes? But he doesn't get up.

Inside I heave a sigh of relief, but I remain brusque. This is just a first step.

In the bathroom. Do you want me to get them?

No.

He studies my bookshelves, though there is no light by which to see titles. His lips move. I leave him and dress myself. Once I have my own clothes on I move briskly about the apartment, turning on lights, straightening things. He has emerged from the bedroom and found his parka. Still naked from the waist down he stand frowning, fishing in the pockets. What are you looking for? He keeps fishing. He stops. As though someone flipped a switch he abandons the parka and proceeds in baby steps to the bathroom. There he stands and looks down at his underwear and socks, as though he thinks they might have something to do with him, but he can't think what. I ignore him and find more to do around the apartment: the theater of my life, enacted to make him go away. I check the kitchen clock. Twenty minutes. I go to the bathroom. He's sitting on the edge of the tub. He holds his socks in one hand. He doesn't look as though he is going to do anything with them. They seem about to fall from his hands. I go turn off the radio. When I come back he is standing. He has abandoned the socks but he is pulling on his underwear, with painful slowness. I feel he is not doing this because I insisted on it; I am just lucky that he happens to feel like doing what I happen to want at this moment. No guarantees about the next. I fold my arms and lean against the doorjamb and watch. He stops and looks around. Terrorists. Only he hears their voices. He depends on them. I wait. At last he has his underwear on.

With twelve minutes to go before my lover's arrival, he is dressed, parka and all. He stands in the bedroom, looking around. He feels his pockets, frowning. What is it? He doesn't answer, just checks each pocket, over and over, kneading the contents. Not looking at me, not even speaking to me, it seems, he says, My pen.

Panic rises in my chest. Breath catches in my throat. As casually as I can I ask, When did you last have it? He doesn't answer. Well, I say, let's look down here. I inspect all around the chair where he draped his coat. Not here, I announce brusquely. He still stands, frowning, feeling his pockets, massaging the contents of each one. He may or may not have had a pen. He may or may not be looking for it. Terrorists don't give reasons, just orders, and he responds. His is many people, and he is no one. They bypass his conscious mind and go directly to his nerves. They tug the axons. He must obey, not knowing why. They make promises, and he believes them, but their promises are never fulfilled. Now they have him on his hands and knees, going over the floor inch by inch. My lover will be here in less than ten minutes.

Look, I'll call you. Give me your number, and I'll call you if I find your pen. He mutters, It was gold. It was valuable. He stands and feels his pockets but doesn't look at me. I get a pad and pencil. He starts to go through the items on top of my dresser, picking up pens and pencils and examining them, as though his next dose (and last hope) are there. Give me your number—I'll call you the *minute* I find it, and I'll *bring* it right to you. He picks up my Swiss army knife. Turns it over in his hand. He pulls open a blade. I freeze. He closes it. Then he pulls open another blade. Looks at me. Then closes it. He puts down the knife and goes back through my pens and pencils. What about these pens? Why can't I have one of these? Sure, I say. You're not doing anything with them. Here, take this one. He takes a pen, looks at it, and puts it back on the dresser. That's not mine, he says. He feels in his pockets again. Mine was gold. It was valuable. All I can think (beside will he *ever* leave?) is, This guy manages to work for the *phone company*? Well maybe that explains some things.

Look, you have to go now. I have to be alone. Understand? No. He only understands what the terrorists say. I have a friend coming over. He won't like it if you are here. What do you mean he won't like it? I'll call you when I find the pen. If I find it. What's your number? He starts to give the number; his voice trails off. I ask him to repeat it. He mutters the last four digits again. I repeat them back. He nods absently. I repeat the whole number. He nods. I'll call you, as soon as I find it, okay? Okay. Step by step he makes his way toward the door, constantly feeling in his pockets.

My Movie

Every few steps he stops and looks around. Each time he stops, it seems he will never move again. It was gold. Step by step, down the hall. He pokes into things as a child would, into places the pen could not possibly be. He feels his pockets constantly. I'll call you. Another step. He stops. Feels his pockets. Another step. Turns back. I'll call you. Turns to the door. Doesn't move. I go to the door, turn the bolt and open it. He looks out. Doesn't move. I'll call you.

I want to look in the bedroom again.

It's not there.

I want to look. It was gold.

I promise I will call you when I find it.

Why can't I look?

Because you have to go.

Why?

I'm expecting someone.

I thought you wanted to be alone.

Look, you'll just have…

Who are you expecting?

In the hallway I hear the elevator. My skin goes cold.

It's not here.

How do you know?

We looked everywhere.

We didn't look in the living room.

I looked in the living room.

I want to look in the living room.

I have your number. The minute I find it, I'll call. Maybe you didn't have it.

I did have it!

Steps in the hall. He hears them, too. Maybe I should call for help, he says.

A key turns in the lock of another apartment.

Everyone here knows me. Besides, you were smoking crack. (Does he have the pipe with him? Was that really his last hit? Is there more somewhere, where he can take them right to it?)

He makes no response. He moves past me, step by step, over the threshold, all the time feeling his pockets.

He is through the door. He is on the other side of the threshold now, but he holds one arm out, stiff, elbow locked, holding the door open. I lean into my side of the door, a little more, a little more. The muscles in his face work. The door trembles this way, that.

If I find it, I'll call you.

Do you have my number?

I have your number?

What is it?

I read it off the pad in my hand. He seems satisfied. I'll call you.

The tension subsides just a bit in his arm. The door closes a few inches. Then he pushes again. I push back.

How do I get out?

Take the elevator. Or the stairs.

Where are the stairs?

There. The end of the hall.

Down there? As though the journey is long and frightening; he doesn't want to go.

Yes!

Oh. He takes a few steps, then stops. In another world, he is funny and smart. A woman holds him in her lap. Then the tick of a clock, a spoon dropped, a scream in the next building, the wave breaks, takes over the village, draws the village away with it, down to where no light penetrates, where your family says light is a rumor, never seen. Down where you can not breathe, where you can not raise your face to the light that is not there.

He takes a few more steps. Stops. Looks uncertain.

So long. Good luck at the phone company.

What?

The phone company. Where you work. Good luck. There.

He says nothing. He looks to the stairs. One more thing should happen before I close the door. I should know his name. It is two minutes to ten. I say nothing. I close the door and bolt it. Immediately that moment of asking his name blows up. There should have been more. I denied him. He should have an entire hour, not like the hour we spent. His name, the name of the woman who held him in her lap, they press the door and though it is bolted I think they will crash in. I must know them. I listen. His footsteps scuff away and are gone. Only the cry of cold air whistling around the doorjamb. I turn and walk weak-kneed back to the living room. One minute to ten.

I go to the bathroom where I am overwhelmed by the acrid smoke. I walk briskly around the apartment, raising each window an inch or two. Cold rushes in. I scan every place I can for his paraphernalia. Could he have planted something? He'll come back any moment with the police. This will be his revenge for being denied. Any second I will hear the violating thud-thud on my door.

I poke in the couch and on the dresser, manic. At last I am convinced he left nothing. I fall onto the couch. Then I sit up. Ten. Is that smell on me? I pull off my clothes and stuff them deep in the hamper, and run to the shower. Naked and wet I am gripped by panic. Where are the rubbers? I flushed one down the john. What about the one I didn't use? I cut my shower short, wrap myself in a robe, and dash around looking for the missing rubbers. And the packets! I can't find them. I decide to assume I flushed the second one, but what about the unopened one?

A key turns in the lock.

Electricity shoots through me. Ecstasy of being fully present and having to manage, now.

We kiss. For a moment I believe he must know, must see everything. I think I will spill it all. How can you live with secrets kept from someone you love? But I will keep this one. I have kept others. Hold it in, hold it in till your soul warps, till it is beyond straightening. I will find a way to live with this withholding as I have with others. We kid, exchange our usual pleasantries. Did you just shower? Do I hear tension in his voice?

That's why my hair's wet and I'm in a bathrobe, I quip. He smiles and dumps his things in the living room. I tip toe quickly to the bathroom to make sure the toilet didn't fail to swallow the rubber. I will get through this. I will figure it all out.

All clear.

I meander back to the living room and make small talk. Cold in here. Oh. I shut a couple of windows. Good excuse to go double check the bedroom.

No, nothing. Wait. I grab the comforter and shake it out and the unopened rubber goes flying like a huge black bug. I grab it and stuff it in my bathrobe pocket. But sometimes he uses my bathrobe. I stroll nonchalantly to the kitchen and deposit the rubber in the waste basket as though it were nothing, as though it did not speak of the power of men and the power of desire.

But it can't be on top! I have to bury it a few layers down. On cue he looks at me. I meet his look, my face blank. My power is gone, too. I go right on burying the rubber. He winks and looks away. What did that mean? After the rubber is buried I come back to the living room. More small talk. He is ready for bed. He goes to the bathroom. I stroll after, heart thumping. What have I missed? What will he smell? Does he know already? What did that wink mean?

Later, when I have slipped the dead bolt on the front door and turned out the lights, we spoon in the dark. My arm rises and falls with his breathing. My eyes stay wide open. That firm ass. Then what I saw when I slid his shirt up. For a second before he shouted to put it back down I surveyed his smooth back tapering, and in the blue glare from the street, along with the bruises, purple-red, I also saw burn marks.

A taxi rattles a manhole cover. Someone shouts. Kids beat plastic drums. A woman laughs, drunk. Where will she sleep tonight? With whom? What will the clear, cold light of day be like? It will be better. It always is.

My arm rises and falls with my lover's breath.

I love him.

I'm sure I do.

The fact of his weight, his bare skin, his pimples and moles, in this bed.

I love him.

But maybe…

…not enough.

Is that what the wink meant? Oh, God!

What if I met again the one whose name I do not even know? What if he begged, sincerely, for a second chance? What if he turned all his pockets inside out and said, *Look*, I don't even have any stuff with me? Search me if you want!

Revealed on those creamy, small feet. No one who so touched the Earth, whose perfectly proportioned frame rose from such innocence could, in the inner seat of him, ever do or mean me any harm.

Please fuck me. You're such a handsome guy. Please fuck me.

What would I do?

Edge

I adjust Sherman's drip, and adjust and adjust it.

"Is this what's left?" Sherman asks.

I keep adjusting. When I have done adjusting, I'll have nothing to do, and I swear I will go bonkers.

Fluorescent light bounces off yellow walls with peeling paint. Sherman sits erect on the edge of the bed. His face is that of a wrecked but still faithful cherub. Full lips, clear eyes. His hospital gown slips, by degrees revealing his back—here a zit, there the golden down of one half his age. Sherman hears angels. He heard them before they became all the rage. An orchestra plays and Sherman hears. Sherman sees cathedrals and choirs and the Sun before it pierces the atmosphere, up where it is pure gold. Up where it burns.

I study the clicking box that controls the drip. Sherman says nothing. Somewhere a symphony has begun; Sherman strains to hear.

The man in the next bed has his mother here from Barbados. Sherman sees through the curtain that separates the two beds. He sees through their skin and through the walls of their hearts. He sees blood filling their atria. He sees the atria squeeze, pushing blood into their ventricles. But he doesn't hear them speak. Not a word.

-o-

I'd like to be under the sea, in an octopus's garden in the shade...

Sherman was right: they have left us nothing. The garbage trucks that pass in the night are tanks. Beggars spy on us. In Sherman's bathroom lace covers frosted glass. Satsumas and lavender saturate the air, and fish stare from the shower curtain. Votive candles rest on the toilet. In the morning I would peer over the edge of frosted glass and see if this morning at last the buses wouldn't look like troop transports. Even on the sharpest blue days they do. You have to lose everything before you can gain anything. Sherman has lost almost everything. I am afraid to lose anything. I just want to live in Sherman's bathroom.

Sherman came home today. He has asked me to come spend the night, in case of an emergency. He moves slowly, eyes focused beyond the walls, on a celestial choir, on gold crosses and candlesticks. Sherman wants no help moving around, but he does ask me, because of the pain in his side, to pull out the sofabed where I will sleep, to spread the comforter, to reach for pillows. Sherman will sleep on a narrow futon on the floor, as he does every night.

-o-

"If our Father in Heaven loves us when we are awake, think how much more He loves us when we sleep and cannot sin."

A saint said that. Sherman will ask which one. Another saint will tell him. Sherman moves slowly, as though he has just arrived here and might leave tomorrow. He touches things as though for the first and the last time, as though figuring out what this world is like—how candlesticks are, how a table feels, a lampshade, a teddy bear. The teddy bear looks as though it landed in a UFO. Silently the bear describes his world to Sherman. Sherman wants to go there.

Before we sleep Sherman asks me to shut the window. Around two in the morning huge, gleaming semis start down the avenue. Sherman's living room faces the route they take into the City, to deliver frozen food to the midtown hotels before dawn.

We both sleep naked. The percale caresses my calves and the hairs on my shoulder blades. From over on his narrow futon I feel Sherman's heart beating—futon frame like a rack, like a ladder.

Though the shades are down, around two o'clock a glow grows in the apartment, golden-gray. The semis start down the avenue, dozens of them, full of frozen fish, frozen orange juice. Sherman was right: there is no stopping them.

Sherman wakes. He lifts himself off his futon and stands naked. How powerful to me is the sight of a gay man's genitals, especially when soft; they must be father to the man, and son. The sight of Sherman's flaccid penis fills my heart, as I twist in damp percale. His caved-in chest and softly hanging cock absolve me. He totters through the kitchen to the bathroom. Truck engines thunder down the avenue. The lights shine brighter. This has to end soon. How many more can there be?

After ten minutes Sherman comes back. In his left hand he holds a dead dove, blood on its sugar-white wings. Sherman comes to the side of my bed. I see the dove is a wad of toilet paper. Sherman looks down at me.

"I can't wipe myself," he confesses. "It still hurts to reach in back."

I sit up and take the dove from him. He turns around. He bends and exposes his anus with the grace and gravity with which he has performed every act—praying, vomiting, singing, kissing—since I've known him. He winces, draws his ass cheeks apart, and I see: he bleeds from his rectum. Dark red runs down his leg like sap on a tree. The light outside grows brighter and the thunder of the truck engines shakes the walls. I have something to do. I have to wipe the blood and shit. And still it comes. It soaks the dove, the dove is useless, it is not a dove. Before I can decide what to do next, Sherman straightens up and thanks me. He reaches for the teddy bear. I squint, and my throat closes to the exhaust.

Sherman's fingers cup the teddy bear like wire holding a crystal pendant. It rests in the soft valley of his chest, a large brown nipple to either side, not like the pale ghost nipples of the boy who might once have held that bear.

Sherman begins to knead his penis. No right word exists for what he does, bringing it to hardness. Not the contemptuous "jack off," nor the furtive "masturbate." He nurses it, encourages it till it stands out from his body—as stout and as hard as he used to be. Still bleeding from behind he positions himself over me and works his manliness with long, loving strokes. He smiles. "I didn't do this the whole time I was in the hospital," he says, and with a sweet convulsion exiling breath after breath as in a boy's first dream his body casts off evidence of his continence, does not squirt but shoots, pours the contents of his vesicle as though it were breath onto me, splattering my torso and face. I believe his virus is his sperm, the mechanism by which I will inherit everything good in him. I scoop it up and smear it on my face. I lick my hand. I grow weak—and strong.

Sherman squeezes the last drops from his cock. He turns away from me and moves toward the window. I get out of bed and stand. I scrunch my toes into the sodden carpet.

The whole world is one roaring semi. As though they have fused into a train. Their lights sweep the window shade. Sherman tugs the shade. He doesn't squint, doesn't blink. Rather his eyes open wider in the horrendous, harsh light. "Would you open this?" he says. I go to him. Before opening the window I look at his feet, covered in blood, standing in blood.

As I pull on the sash I keep my face turned from the parade of semis, from the awful, breathing presence about to take over the apartment, the building, the whole, tiny city. If I look I will be annihilated, yet there is Sherman, staring straight into the long train of exhaust and rage.

I throw up the sash. The air moves over and chills the semen running down my torso. I stagger back from the fumes and vibration. I shield my face. Beyond my folded arms I see Sherman seat himself on the sill. His blood runs everywhere. Slowly, he raises his legs and swings them out, where they dangle in the brilliant light and truck exhaust. He sits with his ridged back to me, his face raised. Beyond him shines the white light that disguises the tons of frozen orange juice.

In a single, pure motion, Sherman pushes with his hands and is gone.

A roar goes up, as though every extinct beast for millions of years were leaping out of the earth. The noise knocks me down and the light imprints my shadow on the floor. The walls crack. Plaster rains from the ceiling.

I cover my ears. I close my eyes. I bear what cannot be borne until it becomes all right. And then the street returns to order and silence.

The walls stop shaking.

The trucks go, and the last night breeze gently angles the shade in the gray glow.

My chest and stomach hair matted with cum and with blood, I rise and stumble downstairs.

There I find Sherman's body so completely crushed that nothing remains for me to bring in from the street.

The Snow Queen

Jo Osbourne had big, hulking shoulders and hair like a little black cap with bangs. Her father, Dr. Osbourne, had delivered me, but he was dead by the time this happened:

My parents introduced me to Jo one Sunday in March 1968, in the choir loft after church. She was standing there, and they kind of had to. She shook my hand and said, "Pleased to meet you, sir!" She raised an eyebrow. "Care to give me a hand putting away some hymnals?" I said, "Sure!" My mother raised her hand just a little way, then lowered it again. She glanced at my dad, and they backed away to say hello to some other friends. Jo put her hand on my shoulder and showed me the racks in the pews where the hymnals went. Right away we were inventing jokes—she invented them, mostly—like pretending we were stevedores on a ship, swinging stacks of hymnals, calling in deep voices, "Hey! Hup! Ho!" It was fun and a little uncomfortable, too. Adults usually didn't play like that. Afterwards, as we were leaving, I asked Mom, "She is, like, a woman, right?" Mom shushed me. My dad chuckled and patted me on the shoulder. "What?" I said.

"People will hear you!" Mom said. She gave my dad a look. "We'll discuss it when we get home!" But by the time we got home, it was like I'd never said it. Like only I could see Jo. I was always making up weird things, and when I mentioned them to Mom we got into an argument, and she'd say, "I don't want to hear another word about it!" Every once in a while, if she was really mad, she'd say, "If I hear one more word about it, you'll wish you'd never been born!" I'd sit alone in my room and think, what terrible thing could someone do to make you wish that? Who did you wish it to? God? What did you say? Actually, Mom never did anything. I just waited, alone, and an hour later suddenly she'd knock, all cheerful like nothing happened, and I'd feel like a pussy for being afraid.

The next week, after Sunday School, I ran over to the church, waved to my parents, and went up to the choir loft before they could say anything. There Jo was, putting away hymnals. I knew then, it was always Jo who put away hymnals. I was afraid she wouldn't remember me, but she looked at me and seemed happy, like I was an old friend. "Well, hey there, Sport!" she said. "Come to do hymnal duty again?"

I wasn't sure, but I said yes. I didn't want to be the one who always put away hymnals, but I wanted to be with Jo and make her happy.

"Wonderful!" she declared. "We'll start here. We'll skin and dress a hundred of 'em and be back in port in time for supper. Did you know, in whaling days, they cut the blubber like pages of a book and called 'em 'bibles'?"

I didn't.

"It's true. So how's life been treating you since last Sunday? School still as boring as it was in 1492? Oops, ahem, I mean 1942!"

She was so nice to me, it was almost like she understood this, like, one certain thing about me—how I couldn't be like other boys, no matter how hard I tried. Including my own brother, Russell. I wished I'd been born like Russell, playing baseball and shouting and knowing what to do all the time. Except I didn't like Russell that much. But his way was the way to be. Jo didn't seem to care what way I was, though. She was different, too. She looked and acted, well, kind of like a man. A lot like a man, I guess, but a nice man, a different man, without the thing that made Russell shout or made my dad so mad and so quiet. I was afraid what it might mean about me that Jo liked me, but it also felt nice, like someone finally understood. I just hoped Jo didn't see that one thing, because, as nice as she was, I didn't think she would like it. Or understand it. What would become of me then?

While we put away hymnals, the sanctuary bright and emptying beneath us, Jo told me her favorite hymns and about the meadows out back of her house on Coe Hill. Then we folded up the extra chairs she had set out for the choir, and that was when my dad came and got me.

"Mr. U!" Jo said. "Sorry. I guess we worker bees lost track of time. You know, you have raised an awfully fine helper here." Dad looked away and nodded once, fast. "Would you folks mind if I offered him a few shekels to help me with some chores up to the Old Manse this afternoon?"

Jo meant her house. I was excited. She'd told me so much about it, it was like a house in a storybook. Dad looked annoyed—not like I couldn't go, but like he was annoyed she asked and he had to do something about it. He said we'd have to talk to Mom. When we did, Mom looked anxious, but I said please. Jo interrupted, saying, "Now, Sport, if it's not convenient..."

"She's going to pay me!" I said. Mom gave me this shocked look. But she ended up saying it was all right. I just had to be home by four. She said it several times, smiling, kind of.

"Four it is, Mrs. U," Jo said. I didn't like it that Mom was impatient with Jo, but I didn't like that Jo seemed impatient with Mom, too. What was so terrible? Why couldn't they leave me alone? It took forever for them to decide if Dad would drive me to Jo's or Jo would come get me. No one wanted to put anyone else out or, I guess, be put out themselves. I thought all the politeness would never end, and I kept being afraid Mom would call the whole thing off. But eventually I we got home and I changed clothes and I had to eat and then Dad drove me to Jo's house, and when I saw it behind the row of trees like its arms were open for me, I wished I could stay and live in that big old family house forever. Inside I saw there certainly was space, with room after room full of old junk draped with sheets, and sun coming in like it was a regular day.

Working with Jo wasn't like chores at home, but more like I lived by myself and was out for a walk, and happened along to help a friend. We had more jokes, like one of us saying, "Want to give me a hand here?" And the other one clapping their hands. Soon helping out Sundays on Coe Hill became a tradition. Jo liked traditions. For example, every Sunday she asked, "Whatcha reading lately, Sport?" Because I liked to read so much—stuff other than what we read in school. Another tradition was knocking off work—"Halt!" Jo would say—and running for the truck with her Bassett hound, Moose, behind, and driving to the cider mill in Granby. "Emergency cider runs," Jo said. Afterwards we heated the cider in her kitchen with a cinnamon stick in the pan (I'd always wondered what cinnamon sticks were for) and drank it with homemade corn muffins or biscuits as the Sun went down.

One time, Jo helped me put a new hinge on my butterfly box, and she let me keep the screwdriver. "My dad passed this down to me when I was about your age," she declared, "and now, I give it to you." I went home and showed it to Mom, who didn't really say anything. "Jo can do anything!" I told her. Mom said, "Well, that's good." Dad said, sort of to himself, "Well, not quite everything." And he chuckled and went back to his newspaper. Mom walked with long strides back to the kitchen.

In April, at the First Church Square Dance, Jo wore the one nice outfit I ever saw her in—gray pants, a yellow sweater over a white turtle neck, and a tiny silver cross on a chain. She came over to me and said, "Handsome sir, might one hope your dance card is not full?" But my dad said, "I think Steve might like to dance with one of those pretty young ladies over there. Am I right or am I right?"

"You go ahead, Sport," Jo said. "We'll see you later." Why did she give in so easy? Was she really on my parents' side? In the end, adults—even fun ones like Jo—were worried about you having too much of what you wanted.

That fall, the day after Halloween, I was out walking the causeway that went from the railroad bridge out over the fields to Wilkinson Academy, where Jo was a carpenter. She came along in her truck and slowed down next to me. "What ho, Pilgrim? What brings you out?"

I told her how, that morning, my brother, Russell, hit me deliberately with his hockey stick, so I tried to yank it away from him, and the end of it broke this vase of Mom's. So she said I was a disgrace and I said she loved Russell more than me, and then my dad came up and Mom cried and said what she always said: "Why do I always have to be the villain?" And she slammed the bedroom door. Dad muttered that I should apologize, and, well, it felt weird and awful all of a sudden because Jo really was listening. You could tell. I don't know how to describe it. I couldn't look at her. I finished quickly, telling how I snuck out to the hardware store, but instead I took a detour down the causeway just to be by myself. Then I asked quickly, "What are you up to?"

"Well, Sport," she said, and I knew I was going to have to stop feeling one thing and feel something else, and I hated it. "I want us to rewind the tape here a second. Why don't you come around and hop in?" When I was settled into the passenger side of the truck ("riding shotgun," as Jo said when we made emergency cider runs), she said, "Now, I think that, really, you know your mom loves you every bit as much as your brother..."

I tensed up my muscles. It was a thing I did when people talked about love and stuff. When I'd snuck out of the house to go to the hardware store, I'd felt like a real boy. But when Jo said that about Mom loving me, suddenly I felt like a girl. Men didn't think about love. If someone said, "Your dad loves you," it was just a thing they said. Love was for girls.

I felt bad because there was other stuff I didn't tell Jo—like how, even though he was a year younger than me, Russell was bigger and more, I guess, masculine, with muscles and all hard. I was plumper and my body was shaped funny. It was like Russell wasn't my brother; he was from outside the family and that's why Mom liked him so much. "Maybe I should give you a lift t'home," Jo said, "so they can know you're okay. She shifted gears and began singing one of my favorite songs she'd taught me: "When I was a lad I served a term..." and I joined in:

"...as office boy to an attorney's firm.
I cleaned the windows and I swept the floor,
And I polished up the handle of the big front door."

And then we sang together:
"Yes, he polished up the handle of the big front door!"

The truck jounced under the bridge and came up to the center of town. At the traffic light Jo shifted gears again and said, "You know, methinks I am getting An Idea..."

She swung into the parking lot by the A&P and Vogel's Hardware and pulled up to the phone booth. We got out, and she called my house.

"Mrs. U! Jo Osbourne here. I found young Steven; yes, ma'am, fit as a viola. He'd like to speak with you..."

Jo stood with her hand on my shoulders while I apologized to Mom. It was funny, but Mom was cheerful, as if the whole thing hadn't happened. It was over real quick, and I gave the phone back to Jo. Jo had done the right thing for most of the world, for the world I wanted to be in. But I was also in another world where what she did was wrong.

"So Mrs. U! I'm doing some repairs on my stone wall this afternoon. You know, 'Something there is that doesn't love a wall!' Or in this case, someone. At any rate, you think you could you loan me a foreman for a couple hours? Yes, ma'am, indeed—five o'clock. Now, is this boy union? Nothing, ma'am. Five o'clock, yes, yup, bye-bye..." She hung up and turned to me and raised a finger in the air. "Tally ho, Jeeves!" she cried.

Five o'clock was so close...

We worked for two hours carrying stones in the field out back of the Osbourne house. Someone had toppled a section of Jo's wall. You could tell it was some guys. It just looked... violent... spread all over without any pattern. I asked her who she thought did it, even though I knew some older guys from church lived up there and could guess it was them.

"This?" Jo said. "Well, I try not to worry about that kind of thing, Sport. Could've been just frost heaves."

"But you told Mom how someone didn't love your wall."

"Well, Sport, I'll tell you." She stopped and braced a rock against her leg, and I wondered if it was a man's leg and then wondered what kind of leg mine was or would be. The way Jo posed was almost like one of those guys would have. "It's a waste of time and energy blaming. Just put things back the way they were."

It was like what my mom would have said. Except she would have used a hundred more words. Maybe it was what my dad would have said. Except he wouldn't have said. You'd just know.

It was hard to say nothing and put things back the way they were. I knew, and I wanted to know if Jo knew, too, that it was those guys—Don Filbert, Jack Wessel, Jack Sheehan. In Sunday school, always sitting together, punching each other and talking about their dicks. Jack Wessel took his out once, under the table. I didn't know how someone did that. And the way he laughed. I'd never seen anyone laugh so hard or look so... beautiful, in a way. Those guys were supposed to worse behaved than me, but I thought they were better than me and I should be like them. Like that's how Mom wanted me to be, and if I was like that she'd finally shut up. I'd sure make Russell shut up if I was like that. Right across his ugly face. But then I couldn't be Jo's friend. I wanted to be careless and boyish enough to wreck stuff, just never anything of Jo's. I went over the wall, out into the long grass after a stone.

"Sport, don't go down there!" she called. "There's poison ivy..." Yes, she'd told me, but I'd forgotten, and now I was there and I had the stone, and when I turned back I saw a bright orange word spray-painted on the other side of the wall, a word I didn't know, but that I understood, sort of, and then I did know and I wished I didn't.

"Come on, Sport, let's bring that back and get it in place!"

Jo forgave. I felt like I'd disappear if I forgave. I was bringing the rock back over the wall and feeling guilty when suddenly Jo held up her hand. "Halt!" she cried. "All hands on deck for an Emergency Cider Run!"

And everything was better. Granby! With Moose following we clambered up the hill and into the truck and took off. The sky was blue and chilly and the leaves were red and yellow and brown and there was smoke in the air and ghosts behind the doors of houses. Back home, Jo made hot cider, and we had short breads. They were my favorite thing she made. Jo finally got me home... I mean, to *my* home... at almost five thirty. "Well," Mom said. "I was worried about you two!" Jack Sheehan's mother was never worried about him. He came and went as he pleased.

"No need, ma'am!" Jo said. Again she seemed impatient or tense. So I was right about Mom. I wished I wasn't. "I've kept a very close eye..." Jo began.

"It's almost six!" Mom said. Then she smiled. "Well. That's no matter..! What were you two up to all this time?" And the thought that I might tell about the word on Jo's wall—though I never would—made me feel like I could not breathe.

–o–

And then, the snow came.

–o–

It danced outside my window at night. It fell on the fields and outside our classroom, and it felt like we were all traveling in a space ship together.

The day school let out for Christmas my dad and I sat in the kitchen having liverwurst sandwiches. Dad loved liverwurst and always offered it to me. I didn't like it, but I took it because it seemed like a grown-up thing to like.

Dad asked, "So, how's the ol' math?" He taught math at the junior high, big kids he loved, kids I'd finally be as good as when I was twelve. I told him the "ol' math" was fine. Then he made a joke, asking how the "new math" was, and I said that was fine, too. If I'd told the truth, that I was getting C's like always, he would've wanted to help, right then. But when Dad helped with my math, I got the feeling he didn't like me. Or he didn't like math, and I felt even worse about that.

"Well," he said, "if you ever need help, you know where to turn. Not many kids have a live-in tutor!"

I nodded vigorously. For the first time I looked at him, and I said, "Oh, yeah, I will!" If I promised this, maybe he wouldn't bring up the other stuff. At the beginning of the year and the beginning of summer they always threatened that I'd have to join Boy Scouts or play junior league sports at the Rec Center. I could never explain why I didn't want to. I just said, "I don't want to!" and "Do I have to?" and they told me I was whining. So far I'd gotten out of it, but every Christmas and every spring I was always afraid.

At six o'clock we had to pick Russell up at the rink. He climbed in back with Mom and poked the end of his hockey stick over to the

203

front seat between me and Dad. Mom tried to stick back on a piece of black tape that was curling off. "Mom!" Russell snapped. "Leave it!" Mom folded her hands and stared at the back of my father's head. "Calm down, Russ," Dad said. Russell hunched forward. I saw his hands gripping the back of the seat. They were bigger than mine even though he was younger. He was growing up right. His nails were big, too, with half-moons. My nails were small, and you couldn't see the half moons. "Dad," he said, "Coach Noga wants me to try out for the All Stars. We're goin' to Springfield, okay?"

Dad put the car in reverse. "I'm sure it is, Russ," Mom said. "For your information," Russell said, "I was talking to Dad!" Mom looked out the window. "That's enough, Russ," Dad said.

We drove up Coe Hill to the McDonald's by the entrance to the highway. Getting out of the car, Mom lagged behind. She walked real slow and looked like she'd cry. Russell ran ahead with Dad and I didn't know where to go or what to do. Inside she smiled and said, "Oh, I don't guess I'm hungry. I'll just watch you people eat." But later she went up and got an apple pie, and came back smiling and chatting about how McDonald's had the best apple pie. I guessed that meant things were okay.

The next afternoon I got to go do my favorite Christmas errand—down to Vogel's Hardware Store to buy presents. I loved the brass bells jingling on the glass when I came in. I went straight to the wooden bins like always. I reached into the one with the finishing nails and squeezed a clump in my hand. I always did that first at Vogel's. I let go of the nails, shook off the last couple that were embedded in, took my hand out, and studied the marks on my palm. It didn't hurt quite enough, but I couldn't do it again. One time: that was the rule.

I reached into the bin with the twenty-penny nails, took one and weighed it in my hand. I had to see the biggest of everything. I moved over to the dowel rack and pulled up the thickest dowel they had. Mr. Vogel was on the phone:

"...so the kid says to his old man, 'Dad, I got a problem: Jimmy wants to sell me his bike for twenty bucks.' And the old man says, 'What's the problem?' and the kid says, 'Well, with you bein' black and Mom Jewish, I don't know if I should jew him down to ten or steal it!'" Then he saw me. He turned his back and kept talking, but I couldn't hear. I put the dowel down and disappeared down the "Home" aisle.

Cards hung with knives and scissors and peelers in plastic bubbles;

sometimes the card showed a woman using whatever it was and smiling. Maybe a child stood by smiling, too. If it was a boy I thought how much I wanted to be like that. If it was a girl I wondered for a second if that was what I really was.

I got a kitchen timer for my Mom. The picture showed a woman overjoyed that the timer was going off. I got work gloves for my dad. They didn't have a picture. I didn't know what to get Russell, so I didn't get him anything yet.

Mr. Vogel rang up the timer and the gloves. He was about to give me change when he stopped. "That business before?" he said. "You know that was grown-ups kidding around. You wouldn't go repeatin' it." I shook my head.

"Atta boy! Wouldn't want to hafta get you in trouble for eavesdropping!" He held his fist out, the curled fingers down. I had to put my hand under, even though I didn't want to. He did this every time I came in, like with my dad, and I thought if I didn't do it he'd get mad and then tell my parents something, some kind of lie I couldn't defend myself against and then... I know it sounds stupid, but I had this idea that somehow I could be sort of sent away. That everyone would agree on it. There was this place in Hartford called The Institute for Living. Mom would mention to Dad or to one of her friends that so-and-so was in the Institute for Living, or maybe should be, but she never said why or what happened there. I think maybe people went there for nervous breakdowns. I didn't get what nervous breakdowns were, or how you'd know you were having one. I had lots of weird thoughts I was scared to say. Was that a nervous breakdown? What could you do about a nervous breakdown if it just decided to happen? I held my hand under Mr. Vogel's. He pulled his fist back abruptly. Then put it out again and waited for my hand. Then pulled it back again. Finally he dropped the change into my hand. "Heh-heh! Good boy," he said. He took a peppermint from under the counter and held it out to me—between his fingers this time—and I took that, too.

On my way out the bells scraped the glass. Outside the snow whirled, spiraling in one direction, then doubling back, doubling again, drifting, going up, going down...

My mom had given me money to get milk and English muffins at the A&P. Crossing the parking lot in the snow I kept thinking how a person would be "jewed down." I didn't know much about Jewish people, except they were usually the smartest kids in class and Mom said the boys were snooty because they were told by their parents how good they were. That actually sounded maybe kind of good to me. And then once a year people from our church went to Congregation Beth Ahm on a Friday night, and kids from Beth Ahm came to our Sunday school the next morning. They sat together and didn't say much. I imagined a hand gripping a black lever and the end of the lever hooked onto the top of the Jewish person's head. As the hand pumped up and down, the Jewish person squashed down till they ended up like an accordion. They bounced around making off-key noises, and people laughed. I squeezed my muscles and walked faster.

In the A&P, I saw a familiar checkered wool jacket stretched over big shoulders. I was excited and then anxious. When I met Jo by accident around town, I couldn't help but wonder what other people thought about her. (As opposed to church, where I guess people forgave her.) Each time I hoped she'd invite me up to Coe Hill, and I'd be afraid she wouldn't. Mom had reminded me that Jo had her own life and things to do.

She disappeared at the end of an aisle and I followed. I came up behind her as she took some bread and said in a deep voice, "You rang?"

Without looking to see it was me she flipped a loaf of bread in the air, grabbed it coming down, and turned around looking shocked. "Gadzooks!" she said. "Sir, you have causèd me thus to fumble my loaf! Scoundrel! Poltroon!" She poked me with the loaf like it was a sword. "I challenge you to a drool. Sweet roles at fifty paces!" Suddenly she changed voices. "So how are ya, Sport? Think fast!" She tossed the loaf and I caught it. "Merry Xmas, ho ho ho, etcetera. You're just in time to help me find some chocolate chips."

"You making by-cracky bars for tomorrow?"

"Nothing less!"

Tomorrow was the annual Christmas choral concert and the party in the parish house. Jo always ran the kitchen for church parties, and she usually made by-cracky bars—a layer of brownies, a layer of graham crackers, then a layer of cake on top of that with chocolate chips in it.

"Those're tricky to make, right?" I asked, but Jo was already saying, "Heavens to Murgatroyd, you're getting big! Ah, me. So—seen any chocolate chips lately?" I was about to answer when she took the bread from me, winked and said, "Who asked ya! Let's go!" I led the way, and she pushed the cart behind me.

"And how's everything t'home?" she asked.

I said it was fine. I didn't want to complain again. I wanted Jo to invite me to her house! Here in the supermarket I was afraid guys from Sunday school would see us. Then tomorrow at church they'd walk around like gorillas holding their arms out, going, "Fee-fi-fo-fum, I smell Jo Osbourne!" I tried to ignore them like Mom said, but they didn't let you. No way Mom ever said to deal with those guys worked for even two seconds. And if I said, "Cut it out!" or "So what's that mean?" I sounded like a doofus. All the teachers ever said was, "Calm down, Donald... Jack, that's enough!" Once in a while they got in trouble, but at the same time there was something teachers liked about those guys that they never said.

After we went through the checkout I lifted one of the bags, so I'd have to go at least as far as Jo's truck. Right then she said, "Methinks I am having another in my series of Brilliant Ideas! What are you up to this afternoon?" I pretended to think about it and said, "Nothing... I guess..."

In the vestibule of the grocery store Jo put down her bags by the phone booth and stepped in. "Number?" she said, and I told her.

"Mrs. Underwood? Greetings. Jo Osbourne here." I could hear Mom's voice coming through the receiver, kind of sharp. "*Jo Osbourne. Yes, ma'am.*" It was funny, her calling my mom "ma'am." "I'm actually down to the A&P, where I was ambushed by your son in the bread aisle. Oh no, ma'am, no trouble at all. It reminded me I could use a little help baking for church tomorrow. I have a fair amount to do and I wondered if Steven might help out at the Old Manse..."

Mom cut in with something that went on a long time.

"Well, Mrs... Would... Would six o'clock be all right, Mrs. U?"

We had to be at the rink at seven for Russell's game. I heard Mom say what she usually said about family outings: "Practically another D-Day..!"

"Of course, ma'am," Jo said. "Yes, six o'clock, on the button. We'll be there. See you, then, Mrs. U. You bet. Six it is! Yes, ma'am, I know how boys are. So long, ma'am."

As she hung up I saw Jo... not *roll* her eyes... they just sort of widened, and she took a deep breath. I thought my mom went on too much; I got embarrassed in front of other kids, but I tried not to think how other adults might think she was a pain. In Sunday school they taught us to forgive. Jo forgave. But there were limits to that Christian stuff, and maybe my family was outside those limits. What did Jo say about Mom to other grown-ups? "The way she goes on! How does the kid deal with it?" I felt awful and squirmy and a thought was coming that I couldn't stop: "How does her *husband* take it?" Oh God I couldn't get through that moment and there was Jo like nothing was happening and I had to be normal just normal no matter what. Not the Institute for Living. Ever.

"I have to bring you back at six, as you may have ascertained." She lifted her grocery bags. I had to get through. "Tally ho, Jeeves!"

Outside snow flew around us, and I felt better because I thought snow kind of got people together, all of us against the snow. We climbed into the truck with our food bags.

"What are you reading these days, Sport?" Jo asked, and maybe life could be the same again.

"Well," I said, "school's out, so I started *Treasure Island*."

"Ah, Robert Louis! Wonderful stuff! Got it for Christmas when I was about your age. Had to battle a bit. With *my* mother. *Little Women* was the extent of, well, at any rate, I'll be interested to hear what you think."

I felt good but like a girl again. Would it ever stop? When I was twelve. As a twelve-year-old I'd be manly, with manly thoughts and a more manly body, and everything would be fixed. Often when I felt bad or weak or like a girl or not knowing how I felt, I thought how it would be different, how I'd be a real boy when I was twelve.

I imagined Jo and I were English teachers, and I lived on Coe Hill, too, without my family, and Jo and I would meet early mornings on our way to school, agreeing it was colder than usual this year and talking books. "What are you reading?" I asked.

"William James! *The Varieties of Religious Experience*."

I'd never heard of it. I imagined a twelve-year-old (first name, William, middle name, James), beautiful and dark-haired and good enough to have his book published, who would think that my family and I were stupid.

"They're making it into a movie with Raquel Welch," she added, and I smiled.

Up on Coe Hill in the vestibule we stomped snow off our boots. Jo's Bassett hound, Moose, waddled in from the living room.

"Moose!" Jo cried. "*Kommen Sie hier, bitte!*" Jo knew German, French and Italian, too, from listening to the opera.

I smelled pine and softly hissing radiators and all the good times before I was born. We tramped through the living room, its Oriental carpets worn, past the huge, spreading tree from out back, dressed up in 1940s decorations. Moose's tags jingled ahead of us.

We clumped into the dim back hallway, then pushed into the kitchen, filled with bright gray light. Canisters of flour and sugar and jars of dried herbs lined the walls. Nothing changed at Jo's. Moose sneezed and his nails clicked the floor.

Jo bowed and asked Moose, "*Mein Hund! Wie geht es Ihnen?*" and rumpled his head. Then she took my coat and hung it with her own on a peg by the back door. She turned on the oven and snapped the radio on to the Saturday afternoon opera. I was hoping she wouldn't turn on the opera. Operas all sounded the same to me, like ordeals. Like liverwurst.

But Jo kept the opera low, and soon we were dashing around the kitchen retrieving bowls and wooden spoons. By cracky-bars required three bowls.

"And now," Jo said, "will the congregation please rise for the reading of the sacred text." She meant the yellow-brown square of newspaper with the recipe on it. As she took it out of her mother's Fannie Farmer cook-book she sang: "*Gloria in excelsis e pluribus unum..!*"

I liked how she joked about church stuff. Most people who were serious about that stuff didn't joke. "*Habeas corpus sayonara la plume de ma tante!*" I also liked that she made jokes that I couldn't completely get. Like she was making me be smarter than I was. "*Et cetera, et ceter-a-a..!*" And while Moose sniffed at our feet, Jo sang cooking instructions to me like they were opera: Vieni, Signor Stefano! First-a we melt-a the chocola-a-a-ta! Suddenly she stopped. "Wait!" She reached and turned the radio up.

She clasped her hands to her chin, closed her eyes and became still, her lips moving as though she were saying grace. She swayed slightly. I stared down at the flour until she snapped out of her pose, almost too fast. Like she wanted me to think she hadn't meant it, when I knew she had. Or had she? Were people really carried away by classical music like that? I wanted to tell her it was okay. "Always have to hear that one!" she said briskly. But I didn't know how to say it, so I didn't.

I wanted there to be something grown-up and difficult like opera that I enjoyed that would make Jo feel a little left out, that would make her ask me questions and look up to me, the way I looked up to her. But all I could think about right then was "jewing down."

Would the handle pull the top of your head off? Would it be bad if I asked Jo what Vogel meant? Would she figure out it was Vogel, even if I didn't tell? What if she thought it was my parents who said it? For some reason I felt like that was the truth. But it wasn't! And then somehow the jewing down got all mixed up with the Institute for Living and Jo's hair in a black cap and I felt angry and like running around the kitchen in circles and I wanted to be somewhere, anywhere else, not even on planet Earth and this was a nervous breakdown, it had to be...

Then Jo called me over to the counter, and things were better.

As we spread the brownie part of the mixture in the bottom of a Pyrex dish I checked the clock. It was after two-thirty. The afternoon was half gone and still hadn't quite become what I'd wanted. Was Jo still thinking about my mother? Did she wish she didn't have to deal with my mother or me?

"Okey-doke, Sport. Now, you are going to be in charge of graham crackers. You want to take the glass and crush 'em still they're uniform and powdery..."

Then we spread the cake batter with chocolate chips on top and slid the whole thing into the oven.

"All righty!" Jo said. "You know what comes next..."

We both cried out: "Clea-ea-ean u-u-up!" Jo put her fist to her lips and made a trumpet call like when horse races start on TV.

"You'll see, Sport," she said, brushing flour off her oven mitt, "no one wants to do clean-up. Want to make a name for yourself? Be Johnny-on-the-spot for all the stuff no one else wants to do!"

I felt like she was making me see some mean part of life. She might even belong to that part, and it made me feel lonely, as though I were home with my parents, who I should be loving... Why did she have to say that?

After clean-up, we peeked at the by-cracky bars. They were tricky to make without burning the bottoms. When she brought them out, one corner was a little too dark, but she didn't care.

"Something burns a little," she explained, peering at the underside of the pan, "you know it's homemade. Stuff in the supermarket has to be perfect. They throw out the burnt Keebler's. No, they make the elves eat 'em! Won't take the burnt ones to church, of course," she added, as she took out the rack for cooling.

While the by-cracky bars cooled, Jo fetched two pairs of work gloves and pruning shears from the shelf by the back door. She hoisted our coats off the pegs, we bundled up, and she led me out into the crisp-smelling snow. She hopped ahead, turned and sat down abruptly, and then lay down on her back and began making a snow angel. "C'mon, Sport," she called, "didn't you ever make one of these?"

No. It was one more normal person thing that I couldn't do. I tried to explain what would happen at home if my coat got wet and Jo interrupted: "We'll just hang it up by the fireplace! C'mon, kiddo..."

"NO!" I said suddenly. She stopped making the angel and I was afraid. She sat up. I took a step back. "I'm sorry," I said. My mouth was dry and my stomach felt like everything dropped out.

"No no," Jo said. "That's all right, Sport. Don't have to do anything you don't want to. Just a thing I remembered from being a kid. Let's get moving and get those boughs before sunset comes."

We walked down along the stone wall that we'd fixed back in October. I hopped on top and Jo held my hand.

"'Something there is that doesn't love a wall, That sends the frozen ground swell under it... And spills the upper boulders in the sun...' Robert Frost, Sport..."

The Osborne property ran all the way to the railroad tracks. Down in Jo's woods we cut holly and pine. I got to choose the carols we sang while we worked. Jo's voice sounded beautiful in the woods, and steam came in clouds from our mouths. "How about..?" And I sang, "O come, O come..." And Jo joined me:

"...Emma-a-anuel, and ransom captive Israel,
That mourns in lonely exile here,
Until the Son of God appear.
Rejoice! Rejoice! Emmanuel shall come to thee, O Israel!"

Jo explained, "Not really a Christmas carol, you know. It's for Advent. When you're waiting for Jesus's birth. That's why it's so beautiful. Waiting for something. Sometimes better than getting it."

I didn't get that.

"Oh, I know!" she said. "You're thinking about those by-cracky bars! But now, which you like better—Christmas Eve, or Christmas Day?"

"Christmas Eve!" Just the thought made the Institute for Living and jewing down go away.

"And you know why?"

"Just... all the getting ready..." But more: the night and the conspiracy of wrapping, pale reflections of electric candles in the cold, things bought that we could have...

"Exactly. And sometimes, well, a person can live a long time, always getting ready. That's why you've got to 'Carpe Diem,' as they say. That's Latin for 'Seize the fish'!"

Was Jo waiting? For a husband? A wife? Was I supposed to marry her? I was afraid I was going to ask.

She pulled a cut bough free and a slice of sky opened. I sang, "O Come, O come..." and she joined me:

"...Thou God, Thou Three-in-One,
And ransom captive Zion.
Disperse the gloomy clouds of night
And death's dark shadows put to flight.
Rejoice! Rejoice! Emmanuel shall come to thee, O Israel!"

"I think this should about do it," she said. That disappointed me. The afternoon might as well be over. Jo must have seen my disappointment, because on the way back she taught me the Pogo version of "Deck the Halls."

"Deck us all with Boston Charlie,
Walla Walla, Wash and Kalamazoo!
Nora's freezing on the trolley,
Swaller dollar cauliflower alley-ga-roo!"

–o–

In the silence after I thought Jo—and God, too—was waiting for me to ask something.

"What is it, Sport?"

"In Vogel's Hardware," I began, "they have these really thick dowels." I pulled off one mitten and held up my thumb and first finger. I hated how small and white my fingers were. "Like this. They're, like, strange. What would you use 'em for?

"Oh...for all kinds of things! I'll show you when we get up t'home."

I tensed my muscles. I looked down and watched my boots plunge into the snow. For a moment I knew I belonged right where I was; not back cutting holly or up in the kitchen, but right there.

On the back porch steps we stomped snow off our boots, and left the holly and pine boughs inside by the shovels and pots and garden implements from summer. In the kitchen, warm and chocolate-smelling, the opera still played. It wasn't an ordeal now. It was nice to come back to the same thing we'd left. I checked the clock: four-thirty. I'd have to go soon.

"Now, come hither, young fellow," Jo said, "and I will show you great wonders."

From the shelf by the back door she took her long red flashlight with the adhesive tape wound around the base. She motioned me toward to the basement door. "Careful." She swung open the door. "And in that same country there was also much mildew," she said. She yanked the string that made the bulb go on over the workbench below. That string had been there always and always would be. "Hang on a sec, now, Sport..." I descended after her into cool, thick, musty air. "Okey-doke. Now: look up there. The flashlight beam quivered.

Above the set tubs, just under the cobwebby beams, ran a big, thick dowel. Empty hangers crowded one end, with paper covers from the dry cleaners; they made me nervous. The other end disappeared in the shadows.

"Nothing special," Jo said. "Just you see there's all kinds of uses for all kinds of things. Now, I believe you and I have a bounden duty to go sample those by-cracky bars!"

Upstairs Jo put carols on the record player. She had so much and all of it just right. When I was a little kid I thought we were like that. But our house was small. The linoleum curled in both kitchens, but at Jo's it had once been grand. My mother always said how rich doctors were. Things were mahogany at Jo's, she understood opera, and even though pine boughs were free, you had to know something to bring them in. I had asked at home, but Mom said, "And get the *whole house* sticky? Oh, boy, you just wait till you have kids of your own some day!"

I cut the by-cracky bars, working hard to make straight lines. We each had a piece of the slightly burnt one with a cup of hot cider, and I made Moose sit up for a dog biscuit. Then we took what Jo called "our spoils"— the holly and pine boughs—and carried them into the living room. It was exciting just to carry them in like that—Jo never said a word about sap or needles on the rug.

The boughs did make my hands sticky and spotted brown. I examined my fingers, and wished again that my nails were bigger. Tomorrow would be Sunday School. What would the guys there say if they saw me weaving pine boughs in Jo's living room? When I was with Jo it was okay; it made sense and I'd forget. But then the afternoon would be over, and I would

213

have to go back to regular life and things just impossible to do.

Tonight, in the light of the fire, holly and pine all around, I wouldn't be here. I wished I could be Moose, asleep on the rug. Or a canister of flour or jar of dried herbs. But I had to go be me. Why wouldn't God make me different? Everyone else prayed to Him, and He gave them what they wanted. I sometimes prayed, "God, please make me normal," but he ignored me. Russell had a game that night. I'd sit on the cold boards and watch guys race up and down and shout. And everyone loved them, God included.

Squares of pale light moved across the wall. A car engine came up next to the house.

"I wonder..?" Jo said. Then, "Uh-oh..!"

She dropped her holly and clumped to the front door. I heard her open the door, and I heard her voice in the vestibule. "What a pleasant surprise! Guess the time got away from us." It was after six! My mom had had to come get me. I'd never be allowed to come back!

"*Completely* my fault!" Jo said. "Took the phone off the hook so no one would call me for shoveling..." She stumbled over her words and something landed—thump!—in my chest, something from the regular world, like a sack of beans. I ran to the kitchen—twenty-five after six! Russell's game was at seven! We'd ruined everything! My knees went weak and my heart pounded. I went through the dining room toward the vestibule. Still my mother hadn't spoken. For a second my eye lit on the china cookie jar, and I thought I would never see it again. I stumbled through the cold study into the front hall...

"Look who's here, Sport!"

My dad.

Jo asked, "Would you care to sample some freshly baked by-cracky bars?" I wanted to tell her to stop. It sounded pitiful. I didn't like her now. I wanted to tell Dad it was her fault...

Dad said no. He told me to get my coat.

"I'll get it, Sport."

While Jo was gone I didn't look at Dad, and he didn't say anything to me. Jo came back with my jacket in one hand and a Christmas present in the other. "Almost forgot this," she said.

She handed me a long, thin, object wrapped in Christmas paper, with curly ribbon and a tag. It looked like a popsicle stick only bigger.

"Go on, Sport," she said, a little sadly, it seemed. "It's for you."

I took it and mumbled, "Thanks." Dad said we should get going.

"Merry Christmas to all," Jo said, following us to the door, "and to all a good night! And apologies again…"

Dad said it was all right. He said that whenever someone did something wrong. Someone outside the family.

We picked our way over frozen slush to the car. I could feel Jo watching. As we backed down the driveway, she waved one last time. I thought maybe I shouldn't wave back. She turned away and closed the door behind her.

Driving down Coe Hill Dad said, "I presume you have the English muffins and milk your mother requested."

I completely forgot! "Well," Dad muttered, "we certainly don't have time now." Waiting at a red light in the center of town he said, "I think this is going to be the last afternoon with her for a while."

"Did Mom say so?"

For a long time he didn't answer. Then, quietly, he said, "I think that after the first of the year we will look into the Boy Scouts. Or perhaps Junior Basketball at the Rec Center." An icy hand gripped me. I held my breath. He didn't say anything more. Slowly, so he wouldn't see, I took out Jo's brightly wrapped "popsicle stick," and peeked at the tag.

"To Steven," it said, "so you'll always know where you are, Love, Jo—Xmas, 1968."

−o−

The next afternoon in the Parish House they had the Christmas party and the choral concert. There were the by-cracky bars I helped make. Mom said I shouldn't have one, though.

After the concert, Jo hurried to the kitchen. She tied a white apron over her gray slacks and turtleneck. She pushed her sleeves up and then she was everywhere—scrubbing, drying, fitting clean pots inside other clean pots and hoisting everything into cabinets. The other ladies stepped to the left or right, smiled and chatted. I turned away. While I waited for my parents I studied the posters on the bulletin board, with birds and rainbows and sayings about love and forgiveness.

What did those ladies think of Jo? Did they know the word I'd seen in *Life* magazine in the article with the pictures of women, like, together? Guys used that word if a girl was fat or ugly. Maybe I'd used it once or twice, just to sound like a regular guy. But I didn't want Jo to be that.

"Hey!" Someone socked me on the arm. "Hey!" It was Jack Wessel.

"Saw ya at the grocery store!"

"Get out!" I tried to go back toward the kitchen but he blocked me.

"Gonna tell on me to *Mister* Osbourne?" He crowded me against the bulletin board. "Think she's got a dick? Yeah and I bet you got..."

"Shut up!" I shoved him. I'd never done that before. His eyes widened and his lip curled. He darted his fist at me, middle knuckle extended. I lost my balance and fell back into the coat rack. He kicked me once, twice, I lunged at him, and then my dad and Jo were pulling us apart.

"What the hell is this about?" Dad asked, and Jo said, "I'm disappointed in you, Sport!"

I wrenched my head away. Mrs. Davies, the Sunday school superintendent, stepped in front of Jo. "I'll take care of this," she said. "Jack, that's enough." She made me and Wessel apologize. Then my mother sent me to the car. As I went for the door I heard my mother say, "Jo, please!" A hand touched my shoulder.

"Sport?" That pitiful voice again. So many people coming at me, and no one caring how I felt or what happened! Not even Jo. I twisted away and shoved open the door.

"Jo," Mom said, "just let him alone to think about it!" I stomped out to the car.

When the rest of the family came no one spoke. Russell and Mom got in back. I got in front with Dad. We slammed the doors and Dad started the engine. Finally, Mom said, "How many times have I told you—just ignore people like that who try to get your goat!" A knock came on the window next to me. "Now what?" Mom muttered.

Jo's face appeared. I rolled the window down. She stood in her apron, without a jacket. Snow blew off the car all rainbow-colored and caught in her hair and sparkled. "Hey, Killer. Almost forgot this."

She held something long, like a spear, wrapped in Christmas paper. She lifted it up—"Go on! Take it, Sport!" she said—and she lowered it in through the open window. It was so long I had to guide the end over into the back seat. "Goodness!" Mom said. "Hey, watch it!" said Russell. His mouth sounded full. I looked. He was eating a by-cracky bar.

"Just something I had lying around," Jo said. It seemed her cheerful voice was back. She stood up straight. "Well, Merry Christmas to all, and to all a good night!" Already she was turning away, waving just a little.

"Say thank you!" my mother hissed. "Thank you!" I wished so much I could follow her. Russell kicked the back of the seat. "It's cold in here, in case anyone hasn't noticed!" "Calm down, Russ," Dad said. I rolled the window up. Russell kicked the seat again. So I don't get something," he said.

"What, Russ?" Mom said.

"How come she always acts like a man?"

"Russell!" Mom snapped. Dad chuckled and looked over and winked at me. He gave me a horse bite on the leg. I gripped my new present till the paper almost tore. Then he was there, Russell, leaning over into the front seat, his breath chocolatey. "So, Dad," he said, "Didja decide about the all-stars? I can go, right?"

–o–

Christmas Eve morning I went back to Vogel's. I squeezed a fistful of finishing nails, hard, then wandered the aisles. I didn't want to get Russell anything, but you couldn't do that. Or get him some twenty-penny nails, but he'd say it was stupid. Then I saw the flashlights. I remembered Jo, leading us down the cellar stairs—and the by-cracky bars and carols in the woods.

I bought a flashlight for Russell.

–o–

Christmas Eve, 1968, the Apollo 8 astronauts orbited the Moon. Walter Cronkite said if a certain engine didn't fire, they'd be stuck going around and around forever, starving to death, I guess, while the whole world watched. It would be funny. Them helpless, still on TV, talking to Mission Control, saying good-bye to wives and kids, millions of people watching and nothing anyone could do.

Christmas morning the sun streamed in on our torn paper and ribbon. Russell said the flashlight was stupid because he had one already that was bigger. Mom sighed, "Russell..!" but she didn't tell him to thank me anyway.

We opened nonfamily presents last. When I unwrapped Jo's "popsicle stick," we were all baffled (except Russell, who was already watching cartoons). It still looked like a popsicle stick, except big: about an inch wide and eight inches long and perfectly stained and polished. Nobody could figure out what it was or what the tag meant... "So you'll always know where you are." I laid it on top of a sweater from my parents, like it was an exhibit.

I didn't want to show my dowel to the rest of the family, but I had to. Mom said, "Well. Two presents from Jo. Goodness!" She asked to see the tag.

"'To Steven. So many uses...'" She looked at my dad. "He must have said something she misunderstood."

Dad grinned. "I would say Jo Osbourne 'misunderstands' a great many things!"

"Well," Mom said, "Be that as it may... We'll be sure and write a thank-you note."

Late afternoon, after dinner, I was alone in the living room having one of the milk chocolate balls that came in my stocking. Mom came in and began picking bits of paper and tape from the carpet. Dad was asleep upstairs, and Russell was in his room playing with his soldiers. I heard him making explosions.

"Mom," I said. "Why does everyone act funny about Jo?"

"About what?"

"*Jo.* Osbourne."

"Oh. Well, I'm not aware that anyone acts funny about her. I'm sure your father just wants you to have more friends your own age." She sat, and we began sorting paper. We threw away Dad's and Russell's crumpled wads and saved the smooth sheets she and I had removed from our gifts.

"But he laughed at her!"

"Steven! When did your father ever *laugh at* anyone?"

"Today!"

"I'm sure he was hoping that you would be a good sport and laugh *with*..."

"...when I opened her present, and you said..."

"Well, it was an unusual present! We'll have to think how to thank her." She smoothed one sheet of paper over and over on her lap.

"He said she 'misunderstood' things."

"Steven, you'll have to learn to take a little good-natured ribbing in stride; it's part of growing up. You don't have to be dramatic. Hand me the scissors?"

"Plus Sunday, after the thing, in the car..."

"Steven! I don't even know what it is we're discussing! Let's just try and enjoy Christmas!" She got up and turned on the radio. A choir sang:

The cattle are lowing,
The baby awakes.

But Little Lord Jesus
No crying he makes...

"Mom?"

"What?"

"Y'know, Wessel said this funny thing..."

"Who?"

"Jack Wessel! At church? He said... I mean, is Jo like...what they call a 'lesbian'?"

"Steven!" She dropped her scissors, but they made no sound on the carpet. "We do not ever, ever say that about anyone! It's a terrible thing to say. Now, we just agreed this isn't the time to go into this, anyway!" She cut a crumpled edge from an otherwise smooth piece of paper. "We can at least rescue part of this." But suddenly she stopped and stared out the window. Her face had that look again, like someone was dying.

I looked down and sorted paper real hard. Mom got up and went to the dining room. I heard her whispering in there, like she was angry, but I couldn't understand what she was saying. I held myself perfectly still in the living room. I thought, if I were a better boy I'd go see what was the matter. But I wasn't, so I didn't...

A few seconds later she came back smiling: "How about some cocoa?"

"Sure!"

She made it in little cups that had belonged to her mother. We sat with it on the living room floor and finished sorting paper. When the room was almost clean she asked, "Did you get what you wanted for Christmas?"

"Uh-huh," I said. I had originally wanted to ask if I had to go to Boy Scouts or basketball. But I couldn't now, not after she made cocoa and everything was okay.

Suddenly a crash came from overhead.

"Oh, *Russell!*" She took off upstairs. I heard her stomping around. I heard words. Then everything was quiet, except for the radio. I thought, yeah, she acted like she was so mad, but she'd rather be with Russell, with his big nails.

I tensed my muscles, hopped up and went to the window. I was bad and didn't deserve to be my parents' son or Jo's friend. I was mean. I ran away from Jo when she was trying to help. When would they let me go to her and say I was sorry?

219

I wanted to climb out that window and go to Coe Hill and have it always be a few days before Christmas and me baking and gathering holly and pine boughs. But real boys didn't want those things—so what did that make me? I tried to see past my reflection. Nothing. Just window criss-crosses reflected forever, till they disappeared. God was with the church people. Real church people, not like us. Maybe I could have my own god, a god of woods and fields, like Jo, not quite a man, not completely a woman, waiting out there to see what I would do next.

That was sacrilegious, though.

I turned back to the bright, hot living room. Jo had her own life, dusting snow off the car, coming into the kitchen for hot cider and the last by-cracky bar, Moose sitting up, begging for crumbs. I wanted so badly to tell her I was sorry. Missing her and wanting to apologize felt like another present, one I would never open.

I hopped over to my real presents. Mom had moved Jo's "popsicle stick" and now it lay on top of a book from Dad, *The Real Diary of a Real Boy*. Now I knew: it was a bookmark! "So you'll always know where you are."

"Thanks, Jo," I said. Tears crept into my eyes. "I'm sorry about Sunday. I hope I see you soon. And Moose." I was afraid Mom would come back and ask what was the matter; and then I was afraid she wouldn't. She didn't. I heard her upstairs, arguing back and forth, back and forth with Russell.

I realized I was all alone on the first floor of the house—the way it would be when I was an English teacher! I took another milk chocolate ball from my stocking. I picked the foil off and ate it. Then I had another.

I sat in the living room with the choir singing, eating chocolate balls. No one came. I was happy.

I was home. It was Christmas. I'd get out of Boy Scouts somehow. I always had. Just avoid them and avoid the subject. And as for basketball, I'd just fail the tryout. I took another chocolate ball. And then soon I would be twelve. And I would be different.

Acknowledgements

My Movie would not have been possible without the enthusiasm, encouragement, and vision of Jameson Currier at Chelsea Station Editions. From many years' worth of stories he culled a thematically linked lineup, suggested critical changes to newer, unpublished work, and published "Calvin Gets Sucked In" in the premier issue of his literary magazine, *Chelsea Station*.

I owe great thanks to all the other editors who shepherded the previously published work: Chuck Ortleb and Neenyah Ostrom at *Christopher Street*; Phil Willkie, Greg Baysans and Patrick Merla at *The James White Review*; Sean Meriwether at *Velvet Mafia*; Patrick Ryan at *Lodestar Quarterly*; Terry Wolverton and Robert Drake, editors of *His3*; Don Weise, editor of *Fresh Men 2*; and Brian Bouldrey at *Harrington Gay Men's Fiction Quarterly*. Some of the journals and Web sites no longer publish, but their creators performed an invaluable (and physically and emotionally demanding) service, putting them out at little profit and launching many writers who have established successful careers. Being part of these periodicals I felt I was part of history.

Over the years, many teachers and peers encouraged me in creating my stories: Donna Allegra, Aldo Alvarez, Benjamin Birdie, Scott Bramlett, Ron Caldwell, Jill Ciment, Karin Cook, Janet Crawford, David Corrado, Tim Driscoll, Sarah Durham, Susan Finque, Fran Gordon, the late Kenneth King, Jenifer Levin, Jeanne McCulloch, Tom Mendicino, Achim Nowak, Eileen O'Toole, Dale Peck, Laurie Piette, Rebecca Shannonhouse, Joe Stamps, Darcey Steinke, Michael Thomas-Faria, and Tom Weber. Special thanks to Felice Picano, aka Miss Bea Oblivious, for believing from the beginning, and for helping book the Chelsea Girls from coast to coast. Thanks also to the staffs and residents of the MacDowell Colony in Peterborough, NH, and the Dorset Colony House in Dorset, VT for their support. Rogério Pinto, my partner, is also my greatest cheerleader and most exacting reader. Some stories might not have gone beyond my laptop had he not so compellingly articulated their virtues, and he lent invaluable help in formulating a final story order. *Je t'adore, Doce!*

Jane Lincoln Taylor starred in and helped me develop a theatrical version of "The Snow Queen," and Regie Cabico selected it for production as a joint venture of HERE Arts Center (Kristin Marting, Co-founder and Artistic Director) and Dixon Place (Ellie Covan, Founder and Artistic Director) in June 2003. Jane also reviewed the final manuscript scrupulously for errors, oversights and story order. The garden imagery in "Another Country" owes a debt to the poetry of Patrick Donnelly. The Alice Munro story alluded to in "All the Young Boys Love Alice" is "Lying Under the Apple Tree," from the collection *The View from Castle Rock*. Joanne Gottlieb created electronic files of the handwritten code in "My Movie," allowing its online publication in the days when you did not try this at home. And my thanks, as always, to Andrew Farber for scrutinizing the fine print.

Finally, my thanks to the booksellers, book lovers, book reviewers, fellow authors, literary conference directors, LGBTQ community leaders, and friends and family who encouraged me and hosted me as I toured the country in 2010-2011 on behalf of my novel, *Bob the Book*. It's a crowded, competitive market out there. Without the warmth, support, and nearly irrational enthusiasm of these people, I might not have felt the impetus to go ahead and create *My Movie*. I owe you all more than I can express.

About the Author

David Pratt won a 2011 Lambda Literary Award for his novel *Bob the Book*. He was born in Hartford, Connecticut and now lives in Manhattan, a stone's throw (or three) from the George Washington Bridge.

"A rare and extraordinary accomplishment. The novel's basic conceit is that each edition of a book has its own personality and name. *Bob the Book* makes a perfect gift—not only to yourself but to friends who love books."
—Wayne Gunn, *Lambda Literary*

Bob the Book
a novel by
David Pratt

Meet 'Bob,' a gay book for sale in a Greenwich Village bookstore, where he falls in love with another book, Moishe. But an unlikely customer separates the young lovers. As Bob wends his way through used book bins, paper bags, knapsacks, and lecture halls, hoping to be reunited with Moishe, he meets a variety of characters, both book and human, including Angela, a widowed copy of Jane Austen's *Mansfield Park*, and two other separated lovers, Neil and Jerry, near victims of a book burning. Among their owners and readers are Alfred and Duane, whose on-again, off-again relationship unites and separates our book friends.

Will Bob find Moishe?
Will Jerry and Neil be reunited?
Will Alfred and Duane make it work?
Open
Bob the Book
to find all the answers...

"This charming novel, recounted by Pratt with seamless insight into the inner lives of books, is told almost entirely by Bob and the books around him—a seductive and eloquent literary accomplishment that, at last, answers the question: What is a gay book?
—Richard Labonté, *Bookmarks*

"This is one of the most delightful stores I've read all year, and the fact that it is a debut novel only adds to the pleasure. On the surface it seems like a whimsical love story, both for Bob and his human owner, as well as several other book couples. But under that simplicity, there are some important life lessons to be examined. There is much Zen-like wisdom woven into this enchanting tale, lessons on taking one's self too seriously, and of striving for things that are not important, just to name a few. Readers who are familiar with the publishing industry will especially appreciate this novel, but all readers can enjoy this wonderfully smart and touching book. Because the main characters are books, it transcends every boundary of gender and sexual orientation, making it an entertaining read for men and women, boys and girls, gay and straight. That's its genius."
—Alan Chin, *Examiner.com*

CPSIA information can be obtained at www.ICGtesting.com
Printed in the USA
BVOW07s2135221113

337103BV00002B/187/P

9 780983 285175